Raunn landed heavily on her right shoulder and rolled once, as she had been taught, coming up into a crouch automatically, with the profane gun braced in both hands. She hated the feel of the smooth offworld metal in her hands, was nauseated by its weight and the awful damage it could do, but used it nonetheless. None of the weapons of Chennidur, not even her beloved blowgun, could reach so far or kill so accurately.

No one barred the way forward. Pivoting, she looked back through the shimmering energy fence and saw the patrol turning away with Merradrix's body hanging limply between two black-clad figures. Taking a deep breath, Raunn steadied herself and aimed the techish weapon carefully at the broad space between his shoulder blades. She hesitated for a single agonized breath, remembering the strength of those shoulders and the pleasure they had given her. As she did, the patrol fell into formation behind their prisoner, blocking her aim.

The men made tempting targets and she did not feel bound by outworld regulations, even though she stood in their jurisdiction. Of course, *shufri-nagai* did not apply to starmen. S̶_____ directly at ____ ____ of the pair and _____ firing mechanis_____ head. Raunn tu_____ med legs, and _____ of a port guard's _____ rifle standing solidly next to her. . . .

# WORLD SPIRITS

## ALINE BOUCHER-KAPLAN

BAEN BOOKS

WORLD SPIRITS

Copyright © 1991 by Aline Boucher Kaplan

A Baen Books Original

Baen Publishing Enterprises
P.O. Box 1403
Riverdale, N.Y. 10471

ISBN: 0-671-72043-0

Cover art by Debbie Hughes

First printing, March 1991

Distributed by
SIMON & SCHUSTER
1230 Avenue of the Americas
New York, N.Y. 10020

Printed in the United States of America

To my husband Seth,
my daughter Simone and my son Morgan
for their continual love and support
no matter what planet I'm on.

# CHAPTER 1

## THE HILLS

Astin loped along the hill track accompanied only by his rhythmic breathing and the soft slap of his shoes against hard ground. He crested one grassy hilltop and started smoothly down the far side without altering his powerful stride. At his back, the last of the sun's rays colored the retreating streamers of the Veil mauve and pink. Ahead, the clear heavens deepened into purple and the Eyestar burned intensely white against the oncoming night. Astin barely noticed that dusk was settling around him, or that it was a beautiful evening. The air was still and cold, not yet touched by the first warmth of Renewal. All of his concentration was centered on running cleanly and maintaining a pace that would bring him to his destination by the appointed time.

A line of diktalls arrowed across his path, gliding toward their nesting grove and safety, oblivious of the foolhardy man who was running away from both. In his quiet uneventful home in the small village at the crossing of the trade roads, Astin's family was undoubtedly finishing their simple dinner, a meal which he had missed completely,

1

and preparing for the evening Call to Prayer. Astin had been absolved of that duty for this one night and his presence at the small temple would be fully, if falsely, supported by the nayya to allay any anxiety his parents might have. Not that they would dare, or even think, to question the nayya, but there should not be even a hint of something out of place, a faint whiff of unrightness for the Tulkan's spies to sniff out. He started up another hill, legs and heart pumping strongly, feeling no guilt for the duplicity and no regret for the secure and ordinary night that he was escaping. A merrain nibbling a seed pod at the path's edge dropped it at the sound of his footsteps and scurried unnoticed into the grass.

Astin thought about his mission; indeed, thinking about it had become a part of him. How could he not have accepted the honor of this assignment? As a Follower of the True Word, how could he have rejected the invitation to be a Runner, refused to take his part in a movement that fought for the greatest right and was of the utmost importance? There was the danger to consider and he was no fool, no soft troi'm boy to weave dreams and ignore the hard realities about him. It was this same reality that drove the Tarraquis and he had agreed to become a Runner knowing all too well that the risk was real and terrifying. In past weeks the number of Runners captured had increased as the Tulkan's government stepped up its campaign to eliminate opposition. They could not kill the Inayyam without martyring a holy man and they were far too cunning to make such a mistake. So they concentrated instead on the easier target provided by his disciples. Now that Astin had joined the Tarraquis, he was as vulnerable as anyone else.

Despite the danger, he was indeed honored to have been asked, for it meant that someone among the Tarraquis had noticed him and valued his loyalty and his potential. That same person, perhaps a nayya, had believed he was mature enough to be trusted with the message and capable of completing the task. That unknown person, he felt certain, had also seen the courage in him, waiting for an opportunity to emerge. Astin knew that he was only one small piece of a small group that fitted into a larger group that was eventually folded into the Tarraquis like the nesting baskets his younger sister Esski used to play with. That was as it should be, for someone just beginning to do his part must demonstrate more than potential; he must prove himself worthy. Astin was young and strong, he felt that he could run all night if that would manifest his worth, if it would help to strike a blow for the True Word against the Tulkan's heresies.

Over the rim of the next hill, Smallmoon's azure disk slipped into the sky, illuminating the night softly and tinting the waving grasses with blue light. Cold air flowed in and out of his lungs as he traversed a game trail that would be invisible to anyone who had not spent his boyhood hunting over these hills and fishing their streams. Astin was at home among the tall grasses and that familiarity gave confidence to his stride and kept the fear of capture away. The path swung around to the left, skirting a large stickybush, and he leaned into the curve, hearing and dismissing the patter of sap that dropped from the bush's leaves. Astin knew that if he could keep up this pace he would be at Bannti's Ford before the Greatwheel was bright and on the bridge over the falls shortly after that. There, in the shadow of the bridge's stone arch, he would give a password masked from any other listeners by the din of falling water and then speak a brief message that meant nothing to him. The people for whom it was intended, another small part of the Tarraquis, would find great import in those words and he took pride in having memorized them precisely. By keeping the Runners ignorant, the Tarraquis hoped to hold them safe from the Tulkan's Puzzlemasters. Failing that, they hoped to keep the message from being understood.

Once his task was completed, Astin would be free and on his own. The temple would cover for him until morning, if his parents were worried enough to ask. There was a drakshouse downstream in Lower Chuktoo where a master blaikist was supposed to create incredible rhythms totally different from the traditional style of play. He planned to hear it for himself before returning to his quiet home where music was a troi'm luxury heard on feastdays but irrelevant to the daily business of living. Astin's smooth stride took him from brightening moonlight into the shade of a ridgepole grove, feeling stronger than ever before. His body was fit and hard. His hair had finally shown its adult color. He had made an important decision for himself and he was making a contribution for all Followers. As his reward, he would have the time to do something that was important only to him. If this was what it meant to come of age and be responsible, he liked the feel of it.

Perhaps this premature confidence caused him to be less than usually observant. Perhaps it was the accompanying elation that lured him into overlooking the thin dark shadow stretched across the trail, nearly identical to the rippled ridgepole shadows which disguised it. Astin's right foot came down on the dark patch squarely and solidly, springing the trap before he was even aware that something was wrong. His forward momentum carried him to the end of the trap's tether, then the chain sprang taut and jerked him off balance. Unable to recover, he plummeted forward and down, snapping his leg just above the trap's grasp.

Astin instinctively got his hands up and broke the fall, then lay stunned in the grass while pain erupted from his leg. It raced along his nerves, shooting red fire up his spine and exploding inside his skull. His mouth opened and closed involuntarily as if that would somehow ease the torment. He clenched his jaw and fought for control while nausea coiled treacherously in his stomach and slithered up his throat. He forced it down. Then, moving very slowly, he turned over and leaned forward the smallest degree necessary to be able to assess the extent of the disaster. It was boundless.

The trap was an off-world abomination—an energy-field leghold that was programmed to send off a signal as soon as it was triggered. It was one of the many godless techish devices employed by the Tulkan's patrols about which he had been briefed a day ago. He had never thought to encounter one. He knew also that he had limited time in which to free himself before a patrol would come in one of their profane flying devices to take him away. The nausea lowered its cold head and he reached carefully for the trap but found that, while he could reach it, he could not touch it. A small energy field surrounding the mechanism prevented it from being destroyed or altered. This meant he could not physically open or manipulate the pulsating "jaws" of the trap and the field numbed his hand when he tried to push through it.

Abandoning that approach, he lay back and wiped away the tears that stubbornly confounded his new maturity. Pushing panic away, he forced himself to think methodically and then checked the chain that anchored the trap to a rock the size of the family table. It was made of a smooth synthetic material that glistened in the moonlight. He slipped his knife from its sheath and, moving slowly, cut at the chain. For a long moment he sawed at it, cold sweat breaking out on his face, but there was no visible result, not even a scratch to show where the knife had touched. Putting the blade carefully on the grass, he gripped the links in both hands, braced his good leg against the ground, and pulled. Pain jolted his body and took possession of it. The trap receded in his vision and a black void roared in his ears. He drifted out of consciousness, away from both the pain and the terror.

Astin came back into awareness with the knife digging into his side and his hands still wrapped around the chain. He did not know how long he had been out, how many critical moments had been wasted. He let go of the links and sat up. Picking up his knife again, he stared at the blade. It was sharp and clean: he kept it that way with diligent use of whetstone and oilcloth. Since he could not open the trap, cut the chain, or lift the stone, Astin knew the only alternative was to remove his body from it. He took a deep breath and fought against the horror that rose in him at the thought. He had known animals to do this; had found sprung traps clinging to pathetically gnawed paws, with bloody tracks marking the way to freedom. Once he had interrupted a tunser that was not far from freedom when his club had stopped its desperate efforts. Desperate. That was the only word to describe his situation.

The patrol would arrive soon and take him to the Tulkan's citadel where he would be delivered to the Puzzlemasters. Their simple job was to remove from his memory the message the Tarraquis had given him. Nothing so crude and imprecise as torture would be used; they would simply fill him with chemicals until they got what they wanted. When those chemicals polluted his body and destroyed portions of his brain, they would not be concerned. Once the message was ripped from his mind, he would disappear, as so many others had before him.

Astin had never thought to find himself in the same position as one of the animals he trapped. He had never thought that "desperate" could be so personal a condition. He braced himself by saying that, if an animal knowing no cause greater than its own survival could do it, he could also. Grasping the knife firmly, he wiped it on his sleeve. Thus prepared, he surveyed the damaged leg: the trap gripped it midway between the knee and ankle. Judging from the swollen flesh and telltale lump beneath the skin, the leg bone was snapped cleanly. He decided in as logical a fashion as possible, that it would be best and fastest to cut right at the break. He was surprised, in fact, at how clearly his mind was working. It was as if the very desperation he felt had shut off any thought that would not aid his escape. It blocked out fear and confusion and doubt and admitted the pain only as an inescapable reality. The sole course of action left to him was spread out in orderly steps.

First he cut the material of his pants leg away, peeling it back. Then he took another irreplaceable moment to chant the prayer that would fill him with the strength of the True Word. With teeth gritted and face set in determination, Astin cut through the skin. The pain was less than he expected but the flow of blood was greater. He pulled off his shirt and cut the sleeves to make a tourniquet. He wrapped one sleeve tightly around the leg above the cut and the other below. It was not adequate to stem the hemorrhage from the great arteries but it would have to do. Since the only anatomy he knew came from skinning small animals, it was only by luck that he did not sever a major blood vessel at once. A second time he cut and the pain grew worse. Astin vomited and fainted again but returned doggedly to the task. He was able to proceed by imagining the leg a foreign object not attached to him at all and admitting nothing to himself of the gruesome nature of his work.

He kept at it when the hum of a light transport floated out of the cold darkness and did not even look up when the grasses around him flattened in the wind from its landing jets. Face drained white, eyes shocked and staring, he continued cutting at the bloody ruin of his leg even as the patrol quartet arrived. He stopped only when a single beam from a nerve pistol sent him back into unconsciousness.

"By the seven suns of Anurreem, look at this one!" exclaimed the gunman as he lowered his pistol.

"I've seen a lot on this hitch," replied his partner, "but never one like this before."

"Rawfin fanatics," said the pilot, "just like all of 'em on this righteous scogging planet."

The navigator remained silent. Not much older than Astin, he was afraid that if he opened his mouth, more than just words would come out. He could not shame himself on his first real duty hitch, especially in front of his seasoned companions. Taking refuge in action, he turned away toward the transport and went for the medikit. It was better than looking at the gore. As he unsnapped the kit from its place in the cabin he heard the pilot hawk and spit. "Just a kid, too," he commented.

Holstering his weapon, the gunman added, "Yeah, but he's going to be a dead kid if we don't get moving. And dead Runners aren't what they're looking for back at the Puzzle Palace."

The second patrolman was neutralizing the force field around the trap when the navigator returned with the kit. Working smoothly together, the four men removed the trap, applied emergency aid to the mangled leg, and lifted Astin's limp body into the transport. There they secured his hands. He would not be strong enough when he woke to fight off one man, much less four, but it was procedure and they followed procedure to the letter. Then the transport lifted off again and swung away into the night sky. They would be back in Nandarri before Smallmoon reached its zenith.

## NANDARRI MARKET

The storm had passed but water continued to drain off the roofs of the buildings around the square, running from the eaves onto cobblestones worn smooth and shiny. It was late, well past curfew, and the slow dismal dripping was the only sound to be heard. The shops that bordered the square were closed up, their awnings rolled carefully in against the rain, the shopkeepers long gone to their warm beds. In the streets behind the market square, larger houses turned blank walls outward, enfolding their family life within protected courtyards. Their shuttered doors were quiet and dark. Even the bright and noisy port, so out of place at the far end of the avenue, was dimmed and silent as if the storm had stifled its alien alertness. Not subject to either city ordinances or the religious dictates of *shufri-nagai*, it still sought no undue conflict with the city which housed it.

This had been haymarket day, but despite the hundreds of animals that had passed through the market, the cobblestones of the square were clean. Between marketclose and curfew, the street cleaners had swept up heaps of manure, baskets full of sodden straw and wisps of hay, scraps of broken harness and the remains of drovers' lunches. The rain had diluted most of the ammonia-reeking pools of animal urine and washed them into the drains. But still the square held an underlying smell of all those things, as if the combined odors clung stubbornly in the cracks between the stones. The eaves dripped, the Great Wheel listed out of the breaking clouds, and the city of Nandarri slept.

Then a faint sound came from one of the side streets, arrhythmic and out of place. The clatter of running feet echoed off solid and featureless walls, growing louder, then softer, but without a source until two running figures burst abruptly out of the shadows and into the moonlit square. They ran at full speed, stretching for distance that would allow them to maintain a lead over their pursuers. One of the runners was large, a man of muscle and height, and he was in the lead. Slightly behind him was the smaller and somewhat slower figure of a woman. Only the size of the runners gave away anything about them for they were both dressed completely in black, with tight-fitting hoods covering their hair and dark camouflage paint on their faces. In the cold raw night, their breath steamed out before them.

They had passed the center of the square when a squad of six patrolmen emerged from the narrow confines of the street and saw their quarry clearly illuminated ahead of them. There was still much open space between the runners and possible safety. To their right lay the dark egress of an alley and a labyrinth of narrow passages that could confound the hunters. The possibility of escape was closer there, but less certain. Ahead of them opened the broad avenue that led to the gates of the port and absolute sanctuary. The man went for the gate even though it meant that he and his partner would be in open danger until they passed the boundary separating Nandarri from land belonging to outworlders.

Now only forty feet gaped before them but the patrol had split in two. The first four men continued in their pursuit without breaking stride. The second two broke away and knelt on the wet cobbles. With practiced precision they slipped a tripod off one man's back, unslung a weapon from the other and connected the two. Aiming carefully through a calibrated nightscope, the marksman took aim at the larger of the two figures while his partner steadied the tripod. For a moment several men of the patrol intruded between gunsight and quarry. The marksman barked a signal that reverberated off the walls and caused the four patrolmen to veer aside without changing stride or losing ground. At that sound, the lead fugitive swerved and the rifleman sighted carefully until the telltales lined up once more. Then, in the split second before his quarry could take another evasive maneuver, he squeezed off a shot.

It was high. The running man swerved again and the rifleman resighted methodically. His second shot reached its mark and a thin beam nearly outside the range of human vision burned into the back of the black camouflage shirt. The quarry stumbled but did not fall. The second runner reached him and hesitated, pulling him up. He pushed her away, slipping on the wet stones as he did so, and said one word. She left him then, running in a zig-zag pattern for the border that meant safety. The next shot caught the man on the thigh and he went down hard, sliding through the puddled rainwater. A fourth time the marksman fired but the woman was already diving through the gap in the port's energy fence. Two port guards emerged, weapons drawn, to ensure that no hostile pursuers followed. Nandarri law and *shufri-nagai* both ended at the gate. The marksman slipped his finger off the FIRE lever and stood up.

When the four patrolmen reached their fallen prey, he was still moving: staining the wet stones with smeared blood as he crawled toward the gates. He refused to give up and for a few moments the patrol stood over him while he pulled himself forward, straining for the sanctuary of the port and its impassive guards. What happened outside the gates in Nandarri was not their concern and unless he reached the port on his own they would make no move on his behalf. Then the marksman gave another clipped command and the men reached down to take their prisoner. A raw cry ripped from his throat as they grasped his arms and pulled him up but they could not tell whether it was caused by the pain of his wounds or the knowledge that his bid for escape had failed. They turned and half-carried, half-dragged him back through the square. They had taken only a few steps when the cobblestones, the shuttered shopfronts, the dripping buildings were illuminated by an actinic light followed by a whump that was felt viscerally more than heard. A split-second later another followed and the dual explosions told the prisoner that he and his partner had succeeded in their mission. One of the patrolmen pulled the man's head back. "What was that?" he demanded. "What did you hit?"

The prisoner grimaced, approximating a smile, but said nothing.

"It sure wasn't the rawfin drakshouse," cut in another patrolman.

"Leave him alone," said the marksman stonily, as he clipped the weapon back into its holster on his partner's back. "We'll find out soon enough and the Puzzlemasters will have more important questions for him."

The patrolman released the man's head and hauled him forward. "Better him than me," he muttered under his breath.

Head hanging, his face hidden from those around him, the man let his fixed smile slip and clenched his teeth against the pain.

## THE PORT

Raunn landed heavily on her right shoulder and rolled once, as she had been taught, coming up into a crouch automatically, with the profane gun braced in both hands. She hated the feel of the smooth offworld metal in her hands, was nauseated by its weight and the awful damage it could do, but used it nonetheless. None of the weapons of Chennidur, not even her beloved blowgun, could reach so far or kill so accurately. "Turn their own weapons against them," the nayya said and he was right. No one barred the way forward. Pivoting, she looked back through the shimmering energy fence and saw the patrol turning away with Merradrix's body hanging limply between two black-clad figures. Taking a deep breath, Raunn steadied herself and aimed the techish weapon carefully at the broad space between his shoulder blades. She hesitated for a single agonized breath, remembering the strength of those shoulders and the pleasure of their embrace. As she did, the patrol fell into formation behind their prisoner, blocking her aim.

The Tulkan's hired men moved off but two of them broke away from the group and took up positions on either side of the port gates. Her escort. The men made tempting targets and she did not feel bound by outworld regulations, even though she stood in their jurisdiction. Of course, *shufri-nagai* did not apply to starmen. She aimed carefully at the first of the pair and was about to shoot when a firing mechanism whirred on just above her head. Raunn turned to see the boots and uniformed legs of a port guard standing solidly next to her.

Slowly she placed her weapon on the wet glasform surface and straightened. As she stood, the indifferent, lethal barrel of a hardlight rifle followed her up. The face above the rifle was tight, impassive and just as deadly as the weapon. Under the port guard's scrutiny, Raunn became abruptly aware of the image she presented. Her black common-weave shirt and leggings, the garb of a *drev*, were soaked with rainwater and some foul-smelling techish lubricant. Her face, camouflaged against probing lights, looked bruised and dirty. The light burn on her neck that had been the marksman's last hit throbbed. Reflexively her hand rose to touch the burn but the guard's lips and fingers tensed at the movement, stopping her gesture midway. Looking him directly in the eye, Raunn held both hands out slowly, palms upward, and kept them level. She knew that from here on her only course of action was to be open and honest. Summoning up the authority she had learned in her family's petition room, she queried in a firm voice, "The port has Code of Trade neutrality?" The guard returned a clipped nod. "Then I claim protection under Section Three of the code's Fifth

Clause." She continued. "And I most urgently request an audience with the Portmaster."

Under the circumstances, the formal offworld phrasing sounded absurd, even to her, but she had studied the protocol well and knew her request was valid. *Use their own weapons against them,* the Inayyam said. The guard remained silent and looked her up and down without visible sign of being impressed. There was a long pause. "Name?" he demanded finally, in bad Chenni.

"Raunn ni Obradi san Derrith," she replied.

The guard cocked one eyebrow and surveyed her again. Raunn could tell that behind those hard eyes he was trying to connect a troinom name and a clan daughter with the disheveled fugitive from the underranks in front of him. She didn't blame him for his skeptical approach. Briefly she wondered how well the port security staff were briefed on the politics of the worlds where they were stationed.

The guard, having reached a decision, nodded his head and gestured with the tip of the rifle barrel. "Portmaster's this way. Come. And don't try anything with me."

He led Raunn silently between several utilitarian structures and then entered a building that was a little larger, but certainly no more impressive. Inside, they rode a techish device to the top floor, paced down a corridor, and stopped before a plain door marked in an alien alphabet. The guard knocked and a muffled affirmative came from within. He opened the door, then stood to one side so she could enter the room first.

What she assumed to be the Portmaster's office held two people, both watching her with some annoyance. She stood facing a battered desk piled with outworld objects that she did not recognize. Even the area her studies told her was a computer access was covered. Raunn thought that no Clanmaster worth following would issue orders from a place so common, so lacking in dignity. Behind the cluttered surface sat a short middle-aged man with a face made older by lines of weariness. His expression said that it was late, he was not yet finished with his duties and did not wish to deal with another problem at this hour. His shoulders were hunched forward and he made Raunn think with a sharp pang of Antikoby hard at work running the Rock. But this man was older, less virile, with oddly thin hair the color of a child's.

Off to the left of the desk, in a battered chair, sat a far younger woman, also tired but noticeably more alert. She was pretty in a careless offhand way that told Raunn she had never thought much about it. The guard closed the door and came to stand close behind his prisoner. At a prompt from the Portmaster, he began to relate, still in Chenni, what had just occurred outside the gates. As he spoke, the Portmaster appeared to sink even further into his fatigue while the woman perked up. The expressions on the faces of both had shifted, however, from irritation at the interruption to curiosity. When the guard finished his statement, the Portmaster looked directly at Raunn. "Is all this true?" he asked.

"Yes, sir, it is."

"Your name, noti?"

"Raunn ni Obradi san Derrith."

The Portmaster's head picked up a little more but his face wore a skeptical look. "Clan, noti?"

"Cliffmaster, sir."

"You think this is a joke?"

"No, sir." Raunn's back stiffened.

"You can't be serious and I'm far too tired to be patient with nonsense."

Raunn remained silent against the insult: she could not allow clan pride to interfere here. There would be more insults, and probably worse, from these heathen outworlders who did not understand proper conduct. And she did not stand on friendly territory. Neutral the port might be, but it was allied by necessity with the Tulkan, her enemy, and she could not indulge herself in a display of pride.

"If you are going to impersonate someone," the Portmaster continued stiffly, "and particularly if you're going to assume a different rank, you should study your role first. Now, what is your name, woman?"

In a tight voice she replied, "Raunn ni Obradi san Derrith." It had never occurred to her that she would not be believed: such a thing was totally outside of her experience.

"All right, I'll indulge your pretense. Let's see how well you do. How does one approach Cliffmaster Citadel?"

"Hand over hand," she said simply. "Once you're old enough to make the climb yourself. Before that you go up on someone's back or you're hauled up in a freight basket."

One side of his mouth twitched upward. "And how many ladders do you encounter on the way up?"

"There are seven," she stated. Then, assessing the expression on his face, she added, "Would you like to know how many rungs there are on each?" Her question startled him and she realized that he had probably made the climb once and had focused all his concentration on simply reaching the top. Only those who had scaled the cliff over and over counted rungs and ledges as they went.

He allowed his irritation to show. "Don't be impertinent. I concede that you have studied, but I remain to be convinced. Proof of identity would be, of course, extremely helpful."

Raunn knew there was only one way to make him accept her rank although, under other circumstances, it would be an outrage. It was an insult even here, but it was nothing compared to what Merradrix would suffer. She tugged the coarse shirt away so that her left shoulder was exposed. "There is my clan mark," she said simply. On her skin, in plain sight, was the dark Cliffmaster tattoo that could not be simulated, even if anyone dared to do so.

The Portmaster's face froze and whitened. The situation had just escalated beyond all his assumptions. He sat up straighter and when he spoke again the tone of his voice was far different. "Sri-nothi," he stopped and cleared his throat as he regained his composure. "Why, sri-nothi, does a clan daughter of the san Derrith family, seek sanctuary in a Quadrant port of trade?"

"The Tulkan's men wait outside the gates. If I leave the port, they will arrest me and I will disappear." Then she added, "Sir," since he had recognized her claim and given her the proper form of address.

The Portmaster scanned Raunn as the guard had done,

taking in the costume of the underranks, the dye-stained skin, the hair bound up, and the blistered burn that seared her neck. He shook his head. "By the arms of Mavi, how did a woman of your station get involved with the Tarraquis? I can think of no other explanation for this state of affairs."

"That is correct," Raunn replied evenly.

"With due respect to your religious beliefs, extremism by the faithful can't win this battle. Your father sits on the Council of Clan Chiefs: he's a member of the very government you're fighting."

"My father is . . ." Raunn began, then stopped, aware that she had almost spoken far too freely. She started again, telling him only what was general knowledge, "My father is a man whose principles were long ago compromised by the Tulkan's strength and the deviousness of his Council Chief. He has been manipulated into voting for things he opposes in his very bones. He is a man of the old code who places honor and duty above all else, you see, and that may just be a trap when your opponent has never known honor and thinks that duty is something owed only to him. When he is without faith; without the grace of the True Word. My father strives still and will never give up but his seat on the council may as well be cold and empty for all the good it does those who believe as we do. That is why he is still alive."

"I see." The Portmaster was silent as he absorbed the implications of a speech that was amazing in its frankness. He tapped something on his desk and then spoke the name of her clan. A thin sheet of a substance like crystal rose smoothly from the desk top. It was blank on the side facing Raunn but the Portmaster stared intently at its opposite face as though reading something of great interest there. "Does your eldest brother know of your activities? Do you expect him to rescue you from the consequences of your youthful zeal?"

"Rushain drowned a half cycle ago while fording a river he knew as well as he knew the Rock."

"My condolences on your family's loss. What of your next older brother, then? Or is he too occupied with the responsibilities of his new position?"

"You have fallen behind the news, Portmaster," Raunn said in a controlled voice. "Cheyte disappeared in mid-Gleaning while riding to meet my father at our town house here in Nandarri."

"Indeed? How disturbing. Is there not an older sister?"

"She dreams. Caught in the web of the stardust your ships bring in to destroy our culture. She went to serve as hostess to my father here and made friends outside the clans. Or at least outside the Followers, for they ignore the laws against pollution of the body. I did what my father had not the eyes to see or the heart to do and sent her back to the Rock for the vellide our mother to deal with."

The Portmaster was obviously taken aback by this calm recital of her family's catastrophes. "You cannot be old enough to assume the duties of your majority."

"If I were not," she replied stiffly, "I could not have come to Nandarri. You can see very well by my clan mark and the color of my hair that I am of age. I came to the house on Cheffra Street because I was needed there and because I preferred not to stay at home, isolated, waiting for my accident to be arranged or, worse, my marriage."

Before the Portmaster could reply, the woman, who had listened quietly but intensely, interjected a query. "Since you have accepted the clan daughter's story, Portmaster, surely she could be allowed to sit down? And perhaps a medic?" She gestured toward her own neck to illustrate the point.

"Of course. My apologies, sri-nothi." He motioned to the guard, who brought a chair, and then spoke briefly into a grid on his desk. Raunn bent stiff knees and lowered herself carefully. Once seated, however, she kept her back straight and her chin high, not daring to relax. If she did, the Portmaster and his alien woman might see through her brave speech and righteous anger to the trembling uncertainty beneath them.

As soon as she was settled, the Portmaster continued his interrogation. "I surely do not have to remind you that Verrer ni Rimmani san Derrith is the Tulkan's Chief of Council."

"You do not have to remind me. How could he be anything but the Tulkan's man, for the stars dance in his eyes. Outworld trade entices him with the lure of profit beyond his imagining. And wealth is power in this new culture you bring us, is it not? His titles are as sand compared to what he dreams of acquiring. He is a man for whom power and wealth have replaced all else and no amount of either will satisfy him. He and the Tulkan together have sold Chennidur and the freedom of our people for his own gain. Only the True Word, the Inayyam, and the Tarraquis oppose him."

"He is still your father's cousin."

"He is no part of our family," she said coldly.

The Portmaster wondered at what doors she had been listening to have absorbed such opinions. If her brothers had taught her this, it was no wonder the Tulkan had removed them. The silence in the room was broken when the door opened to admit a grey-haired woman, tall and of an impressive stature. She looked at the Portmaster and then gestured at Raunn. "This is my patient, I assume?" At the Portmaster's nod, she gave Raunn's wound a quick examination that missed nothing. She looked up seriously. "This is worse than it looks. I would prefer to treat it in Sick Bay as soon as possible. Preferably right now." Her tone matched the Portmaster's authority and Raunn was surprised to hear what she interpreted as insolence in one who served under the Portmaster in the outworld hierarchy.

Her assumption proved correct when the Portmaster held up one hand in a forestalling gesture and replied, "In a few moments, Doctor. There are some questions that need answering before I can release her to your expert care." The doctor made a noise that indicated clearly her distaste at being called from her sleep and then required to wait.

"So," he continued, "you have decided to run with the Tarraquis in defiance of your family obligations."

"If that is how you wish to see it. That is not what I said."

He ignored the comment. "Was the mission you went out on last night your first?"

"Yes."

"Hmmm. And they sent you out with explosives. A bit dangerous for amateurs, don't you think?"

"We understood the danger. And we learned how to use your techish bombs."

"You must have learned well. Two warehouses are now heaps of rubble and the Tulkan's quartermaster will feel the pinch before the next supply run. You succeeded at your mission. Too bad you were caught."

"I was not caught."

The Portmaster waved his hand in acknowledgement. "I stand corrected. Had you been captured along with your partner, you would not now be my problem." He studied the look on Raunn's face. "You knew your partner well?"

"Yes. Very well."

"And who was he? The Patrol has released no name. Another troinom, perhaps, fed up with the status of things and itching to set his own course?"

"His name is Merradrix," Raunn replied shortly, stung by his goading. Let him draw his own conclusions.

The Portmaster stopped his acid questioning and stared at her. He had, in fact, no trouble arriving at a conclusion. Blue dirt. In addition to everything else, the troinom woman had a blue-dirt lover. It was not unknown, of course, in fact it was quite common among the troinom of both sexes both before and after they married others of their class. This woman was honest and entirely his problem: that was why he was being blunt with his questioning. The last thing he needed with a member of the Family sitting in his office was a political time charge, and the arrogant troinom woman in front of him had all that it took to assemble one. "I assume," he said finally, "that this Merradrix was as deeply committed as you are to the Tarraquis and your mission?"

"Certainly. He is a devout Follower and prepared to give his life to help it succeed."

"He's about to do just that, sri-nothi." Raunn allowed a cry to escape and he relented. "I'm sorry, to be so blunt, but you have to face some hard facts and face them now. The Tarraquis is outlawed and working with them in any way is a criminal offense under civil law. The Puzzle-masters will interrogate him and the courts will sentence him. It will be a long time before you or the Tarraquis will see Merradrix again."

"The hard facts, as you insist on presenting them, are a great deal worse than that, Portmaster," she countered. "Merradrix will have what little he knows ripped from his brain by drugs that will take much of his mind along with it. He may be tortured. Not for information they already have, but just because the Tulkan's men enjoy it and it serves to frighten the opposition. Then he'll disappear, like all the others. No one on Chennidur will ever see him again. If you face those facts, perhaps you will help me!"

The Portmaster shook his head. "I represent the port and the port trades with the legitimate government of Chennidur," he replied in a stony voice. "It is not in our interests to deal with, much less assist, a rebellious group of troublemakers whose goal is to break off the very business on which the Trading Family, this port and the Tulkan's government all make a satisfactory profit. Further, it is not in my personal interests to encourage religious fanatics who wish to take this world back a hundred STUs and return the culture to the feudal isolation in which it stagnated for so long. The Tulkan's government may have rough edges but it is our ally and business partner and it is the one thing that will keep your world from strangling itself." The sudden fire of his conviction died down and he ran one hand through his thinning hair. "Besides," he added, "your Merradrix is beyond my help."

"All I ask is that you help me to find him," she countered. "If I hadn't missed my shot, he would not need anyone's help. But I failed in my obligation to him and now I have to try and free him any way I can."

The Portmaster looked at Raunn in disbelief. "You tried to kill your own partner? Your lover! And you speak to me of obligations! I think you have forgotten the *shufri-nagai* you learned at the nayya's knee."

Blood rose in Raunn's face and she was struggling to maintain her composure against this insult when the quiet, self-assured voice of the young woman who had named herself Aurial broke in again. Her Chenni was rough and strongly accented but understandable. "It is possible, Portmaster, that the sri-nothi has not forgotten the obligations of her Clan and faith but knows them only too well."

The Portmaster turned to her angrily and then caught himself so that his reply, almost deferential, belied the emotion plainly visible on his face. "Indeed. I'm sure you are quite correct, sri-nothi. I spoke in error."

Raunn was brought up short by the troinom honorific. She looked hard at the woman who had a simple drev name, and saw Aurial's expression change, as if she had caught herself overstepping self-imposed bounds. Aurial's next words confirmed that impression. "Your pardon, Portmaster, I intrude in your affairs. This has nothing to do with me."

He shook off her apology. "Your comments are most welcome, sri-nothi, I have been here a long time and am perhaps more involved in the local situation than is wise."

"Just call me by my name," Aurial replied. She shifted in her uncomfortable chair and looked at Raunn. "Now then, how do you expect us to help you? That's a big request from someone in such a tight spot."

Raised in a highly political environment, Raunn recognized a possible ally when she saw one and had not missed Aurial's use of the word "we." "Just get me out of here, somehow, past the Patrol. That's all the help I need. Once I'm back in the city, I can reach the Tarraquis and we'll find Merradrix."

The woman looked at her coolly. "If the Tarraquis can do that, why do they need you to lead the search? Surely they know he has been taken. If the Tarraquis are capable of freeing your Merradrix, why have they not done so for the others who have been captured fighting for the True Word?"

Raunn caught her breath, sat silently, and searched her wits for an answer that did not exist. The lady, Aurial, was right. Before she could reply, Aurial followed up with another hard question. "And what if you could find him? What then?"

"Then I'll either get him free or I'll kill him. I'll do

whatever I have to do," she replied, but her voice lacked conviction.

"No one doubts your courage or your commitment, but I doubt if it is really that simple, even for a Clan daughter. Perhaps especially for a Clan daughter." She turned to the Portmaster and asked, "What will truly happen to her . . . to Merradrix?" He looked down at his hands and took a breath but before he could speak she cautioned him, "The truth. Not the official line."

The Portmaster looked at Raunn and his eyes held a knowledge he would have preferred to deny. "All right, the truth is very much as she has stated. He will be drugged and questioned and possibly tortured as well, although his wounds might save him further abuse. When the Puzzlemasters and the Tulkan's men have finished with him, they'll sell what's left to an independent labor merchant. He'll be shipped offworld, most likely to a developing planet with a contract out for cheap, disposable workers. If he's not dead by the end of the contract, he's free to earn his passage out."

In a very small voice Raunn asked, "How many survive to the end of a contract?"

"Virtually none. If a hostile climate doesn't kill them, then overwork and starvation rations usually do. It's slave labor hidden behind a nice businesslike front. Besides, the contractors and buyers don't really want anyone coming back to talk about what it's like in a labor camp. Too many governments use them as a convenient way to rid themselves of undesirables and make money on it. Nobody wants any inquiries to disturb their smooth and very profitable arrangement. Everyone's happy but the laborers and, once they've disappeared, no one cares about them."

Raunn sat frozen with a stricken look on her face. There was silence in the room as the other two looked at one another. Offworld. The possibility that Merradrix would be taken off Chennidur had never occurred to her. Once away from the soil of their world he would be *parostri*, lost to her, to the Tarraquis and to the True Word. His body would be worked to death and his spirit cast into the timeless dark, for the Raveler to own.

Finally the Portmaster spoke and his voice was almost gentle. "Think about all of this, sri-nothi, and decide what would be the best way out. I will make additional inquiries and in the morning we will speak again when we'll be able to think more clearly. For now, go with Dr. La and she will see that you are taken care of."

The medic made a sharp noise that said it was about time and came over to Raunn. Deciding that the Portmaster was most likely right, she stood with the medic's help and went out.

## NANDARRI

He who had once been a boy named Bikkle but was now Shaman of the Living Hills People kept still and silent. Seated on the floor in the center of an empty room, he maintained his stillness within and without. In this place of walls, floor, ceiling, he was shut off from the world that was as much a part of him as his own skin. Without the voice of the sky, the touch of the soil, the scent of the rain and the taste of the wind he was crippled, as if his limbs had vanished. He was surrounded by men and women of the hive they called a city but cut off from the People so that he could no longer hear their needs and feel their pain. The mark of the shaman on his forehead, created when his Allsight had opened, was occluded. He could not know when he was needed. The joys and sorrows of his people no longer involved him and he was as a bikkle whose podmate was dead.

Yet he was not being punished: no one had forced him to leave the Living Hills and enter this city of the walking dead. His path had brought him here and the People had wailed at his going. Although his soul had mourned with them, still he had come here not knowing why or what he must endure before he could return to the hills and the

People that were his life. Now he remained in the city where the Silent Ones shut themselves away from the Provider in rooms like empty skulls and jabbered at one another but could not listen to the voice of their mother.

Following his path, he paid attention to words that were like the clicking of pebbles until he could understand more than the few that were known to the People and speak them as though they were his own. He covered his hair, which marked him, and did not intrude upon the Silent Ones. Thus, they did not see him, for they were blind as well as deaf. He did all of these things diligently but still he could not unlearn how to listen and the silence that surrounded him was a prison. He did not move because there was nothing for him to do and he waited between walls like bone for the next portion of his path to reveal itself.

He would not wait long, that he knew and the knowledge was a small comfort, for every moment that he spent in this place was dangerous. Whenever the People and the Silent Ones met, always there was the risk of violence to the People. The Silent Ones feared them and fear breeds anger. The risk was far greater for a shaman. These things he knew and yet his path took him to a crossing point not with the Silent Ones, who lived on the Provider but were not of her. He waited for the Others.

The room was lit dimly by a single window on his left and now that light began to fade with the setting sun. The shaman's body was hungry and thirsty but he set those needs aside. The time was almost upon him and his body would receive what it needed later. He emptied himself of all thought, ceased for the moment even to listen, and concentrated on drawing the path's nexus to him. He felt his soul's energy radiating out, reaching down into the soil, out through the walls and up into the night sky. All the radiant energy had but one focus, one meaning. Come to me, it said.

There was a rumble of steps outside the door and then the rough boards were wrenched away. A new light flooded the room, one that was brighter and harsher than any he had ever seen. Men pushed their way into the room behind the light and formed a circle around him. The shaman could not look up at them without being blinded, so he continued to stare straight ahead.

"He don't look so terrible to me," one of the men said.

"Yah, he's still sittin' down," another replied.

A hand reached out and pulled the hood away from his head, revealing his fine hair, as changeless in color as the Veil. "Yup, he's one of them," said a third voice. "The old snitch was right."

"Stand him up," ordered the leader in a matter-of-fact voice.

Hands gripped his arms and the shaman stood in response. His eyes had adjusted and he regarded the ring of Patrollers, seeing nothing that surprised him.

"Well, scog me," said the first man. "He is a tall one, ain't he."

"Still doesn't look like he's going to start any trouble," added his companion.

"He doesn't have to do anything," said the commander, who looked the shaman over coolly. "All it takes is for one nayya to get wind of a Rugollah in the city and we'll have our hands full. Let's get him out of here while things are still quiet."

The hands tightened their grip and the shaman obliged them by walking calmly toward the door. Before he reached it, however, he shook them off and pulled the hood back over his head. There was a frozen moment while the patrol waited for him to make a wrong move. When he continued walking quietly, they fell in before and behind him. Then the group filed through the open door and out into a chill Nandarri night.

# CHAPTER 2

## CITADEL CLIFFMASTER

Tuupit Antikoby stood at the edge of the terrace with his fists clenched upon the broad stone railing. Before him, far out above the crown of the forest, the sun sank toward the horizon, illuminating the ragged edges of the Veil with its final glory. Trees waved in the evening wind, clattering and tossing their branches like live creatures. Fields and pastures rolled up to the overgrown talus slope guarding the base of the Rock's sheer walls. Above those walls, on the terrace immediately below Antikoby, a hauling crew strained to lift crates of supplies while the daylight lasted. The shouts of the overseer and the work chant of the crew mingled with the shriller cries of children playing behind Antikoby on the broad temple terrace. These little ones also pursued the short time remaining in the day, racing about with a frantic energy to hold mothers and darkness equally at bay.

Standing by the high rail, however, tuupit Antikoby was shut inside the narrow room of the worries that haunted him. All he could hear was the repetitive sound of his own circular arguments; all he could see was the blank wall of

26

his own confusion. Fear burned hard and cold in his gut. Oddly enough, Antikoby was not at all confused about what needed to be done; nor was he uncertain of his abilities to carry out the plan he had devised. He had fitted the necessary steps into place over days of careful deliberation with himself. But it was neither his position nor his responsibility to take the actions required. That particular initiative, that authority to grasp a situation and act decisively to change the course of the Clan's events, lay only with members of the Clan.

It was not that Antikoby was incapable of decisive action; as tuupit of Citadel Cliffmaster he was quite accustomed to it. When there was an emergency, broken bones and severed veins did not, after all, wait upon the presence of troinom authority and neither could the care of them. Antikoby had seen and dealt with many such crises while serving the Clan and the san Derrith family in the highest position to which any drev could aspire. Such problems as he was accustomed to resolving, however, were the common, house-and-garden sort. Difficulties such as the one which now circled endlessly in his mind, difficulties that involved the future of the House and the Clan, were the rightful province of the vellide Rutin-Xian. Yet she was consumed still with the grief that had enveloped her since the death of her second son. Her awareness of reality was shallow and limited to the daily round of activities in which she moved like a graceful figure in a shadow play. Beyond a formal greeting and a few pallid words of welcome, she had paid no real notice to the return of her daughter, the su-vellide Torrian-Xian, to the Citadel. Nor did she seem to be aware that her daughter had arrived accompanied by a "friend" of unknown pedigree from Nandarri, his servants and what Antikoby suspected to be a supply of the profane stardust.

One look at the su-vellide, a few moments of talking with her and seeing the arrangement of her entourage, had told Antikoby what needed to be done. Later events had only confirmed that knowledge. Yet still he juggled the realities of need with the visceral dread of overstepping his position and his rank. The sun rolled below the horizon, accompanied by the Veil's last edges. The trees below him dulled to a uniform shade of grey. The hauling crew locked the windlass in place and dispersed. The children were herded, protesting, into washrooms so that they would be clean and presentable for the evening Call to Prayer. In a twilight suddenly silent, Smallmoon lifted into the sky and Antikoby made up his mind. The vellide could dismiss him from his position, banish him from the Citadel, declare him pariah among the clans. She could even take his life. Yet he would leave, or die if it came to that, with a clean conscience. What he could not do was stay silently here on the Rock, going dutifully about his tasks as tuupit, and watching as the House was destroyed, the True Word mocked, the impregnable Clan fortress corroded from within.

The Eyestar burned hard and bright in a sky now lavender-black and the evening wind raked his hair with a cold touch. As the first melodic chants of the evening service drifted out of the temple, Antikoby breathed deeply of the clear air then released it slowly. His place at this moment was inside, at the head of the household staff, leading their responses to the nayya's calls. The compelling need for action had driven all other obligations from his mind, but it was time to assume those duties once more. Fortunately, he could also use the evening service as a steppingstone for action.

He crossed the terrace and stood by the temple's small side door, waiting for a pause in the ebb and flow of the prayers. When it came, he slipped silently into the big hall and moved as unobtrusively as possible down the aisle and into the space reserved for the tuupit. He was not often late but it was known to happen and no one took notice. The smell of the rennish incense filled his nostrils and made him briefly giddy. Grateful for the opportunity to lose himself in the observance of his faith, he let the familiar ceremony wash over him, responding from his heart when the ritual called for the participation of the underranks. For once, his over-active mind was still, caught up in something greater than he, with all his worries, would ever be.

It was a short respite, however, and soon the words of
the last chant brought him back to the business at hand.
The service over, he made his way through the predicta-
ble confusion of people as the underranks lined up for the
Sharing of Water. He stopped at the front of the temple
where the vellide Rutin-Xian remained seated, still and
apathetic, in her ornate chair. Antikoby stood before her,
looking sadly at the wreck of a woman who seemed barely
aware of his presence. Once lithe and almost athletic, she
was now gaunt, her skin slack over hard bone. She had
never been a beautiful woman and was now not what
people would tactfully call attractive. Yet her inflexible
dignity still lent distinction to the square face with its pale
eyes, solid chin and narrow mouth. An inbred confidence
made the wrinkles on her face seem more a badge of office
than a mark of age. Only her hands, once so firm and calm
but now thin and trembling, gave her away.

Antikoby held out his hands for her to take and raised
her from the vellide's chair. Her *dorchari* fell in straight
folds to the floor, as if no body stood within it. This also
was not his duty: the vellide should be escorted by her
husband or by the sons or brothers of the family. Here on
the Rock, however, there was none but the tuupit left to
walk with her. Absently placing the unsteady fingers of
her right hand on his left, she walked by his side toward
the great doors that led from the temple to the main
courtyard. This ceremonial exit was part of the household's
ritual life, and they moved through it mechanically.

It was futile, he knew, but Antikoby was compelled to
make one final attempt, try one last time, before taking
the initiative into his own hands. "Sri-nothi," he said
easily, "the su-vellide Torrian has returned to the Citadel
and is in her quarters. She is not well. She cannot come to
you as is proper. Do you wish to see her? We can walk
there now and I will wait until you are ready to return to
your rooms."

There was a long silence in which no sound intruded
but the measured tread of their steps and the cries of a
night flyer wheeling overhead. For a moment he thought
that she would not reply at all, had not heard his query

any more than she had acknowledged his presence. Then came a deep sigh as though the vellide found the necessity for speech an annoyance, distracting her from the grief that consumed her. "No, tuupit," she said finally. "Later. Tomorrow. I am tired and I wish to retire. Take me to my quarters directly."

It was virtually the same answer that he had received on the other occasions when he had attempted this query. He knew there would be no tomorrow. This time he added another comment, just to make sure that she knew of his intentions and did not disagree with them. "I will visit the su-vellide tonight, then. For I wish to help her become well again and to be certain that she walks with the grace of the True Word and in the presence of the Chenni-ad."

"Yes, tuupit, that would be good," she responded in a soft voice.

So, he had his assent: now he could act with a clean conscience, if no less fear. He walked the vellide slowly back to her quarters, making light conversation all the while, filling her in on the daily details of running so large and self-supporting an entity as the ancestral citadel of Clan Cliffmaster. These were the things they had once handled together, discussing them daily. Now they were merely words to her. Rutin-Xian said nothing although she was almost certainly listening in her distracted and disconnected way. Her maid opened the door to her chambers and Antikoby left her there with an innocuous wish for pleasant dreams. The moment the door was closed, he pivoted and strode decisively down the hall on his way to putting his plan in motion.

The su-vellide's quarters were not far from the chambers of her mother but, despite his consuming impatience, he did not move in that direction. Before he ever spoke to the sri-nothi Torrian, he must prepare the room. This work was something he must do himself for he could trust no-one else, and could not risk a whisper reaching the wrong ears. He moved through the enormous structure cloaked in an authority he had never needed more than now. It was a mantle that was expected of him and would be remarked only by its absence. There were people everywhere and while servants were the most observant of all the house's occupants, they were also the least discreet. With strangers in the house, out-clan people to carry stories back to the city, there could not be even a hint of suspicion. He did not wish to have anyone speculating outside these walls, far less off the Rock, about why the tuupit left the vellide's door and went to a little-used part of a distant wing.

He fetched a heavy sack which he had filled earlier, despite his anguished hesitation, with the necessary supplies. Swinging it over his shoulder, he continued through rooms and hall to the base of the moon tower. Climbing carefully up the worn stairs that curved around the inside of the tower's walls, he reached a small octagonal room clinging to the very top of the old structure. Barely breathing hard, though it had been a long climb, he dropped his sack on the floor and looked around. The moon tower was very old and had been virtually abandoned, providing a seclusion that suited his needs exactly. The room was still well enough equipped although the furnishings were not of the quality or comfort expected by a troinom. He shook his head: it was of no consequence. This guest would not notice such details for a while to come.

The dust of decades was settled comfortably on every surface; the air in the room was still, dank and cold. On the wall a frieze of scenes depicting how Aahks the Planner had spun the world was black with old smoke and cobwebs. Antikoby began by opening the shutters and checking the porcelain stove to ensure that it was sound and without cracks despite long disuse. He took wood and kindling from the sack and filled the grate. It took a while to get the fire going but eventually the stove purred hoarsely and sent out tentative ribbons of heat. While the room warmed, he shook out the bed's thin mattress thoroughly and made sure that it had no unwanted occupants before covering it with fresh linen. He would have preferred to replace it but lacked the time: a comforter would come up on his next trip. He swept up debris and cleaned things as well as possible without hot water and a scrub brush. That, too, could come later. This was underservant's work and heavier labor than any he had done in a long time but he was working toward a worthy purpose. He offered his efforts to the Chenni-ad, hoping to mitigate the effect of breaking the rules. If all went well, there could soon be a servant here to take over such menial tasks, but for now he was forced to rely only on himself.

When the room was swept and neatened, the extra wood piled in a rusty holder, and a few other supplies stacked on a shelf, he uncoiled a length of fine rope from the bottom of the sack. It was the same tough fiber that hauling crews used to lift heavy loads up the cliffs, but thinner and more supple. Cutting it into four pieces, he set to work.

Finally everything was ready and he proceeded methodically to the next step. Antikoby wound his way back down the tower, through the old wing to the family quarters and then toward the apartment where the su-vellide remained in seclusion. The next part of his plan would proceed much more smoothly if he could elicit the cooperation of her maid and he was counting on the woman's loyalty. Because Maitris had known him all her life and because she looked up to him as the ultimate authority for all servants, he had considerable leverage. He did not know, however, if she had changed in the time spent with her mistress in Nandarri. She, too, might have been corrupted by the outworld influences that abounded around the port. Anything could happen in a place where starmen walked among the Followers, spreading their heathen ways and techish wares.

He knocked loudly at the door and it was opened with startling abruptness by a slim dark woman with a tense face and anger smoldering behind her eyes. Her shining brown hair was pulled severely into a tight knot at the nape of her neck, a style that made her appear older than Antikoby knew her to be. She had a smooth skin and full figure but held herself stiffly. At first Antikoby thought that she would snap at him but then she recognized his face and closed her mouth again so that her lips formed a straight line. She stepped aside for the tuupit to enter and closed the door behind him quickly and firmly. Who, he wondered, was she seeking to keep out? As was proper, the maid waited for the tuupit to speak first. Antikoby decided on as direct an approach as his position allowed. "I must speak with the su-vellide Torrian-Xian immediately. Please inform her of my presence here and tell her that I most respectfully request a few moments of her time."

Maitris straightened into an almost defensive stance. "My mistress is not well. She is resting and does not wish to see anyone." Her hard words resisted any argument.

"Yes, I have heard of her illness and that is why I have come," he replied firmly. "As tuupit, any sickness on the Rock is my concern. Yet, though the su-vellide has been ill for several days, no help has been summoned—neither the infirmarer to ease her body nor the nayya to comfort her soul. No help of any kind has been requested. Now I must see and speak to her. It is my duty."

Maitris shrank from the truth of his words yet she did not back away from what she understood to be her own obligations. Instead she went to the door that led from the anteroom to the inner suite and stood with her back against it, barricading passage with her body. "My mistress is unwell in the way of women," she replied, tilting her chin in the air. "It has come upon her before and she has chosen to lie down until it passes. No help is required. She does not wish it. She has been most firm."

"Surely the infirmarer might have brought something to help—a soothing tea, perhaps, or a warm poultice."

"She wishes neither food nor drink, only a quiet room, shielded from the light, for her head aches as well." Maitris's voice had grown tight and combative as she searched for answers to his quite reasonable questions. She was uncertain in what direction this meeting would go but she was absolutely sure of the rules of conduct in such situations. Eventually the tuupit would exhaust his polite inquiries, reiterate his concern and leave. She would retreat also and marshal her forces for his next visit. No other behavior was permissible and her stance in front of the door was purely symbolic.

Antikoby, however, had embarked on a course of breaking the rules and understood fully the need to keep on breaking them. Polite verbal fencing would get him nowhere, as the maid understood only too well. To Maitris's astonishment, he moved quickly across the room and grasped her shoulders, crossing at the same time the boundaries of social convention and religious dictate. He would atone later, when the job was completed. Gently, yet brooking no resistance, he moved her to one side and opened the door. Ignoring her protests, he entered the su-vellide's apartment, went through the sitting room and found the bedroom beyond. Followed closely by a maid frightened now into silence, he entered a bedchamber that was dark and close, its atmosphere stifling with a sweet scent. The su-vellide Torrian-Xian lay in total stillness on the elegant bed, hands folded on the comforter and hair spread across the pillow. Her eyes were closed, her breathing shallow and slow. He stepped closer and carefully raised one eyelid: the eyeball was rolled back. Next he held her wrist, timing the sluggish pulse. Her arm, like the rest of her body, was weak and emaciated. Her skin was dry and peeling. The wraith who lay on the bed before him was far different from the mature and composed young woman who, brimming with enthusiasm, had left her ancestral home to keep the family's residence in Nandarri for her father.

Antikoby leaned over the etiolated figure and sniffed her lips. From between them came the sickening smell that permeated the room. He turned calmly to regard Maitris as she watched him, her expression shifting through horror and embarrassment to relief. He seized on the last emotion. "If I look below her tongue, woman, will I find it red? Will there be, perhaps, a few sores?"

The maid nodded jerkily, as if her head moved of its own volition while the rest of her body was frozen.

"And that is why she is so thin, isn't it? When the stardust owns her, she dreams and neither eats nor drinks. Yet even when the drug has faded, she cannot eat or even swallow for the pain in her mouth. Is that not so?"

Again the marionette head nodded.

"And how often is she like this?"

Maitris stared at him and her hands clenched into fists. She gritted her teeth but he could see the words pushing to get out even as she struggled to decide what was the right thing to do. Then, with the force of water bursting through a dam, she cried out, "Almost all the time—now. At first . . . For a while . . . I didn't even know! It was them, her troi'm friends. She met them outside the house in other places where I couldn't go. When she first took the stardust, or at least when I first noticed a difference, it was almost nothing. She was silly, wild, full of a flighty kind of energy. I thought it was being in the city that did it, with the young men around her and all. You know, on her own, with grown-up responsibility." Her hands wrung themselves, fingers twisting and pulling. "She was always so serious about doing her duty that I thought it was time she learned to enjoy herself. But then when the wildness passed she was tired and slept for hours as though she had been working the fields at harvest time. Still I wasn't alarmed. Those things happen, can happen for no reason. I never thought of the dust, you see." She hung her head, hiding her eyes and her shame at having failed in her duty.

It had happened almost exactly as Antikoby had imagined it. Still, it was truly not the maid's fault and guilt would serve no purpose now: they had more important things to do. "You could not have known," he said gently. "Living here on the Rock, you had no experience of such evil or how seductive it can be."

Her head came back up and her eyes flashed with anger. "Evil, yes! Those 'friends' she made," she nodded in the direction of the guest wing, "and him. Troi'm trash. All he wanted was to ruin her and make her as evil as he is. To corrupt her." She looked away from him for the first time, toward the silent figure of her mistress. "When I first saw it, the dust, I couldn't believe what my own eyes were telling me. There they sat, tipping it under their tongues, and I wanted to vomit. That's when I tried to talk to her, to warn her about what was happening. But already the stardust had changed her and she would not listen. It got worse. After that, everything went so quickly."

"And what will you do now?"

"Do? What can I do but attend to her and keep people away so that they won't see her shame."

"Then it will only go on like this."

"No, tuupit," she replied bitterly. "It will get worse. This is agony. Watching her waste away while she dreams and then starve when she's awake. Watching her lose her pride, her dignity, her strength. She used to be so strong, so sure of what was the right thing to do. And now she's just a shivering thing, dying in front of me and all I can do is watch."

She looked at Antikoby again as if challenging him to question her. After holding it inside herself for so long, after dealing with it all alone for day after frightening day, she needed to tell him everything and yet was terrified that he would find her lacking. Antikoby nodded and made an encouraging sound. Maitris drew herself together and continued. "All I could think of was to get her home. Get her back to the Rock where there is no dust. I talked to the tanzl and he did not believe me." She paused again and Antikoby could tell that this blow had been the hardest of all for her to take. "He did not believe me, but he must have known something was wrong because he sent for sri-nothi Raunn. But even then, when she came and took charge and sent us back here, those awful friends whispered and persuaded and the tanzl listened. He came along. Now the dust is here on the Rock and he will spread it, finding new victims. I haven't saved her. I've brought evil here instead."

There was such anguish in her face that it struck his heart and he knew that they were allies. Still, he must hear it from her. "Then will you help me?"

"Help you? How? Has vel Rutin sent you? Tell me what you are planning."

Antikoby started to answer her with the bleak truth but caught himself. If she assumed that he had orders from the vellide, she would follow him more readily. There was really no need to force her to make a difficult decision: she would hear what she wanted to hear. "Only I know and you must be my helper. Can I trust you?"

She nodded forcefully. Her body had lost the appearance of a mannequin. Now it was taut with enthusiasm and her eyes were gleaming with hope.

"Good. We'll make sure that no more evil comes to the Rock," he said firmly. "You're not alone with this any more. I want the same thing you do and there is a plan. We'll work together to get rid of the Wordless ones who want to keep suv Torrian in their grasp, to pollute others with their wickedness. Together, Maitris."

Without hesitation she asked, "What shall we do? Tell me. I'll do anything."

"Right now, we have to get her away from everyone. We must move her quickly, before anyone knows. I have a place prepared where she can be hidden from the one who accompanied her."

"Child of slime," she spat.

"Yes. We will be the only ones to tend her. There will be no dust, no evil, no false friends around her and we will make her well. That comes first."

"But she'll be wild. When the drug's lethargy wears off, she'll want more. She'll go out of her mind with the craving and we won't be strong enough to keep her from it. From him."

"I have heard what the stardust can do to those it holds enthralled. I have taken precautions. You'll see. Now, put together the things you'll need for both of you. I'll wrap her in the bedding so that, even if we are seen, no one will recognize the su-vellide. You and she will disappear while they are sleeping. Move quickly."

Maitris whirled and began pulling clothing, toilet articles, and a variety of other items from shelves and drawers, heaping it hastily and wrapping it in a spare quilt. In only a few moments the conspirators were ready, each cradling an oddly-shaped bundle. Then they moved in silent haste through the dark halls, encountering only a few of the under servants who toiled with their own heavy labors and who were not curious about the activities of their betters.

They reached the stairs to the moon tower and Maitris went first, holding the lamp she carried as high as she could without dropping her burden. They spiralled around and up, climbing until Antikoby began to feel the weight of the fragile body he carried. At the top Maitris set down the lamp and dropped the quilt, looking around her at the austere room. Then she rushed to help Antikoby as he lay the su-vellide down on the small hard bed. They made the limp figure comfortable but then Maitris stepped back, gasping, as the tuupit took the ropes from each bedpost and knotted them around wrists and ankles with sure hard knots.

He looked at Maitris and said, fiercely, "You are not to remove these for any reason. *Any* reason. No matter how much she might plead or cry or threaten. If you release her, she will go after the dust and all our work will be undone. She will be lost. If you cannot listen, go out of the room, but do not touch these ropes. When you think she is well again, tell me and I will untie her. Do you understand?"

She nodded wordlessly, then said, "But . . ." and gestured toward the chamberpot in the corner.

"If she cannot use that, then let her soil the bed. We can always get clean linen. We can burn the bed afterward. But do not untie her!"

"Yes," was all she said but the indecision was gone, replaced by cold determination. Then she set briskly about putting away the things she had brought and settling the two of them in while her mistress slept on, unaware of the unprecedented actions which had just transpired, unaware that her future had just changed completely. After checking out the room thoroughly, Maitris gave Antikoby a list of things for him to bring when he came again. That done, Maitris sat down to begin her vigil, not knowing how long or difficult it might be and not caring. At last her long anguish was over. Once again she could devote herself to her job—caring for her mistress. If a daughter of Clan Cliffmaster was not strong enough, if the eldest daughter of Krane ni Srinnioth san Derrith had neither the wit nor will to withstand temptation, then she, Maitris, would have strength and character enough for them both. They would see that courage was not given to the troinom alone.

# The Puzzle Palace

The man opened his eyes and looked around slowly, blankly. He was in a room. It was large, with a ceiling high above where he lay on the floor. There were other people lying, sitting, squatting, standing around him. He did not know who they were. He did not know what room this was, or where it was. He did not know why he was here. Or even who he was. Those were important things; he should know them. He raised himself up on his elbows and scrutinized the room once more. Painstakingly he pieced together the facts of what he saw, trying to pull those pieces together. If he could only do that, he could make a picture in his mind that would make sense. Somehow he knew that, but building the picture was difficult. Thinking hurt. Why?

The room was rectangular, its walls constructed of stone blocks fitted closely together. The stones were dark and smooth. Moss grew in the chinks and crannies higher than the level of a tall man's head. There was light. It spilled into the room from a single window set high in each wall at either end of the room. They looked out only onto a dull sky. It was daytime. What day?

His eyes drifted back down to the wall and followed it around until they encountered a door to his right in the wall on which he was leaning. Pushing himself forward, he crept out into the room until he could see the thick planks bolted together with bands of iron. There was no opening in the door. No handle to pull or latch to lift. That meant something. What?

He tried to assemble the pieces of information into a picture but they slid smoothly apart before he could make something of them. Something pulled at his mind, scattering his attention further, keeping all the pieces shifting around. It was a bad feeling in his body. No, not just bad. Hurt. Pain pulsed and burned somewhere. Where? He looked down at his own body, seeing it as if for the first time. He was clad in a rough shirt, torn and dirty, over heavy trousers that had only one leg; the other had been ripped off. His feet were bare but between the right foot and the knee a bandage encircled his leg. That was it: the bandage was hurting him. No, not right. Under the bandage. Yes, the pain came from there; he would look. Before he could find the end of the bandage, however, the thoughts uncoupled and went spinning away.

He crawled back to his place along the wall and leaned against the cold stones. Hard. Why was thinking so hard? His brow furrowed as he tried to connect one thing to another but no two thoughts would stay in one place long enough for him to put them laboriously together. He cried with frustration and the tears flowed easily, running down his cheeks unhindered. Putting his head into his hands he wept with the freedom of a child. No one noticed. When the tears had stopped, the thoughts still would not come.

Keep trying. Other people. Look at the other people. Holding out his hands straight in front of him, he lowered one finger for each individual beginning with the man on his right. He worked slowly and carefully so as to keep the people and the fingers from becoming separated. When he had completed the circuit all his fingers were touching his palm except for the thumb on his left hand. There was a number for that many things but it floated in the veiled sky outside the window and would not come close enough for him to see. He closed his fingers into a fist and pounded the stone floor.

Some of the other people watched him. Some slept. A few stared straight ahead as if there were something happening in the middle of the room that was invisible to all eyes but theirs. Their faces were pale ovals, meaning nothing to him. Most were men although there were a few women. This room was a terrible place. Something awful had happened to the people in this room. What? He did not know. The women seemed no different from the men. All were the same. He did not know why.

A sound entered his consciousness. Thud. Thud. Thud. Thud. Heads picked up and eyes moved around the room, focusing gradually on one portion of the wall. He followed the direction of their eyes and found that they were looking at the door. More sounds came. Voices. The others began muttering and repeating one sound over and over. Ooooo. Oooood. Foooo. Food. A hollow place inside him made itself felt. He attached the hollowness to the sound. It was a need of the body, beyond thought and so the idea of food became clearer. The thudding stopped and was replaced by a creaking, groaning noise. More light. More voices. The door was opening.

A man walked into the room carrying round things in his arms. He was followed by another man with a pail that had a shiny straight thing sticking out of it. These men were different. Why? No, there were no answers to why. How? They moved quickly, taking the shiny thing out of the pail and tilting it over one of the round things. Something poured from the shiny thing to the round thing. Each person got a round thing and began taking food from it. When it was his turn, he found the round thing filled with a kind of food he knew. What? Sooo. Stoooo. Stew. Warm liquid and chewy solid pieces. Good. He ate with his fingers like all the others (every finger on both hands except for one thumb), then drank the warm liquid. It felt good in his mouth and tasted like the first food he had ever eaten. When the round thing was empty, the hollow feeling inside him was better. His head felt better. He would try again.

He looked at his fingers. No, he could not use those: they were for people. He needed something else. The food things were gone. The food men were gone. The light was almost gone. Where? Now the door sound came again and the food men were back. They carried big pieces of cloth. Again, each person got one. Some wrapped themselves up. Some crawled underneath. One man held his against his chest and rocked back and forth. The pieces of cloth had lines on them, black and red lines. He stretched his cloth over his legs to cover the pain and looked at the lines. He could use those. One line for each thing: the cloth would hold them together for him. He started at the beginning. The room. Stone walls. Windows. Door. People. Pain. Food. The pieces stayed in place, anchored by the lines and he could look from one to the other. When all the lines were filled, he could fit other pieces in between. High walls. No handle. Thinking hurts. Door closed. Better. That was better.

He was not there yet, where he needed to be. Not anywhere near it. But he had come a long way. The cloth, the blanket, would hold the pieces for him. Tomorrow he would think a little more. Now he could let go and slide back into the darkness that filled the window, flowed down into the room. He would sink into the pain that consumed his leg. He would let the darkness and the pain fill him and block out the confusion that was his mind.

## THE PORT

Raunn woke slowly from a sleep that felt as deep and dark as the Chasm of the Spring. It was difficult to fight her way up from the darkness of exhaustion, to relinquish complete relaxation and the oblivion of avoidance. It was even more difficult when memory returned, opening the floodgates to recognition of her surroundings, the pain of the events one day past, the horror of Merradrix's circumstances. As if that were not awful enough, she hurt. Muscles in her legs and shoulders that had been pulled protested their mistreatment each time she moved. Sharp needles of pain radiated from beneath the clean bandage on her neck. She tested the new dressing and then rubbed several of the spots on her arms and legs that ached the most.

Rising slowly, like an old woman on a cold morning, Raunn looked about her at the room she had barely noticed before falling onto the bed last night. It was small, very plain and very white. A bed, a dresser, a mirror and a tiny sanitary cubicle filled it completely. Light from one small window illuminated all the whiteness, making the walls seem to be lit from behind. The air was flat and artificial, smelling faintly of some chemical antiseptic. It was a room that did not encourage one to linger.

Hunger was beyond her and eating was out of the question. When Dr. La entered, however, she insisted that Raunn drink a container of clear fluid that was supposed to be filled with vitamins and nutrients. Because it looked and tasted like water, Raunn was doubtful of any beneficial effects but she drank it anyway. She got dressed and was at least on her feet and presentable when the door opened. Expecting to see a port guard, she was surprised when instead the woman from the Portmaster's office entered. Perching on the edge of a table with one foot dangling in the air, the woman, Aurial, smiled at Raunn and asked, "How are you feeling today?"

"I am sore," Raunn replied briefly, "but Dr. La has taken excellent care of me. What time is it? There is much to do and I cannot do any of it here. Are the guards still outside the gate? Has anything happened to Merradrix?" She stopped and flushed, uncomfortably aware that she had sounded more like the adolescent the Portmaster had supposed her to be than an adult.

The woman appeared not to notice. "It is early yet. You did not sleep long. The guards are still there and won't be going anywhere soon. No, we do not know what, if anything, has happened to Merradrix. Are you hungry?"

Raunn blinked slowly as the memory of yesterday's failure twisted her insides and replied, "No. Not at all. But Dr. La gave me a drink."

"Well, that's understandable I suppose. You'll feel better in a while, when all of this seems a little less strange. But for now, the Portmaster's waiting, with more questions no doubt. Come, I'll take you there."

It was a cold morning and their breaths bloomed in front of them. Sunlight gleamed brightly through the Veil, however, promising a warmer day. Renewal was only days away but the sun was fighting a daily battle to achieve the proper warmth. Walking through the ugly functional spaceport, Raunn looked somewhat suspiciously at her companion. She was slim and dark. She wore an air of confidence along with a natural assumption of authority that belonged on a woman far older than she. Raunn did not recognize it, but in this they were much alike. Aurial's skin was pale, as if it had not often been out in clean air and sunshine. The deep-set black eyes gleamed with intelligence and her mouth was set in a firm, take-charge line.

Who was this alien woman? Why was she suddenly involved in Raunn's affairs and, most particularly, why was she being so friendly? It was time to seek some information. "You have me at a disadvantage," she began. "In last night's confusion, you heard me speak my name but we were never, well, introduced." That should be clear enough.

The woman looked at her with surprise and a hint of amusement. "No," she answered, "I guess we weren't. But you spoke your name loud and clear and I will do the same. I'm Aurial il Tarz." Her gaze intensified as though she were seeking or expecting some reaction to that name. When she met only a blank gaze, her features relaxed.

"Are you a crew member on one of the ships?" Raunn pursued further information.

"No. I am on . . . I'm just here to learn."

"To learn?" Raunn's eyebrows arched upward. "I did not know that Chennidur had anything to teach a starwoman."

There was more than a little sarcasm in her words and Aurial picked it up, then fielded it neatly. "Oh, well, this is only one of the places I've been sent to."

"And what are you supposed to learn here?"

At that Aurial looked truly perplexed. "Actually, I don't know. Perhaps you can help me find out."

Raunn had no reply to so puzzling a statement: Aurial's words were incomprehensible to her. But if she could not understand what the woman was talking about, at least she had learned her name.

It did not take them long to reach their destination. They rode the lift to the Portmaster's office in silence. The morning sunlight was as cruel to the cluttered, utilitarian office as it was to the rest of the port. It was even less impressive by day than it had been last night. The Portmaster himself was rested and a renewed energy had straightened his back, firmed up his shoulders. But the harsh light revealed every worry line on his face and threw the deep bags under his eyes into shadow. He offered the two women a hot drink and waited while Aurial filled her cup. Raunn sat down without waiting for an invitation: she refused to be put at a disadvantage. When he had inquired after her health and comfort and Aurial was sipping from her cup, he returned to his questioning. "So, now that you have been tended to and we have all had a chance to rest, we can continue. I have checked on your story and find that it is, regrettably, accurate. There can also be no doubt that you are who you say you are." He paused and looked at her carefully. "No one has reported you missing, however. As far as everyone is concerned in your government, the Tarraquis bombed two storehouses last night. The perpetrator was caught and is being held for interrogation. There is no mention of participation by any other person, particularly a troinom, particularly a clan-daughter. Our very discreet inquiry at the san Derrith house on Cheffra Street learned that you are indisposed. So. Everyone is covering up the truth and I have a very sticky situation on my hands.

"The guards are still at the gate, although no one mentions why, and you are in here. That brings us to this morning and the question of what we are to do with you."

Raunn grasped at a wisp of the Veil. "Can I just wait? Will the patrol go away when I don't come out after a while?"

"Not a chance," he replied. "There are only two ways out of this port—out the gate and up the well. The Puzzlemasters know you have to go one way or the other and they will persist until they know which of those two ways you have taken."

Raunn brightened. "Where is this well? How can I go out through it? I'm strong and I'm not afraid."

Both the Portmaster and Aurial smiled. "I'm sorry," he added, "that's our expression for taking one of the shuttles up to a ship. Think of sitting here on Chennidur as being at the bottom of a huge well with the sides made of gravity. At the top is space, outside the range of Chennidur's gravity. When you climb from the planet's surface to space, we say you have climbed the well."

"Oh. I see." Raunn felt foolish. She sighed. "They'll

know if I come out the gate; that's simple. But how could the patrol or the Tulkan know if I did ride up on one of the shuttles?"

"Information on cargoes and passengers in and out gets logged into the base records," the Portmaster replied patiently. "That data is sent instantly to the ship and to the master computer on the nearest distribution center. I provide a printed copy of the record to the government on a regular basis. If you went up the well, you would be listed on the manifest. If you aren't listed and you haven't walked out the gate, you're still here."

Raunn thought the solution was ludicrously simple but she refused to say so. Everything here was different, more complicated even than the politics she was used to. She would not give them another opportunity to smile at her naivete. Still, she would make the suggestion. "Perhaps you could 'accidentally' put me on the passenger list. Then, after the patrol left, I could just walk out the gate. That would be much less trouble for you."

Aurial spoke up suddenly. "Less trouble? No, just the opposite. As the Portmaster said, that data becomes part of the shipping records for this quadrant. The records have to balance with mass hauled, fuel burned, inventory shipped and revenue taken in. Listing imaginary cargo, human or otherwise, would unbalance the records and trigger an alert. Then a whole lot of computer links and a great many people would be subjected to time-wasting inquiries while the discrepancy was tracked. In the end, someone would be responsible for the error; someone would be to blame. The amount of money blown out the hatch in auditors' time and lost productivity would be almost incalculable. There would have to be a very, very good reason to stir up a mess like that."

"To be blunt, sri-nothi," the Portmaster added, "getting you out of the hands of the Tulkan's patrol is not good enough."

Aurial shrugged apologetically. "In fact, getting involved in the political turmoil on a single, moderately-profitable planet is not good enough."

Raunn looked from one to the other. Who was this

woman? And what was really going on here? After a moment, she said, "I see. Well, since just walking out the gate is equivalent to committing suicide—worse in the eyes of the Clan—my only alternative is to stay here for the rest of my life."

The Portmaster smiled dryly. "This is a working port and, although I'm sure you are quite a pleasant young woman, there is no room here for you. Neither do I wish to have a bloody battle fought on my front doorstep over whether you stay or go. No, I'm afraid the only alternative that is really open to you is to somehow go up the well."

Raunn hesitated, wondering why those words, now that she knew what they meant, should give her such a feeling of excitement. For all Followers, the way was clear and uncomplicated: alien technology was forbidden, poisonous. Now she contemplated giving her body over to it. Not to mention leaving the surface of Chennidur, where humans had been placed by the Chenni-ad, and flying, *flying*, in the air. She should find this prospect appalling. She should be terrified. Or outraged. Instead her heart pounded and a thrill ran up her spine as she anticipated this proscribed experience. Up the well. She wanted to do this, to look down on the world that had always held her close and wrapped her life so carefully in its customs and traditions that she had never had to really think for herself until a few weeks ago. In fact, until yesterday she had never faced anything more dangerous than an animal at bay on a hunting trip. Up the well. Just thinking those words gave her a frisson of excitement that she could neither explain nor deny.

Pulling herself back to the business at hand, Raunn asked, "But what then? Cargo going up to a freighter costs money, right?"

Aurial nodded solemnly.

"Then I somehow have to give you enough money to make up that cost and leave you with a profit."

"You learned that well enough," the other woman replied. "Can you pay for your passage?"

"Passage where? After I go up, I have to come back down somewhere. If it works here the same way it works on Chennidur, the cost of passage depends on both the length and difficulty of the journey."

"That's true. How much money do you have?"

"Here with me now?" Raunn's voice was scornful. "None. One does not carry money on a mission. Back at our house on Cheffra Street I have money and on the Rock there's a lot more. Unfortunately, I can't reach any of it without getting off the base first."

"This is a real sticky valve, isn't it?" the Portmaster commented. "But it certainly sounds workable."

"Indeed," commented Aurial. "I could stake your passage against my personal account."

Once again Raunn had the feeling that something was going on that she didn't understand. The real meaning seemed to lie between the sentences, not in the words themselves. The two outworlders were careful not to give away anything in their expressions to help her feel her way over this treacherous ground. "Then my passage must be cheaper than I thought," she tested. "Or you have a great deal of money in your personal account."

Aurial looked serious. "Actually, the cost of your passage is not inconsiderable. I do not, in fact, have that much personally. But I do have access to, well, a form of credit that would suffice."

"Why would you extend this credit to me?" Raunn challenged.

"For the simple reason that I want something in return," Aurial replied bluntly.

*Well, at last,* Raunn thought. *Now we begin to negotiate.* "What could you, an outworlder and a heathen, possibly want from me?"

Aurial's reply took her completely off guard. "I want to go with you," she said.

"Go with me? Why? You can go up any time."

"Yes," Aurial nodded. "But as you just pointed out, you have to come back down somewhere. You come up with me, I come down with you. I told you that I was sent here to learn and I can't learn what I need sitting inside the Port. If I understand your culture correctly, the Kohrable calls for all the Followers of the True Word to remain isolated from the Quadrant's civilization and have nothing to do with technology, which it says is evil."

"Yes, that's right."

"Then in order to go outside the port and learn anything, I need to look, act and speak as an inhabitant of Chennidur and be accompanied by someone who will help me to meet the right people."

"Only a troinom can do that, or a nayya. And none of the nayyat would compromise himself so."

"Exactly," Aurial said. "But you are a troinom of the Cliffmaster Clan. You could do it."

"Yes," Raunn agreed slowly, "yes, I could, although you would have to improve your accent. We would also have to create some tale to explain your presence. And you must understand, that being discovered in this deception would be a disgrace to me, to my family, and to the Clan."

"Even if the evil outworlder saved you from the Tulkan's patrol?"

Raunn thought that one over carefully. She hated to admit it but the "evil outworlder" was right. That act would carry a great deal of weight with the Clan. Except for Verrer. She picked up her chin: she would not think about him. Besides, this agreement gave her a great deal and cost her little in return. "Yes, all right," she replied. "But where? Back to the Rock?"

"No," the Portmaster interjected. "If you're to carry this off, you can't be connected with a shuttle and they make enough noise and glare to be noticed if one sets down anywhere near people. More importantly, though, we have to assume that the Puzzlemasters track our shuttles regularly—they have the equipment. We need to set down in a location that would not concern them if we claimed engine malfunction. That means a place isolated enough for the shuttle to land unremarked but close enough to your people for you to reach them quickly." He brushed some of the clutter off the computer grid on his desk and spoke into it. The air in front of the desk wavered, colored, and turned into a map.

Raunn rose from her chair with a cry of surprise and walked to the map, which now appeared as solid as a new wall. Examining it carefully, she identified landmarks and then said, "Here's the Rock."

The Portmaster came around the desk to join her and soon all three of them were examining the terrain in concentric circles around the Clan's citadel in an attempt to find a suitable location. They discarded site after site, with the Portmaster shifting the map several times until finally Raunn said, "Here. The Perimeter is far enough out and yet the house of my father's brother is an easy walk."

Calculating carefully, the Portmaster developed a trajectory that would place them in the desired location. "It can be done," he said. "But you will need provisions for the walk from the shuttle to the house."

"That shouldn't be a problem, considering the supplies you have at your disposal," Aurial prompted.

Raunn added, "We'll have to carry them ourselves. Once we get to Perimeter House, we can obtain more food and a pair of burrkies. After that it will be only a day's ride to the citadel. On the way, we'll have plenty of time to come up with a story that will explain your unusual accent and odd ways." She stopped and the light went out of her eyes. "By the time we get to the Rock, Merradrix will be beyond saving."

The Portmaster gave a clipped command and the screen disappeared. "Merradrix is beyond saving now," he said, with the cold tone he had used the previous night. "You may get yourself out of this, and the sri-nothi Aurial's plan might succeed, but you can't save him. Even the nayyat can't save him. Give it up and thank your Chenni-ad that you weren't taken too."

Raunn could not deny the truth that he spoke. Neither could she face it. Instead she rose abruptly and left the room.

# CHAPTER 3

## THE ROCK

When she was halfway down the winding staircase, Maitris stopped running and leaned against the tower's convex inner wall. Tearing the scarf from her neck, she wadded it over her ears in a frantic attempt to block out the sounds echoing from the stone walls. This was the worst of the ordeal, and it had been very bad. She was at the end of her endurance, beyond the ability to cope with what was now occurring. For days she had battled the stardust while it clung with chemical hooks to Torrian's body, leaving biological wreckage as it withdrew. She had cleaned up the aftermath of nausea and incontinence, wiped away cold sweats and bathed ruptured mouth sores. She had fought fever with cold compresses, dehydration with tiny sips of water, delirium with a soothing voice. Through the hard and lonely conflict, while day slipped into night and night crept back to dawn again, her only concern had been to ease the awful process in whatever small ways she could. Often, keeping Torrian as clean and comfortable as possible was all that she could do.

Now the physical debilitation with its awful fluids and

51

vile smells was behind her and that had been easy compared to this. For what the su-vellide's body had relinquished, the mind still craved. Just past sunset Maitris had looked up from her sewing to find her mistress regarding her with lucid eyes. Maitris had been flooded with relief to see Torrian once more in her right mind and recovery seemingly at hand. The first request, for a cold drink, had been easily and joyfully satisfied, as had the next one and the one after that. The request to be untied, made in an equally calm and even voice, had been no less reasonable. Maitris had, to her great shame, been halfway to the bed in response before Antikoby's words came back to her. A footstep's hesitation had saved them both. Not yet in possession of the control she feigned, Torrian had swung instantly from request to command. Maitris, brought up by the abrupt change, had looked closer and penetrated the facade of good health. She had seen eyes bright and glassy, jaw muscles tensed and knuckles whitened and then sat down firmly.

Following her refusal, Maitris had been buffeted by an emotional whirlwind of pleading, demanding and raging. Finally, appalled and embarrassed, she had backed out of the room and sought refuge on the stairs. Now she slid slowly downward until she was sitting on the steps with her shoulders against the wall and her legs stretched out before her like a child's. With the cold stone etching its grain into her back, separating her from the raging woman above, still she could hear the echoes of that fury ricocheting through the tower. How long, she asked herself wearily, how long could this go on? She had no experience with the stardust sickness and knew only the rumors passed among the domestic staffs of the troinom houses on Cheffra Street. Here on the Rock she had no one she could ask but Antikoby, and he was not a healer of any kind. Tears welled up as a sense of enormous helplessness filled her: she couldn't go on and she was alone. All she had to hold on to was her own strength and determination, her duty to Torrian and to the Clan. Wiping the tears roughly away with her scarf, she realized that those things were all she had ever had and they were enough. They had always been enough. She was not at the end of this ordeal and there was work still to be done. This was no time for sitting and weeping and feeling sorry for herself.

Blocking out the cries from above, she pulled herself into a kneeling position and regained her composure. Beginning with the very first one she began to recite the tenets of the True Word. Speaking each out loud slowly and precisely, she focused her consciousness on the well-known words, letting them fill and soothe her. As she went from one tenet to the next, the storm of emotions within her drained into her arms, down into her hands, then into her fingertips and flowed away. Only peace and tranquility were left behind. This was a technique she had used many times in the dark nights of her childhood. Awakened, alone among the bodies of sleeping children, she had listened to slow, mysterious sounds that seemed to emanate from the bedrock itself. Terrified of the noises, even more frightened of waking guardians sunk in exhausted sleep, knowing that the other children would only mock and tease her, she had turned to the nayya.

Nusrat-Geb had not believed her either, but he had given her this method of holding off her fear. She had learned the tenets well as she grew, repeating them over and over in the dark until sleep finally overcame the fear. It worked once again here as, reaching the end of the list, her voice slowed and thickened. It faltered and the pauses between the words stretched out until finally her lips stilled. Her head dropped back against the stone and she drifted into slumber. As she slept, however, the mad voice from the room above continued its ravings. Threats followed demands and pleas replaced threats, heedless of the empty room into which they fell. The thick stone of the tower absorbed them all impassively and gave nothing back.

Sometime later, having no idea how long it had been, Maitris crept back up the stairs, approaching the open door of the tower room with trepidation. It was quiet; not a sound emerged from the doorway and this sudden silence, as deep as the chaotic noise that had preceded it, was frightening. When she awakened once again and listened for the tirade which had driven her away, she had heard only this stillness. At some point during her drained sleep the raving had been replaced by a quiet as deep and solid as the stones around her. Anything could have happened while she lay exhausted and oblivious to her surroundings. All the dreadful possibilities presented themselves to her with stark clarity while she mounted the steps one after the other. Approaching the circular chamber, Maitris expected to be confronted by the worst, believing that disaster was the least she deserved as punishment for her lapse. She peered around the doorjamb into the room. In the rumpled bed Torrian slept soundly and peacefully.

Maitris exhaled in relief, then pulled herself together and entered briskly, more nurse now than lady's maid. The bedclothes were a tortured mess, stained with sweat and tears and blood from blisters not fully healed. The linens needed changing but she did not want to disturb the soft regular breathing nor waken her patient and bring on the awful screaming again. She did not even dare to wipe her mistress's face with a cool cloth. Suv Torrian had not slept this deeply since the beginning of the detoxification process. Instead Maitris straightened up the room, set water to heat for tea, then went to her chair at the head of the bed and sat watching her sleeping charge.

She settled herself calmly to wait. She was used to waiting for Torrian although she usually had some work to keep her hands occupied the while. Around her the room was quiet, as if a bubble of silence enclosed the top of the tower and separated it from the rest of the citadel. Inside the bubble were just the two of them, as it had been so many times before. They had been together for a long time, since Maitris was selected from among the junior chambermaids to attend the new troinom lady. That was on Torrian's Coming of Age Day, when she had left the nursery and moved to one of the adult bedrooms on the upper floors. On that day she had begun the more serious training required of a Clan's su-vellide, or eldest daughter, and Maitris had begun learning the skills of a lady's maid.

It had been a momentous day, signalling great changes in the lives of both young women.

They hated each other. Maitris hated because she feared all troi'ms and resented having to serve one particular mistress. Torrian hated because she, too, was frightened. Having her own maid was a symbol of an adulthood that represented the acquisition of enormous responsibility and, worse, the inevitability of a political marriage. Had they both been only a little older, the pairing would have been disastrous. What broke down the barriers and allowed them to learn from one another was a storm.

Billowing out of the mountains in the depths of a hot summer night, it broke virtually on top of the Rock. Great flares of lightning flashed into the room with shocking intensity, followed almost instantly by thunder that rebounded off the cliffs and outcrops surrounding the citadel. In the nursery below, troi'm children were comforted by nursemaids, soothed with kisses and distracted with songs and treats. Upstairs, among the adults, no such fear was acknowledged, if it existed at all, and people simply kept to their beds until the storm passed and they could drift back into sleep.

Maitris knew that Torrian was terrified but could not seek comfort because that would have demonstrated that she had not outgrown childish behavior. No adult would come to her aid then, not even her father, the tanzl. But in her own room she cried out with each slash of lightning and explosion of thunder until Maitris's lack of response shamed her into silence. Maitris had sat, wide-eyed not at the storm but at her mistress's histrionics.

Telling herself that only a troi'm would behave so, Maitris had found herself feeling in control and the more grown up of the two by far. So when Torrian said, "I'm frightened," in a voice that was almost inaudible, Maitris nodded a silent affirmative and then scrambled over to the big bed. There, seated on the feather spread and surrounded by draped curtains, she held her mistress until the storm crashed its way out across the rocky peaks.

After that they had gotten along, although cautiously, then learned to rely on one another as they negotiated the difficulties and confusions of the adult world. It was an alliance of opposites and at no point did it ever go beyond the distinctions of troinom and drev. Finally Maitris came to feel that she was a part of Torrian, the key support that made her successful. This work that she was doing now, driving the starmen's poison out, was the most important task that she had ever undertaken. She would stay where she was until it was over, even if there was still a long, hard way to go.

She smiled a tight smile of triumph to herself: the drug was nearly vanquished. When its evil claws had been drawn, she would work hard to restore Torrian to her former beauty. Her mistress shifted on the bed, fingers pulling at the bedcovers. Maitris looked sadly at the poor nails, broken and dirty. Once they had been Torrian's pride and she grew them long, insisted that they be oiled, shaped and buffed. Maitris would begin with those sad hands. Cups of hot marrow broth would make the nails strong again. Pureed *durric* placenta would bring body back to the hair, now lying dirty and stringy with sweat against the pillow cover. A good rinse with beer would add luster. After that . . .

She busied her mind with planning the reclamation of a beauty devastated by chemical pollution. The wreck of that beauty offended her for she felt that it belonged to her as much as to its possessor. Torrian's appearance was Maitris's achievement, her masterpiece, the finished product. When Torrian left the room with every fold and seam of her gown hanging just so, with every hair carefully arranged in its place, with every detail attended to, Maitris could be justifiably proud of her handiwork. She was a craftsman, constantly perfecting a work of art that shifted continually. The beauty was gone to ruin now, like a garden given over to weeds, but it could and would be restored.

# THE PUZZLE PALACE

When the light came again it drew the man back into
the world of the strange room, filled with pain from a leg
that would not work, hunger, and overwhelming confusion. He was still surrounded by people he did not know,
adrift in a stream of facts that eddied by and around him
but would not linger. The pain in his leg was worse, or
perhaps he was simply more aware of it than he had been.
Now his leg throbbed beneath the bandage like the heartbeat of an animal and would not be ignored. Part of him
wanted to peer under the dressing to see the wound itself
and try to understand, to remember, but it was countered
by fear. Lying still in his blankets, he stared at his hands
and groped for a memory, one simple picture, that would
connect him to the person he had been before this room
existed. There was nothing.

The light brightened, and around him the other denizens of the room began stumbling up from their thick
sleep. Like him, they rose into damp morning air fetid
with the smells of unwashed bodies and human waste.
Feeling a pressure in his gut, the man drove his gaze
around until he found the buckets, one in each corner.
Like hunger, this drive went deeper than thought, pulling
him up, but his leg was too stiff and the pain was too
great. Giving up the effort, he crawled instead on two
hands and one knee, dragging the useless limb behind
him. His movements antagonized the pain creature that
lurked beneath the bandages and each bumping "step"
roused it more. Its sharp jaws bit into his leg, sawing back
and forth. When he had relieved himself and gotten back
to his place, he had to lie still for a long time, clenching
his teeth until the pain diminished.

After that he took up the blanket and drew his fingers
from line to line, pulling from each thread the meaning
that he had given it the previous night. It took longer than

before but finally he assembled the complete litany of words and arranged them in the correct order. Then he returned to the beginning and began counting off the other figures in the room on his fingers. It took several tries because his cellmates were active now and their movements confused him. When the count was complete, all the fingers of both hands were folded down. He frowned at them. That wasn't right. His forehead creased with puzzlement when he repeated the entire process but the results were the same. There was another person in the room. One. Another. All the fingers. He scrutinized each face, one by one, but it was hard to distinguish individuals. All were as dull and unfocused as they had been before and looked much alike. Persevering, he finally located a supine figure rolled up in a blanket and motionless by the door. One more.

The door noise came again, prefacing the entrance of the food bringers. The sound stimulated the inmates. There was a wordless rumble and people began moving in the direction of the door. It opened and two men, not the same as before but wearing the same clothing, carried in a basket and a pail. There were no bowls this time, only rolls of coarse bread and fruit and water from the pail. Although people were hungry, no one pushed for first place or fought over the food. Instead quiet figures shuffled with mindless patience, awaiting their portion, or lay in complete oblivion until food was put in their hands. Like the others, the man took his food and waited for a drink dipped from the single pail. The silent figure on the floor did not move.

As they worked, the food bringers talked and the man, chewing slowly on his bread, listened intently. He hoped to hear new words that would help bring the pieces together. He did not understand all their words and much of what they said made no sense to him but nevertheless he paid close attention.

"Give me the shivers, they do, all quiet like and no more thought than trees."

"Can't blame them for that: the Puzzlemasters don't

leave much. Some more than others, though. Look at the eyes; that's how you can tell."

"You look at their eyes. I've ridden animals that looked smarter than these hulks."

"Sure, but those animals weren't shot full of chemicals that burned their brains out."

"So they're just burned meat?"

"That's right and they won't ever be much more than that. I've heard that coming out of chemsleep brings them back around some but I've never seen it."

"Makes my skin crawl."

"Yeah, well. That one now, number ten, he's got something left under his hair."

"Over there? He's just a kid. What happened, did the Puzzlemasters decide he didn't know anything worth digging for?"

"No chance. They got whatever he had. I don't know why, but he still has more rods firing than the rest of them. Lucky for him. Let's collect the blankets."

"Lucky, hah. As if you could call anybody in this rawfin place lucky. Be glad when I rotate off this duty."

When the door was closed again and he sat in silence, the man thought over what he had heard. Most of it had been beyond his comprehension and he had picked up only a word or two. Puzzlemasters. Meat. Kid. Shivers. They were words he knew but the only one that meant anything to him was meat. There was meat in stew. But the men had looked at him when they said kid. Ten, one of them had said. What was his name? Ten. It didn't sound different from any other word. Wouldn't his own name sound different? He didn't know. He decided to try it; it was something and he had nothing.

He gave up his blanket to the men when they came to collect it. As the woven pattern disappeared, he thought that he did have something. He was awake. He was trying to think. The new one didn't have that much. He didn't move. Wrongness. There was something wrong with the new one. Ten had a bad sense about that. The new one was wrong and all alone. The bad feeling built up until it pushed him out of his spot. Once again he dragged himself painfully across the dirty floor over to the still bundle of blankets. Slowly he edged alongside the shapeless mound until he reached the head. Moving the edges of the blanket carefully, he exposed the face. He saw a man. New beard. Scraggly. Eyes sunk deep and bruised. Mouth twisted. Bad.

Ten shifted himself around until he could rest the man's head against his good leg. He pushed the blankets down and smoothed the man's hair away from his forehead. Then he leaned back against the stone wall. The pain creature was eating his leg again but he felt oddly better. Helping the new man made him feel stronger. It gave him an even better feeling: he was no longer alone in this terrible place. All that day Ten cushioned the sick man's head and soothed him when he twitched or moaned in his sleep. At the next meal he accepted the man's food for him and tried to help him drink. When the water ran from between the slack lips and puddled on the floor, he set the food aside for the time when his charge would awaken and need it for strength as Ten himself had done. When he had done all that he could think of to do, he sat quietly, stroking the man's hair. He felt that this contact was healing and positive, not only for the injured man but for himself as well. In the long quiet hours he tried over and over to put thoughts together like shards of pottery to reform a jar that had been broken. Although he did not succeed, he did manage without knowing it to assemble pieces that were the same shape or size.

When the light outside the windows began to dim, the men from last night came back with what Ten thought of as the dark meal. They first fed the group that waited for them, then handed out bowls to the few who remained on the floor. As they worked, one of them grumbled about their task. "Don't know why the Tulkan needs the Patrol to guard this lot," he said. "I joined to fight, not to nursemaid a roomful of hulks."

"Fine," his partner replied equably. "Why don't you go and tell the Tulkan that. I'll stay right here and take care of the meat. Then I'll break in your replacement."

"I'm not scogging stupid," protested the other. "I do

what I'm told alright, just like anybody else. It could be more exciting, that's all. A lot more exciting."

"Big man," the second scoffed. "If you want excitement, just go on thinking there's nothing in this room worth keeping your wits about you for. When you're not alert, anything can happen. Even here." The only response was a snort. "Of course," he went on, "most of them wouldn't know what to do if we took them out on the street and left them there. But the kid over by the wall is different. And the new deposit, too."

"What do you mean, different?"

"The Puzzlemasters are lightening the doses. The less juice the prisoners get, the more they have left to think with. And if they can think, they can act. Keep that in mind. If they act and you're asleep, you may see all the excitement you're ever going to get."

"I heard something about that from the first shift." His voice was sullen, but interested. "They didn't know why. Whaddaya mean less juice?"

"Money, what else? I heard, from nobody I can talk about, see, that the contractors complained. The meat they were getting was so burned they couldn't follow orders. Couldn't remember what to do next, you know. Can't get much in the quad markets for workers too fried to work. And a lot of them didn't last long, either. Probably too dumb to watch out for themselves."

"Sooo— If the contractors don't pick up the shipments, the Tulkan doesn't get his money. No profits plus he's stuck with the bodies."

"You got that right. So they cut the juice and our new guests are going to have more left behind the eyeballs than the rest of them. Ten and Eleven over there, for starters."

"Okay. I'll look out."

Ten and Eleven. If he was Ten . . . He looked at the man still sleeping. Was he Eleven? What did that mean? Juice. Contractors. Quad markets. More strange words. He still understood nothing and now there was more to learn. His brain had to start working soon. In his lap, the sleeper's head stirred, moving sluggishly from side to side. A shudder ran through the man's body. Ten stroked Eleven's head and found it hot and dry. He was hot but he was shivering. That was wrong. The badness was worse. He had to think. He had to do something. What? He looked at the guards, who were gathering up the utensils and preparing to leave. "Hot," he said, and then repeated it more loudly. "Hot."

The two men stopped and looked at him with the same expressions they would have had if the water pail had suddenly spoken. They did not move. He tried again, "Hot. Wrong." The older one looked at the other. "What'd I tell ya," he said. Then they left the room, swinging the door solidly shut behind them.

Time drifted by and the sad denizens of the cell drifted with it. Night flowed in and they slumped down to sleep, wrapped in their blankets. Ten covered Eleven. He wished he could cool the man's face with the unused water from their last meal but the guards had taken it away. Eleven continued to twitch and shiver. He began to murmur but only in broken fragments of words and sounds. Ten held on to his hand and squeezed hard. He wanted to make the wrongness go away but there was nothing he could do. He squeezed again and said, "I'm here. I'm here." Eleven could not hear him but it made him feel better to say those words. Perhaps Eleven could feel that there was someone near who cared. The high windows were black and featureless. Ten felt like he was anchored to the floor by his stiff and throbbing leg and the leaden weight of Eleven. It had been all bad but now it was getting worse.

Then the door opened even though the last meal was over and the blankets had already been distributed. The guards entered again, accompanied this time by a third man. The guards remained by the door but the strange man approached Ten and Eleven. Ten heard the older guard whisper, "First time for a medic in here. I told you: no profit in dead meat." Medic knelt by Eleven and unclipped a pouch from his belt. He removed a shiny box from the pouch and placed it against Eleven's neck. He looked intently at the box and muttered to himself. Then he looked directly at Ten and asked, "How long?"

Ten searched Medic's face. What answer did he want? How long? How long what? He wanted desperately to give the right answer. Why couldn't he understand?

The Medic made another attempt, "How long has he been this bad?" Bad. Ten knew that word. Eleven was bad but what was how long? How could he know how long? But he had to say something so Medic wouldn't give up and go away without helping. "Long," he repeated. He pointed at the dark window. "Light."

The Medic interpreted. "It was light when he became 'bad'?" Ten nodded enthusiastically. The medic rolled Eleven over so that he lay on his side, causing the unconscious man to groan with pain. Sliding the blanket off his patient and, rolling up his shirt, the medic exposed a large patch on the man's shoulder. He held the shiny box over the patch and watched it for a moment. Then he replaced the shirt and removed a thin blade from his pouch. With one swift stroke, he slit one pants leg to reveal another patch on the man's leg. Again he looked at the shiny box.

Ten was confused but that had become such a familiar condition with him that he did not fight it and simply watched. Medic became very busy, using strange implements to give the unconscious man medicines, and placing clean bandages on the wounds. Ten felt better when Medic put the box down and looked at him. "You were right to call," Medic said. "He needed help. Now, what about you?" Handling the stiff leg carefully, he cut the bandage away. Ten gritted his teeth against both the pain and the fear of what he would see. There was nothing beneath the wrapping, however, but a raw and swollen line of stitching girdling the leg. When Ten looked at it his throat tightened. The sight of it terrified him, as if it revealed something dreadful about him. The emotion swelled up inside him uncontrollably. "Aaaahhh," he cried out, and then the tears followed. This was what he had feared. It was awful. What had happened? Who had done it? What would happen next?

Medic looked up, "Is there much pain?" he asked, unmoved by the tears and Ten's great distress.

Ten nodded wordlessly. The tears continued to stream down his cheeks.

"Can you stand?"

Ten shook his head.

The medic looked around them at the dismal room. "Well, stay down, then, as long as you're here. That shouldn't be a problem. After that, well, when you leave here I can't help you. We fixed your leg as best we could, reconnected everything you severed. But there's no telling with something as severe as this. I'm not supposed to but I'll give you the same sedative I've given your friend. You'll sleep for a while and the pain won't catch up to you right away even after you wake up. That will help. About all you can do to help is to think yourself healthy and strong. Take all the nourishment you can. Don't push the leg unless you have to." He looked away, adjusted his instrument and then put it against Ten's neck. The sleep that followed was deep, untroubled and welcome.

# THE PORT

By the time they left the Portmaster's office, the Veil was thick, shielding them from mid-afternoon light. The outworld woman never looked up, seemed oblivious to the day around them, but asked, "Are you hungry?"

Raunn shook her head. Her stomach was a hard, sore little knot and everything about this techish place made it tighten even more. The harsh smells of substances she could not even begin to identify, the stiff regimentation of the people, the different clothing, language, gestures, the overwhelming alienness of it made her want to vomit. She stole another glimpse of the familiar sky and tried to remind herself that she was still in Nandarri, only a brisk walk away from the house on Cheffra Street. She thought about opening the door of that house, entering the courtyard and crossing the tranquil garden. Just up the stairs was her room where Chewtti would assemble a hot bath, a soothing drink, clean clothing, all for her comfort. When her father returned from the council, she would attend the evening Call to Prayer with him. Then, while he presided over the evening meal, she would listen to the account of his day and try to ease his frustrations. The wonderful familiarity of that routine filled her with longing. It had been her normal life until only yesterday. Here in the Port she was forced to acknowledge for the first time the magnitude of what she had risked and lost.

Aurial interrupted her thoughts. "Well, I'm starving. Breakfast was a long time ago and I thought we would never finish in there. Why don't you come with me to the commissary? You might surprise yourself and eat something, just for the enjoyment of it."

Raunn nodded. It was easier to go along than to force words past the rough obstacle in her throat. Besides, what else did she have to do? The few days before they would board the shuttle and put their plan into practice stretched endlessly before her. Surrounded by noise and activity, they crossed the Port in silence. Despite her anguish, Raunn could not help being curious. She took in the Port as she always observed her surroundings, noticing especially the small things that most other people never saw. Finally she swallowed the obstruction and broke her silence. "This isn't what I expected."

"What isn't?" Aurial said.

"This place, the Port. I knew it didn't harbor monsters and evil creatures from the stars; that's the kind of story the nayyat tell to frighten children and keep the underranks in line. That's not what I mean. It's just that I was expecting something more—well, impressive. Where are the ships that cross between the stars? Where are the great machines that let you talk across the void? It's all so ordinary here. These buildings are just offices and warehouses like the merchant compounds by the river."

Aurial stopped and pivoted to look at the spaceport with

her companion's eyes and barked a short laugh. "That's exactly what they are," she replied. "They're all that's really needed down here. The interstellar freighters are up there," she pointed at the bright sky, "in parking orbit above Chenridur. They don't ever land."

Following her gaze, Raunn said, "Oh. I remember. The shuttles get the merchandise from the warehouses to the ships. Up the well, right? That seems to be extra work. Like using a lot of little wagons to load up a big one."

"Not all of it goes up on the shuttles: most of the small stuff can be transported. I'll explain that to you later. The shuttles take up anything that's too unstable for transporters, or too bulky. Or alive. The port has three shuttles; they're all up right now but one of them should be down before tomorrow morning. You've been living in Nandarri for a while so you must have seen the glare from the thrusters and heard the noise they make. We baffled them as well as we could to meet the requirements of Nandarri's civil code but we couldn't make them completely silent. As soon as the next shuttle comes down, we'll go through it so that it will be familiar when we take our trip. I can show you around the transporter base, too. That may be a little more exciting than the rest of this place."

They started walking again and Raunn thought for a bit. Then she asked, "Will I get to see one of the interstellar freighters?"

"It's not likely," Aurial replied right away. "We'll be taking a short, sub-orbital hop while the freighters are parked in a much higher orbit. But you won't be missing much. There's nothing pretty or impressive about a freighter and there's not too much to see. They're designed to carry merchandise from one star system to another safely, reliably and with a minimum of damage. That means they're big and bulky and functionally ugly. Building one strong enough to withstand the force of gravity and hold up under the acceleration necessary to get its payload out of a planet's gravity well would take an enormous amount of money. It's really far more economical to use tough little shuttles that never go outside of Chennidur's orbit and get the merchandise up and down cheaply." She looked at

Raunn briefly and glanced away again. "It's business and business is profit and loss, risk and reward. You figure out how you can make the most money when you sell or save the most money when you buy. It's not very glamorous or exciting but it keeps the economies of whole systems in the quadrant running pretty well."

Raunn's head was still trying to make sense out of the harsh words from the common language that Aurial had used when they arrived at another plain, ordinary building slightly smaller than the others. On the side of the structure next to the door a stack of words was printed in several different alphabets. Raunn recognized only one of them, the Chenni word for food. Inside, they were assaulted by the smell of cooking food and a rushing tide of noise—voices talking and laughing, the clatter of utensils, the crash of a chair falling over. It brought Raunn up short for a moment before she straightened her shoulders, raised her chin and walked behind Aurial into the chaotic room. This may be an alien environment, she thought, but she had been entering crowded rooms all her life and had been trained from childhood to do so with grace and dignity. The port staff, however, kept right on eating and talking without taking any notice whatsoever of the two women.

Following Aurial's lead, refusing to feel abashed, she helped herself to a minuscule portion of what food she recognized and then went to sit at a table. It was so crowded and noisy in the room that conversation was difficult. She concentrated instead on attempting to swallow something and keep it down. The talk around them was fast, complicated and used, as Aurial did, many words that Raunn could not understand. In spite of that, she found it oddly compelling. Raunn reminded herself dutifully that all this was corrupting, forbidden: the nayya would instruct her to shut her eyes and mind to it. Instead, she found herself trying to hear and remember everything. A buzzer went off and people all over the room responded by rising from their seats, taking their trays to the drop-off and heading out the door. In only a few moments, there were few diners left and the room was a great deal quieter.

"Feeling any better?" Aurial inquired.

Raunn looked at her, startled that she had, if only briefly, forgotten her situation and that of her partner. She pushed her tray away. "A little. But I won't feel right until I'm out of here and trying to help Merradrix."

"If you can," Aurial said in a neutral tone.

"If I can. Tell me something. Last night the Portmaster said something about the Tarraquis undermining an organization he called a Trading Family. What is that? Do they own this port?"

Aurial sighed, as if the answer carried great weight. "He was referring to the Trading Family that controls most of the business operations in this quadrant of the galaxy and certainly *all* of the important business. No, the Family doesn't own the ports or the ships but they license their use and without the license and the authority it confers to trade with the Family, no one can make money legally. That's why the Family is so important."

Raunn looked across the table at her affable companion. Once again she had the feeling that some hidden goal was being pursued and she was excluded from that knowledge. If she wanted to know, she would have to keep pushing and pay the most attention when they stopped answering. "Who runs this Family?" she inquired bluntly. "One person has to be the head of an organization that powerful. There can be only one brain in such a strong body; one person to have the vision and control the power. Am I correct?"

"You are," Aurial replied calmly.

"What is his name, then?"

Aurial looked suddenly amused. "Her," she said. "Her name is Nashaum."

"That's all?" Raunn could not keep the incredulity from her voice. "Nashaum? How could anyone in such a powerful position have but one name like some blue-dirt farmer. . . ." She broke off abruptly to avoid inadvertent insult.

The outworld woman was unfazed. "Be careful when

you deal with other cultures," she cautioned, "they rarely have the same referents as your own. Names in other places do not necessarily carry the import that they do here. Her name is simply Nashaum il Tarz but she carries more titles and honorifics than I can even remember, let alone recite. I doubt if she knows them all."

"Il Tarz," Raunn repeated numbly. "And you are . . ."

"Aurial il Tarz. Yes, you heard correctly. I am her daughter and a working member of the Family."

"Then you have rank and power. You can make things happen. All that talk about profits and fees was just to get me to do things your way. Getting me out of here would be simple for you."

"No, not simple. But possible, as it would not be for anyone else, even the Portmaster." Aurial's voice was stern. "That is why we have an arrangement and you can look forward to seeing your own family again."

"You could free Merradrix!" Even to her own ears, Raunn's voice sounded affronted.

"No," Aurial replied sadly, "not even I can do that. I am my mother's daughter, after all, and I will not interfere to that degree nor take such an enormous risk for one man's life."

"You're just trying to raise the price." Raunn knew that she was pushing now but she had to push to learn. "You already have trading rights on Chennidur and that's how your family makes money. You already have what you said you came here to get, entree to troinom society. What else could I possibly give you to make it worth your while? What else could even interest you?"

Aurial simply shook her head. "All I want is to meet and talk with the clan council."

"Yes, that is what you said. I agreed to arrange it and to disguise you from my own people until the time is right. What you don't understand is that there is nothing you can say to the clans that they will listen to. There is nothing you can do here that will make any difference."

"I must try."

"Clan Cliffmaster will be very polite to you and treat you with faultless courtesy even after they discover that you are not a Follower and, worse, an outworlder who trades in stardust. No prejudice may abrogate the rules of hospitality. But they will not discuss trade with you. Nor will any of the other clans."

"Why not? Why is trade a forbidden subject?"

"Because the Kohrable demands that the Followers of the True Word remain isolated from outworld civilizations. You know that. We are forbidden to have anything to do with the evils of your technology."

"Why is technology evil?" Aurial asked, her voice still calm. "It is people who are good or evil, not things."

"The Tulkan opened up trade and look what happened," Raunn replied with stubborn logic. "Machines replace honest workers, the old values are mocked and discarded, the stardust pollutes our society. People read books that foster heresy and dissent. They eat food forbidden to us by the Kohrable. The words of the nayyat are disregarded. The strength of the True Word is weakened."

"Ah, but trade brings other things as well. Medicines that keep your children from contracting fatal diseases. Materials to build houses that are warm in the cold and cheap enough for the poor. Lights for the darkness. A better standard of living for everyone, not just the troinom."

"We were fine as we were," Raunn protested. "The Tulkan opened up trade only for his own glory and power."

"Perhaps," Aurial countered softly, "the Tulkan opened up trade because he believes that this world will stagnate unless it has contact with the rest of the quadrant."

Raunn persisted. "The Tulkan is a traitor and a heretic."

"Are you that sure? Perhaps he is a man with a vision and being vilified as a traitor is a price he is willing to pay. Please, don't interrupt, just listen. Trading rights with Chennidur exist only as long as the Tulkan is in power. If the Portmaster is right, and you are proof that he is, the Tarraquis is part of a growing fundamentalist movement to depose the Tulkan and return Chennidur to a state of 'pure' isolation. The Tulkan is strong, a man of history, who will take enormous risks to do what he believes is right for his people. But he is human and men are vulnerable.

"If none of the clans will meet with us, then the end of the Tulkan's reign will mean the end of trade here. It will also mean the beginning of a long decline for the economy of Chennidur and for the society which depends upon it. No, you may not believe any of this: you are bursting with denial. But it's true all the same."

"It will also mean the end of a significant source of revenue for the il Tarz Family, no doubt," Raunn replied with sarcasm.

"Certainly. I never claimed to be a disinterested party. That does not make the rest of it less true, however."

Raunn's outrage vied with horror and fury. With a few well-chosen words this outworlder had created a picture that turned all of Raunn's beliefs upside down. The Tulkan, a man of history! Trade with alien non-believers necessary for Chennidur. The True Word, narrow and short-sighted. What would she say next? Raunn was afraid that if she listened any longer she would hear the Kohrable called false and the Clan Council named the real enemies of her world. She wanted to block out the words but knew that she could do nothing to remove the ideas that had found their way insidiously into her mind. Worse, she could not stop herself from thinking about them. She felt disoriented. Everything had changed and she could not simply pretend that the words had never been spoken. She wanted to hurl another outburst at Aurial but was too confused to voice it. Instead she said something that she knew was true even if it seemed tangential to the issue. "He kills people. His patrols torture them and the Puzzle-masters destroy their brains with chemicals. Anyone who disagrees with him disappears. How could this be good for Chennidur?"

Aurial sighed and ran her fingers through her hair. "Yes, I'm sure he does and I am as appalled by it as you are. Powerful men often use brutal methods to achieve their ends quickly, for they have no patience to do it slowly. They cannot take the time to persuade, to negotiate, to bring people around to where they can see the same vision. That brutality is usually their downfall because it generates hostility and organized opposition. The opposition really wants to get rid of the reforms but it's oppression that fuels the rebellion. I would wager that most of the Followers who support the nayyat oppose the Tulkan blindly and do what they are told. They most likely have no conception why the two forces are truly in opposition."

"They know when people disappear," Raunn said stubbornly.

"Yes, they do. But people get killed on both sides, don't they, Raunn? Runners like you and Merradrix are captured and presumed killed but the nayyat are never at risk, are they? I'm sorry. I know that I'm treading on treacherous ground here and it is neither wise nor politic to attack another person's religious beliefs. Particularly when politics and religion are as closely allied as they are here. I should not have said anything."

"Yes, you should," Raunn said slowly. She tugged on a strand of hair. "I think. Clans don't see religion as the underranks do but still you have managed to shock me. I can't deal with all of this right now. Don't expect me to change what I believe, how I think, all my values because of what you say. It's too much. You have told me what *you* want. I want only two things: to find Merradrix and free him from whatever the Tulkan's men have in mind, then to get home again. I need your help. It is a hard thing for me to ask at all, and even harder to seek aid from an outworlder. But I must. We have agreed to help one another." She paused. "Please. Life is at stake here, not just money."

Aurial stared blankly off beyond Raunn's shoulder and said nothing. Then she gave a shrug and a smile. "Perhaps. Let me think about it." I'll probably catch it later, she thought, but then Mother and Itombe *did* say that I was to learn as much as I could on this assignment and I'll learn a lot more this way than by just observing. One of the first things they taught me was the value of favors wisely used. "Why don't you go back to your room and rest a bit more. We have a lot of work ahead of us. I'll stop by later on and we'll talk again." Watching Raunn walk away, Aurial thought, yes, Mother said learn. She also said to find a way to prevent either religious rebellion or the hostility of the fundamentalists from destroying trade by taking Chennidur out of the Family's network. Just a small assignment, really. Nothing to it.

She shook her head and went back to her quarters to draft a message for transmission to the Beldame. After that there would be time for some additional language study. She had found her way into a culture that was almost impossible for any offworlder to penetrate. Now she had to carry it off.

# CHAPTER 4

## THE ROCK

The next step would be more difficult. In need of guidance, Tuupit Antikoby sought the deserted clan chapel. No better place existed on the Rock for the solitude and contemplation that led to clarity of thought. In silence he began the preparations required for the Ceremony Summoning Strength. The small, oval-shaped stone chapel in which he moved with quiet purpose was simply laid out but elaborately and exquisitely furnished. Several rows of heavy chairs weighted down a lush jewel-weave rug of a matching oval shape. At the front of the room stood a carved and polished wooden table which held four objects, all of beaten silver inlaid with a pattern of the finest green syddian stone. Next was a delicate rennish bowl in which rested a single root. Beside it stood an incense burner with firestarter attached. On the other side of the table rested a fluted pitcher containing clear water from the Heartspring. The final object was a bookstand on which rested an ancient copy of the Kohrable, the book of the True Word.

Old and precious as they were, these objects were but a

few of the many, equally-priceless artifacts in the room.
The chapel was lit by lamps fashioned of the finest materials and worked with dedicated craftsmanship. The chairs
were upholstered with embroidered cushions worked by
the hands of devout troinom ladies. Bound in soft leather,
the chanting books were illuminated with brilliant colors.
All of these varied works of art were the gifts of many
generations of troinom gentility, the proof of the dedication of Clan Cliffmaster to the True Word. At the same
time they served as talismans, offered to the Chenni-ad
to protect the clan and its domain from the Raveler's
destruction.

Offerings, gifts, displays of wealth and pride, they should
have gleamed softly in the rennish-scented air. Instead, a
film of disuse dulled the luster of these marvelous objects,
for despite its ostentation, the chapel was now little used.
The deaths of two troinom sons and the extended absence of the tansul had gutted the soul of the family so that
it was now indrawn and focused solely on its own problems. The vellide could have kept the family going, maintained the old traditions and adherence to *shufri-nagai*,
but she was too far sunk in despair to attend to uxorial
duties. Antikoby paused in his preparations long enough
to note that the attentions of the underservants were needed
to restore the room to its former brilliance. He would
speak to Nusinnith about it.

Methodically he moved aside several chairs until he had
cleared a space on the rug. From the bowl he removed the
single rennish root, a long slim rhizome that was well
dried. It would burn just long enough for his needs.
Placing it in the incense burner, he struck the firestarter,
lit one end of the root and blew on it until it burned
steadily. From a tray that stood to one side of the room he
removed one cup of a set carved exquisitely from luminous
grey kristopresh. Tilting the pitcher, he filled the cup with
the clear and slightly effervescent water that rose from the
spring at the very core of the Rock. The smell of rennish
intensified as faint wisps of smoke curled around the room.

Antikoby began the set of exercises that prepared him
for the ritual. Breathing in, stretching his muscles one at a

time, pausing, breathing out and relaxing. Because he was pressed for time, he did not complete the full set prescribed in the Commentaries for the Ceremony of the Drawing of Strength. Instead he took the short path. It was neither proper nor recommended for one who was not a nayya or suitably trained but it would have to suffice for this one occasion.

When he had finished, he settled on the rug at the center of the circle. Taking up the cup, he quaffed the water in a single graceful motion, heedless of the bubbles or its strong mineral taste. Then, composing himself with his legs crossed and his hands resting limply on his thighs, he again breathed deeply. This time he held the smoke deep within his lungs for three heartbeats before releasing it. At the same time he began the Chant of Strengthening.

First came the indrawn breath, then the pause followed by a line of the chant repeated mentally, then the exhale:

> *"I am strong.*
> *I attempt many things.*
> *I achieve what I attempt.*
> *My goals are without limit.*
> *My strength is endless.*
> *My actions are guided by the True Word."*

The words reverberated in the expanding vault of his mind and in his veins, the rennish sang like fire.

> *"The strength of all life fills me.*
> *The power of life strengthens me.*
> *My will has the force of water,*
> *   which flows through small spaces.*
> *My will has the power of wind,*
> *   which bends trees before it.*
> *My will has the strength of stone,*
> *   which remains for all time."*

The blood surged through every cell of his body and the words suffused it, becoming reality. The rennish smoke, the rhythmic breathing, the power of the words and of the ceremony were all one reality and that one was within him. Determination to achieve his goal was forged, becoming the sole focus of his will.

> *"I draw to me those whom I need.*
> *We shall work together toward the goal,*
> *blending our many strengths.*
> *We are one with the goal.*
> *Our strength is the strength of many.*
> *Our strength is the strength*
> *of water, wind, and stone."*

Antikoby completed the entire chant methodically and precisely. When it was done, he concentrated on channelling the strength that he had summoned. He would need it all for what came next as well, and more. When he finally arose, slowly, the rennish root had burned down to a thin line of ash. He felt light and graceful: he was also flushed. When everything had been replaced, however, and the ornate doors of the chapel had closed behind him, he was indeed stronger and barely able to contain the force within him. Once again the True Word had proved itself worthy of his faith and fulfilled its promise to him as a Follower. Only this time, he was keenly aware of the ways in which he was defying its total authority over his life. The ceremony had reinforced his faith and yet he knew that his actions, not sanctioned in any part of the Kohrable, were correct. He determined that the path he had chosen must be true or his faith would have deserted him when he turned to it for support. The Chenni-ad watch, he thought, and approve.

It had been the ragged end of the night when Antikoby entered the chapel and now the sun's veiled light glowed well over the tree tops. It was time for him to be about his duties, both those which kept the fortress running and the others that he had taken upon himself. Fortified in spirit, humming with energy, he went directly to the large room that served as his office and was the operating heart of the Rock. It was filled with clear morning light and with his staff, who were waiting patiently for him to conduct the daystart meeting. Most of those present served the needs of the huge complex that made up fortress Cliffmaster. They did not serve his other purpose, not yet, and that was as it should be. The regular household routine must go on, could not falter for a moment, and would serve to cover his movements whenever he deviated from this daily schedule.

In his usual efficient fashion, therefore, he dealt with the tapits of house, staff, security, sanitation, fields and stables. Fortunately there were no problems this morning greater than the usual issues handled easily by the tapits, who required only his knowledge and approval. When this agenda had been completed, he dismissed everyone except Tarshionit, the tapit of security, and Nusinnith, the tapit of staff. They conferred quickly, then these two most trusted of his underlings left to execute his instructions, which they accepted without question.

He removed from its hangar the robe of authority that he wore seldom and only in the presence of those who did not belong to the Rock. He was tying the sash in a ceremonial knot, rehearsing his words for the next step in his plan, when the door of his office was flung back with such force that it smashed against the wall, its knob splintering the wainscoting. A strange man strode into the room, bringing discord into its sunny spaces. He was tall and slim, dark of both hair and eye, possessed of a grace and confidence that Antikoby knew well. His appearance, from the elegant clothing to the thin braid draped over his right shoulder, branded him as a troinom before he spoke one word. The tuupit was startled for a moment out of his composure as even the strength and certainty that he had gained so carefully in the chapel wavered. No one of such status ever sought out a drev. Even the tuupit of a great holding was summoned into the presence of a troinom at his or her convenience. Members of that class called, demanded, ordered the underranks and reserved consideration for those of their own status. By coming here, this man had acted outside of his position. But then, Antikoby thought ruefully, so had he also.

He waited for the stranger to address him, as was proper,

and was prepared to reply with courtesy and respect, as was required. The stranger's words, however, were even more direct than he had expected. "Where is she, tuupit?"

"She? Sri-noth, if you would specify to whom you refer . . . ?"

"Don't play games with me," the troinom interrupted. "I am not a patient man. The su-vellide Torrian-Xian, your mistress, tell me where she is."

"My mistress is the vellide Rutin-Xian," he replied with a calmness that surprised even himself. "At this hour, the su-vellide Torrian is normally in her apartments."

"She is not there, and I believe you know that well. Very well, in fact."

"With all respect due to you, sri-noth, the su-vellide does not inform me of her plans unless she requires something of me. She has made no request for my services since arriving here. Perhaps her maid . . ." Antikoby found that, as the troinom became more excited, he himself became calmer. His years of training had prepared him to deal with emergencies and this was no exception.

"The su-vellide's chambers are empty. If she has made no request of her tuupit and he knows nothing, then she must have vanished into thin air." The man's voice was heavy with sarcasm. "And that is not likely. None of the servants knows anything except, perhaps, her maid, who has also vanished. How very typical of servants to know nothing. But the tuupit knows, oh yes. The tuupit always knows." His tone sharpened again. "Now, where is she?"

Antikoby was annoyed that any guest on the Rock, even a troinom, would be so demanding. He was, after all, in a strange household. Such a bold offense often masked a position of little strength, as it did here, and the best way to counter that was with the facts, stated calmly and with certainty. This approach gave the man nothing to grapple with and no information to twist.

Antikoby therefore smoothed the collar of his robe and met the man's hard gaze straight on. "If the su-vellide Torrian did confide her activities to me, I would be unlikely to communicate that information to a complete stranger, one whose name and family are not known to me and who is a guest in this house. Clan matters, as you must know, are entrusted to clan members and sometimes to those who serve them. I am a loyal servant of Clan Cliffmaster and the senior servant of this household. I must request that you identify yourself."

Fury rode the man's features for a moment and Antikoby could see that violence surged not far beneath his surface sophistication. This troinom was not accustomed to being answered by the underranks, much less contradicted by one, and serving in his household must surely be a job done cautiously. In a clipped voice, hard and cold, he answered, "I am Surrein ni Varskal san Cannestur. I am, in fact, a guest of the su-vellide's. I am also her intended husband and therefore have every right to demand of you the whereabouts of the sri-nothi Torrian."

Antikoby flinched. Fear raced through his veins and panic followed close behind it. What had she done? Was it possible that Torrian had actually agreed to such an arrangement? And what of the tansul, her father? Did he know what sort of man this was? He drew his thoughts together and replied with somewhat less composure, "If you say it, then it must be so, sri-noth. However, there has been no ceremony of betrothal here and the vellide Rutin-Xian has been in seclusion since the death of her son. I have received no confirmation of such a claim."

"Unbelievable!" The troinom interrupted again with scarcely concealed rage. "You insult me, servant. Were you in my household, no matter what your status, you would be punished for such impudence, and severely. Indeed, I would supervise it myself." He stopped and drew a deep breath, making a visible effort to control himself. "Nonetheless," he continued in a more reasonable tone, "I am a guest, and I recognize that you must do your duty. The betrothal you question took place at the tansul's home on Cheffra Street and the tansul made the responses for his daughter. She was present but, shall we say, 'indisposed' at the time. The Tulkan's Staff Chief, Verrer ni Rimmani san Derrith also graced us with his presence. All was accomplished in the most proper fashion. Now, I have been patient with you, tuupit, more patient than you deserve. Before my forbearance disappears completely, tell me where I may find the su-vellide. I will not ask again."

The blood was cold in Antikoby's veins. "You are most gracious, sri-noth. As a Clan member yourself, however, I am certain you understand my position. Until I hear from either the vellide or the tansul that a betrothal has taken place, I cannot accept it as fact. Since I now know who you are and that you are one of the su-vellide's trusted companions, I can tell you what it is that you ask. The su-vellide is ill. Gravely ill. After consulting with the infirmarer, we have placed her in seclusion. The infirmarer fears that it is the choking cough. We will know soon enough. I do not have to tell you how serious it is, sri-noth, both for the su-vellide and for those who have been close to her."

Until now, he had spoken only the truth. His untruths must be forgiven along with the other trespasses he was committing for the good of the True Word. The Chenni-ad knew that he uttered them in a desperate cause.

"That is impossible!" the man exploded, then stopped abruptly. Antikoby watched as he thought quickly, sorting out possibilities and consequences before he continued in a more rational tone. "You don't know for sure. I insist upon seeing her myself."

"With respect, sri-noth, the impossibility is your seeing her now. The choking cough is extremely contagious. May I ask, when was the last time you were with her?"

Again Surrein thought his position through before replying. "I? Why, not since we arrived. That is why I am worried. That is why I actually sought you out for news of her. I thought I made that perfectly clear."

Antikoby barely heard the jibe. "It is as her maid said as well. Then neither you nor anyone in your party is in danger—as long as you do not see her. The su-vellide and her maid must remain isolated from everyone on the Rock but our infirmarer until they are well." He paused. "Or until they are beyond illness. You must prepare yourself for that possibility, sri-noth. It is not unthinkable."

"Don't tell me what to think, tuupit," he spat. "If the su-vellide truly had the choking cough, she would be isolated in her chambers and she is not. I'll find her if it takes me weeks to do it. This pile of stone may be big but it's not so big that I can't find my way through it. And I promise you, drev, that if you get in my way . . ."

"Your pardon, sri-noth." Antikoby felt more confident by the moment. Despite his subordinate rank, he was in control and beginning to actually enjoy it. "Your pardon. You may, of course, consult with the infirmarer if you doubt my word. It is simply not possible for you and your party to remain here in the citadel. The danger of infection is great and the risk of contagion must be kept to a minimum. You must all leave immediately. Again, with respect, that is not simply the desire of the tuupit but the law by which we all live. *Shufri-nagai* demands it."

Surrein's eyes narrowed and his face tightened with anger as he saw the trap that had been prepared for him. They both knew *shufri-nagai* only too well and were aware that it left him no honorable alternative. To disregard it would be to render himself unclean. It was not to be considered by any troinom. "Are you dismissing *me* from this house, tuupit?" he replied in a cold voice. "Or do I only imagine that you take upon yourself the privileges of your mistress?"

Antikoby winced mentally but gave no outward sign of it. "My mistress," he replied evenly, "remains secluded, as I have said. She grieves and does not concern herself with such matters as a quarantine. You may, of course, seek an audience."

"Yes, and I could speak with the infirmarer as well but I'm sure that you know better than I what I would hear." Seething, he glared at the drev scum who balked him.

"When you return to your quarters, you will find that my staff is helping your retainers to pack your belongings. Mounts are being prepared." Once again Antikoby paused, reinforcing the importance of his words and relishing the look of frustrated fury that suffused his opponent's face. "To assist you in every way, and to assure your safety on the trail, I have also instructed members of our security force to accompany you down from the Rock. They will even escort you to the hostel at Trailhead."

White with anger, Surrein appeared on the verge of striking out. Antikoby almost hoped that he would: a blow from a troinom was nothing and it would show the man for what he was. Instead Surrein said tightly, "You are more than the tuupit here, aren't you? We both know that, you and I, but it will not help you in the end. I will marry the su-vellide. I may even request that you come to be the tuupit of our new household, as a wedding gift from the tansul. That would be interesting, would it not? We will certainly meet again here when the vellide and the tansul follow their sons." He turned stiffly and left the room.

Antikoby watched the door long after the man had disappeared, as if frozen. His nerves screamed danger signals at him and yet he felt oddly serene. He had won, at least for the moment, and he wished to prolong his fleeting victory. To face down a troinom and send him into retreat was a two-bladed knife that could turn in a drev's hand, drawing blood before he even felt the wound. He would savor this victory all the more because of its rarity. He turned his face toward the sunlight streaming through the window and closed his eyes. There was no sound in the room except the slow calling of a newly-hatched puffer.

# THE PORT

"And this is the transporter. It's very good at moving some things. Not good at all with others." The transporter had lived up to its advance billing and provided an impressive display of technical prowess. With its massively detailed control panel and four dark platforms aligned beneath matching ceiling grids it was sufficiently alien and menacing in appearance. When it operated, however, the columns of iridescent light that leaped from ceiling to platform, enfolding the cargo, were dazzling. Aurial had arranged their visit for a time when cargo was scheduled for transport and that had given them the opportunity to watch several transfer operations. Aurial watched Raunn's face as the transporter's high-frequency whine grew then diminished and saw on it the same expression that she had seen on board the shuttle: fascination. She had expected the troinom woman to demonstrate fear or shock or distaste. Instead, Raunn seemed drawn against her will to anything related to interstellar travel. She studied alien mechanisms and machinery with intense interest, listened to explanations that dealt with concepts far beyond the technological level of her own world. Then she asked questions, lots of them, and good ones, too. Like a fuel absorber, she soaked up everything Aurial had to say and then pushed for more. How much of it she understood, Aurial could not imagine. Perhaps all of the scientific details were beyond her comprehension but there was no doubt that she grasped the underlying concepts. "So, what is the difference?" Raunn asked. "Why don't you just use it to transfer everything up to the freighters? That seems to be a lot easier to do than loading and unloading shuttles."

"It certainly is. Unfortunately, operating a transporter big enough to handle large, heavy-mass cargoes requires a great deal of energy. The energy cost grows higher as the mass increases. At a certain point, it's so expensive to operate the transporter that you can't recover the cost by selling the goods. But the shuttles are designed to move a lot of mass and it's far more economical to run a full shuttle than one that is, say, half full. With heavy cargoes it becomes more efficient to run the shuttle than the transporter."

Raunn thought about that. "Yes, I can see where that makes sense. But what about people? We're not large, heavy-mass cargoes; why not just transport us up to a shuttle that's already in orbit?"

Aurial laughed. This woman was quick, all right. Give her a high-tech education and she'd do very well offworld. "Sure. That would be just the thing. And we could do it, too, if you didn't mind being dead when you arrived. For some reason, the transporter is unpredictable when moving live cargo outside a planet's atmosphere. Sometimes living things get through just fine and sometimes they show up at the other end in one piece and looking fine but very dead. If we were talking about some commodity, we could accept a certain level of damage as a cost of doing business but even with livestock, not to mention people, it's got to work right every time. That's why the M'Gwad Technocracy, among others, has been working on this problem ever since the transporter was invented. No answers yet."

"What about inside the atmosphere?" Raunn fired back. "If it works on the planet's surface, you could just transport us to the Rock and do away with the hike through the Perimeter. That would save a lot of valuable time."

"It certainly would and we certainly could," Aurial responded. "If we had a transporter grid established across the surface of Chennidur. Unfortunately, the only transporter on your no-tech world is right in front of us. Using one transporter is like using one message tower: you can send but no one is listening."

Raunn paused for a moment. Aurial could tell her circuits were firing in rapid bursts. "So, anything that's alive goes up to a freighter on a shuttle?"

Aurial could see where she was going. Raunn looked up at her with widened eyes and Aurial knew that she had made the final connection—put all the pieces together. Here it came: she braced herself.

"That means," Raunn said in a deliberate way, "that when the Tulkan's prisoners are sold off to the labor contractors, they're shipped out of this port on shuttles licensed by the il Tarz Family to freighters licensed by the il Tarz Family."

Aurial kept her face impassive and her voice as neutral as possible. "Yes, that's correct," she replied.

Anger rose in Raunn's eyes and flushed her cheeks. "That makes you more than just business partners with the Tulkan," she said and her voice was hard. "That makes you slave traders."

"That's one way of looking at it."

"Oh? Tell me, what other way of looking at it is there?"

"The il Tarz Family are merchants. We carry goods from one destination to another. We also trade in certain merchandise and commodities. Laborers are simply cargo. We charge for their transportation and deliver them as scheduled."

"Cargo." Raunn shook her head in disbelief. "You're talking about people, not things. Or are people just commodities in the 'quad markets' to be bought and sold like everything else?"

"Call them passengers then. Guests, if you prefer. Whatever you or I choose to call them, the il Tarz Family does not profit from the exchange between the supplier and the labor contractors. Transportation fees are the extent of our remuneration." Aurial found that holding her ground was more difficult than she had expected; or perhaps the ground she stood on was less firm than she had thought. She had been schooled in a sophisticated and pragmatic environment but there was something about what Raunn said that bothered her.

Raunn may have seen it in her eyes because her rejoinder was swift. "You're quibbling. You can put a different name on it, Aurial, you can distance yourself from the dirt of it and you can even deny that you're really involved. But the fact is that if you touch it in any way, then you own a piece of it. If slaves are on your ships, you're in the slave trade and that's immoral. At least, it is under the tenets of the True Word."

"Now you listen to me," Aurial responded with more heat than she had intended. "What's immoral depends on where you are. Your perspective on life is based on the teachings of one small and restrictive religion. You see the universe from this undistinguished planet revolving around a middle-size sun so far in the Outback that you're barely on the charts. What is good and moral and right here on Chennidur is anathema, insanity or perversion on older worlds you're never heard of." Raunn started to interrupt but Aurial held out her hands in a gesture of denial. "No. Listen. If you were to think of the three most hideous and unnatural practices that you can imagine, I could spend a few moments with the port computer and find worlds where those things are normal and natural and accepted."

"What if you can," Raunn burst out. "You still can't tell me that right and wrong depend on where you are. There are evil things like slavery and murder that are bad everywhere. Just plain evil."

Aurial brought some of her more extensive experience into play. "There may be the morality of the Kohrable and the morality of Chennidur, but there is no universal morality, no right and wrong that applies to all races, species and cultures at every stage of their development."

"I don't accept that," Raunn replied, biting off her words. "Yes, there may be different ways of looking at good and bad. And the sentient species of the galaxy probably also have different ways of interpreting it depending on how far each has evolved. But there has to be something, some goal, that we're all reaching toward in our imperfect ways. That goal must be a concept of good that applies across the galaxy—or the universe."

"You may be correct," Aurial conceded, deciding that it was time to end the discussion before it got out of hand. "I hope you are. Even so, that changes nothing. Given the diversity of cultures and ethoses, the il Tarz Family cannot make judgments on the morality of its customers. It would be impossible to do, much less stay in business doing it. Imagine being a shopkeeper in the Nandarri bazaar. A man comes to your shop and asks to buy a pot. You don't question where he got the money from before you agree to sell him the pot. He may be a thief, but even if you suspect that he came by his money dishonestly, you would still sell him the pot. You cannot find a merchant in the stalls outside the port who would refuse to make the sale on such highly moral grounds."

Raunn shook her head stubbornly but did not reply.

"Mother has set some basic rules that we follow and one of them is not to trade in human beings. But transporting them is different."

"Even when it's against their will?" Raunn was not willing to let the argument go.

"Who makes that decision?" Aurial replied. "The labor

contractors are not stupid. They have documents signed by each laborer stating that he or she is employed by the contractor and willing to travel to the work site at the contractor's expense. Slavery may be legal on many worlds but the interstellar transportation of slaves between those worlds is proscribed by the laws of the Quadrant. But how do you prove that the signatures on those documents are forged? Or that the laborer was coerced into signing? Who, then, decides whether these people are free workers or slave laborers?"

"All right," Raunn conceded reluctantly. "You and they and the people who enforce Quadrant laws can equivocate and look the other way while someone makes a lot of money. I can't change that. I can't change the universe, or the Quadrant. Right now all I want to do is save one person, one man. That's my reality. I'll settle for that. If you won't change what's truly happening, will you help me to keep Merradrix on Chennidur?"

Aurial swallowed. How could she say no? Yet there was no way she could agree. She shook her head. "Regrettably, no, I can't."

Raunn seemed to bite back a barbed reply. "Can you at least help me to talk with him before he is sent offworld?"

Again Aurial shook her head. "Please understand. They're shipped out in sealed SA modules. He'll be in chemsleep—shot full of drugs that allow the human body to travel at hyperspeed without need for anything but basic life support. That way there's no need to carry and prepare food or handle waste matter. Temperatures can be kept much lower. Light and living space are unnecessary. It's much cheaper."

Raunn started to argue but then lowered her head into her hands, defeated. "Then there's nothing I can do to help him?"

"No," Aurial said sadly, "I'm afraid not."

"You said you would think about it. Now there's nothing you can or will do to help him."

"I didn't say that. Only that I can't do the things that you asked of me."

Raunn's head came up. "Oh? Then what can you do?"

Aurial spoke slowly, as if against her better judgment. "I can call my . . . contact at the Family's headquarters and have him track the labor shipment that includes Merradrix. Following the data trail, it should be simple to find out which contractor's base station the shipment is going to. That's a sort-and-assign facility where they break shipments from different planets apart and distribute the workers according to sex, skills, strength, age and health. They also assign a number to each body—they never use names—and the tricky part will be identifying Merradrix's number. Once we have that, Rolfe can track his movements almost anywhere. My guess is that they'll send him to the Caris IV system where there are some developing worlds in need of heavy labor."

Raunn was interested. "Caris IV, where is that?"

"It's on the outside edge of the same spiral arm as Chennidur but near the tip. It has great mineral resources that were bid out to developers about five STUs ago. The winners in the bidding have just gotten their operations established and ready for the workers to set up. It's a fit. And it's close."

"If this person tracks him there, or wherever, what then?"

"Then we can try to get him out. The il Tarz family resources are extensive and, in the larger scheme of things, one worker on a developing world is expendable anyway. The up-front method would be to send in an operative and buy out his contract. That would probably work but be very expensive."

Raunn waited for the catch. "If he's expendable, why would his contract be expensive?"

"Simply because the developer is free to assign the cost of the contract over and above the amount he has already invested. Once the developer receives an offer, he knows that the individual is valuable enough for someone to make the effort to retrieve him. Once aware of that, he would assign the contract's value upward. Way upward."

Raunn ran both hands through her hair, causing it to

stand out from her head in rough waves. "That's clear enough. What's the not-so-up-front method?"

"To send in an operative with a different set of skills and break him out. This approach, needless to say, is cheaper but a lot more dangerous. The odds on a successful operation decrease. Rolfe will have to evaluate the situation, decide which approach to take, which operative to use and how far to go with his plan."

"Oh. What do you think?" Raunn asked.

"I think that Rolfe needs to look at all the information and make a decision. He may even have to go to the work site before putting a plan together. You and I are out of it at that point, though. Don't worry—Rolfe is good and he's tough. He has spent a lot of time out here and he'll probably enjoy it." *If Mother allows it*, she thought to herself.

"But where will you be?"

"Here," Aurial replied, stifling an impatient reply. "You may have forgotten in your concern for Merradrix, but we still have a tricky operation of our own to execute."

Raunn looked at her warily. "What's tricky?"

"Set up a dialogue with the Clan leaders that will help me persuade them of the advantages of expanding trade."

"And, just by the way, making sure that the Family keeps right on making a profit."

Aurial cocked one eyebrow. "Certainly. Do the merchants in the bazaar give away their merchandise? Do the drev craftspeople give away their creations to the merchants? Do the 'blue-dirt farmers' simply hand out their crops to passers-by? Of course not. Commerce is the platform on which economies and cultures are built." She smiled. "Religions too, for that matter, although they prefer to disguise it." She held up one hand against Raunn's protest. "The True Word may be an exception but there's more to it than that. I've already tried to explain it. Cultures are like people. They can choose to grow and develop even though it might be scary and involve taking risks. Or they can choose not to take those risks and maintain an ever-more-stagnant status quo. Or they can choose to turn away from progress altogether and go backwards into a simpler and more comfortable stage."

"Nonsense," Raunn protested again. "Who would not want things to get better for one's people? It's how you define 'better' that is the crux of the issue."

"Perhaps," conceded Aurial. "Just consider that progress is the scariest way to go because it means change and most humans are more afraid of change than they are of death. But it's the only way those cultures can grow and move ahead, 'get better,' move closer to the universal goal, Raunn, if there is one. Stagnation is easy; just replace questioning and choice with tradition and follow the seasons around and around until you die. Going backwards can be very seductive, especially when it's placed in the framework of a return to religious beliefs that are valued and valuable. But it's still a trap and when you walk voluntarily into a trap, you'd better believe that someone is going to spring it on you. Any time you give yourself over to the directions of another human being, even if he claims to be more right, more holy, more touched by the spirit of truth, you've given away your power of choice. If you want to change your mind after that, it's too late. Way too late."

Raunn looked at her with a straightforward and intense gaze. "And that's the trap you see Chennidur walking into? The trap you're trying to save us from?"

"Save you? No, I'm no savior. I just want to point out some alternative choices and keep trade going while the Clan Council chooses for themselves."

"And you think talking to the council will let you do that? That's asking a great deal of us and of yourself."

Aurial shook her head slowly and smiled. "A culture is nothing but people. You start not by talking but by listening and observing—something impossible for me to do when Chennidur is closed off to me. But with your help, I have a chance to learn all that I need so that when I finally reach the right people and have a chance to talk to them, I will be able to say the things that count the most. And if I can reach them before they know that I'm from offworld, well . . ." She stopped. It was time to stop arguing and let

Raunn think for a while about the help she would be
getting and what she would be giving in turn.

## THE PUZZLE PALACE

Number Ten, who could no longer remember the name
Astin, and Number Eleven, who had forgotten being
Merradrix, slept deeply. The windows darkened and lightened. The door opened again and again to admit guards
with food and blankets and to admit new prisoners. Like
leaves piling up by the garden wall, the prisoners drifted
into the room and settled on the floor. When the space
along the walls was gone, they took the middle of the
room. Astin and Merradrix were jostled and pushed together but they did not notice that any more than they
noticed the passing of the days. The room was now crowded
with bodies long unwashed. The smell of their sweat, dirt
and excretions was like an invisible wall that the guards
pushed through every time they entered.

The morning shift brought the first meal in but now
each guard had to carry a basket and two cans to make
sure there was enough for everyone. The older guard
dropped his burden just inside the door and made a noise
of disgust deep in his throat. "This is worse than a stable
that ain't been mucked out for a week," he said. "Animal
manure smells better than this. It's clean, like, if you
know what I mean."

His companion cast a wary eye at the shambling, hollow-
eyed mass of people converging on the pails that held
their meal. "Yeah," he concurred, "and animals don't smell
worse if they're dirty. They just smell like animals all the
time. But if people aren't clean, it's unbearable."

The older guard started slopping cooked grain into the
bowls. "I thought I smelled some pretty bad things in my
time. Once I pulled duty on Uri★na-sh and spent some

time in the swamps there. I still have nightmares about it and I can smell that mungerin' swamp after I wake up. It sticks in my nose for half a day. But this is worse."

Handing out bread, the other one added, "Well, it can't just keep going on, can it? Another week or so and they'll be sleeping on top of each other. They're still too burned for any trouble but there's nothing like pushing and shoving to get something started."

"Nope. Time for another run up the well, I'd say. The hackers over in GenAd are probably setting up a shipment. Then we'll just line them up and march them into the old chemsleep lab. Carry them out of there and stack them in a shuttle like crates and then they're gone. Whoosh. Up and out of our lives."

"Until the next batch."

"Maybe we'll get lucky and pull another duty. Let's go check our sleeping twins." With breakfast distributed, they went to look over the two men they thought of as Ten and Eleven to make sure that they were still alive. If not, they could blame the loss of two salable workers on the previous shift. Once again, however, they found that both were sleeping soundly and breathing evenly. The illegal sedative would wear off soon but, until then, the men's bodies were working hard to repair damage and rebuild tissue. Food would have helped but, as the doctor had known, sleep was even more important for their recuperation.

The guards were relieved. They wanted no black marks on their tour of duty here that would make re-assignment to it more likely. Once this lot was up the well, they could put in for transfer and hope for a new post that would include clean air and a chance for them to make use of their martial skills. Let someone else nurse the next round of prisoners. Meanwhile, it was time to empty the scogging buckets.

# CHAPTER 5

## THE ROCK

Antikoby climbed the stairs to the message tower with trepidation. There was certainly nothing unusual about a message coming in at any time, not even one that was coded. True, one of the troinom would ordinarily take such a message and inform the tuupit of its contents should it be necessary. Now, as in so many other ways, he must assume that burden himself. Doing so gave him more control over his plan and how it would be affected by the activities of the Rock. It also made it less likely that he would receive any unpleasant surprises. Each time he took control, it became easier to do it again but he still carried a heavy burden of guilt and fear. His apprehension came equally from the knowledge that things were going well now, were proceeding precisely as he wished them to, and he did not need bad news from Nandarri to interfere. Climbing the steps of the Message Tower reminded him of the similar ascent in the Moon Tower and he reminded himself that, if he wished to avoid surprises, it was time for him to check on progress there.

He topped the last step and entered a room structurally

similar to the one where the su-vellide lay but different in
every other way. It was larger and brighter, with a huge
disk of beaten metal mounted on a frame in its center. A
fire pit, blackened and cold, waited in front of the disk for
its turn to come alive and send messages flying to other
towers on beams of light. The disc could swivel up to hook
the sun's rays or down to reflect the light of the fire. Eight
large windows were open to the sky and air. Catching his
breath, Antikoby pulled in the distinctive aroma of a message tower that was the bitter smell of old charcoal combined with a brassy tang of metal polish. A high thin wind
sang through the tower's windows and Antikoby, still flushed
from his climb, shivered more from the sound than the
cold.

The duty guard sat riveted in the window which faced
Nandarri, his eyes fixed on a distant point of light that
winked on and off. He did not register Antikoby's arrival
and his attention did not waver but the assistant pulled out
a seat. Antikoby settled himself—one could never tell how
long transmitting a message would take—and focused his
own eyes on the beacon. It was difficult to read a message
when starting in the middle and impossible when it was
coded but he tried anyway. He had made no progress
when the beacon blinked out the standard ending sequence. Antikoby pulled his attention back to the room,
then surged out of his chair as the duty guard rose. *Let it
not be bad news*, he thought again, no longer daring to
make it a prayer, and accepted the paper with the coded
message on it.

He had turned to go when the guard said, "Tuupit, a
moment, please."

Apprehensive again, Antikoby stopped and faced the
man. "Yes?"

"Tuupit, the duty guard on the third shift reported
seeing what appeared to be a light in the Moon Tower last
night and the night before. He noted it in the log but I
thought you should know."

Antikoby hesitated. It would not do to snap at him for
being conscientious. Or the night guard for being observant. The men were only doing their duty. "My thanks for

this information. It is most likely nothing but I shall investigate." The guard nodded gravely and Antikoby could see by his expression that the issue had been laid to rest.

He leaped recklessly down the stairs, taking them two and three at a time, and hurried down the long corridor to the tansul's private office. Once again he was trespassing on troinom territory but the code book was locked here and the vellide was neither able nor willing to get it for him. At the door he paused only to isolate the room's key on his master ring and thrust it into the lock. Then he was inside and pulling the small book from its special place on the shelf over the massive tansul's desk. Working swiftly and precisely he decoded the message, his heart sinking as he proceeded. Bad news, indeed. Antikoby knew it could be worse but not by much. The sri-nothi Raunn was missing. Vanished.

Since the tansul had framed the message for the vellide's information and coded it so that no eyes but hers would see it, he had speculated. He mentioned the possibility of rash involvement with the Tarraquis, of capture by the Tulkan's patrol. He would use all his influence with the Tulkan to find her and, if she was in one of his prisons, to free her. Antikoby had no doubt that the tansul could grease the governmental mechanisms sufficiently to accomplish this. He had heard enough about what emerged from the Tulkan's prisons, however, to think that this would be little more than a token victory. The Rock already held two damaged women, and the sons were dead. Raunn, level-headed pragmatic Raunn, had been his hope for the future of the Cliffmaster Clan. But Raunn was also impatient, as he well knew. What had she done? How could she have done it?

He sat back in the tansul's chair and thought through what came next. The duty guard would have automatically sent a message confirming receipt of the code from Nandarri. No reply had been requested so he did not have to write one that either deceived the tansul or made it clear that the tuupit had assumed control. All that could be done in Nandarri the tansul would do and it was far more than Antikoby could, were he on Cheffra Street. Raunn would be found or she would not be but he could not affect the outcome in any way. His plan was now more important than ever, for the future of the su-vellide Torrian had become of the greatest importance. It was time for a visit to the Moon Tower.

Locking the tansul's office behind him, Antikoby first made his way to the vellide's chambers. His duty was to inform her of the message but he dismissed any thought of actually doing so. The call would be for appearance only. By the end of the day everyone on the Rock would know that he had accepted a coded message and he could not afford to be blatant about his assumption of authority. But he knew that, even if she understood what he was saying, the news would only drive her deeper into herself. The old lady sat in the sun surrounded by flowers and looking out the window while her maid brushed her hair. Antikoby spoke briefly, relating small news and little pleasantries as always. She asked no questions and seemed content in her comfortable unthreatening world. He left as soon as he could.

From there he made his way methodically to the abandoned wing, speaking to servants and checking up on their work as he went. This attention to the detail of his job helped to calm him and keep his thoughts from racing off in pointless speculation that would only distract him from his plan. On the steps of the Moon Tower, however, he heard voices engaged in a conversation above him. He stopped, heart pounding. Had someone discovered his secret? Who could be up there talking with Maitris, while the su-vellide slept? Had Surrein slipped back and found her? More bad news seemed likely and he hastened upwards to confront it and do his best to contain it.

At the top of the tower, however, he was surprised to find that Maitris was not defending her helpless mistress against the attentions of some uninvited stranger. Instead she was quietly conversing with the su-vellide Torrian. Both women looked up with pleasure when he walked in. "Ah, tuupit," Torrian said quietly, her voice hoarse. "I am truly delighted to see you. Now perhaps you can convince our fierce one here to release me from your bondage."

She looked like the Torrian who had left the Rock for Nandarri, composed and confident, but far thinner. Her skin was pale and the smile on her face was weak. Antikoby looked at Maitris who gave an affirmative nod. "She is well, tuupit," she said with a smile. "I was not sure that we would both survive until now but she is truly well."

He crossed the room to the bed. "Then releasing you is a duty and a privilege." Without waiting for any response, he began to work on the knots. The ropes had been pulled and twisted for so long, however, that in the end he had to take the knife Maitris offered and cut her free. With the ropes removed, the marks of friction burns stood out clearly on the pale skin of her wrists. Torrian flexed her fingers and Maitris rubbed her mistress's hands but it took a long time for the circulation to return. When the pain had abated and she could trust her hands to do her bidding, she took up the cup of water Maitris had left for her and drained it. "You have no idea how good it feels to be able to do that," she commented. "When you are really thirsty, depending on someone else to give you little drinks is not acceptable.

"Now, tuupit," she continued, "tell me what is happening. You did well in releasing me from the stardust's thrall, although I, too, doubted that Maitris and I would both survive the process. I shall seek guidance from Nusrat-Geb and do long penance for my weakness. But now that I am free, I must know what I will face when I come down from this tower."

Antikoby was relieved to be able to put some of the responsibility back in the hands of a troinom, who owned it by right, yet also reluctant. He told her what he had done, from the beginning. Although Antikoby meant for his account to be as complete as possible, he found himself altering it, changing a piece here, leaving out a bit there. In the end it sounded more as if he had responded to the needs of the situation, reacting as a good drev, rather than that he had developed a plan and put it methodically into place. Some details he held closely to himself, reasoning that he would tell her more when she was stronger and when it was necessary. Antikoby reported his conversation with Surrein as accurately as he could recall and, at the end of his tale, read Torrian the message he had just decoded. She made a sound that conveyed anger and disgust.

"What do you think, tuupit? Is my impetuous sister in the Tulkan's prison?"

"I do not know, sri-nothi. It is possible. You know her better than I and I know her impatience too well to discount the possibility. The sri-nothi Raunn always wanted things done, fixed, changed immediately. She wanted to know things without taking the time to learn them, to have skills without practice. The Tarraquis could easily have lured her with the chance to act and then, as I said, anything is possible."

"They may have lured her in other ways, as well," Torrian added in a low voice.

"Sri-nothi?"

"There was talk of a man. Before I became—ill. A drev." She looked away, over his shoulder. "I do not remember much and who knows what happened after I returned here. She is of the right age for such temptations." Torrian smoothed the covers fussily and then looked up again. "Was anyone captured on the night that Raunn disappeared?"

"I do not know, sri-nothi. The message did not say."

"Yes, well, the tansul, my father, shall find out. Where is Surrein now?"

"He and his retinue remain in residence at the Trailhead hostel."

"Not far enough," she replied shortly. "I shall remain here in the tower, tuupit, until we have reviewed the situation in more detail. Once I come down and my 'recovery' is reported, he will return. Then, neither you nor I will be able to refuse him entrance. Not even the vellide, my mother, may prevent it. For now, however, the most important thing is a bath. I must be clean again."

Maitris, who had been following the conversation intently, rose swiftly. "There is no tub here, sri-nothi," she said, spreading her hands in a rare gesture of futility, "but I hasten . . ."

"I will carry one up myself," Antikoby interrupted. He went toward the stairs, then turned again. "Then it's true, sri-nothi," he said, almost as an afterthought. "Surrein is your betrothed."

Torrian held his eyes for a moment and then looked away. A flush spread into her pale cheeks. "It's true," she replied.

## THE PERIMETER

Aurial waited patiently while the shuttle's engines dwindled and its bright exhaust vanished into the morning sky. When the tumult diminished, she examined the landscape on which she and Raunn stood. Its grandeur rapidly transformed her enthusiasm and excitement into silent wonder. The perimeter country which they were about to cross would have taken the breath of even a native who had not gazed upon it before. They stood on the swelling crest of a hill and from its base other hills rolled away in unbroken sweeps. Although their heights varied, the ranks of hills humped unbroken all the way to the horizon. They created a cabochon landscape patterned with different colors and textures. Trees grew thick and tall in the valleys and covered the lower slopes, but thinned out and diminished in height closer to the hilltops. The apex of each hill was left to long grasses, scrubby bushes and rocks. The effect was that of looking out onto an enormous herd of immense sleeping animals whose backs had been shorn of their fur. Rearing its luminous canopy over the panorama was a vast sky filled with thin streamers of cloud beneath the protection of the Veil.

Pivoting on one foot, Aurial surveyed the full circle of their surroundings, then whispered, "It's so—so big. Enormous. The land goes on forever."

Raunn, who had been taking her bearings with a practical eye and comparing her sightings to the map in her hands, looked at her companion with a puzzled expression. "It's just hills," she replied. "Not even mountains. Hills and trees and grass and sky. Nothing worth whispering about."

"Yes, and sky," Aurial added. "The sky is immense. It makes me feel tiny. Insignificant."

"Out here, we are insignificant. These hills aren't very big, though, at least for Chennidur. There are mountains to the south and east of here and around the Rock, but we won't encounter anything impressive between here and Perimeter House."

"They look high enough to me," Aurial stated.

"The Perimeter is deceptive. Things are often different than they appear at first." Raunn stopped and looked out over the hills. "It's not quite as empty as it looks, for instance. There are animals everywhere in those hills. The Rugollah live out here, too, but there are not many of them and we're not likely to see one."

"The Rugollah?" Aurial queried. She tapped into her databead but received a NO DATA message. She took a guess. "Are you going to tell me that they are small and live inside the hills? That they do odd things and can disappear in the blink of an eye?"

"Why, no," Raunn replied, looking puzzled. "Whatever gave you that idea?"

Aurial brushed off the question. "Oh, just some old stories. It seems to be a popular kind of legend."

"Well, the Rugollah are about the same size as regular people, maybe even a bit taller, and a lot stronger. They're nomadic and drift about the Perimeter. They don't believe in domesticating animals. That's a philosophy that makes more sense out here, somehow, than it does back in Nandarri."

"Do they have regular campsites?" Aurial asked.

"No one really knows where they live. I've never met a person who's seen one of their camps, and if anyone has, they've kept it to themselves. If the Rugollah did have places they visited regularly, we would know more about them."

*The orbiting freighters could track them,* Aurial thought and made a mental note to have Rolfe check when next she sent him a message.

Raunn folded her map and then regarded the other woman with a wary expression. "Is this a new experience for you?" she asked apprehensively. "Being out in the country, I mean. I thought you would have seen panoramas on other worlds far more splendid than our little hills."

With her eyes riveted on the landscape Aurial replied, "Actually, no. I haven't had assignments on more exotic worlds so this is a new experience." She pulled her eyes back to Raunn and continued. "I was raised on the Beldame; that's our headquarters. It's an artificial satellite that's in stationary orbit in the Thulin system. The Beldame is huge, even as orbital stations go, easily the equal of a large asteroid like your Smallmoon. Inside, though, it's just a lot of small enclosed spaces attached to one another. There's nothing big enough to give you a sense of distance and there's no horizon, of course. As for other worlds, well, Mother kept us all on a pretty short tether until we were old enough. Then, like my sisters, I was sent out on Family ships to learn. Ships, like trading stations, are more small enclosed spaces. I've been to other worlds but stayed mostly in the cities and trading compounds. This is my first time away from walls and outside of the cities—on a full-sized planet."

"But in Nandarri you must . . ." Raunn protested.

"I wasn't there long and I stayed inside the Port. Even the city itself keeps you closed in. I was comfortable with that: it was familiar."

"I understand," Raunn responded. "In that case, I'm going to start teaching you to feel comfortable in the open. You have no choice: there are no walls or doors to hide behind for an awfully long way." She hoisted her pack up and added, "Come on, let's get started. We've got work to do." Raunn turned to Aurial and stopped abruptly as she saw the outworlder struggling with her own pack. She held the pack steady so Aurial could get her arms through, then helped her to adjust the carry straps and the frame. "There," she said when it was done. "How does that feel?"

"Heavy," Aurial responded with a grunt. "But I can handle it."

Raunn started downhill, then turned again and looked at Aurial suspiciously. "If you haven't been in the open much," she said warily, "that means you haven't done much hiking."

Aurial looked abashed. "Well, strictly speaking, that's true," she replied. Then she hastened to add, "But I do keep in shape. My sister Gwynn absolutely insists that we all exercise regularly. When I knew I was coming to Chennidur, I did special training, too, for adaptation to natural gravity. It's not supposed to be different from artificial gravity, but it is."

"This is going to be a long walk," Raunn said slowly and with no hint of amusement. "A long walk carrying heavy packs. I plan to travel at a rate that will get us to Perimeter House in a day and a half. Then, if we can get mounts there, it will be a few more days' ride to Cliffmaster citadel. It's not going to be a pleasant stroll through some artfully-designed park. You've seen the hills. Some of them are steep and some aren't but they all go up and down. Then there are streams to cross, rocks to climb, obstacles to evade. I assumed you could manage all that; now I'm beginning to suspect that you can't."

"I'll handle it," Aurial said in a tight voice.

"You'll have to." Raunn sounded almost angry now. "It's too late to catch a ride back."

"Just because I grew up on the inside doesn't mean I'm weak," Aurial protested. "Why didn't you give me this lecture before?"

Raunn looked astonished. "It never occurred to me that anyone could live practically her whole life without ever doing something like this. Even my mother and Torrian had to climb up and down the Rock, walk at least part of the way to Nandarri and to other citadels. We all live outside, especially as children, and Clan Cliffmaster grows up climbing rocks. I never thought to ask about you."

"That's just as well," Aurial retorted. "Or we'd still be in the Port arguing about this instead of doing it. Now, let's get started."

Raunn pulled on the straps of her pack. "Good idea. But

we'll start off slowly and take lots of rest breaks until I can see how you're doing. You'll be sore for a while, there's no way around that, but I don't want your muscles so cramped up that you'll be crippled. After that you'll toughen up and we can go faster."

"I'll handle it."

Raunn started off and Aurial followed. There was a faint trail, no more than bent grass, that marked where animals had passed. They followed it along the ridge of the hill but when it dipped downward they struck off in a different direction. "We'll follow the ridgeline as much as possible," Raunn explained. "It's windier on the hilltops but there's less underbrush to slog through."

Aurial just kept walking, concentrating on what she was doing. Walking had always seemed a simple mindless exercise but then she had never had to be attentive to so many things before. She had to adjust her center of gravity to accommodate the pack's weight, watch for rocks, branches, roots and holes, keep an eye on what Raunn did so she could duplicate it. In spite of the beauty of the landscape, her world quickly narrowed to the part of it that they were walking on, over or around. The pack seemed heavier than it had been when she swung it on and off the shuttle. It was well-balanced and sat comfortably on her shoulders but it pulled on her at the same time. She picked up her chin and kept moving.

Protests to the contrary, however, Aurial tired faster than she had expected and was ready to rest when Raunn was still striding ahead energetically. She refused to ask for a break and clenched her jaw in determination. Fortunately, Raunn called a stop shortly afterward and Aurial sank to the ground with relief. *Days,* she thought. *They were going to be doing this for days.* It was plain to Aurial that the break was solely for her benefit because Raunn was still charged with energy and fairly twitching with the desire to continue. Aurial was embarrassed at needing special consideration, nonetheless she slipped off the pack to get the most benefit from the rest. After a moment, Raunn sat also and they used the time to review the geography of the territory they would be crossing. "As you can see, the land between here and Perimeter House is not bad country. The underbrush can be an obstruction, mind you, but other kinds of vegetation present problems as well. A few of them are dangerous and I'll point those out to you. Make sure you stay pretty close to me and watch what I do until you learn.

"This far away from settled country there can be animals to avoid as well and they aren't afraid of humans. I'd rather not have to use that techish gun of yours but we may have to. Once I can get a blowgun from my uncle's rack, I'll be happier. I'm good with a blowgun. Even Rushain admitted it before . . . Before." There was a pause in the monologue, then she asked brusquely, "Are you ready? We have to keep going."

Once again the packs went on and they resumed their journey up and down the hills. Aurial was glad that the shuttle had dropped them at mid-day, leaving only the afternoon to walk before setting up camp. Even with several rest breaks, however, she was exhausted before the sun touched the hilltops. The mental picture she had painted of herself striding energetically through an alien land, in control and enjoying the adventure, crept away into some dark corner of her mind and hid. On the Beldame, the overall health and well-being of the individual were important. While some people cultivated physical strength, it was not admired or rewarded for itself. In Nashaum's world, strength was more an issue of the mind, of character, and the il Tarz family despised weakness. Gwynn had forced Aurial, sometimes literally, into the gym and Aurial had hated every minute of it, never understanding why it was necessary. Now she comprehended what Gwynn had been trying to do for her.

Plodding through the wilderness of an Outback planet, she began to grasp the several meanings of strength and how important simple muscle power was to that concept. The idea that strength of will could be undermined by a weak body was new to her and radical. It was illuminating because the corollary was how a powerful body could help. She saw that the hike she had agreed to so readily could begin to give her that strength. It would be painful, was already painful, but somehow she would overcome that and become strong.

The sun moved sluggishly through the sky, seeming to hang at a fixed distance from the rolling horizon. Time stretched for Aurial as well, turning eventually into an unending nightmare where thought was impossible and there was room only for endurance. Gravity became a living force, not a concept studied in a lab or a temporary opponent in the gym. It surrounded her, it moved with her, it was inescapable. Gravity sat on her pack like a relentless and malevolent entity, pushing it toward the ground. It wrapped itself around her feet, clinging with silent tenacity each time she lifted one, pulling it back down so that she nearly stumbled. Still, she kept on obdurately, waiting for Raunn to locate a good place to camp and put an end to the torment.

Finally, when the shadows were welling out of the valleys and Chennidur's satellite was brightening over the horizon, Raunn found a small stream that ran into a grove of trees and led Aurial to a clear spot under the branches. Aurial sat, stupefied with fatigue, while her companion built a fire and heated some of the supplies from their packs. Aurial heeded the other woman's advice and choked a portion of the food down, knowing that her strength the next day would depend on it. Without her noticing when or how it was done, a groundsheet was laid down, a tent put up and their blankets unrolled. Almost before the last bite had been swallowed, she crawled into her blanket and fell into an endless abyss of sleep.

Early the next morning, before the sun was fully over the horizon, Raunn woke and rose, impatient for the day to begin. Leaves rustled in the trees around their crude camp as diktalls hitched their way along the branches to stretch out their flying membranes. A new clutch of puffers hissed in the undergrowth, pumping up their float bladders. The air was sharp with the night's chill and the vapor of her breath floated briefly in front of her lips. Shivering, Raunn uncovered the coals of their fire and added kindling. Soon she had a blaze built up and giving off a welcome warmth.

Raunn looked down at the sleeping woman beside her with sympathy and disgust combined uneasily on her visage. She could comprehend the exhaustion only too well, having felt it often enough herself and seen it in others as well. Here, outside of cities, where the sky was so big and the land so demanding, it was easy to overstep one's strength. She tried to imagine living all her life in Nandarri, never knowing the forests and cliffs, never stretching her muscles on a hard climb or breathing the sweet air of a cold night. She began to see the Perimeter from the eyes of a person who had always been a voluntary prisoner of rooms and walls and ceilings. Suddenly she wanted to show Aurial the beauty of Chennidur and let her sample the pleasures she had missed shut up in her artificial asteroid floating in the middle of nothing. She wanted to pull her from one place to another, saying, "Look at this, smell that, taste this other thing, feel over here."

At the same time, Raunn was consumed with the need to move on as far and fast as they could. There was so much to be done and they needed to be about it as quickly as possible. The rest stops had cost them time. Right now she wanted to be up and on the move before breakfast but realized that Aurial needed more rest and a hot meal before setting out. The taste of last night's dinner, techish processed food from the Port's stores, still tainted her mouth and she wanted to start off the day with more nourishing fare. In addition, they were going to be longer on the way to Perimeter House than planned and needed to conserve the supplies in their packs. She had time yet to search out what the land provided. It was early in the season, Rebirth was new; that meant there would be sparse new growth but little of the bounty the land would later provide. Raunn knew that with her blowgun she would have been able to bring down some game, but she could still forage what was available. Selecting a stout stick, she slipped quietly off into the new morning.

Following the small stream uphill, toward the spring

that was its likely origin, she went from the grove of trees where they were camped over a clean grassy area and through light scrub. Backtracking the quick-running stream, she climbed into a more heavily overgrown area and then up over a narrow rock lip onto level ground. Here the stream had spread out, backed up by the rock, until it formed a slough. A number of plants had established themselves in the mire, taking advantage of the boggy conditions, but most of these were still dormant, or so newly budded as to be of no use. Nevertheless, Rauun began to search the muddy pools carefully, using her stick to bend back dried grasses and dangling branches. Small shoots marked a clutch of dumpling bulbs that was her first find. Digging carefully around them with the stick, she unearthed two handsful. Selecting several of the fattest, she pulled them from the clump and washed them of their muddy coating. Rauun put the bulbs in her pouch and smiled in anticipation. This was the best time of year for roasting these delicacies when they were still sweet with unsprouted growth, and untainted by the toxins that would later develop.

Her nose led her to the next find, but the spicy odor of the jura bush was faint. Its new buds were barely visible so she had to make do with collecting a few of last year's leaves, still clinging tenaciously to the branches. They were dry from exposure to the cold but retained flavor that would be released by boiling water. Moving on past the small bog, she located a stand of rigorbean that yielded five or six of the long pods still intact from deep inside the thicket where animals could not reach. There was wild watergreen, too, but it would not be edible until much further into the season and she left it to mature.

Rauun climbed a final slope where the stream rilled downward over bare rock, glittering and rushing with the bright force of water unleashed from an icy prison. Scrambling over the top of the slope, she reached the spring for which she had been searching. It was a small pool and no deeper than her arm could reach but clear. Rolling up one sleeve, she plunged her arm into water that was only fractionally warmer than ice and probed with her fingers under the shelves of rock that jutted from the sides of the pool. Working quickly against the cold, she located the spiky shells of springborers that had ground out the basin from the rock. Pulling against the suction that held them to the stone, she plucked them from their hiding places. These were little bigger than a nut and nothing to compare to the venerable specimens that lived in the Heartspring, but they would be the more tender for it. Her bag full, Raunn dried off her arm in the warming sun and started back down toward camp. From the grove of trees ahead she could see the flock of new puffers, their air bags filled with warming gas, lifting slowly and with budding grace into the sunlight.

Aurial had not yet stirred by the time Raunn returned, so she set about preparing their meal. A flexible folding tripod that was easy to pack but completely stable earned her grudging admiration as she set it up. The device was techish, but useful. She hung a pot of stream water over the fire, then wrapped each dumpling bulb carefully in one of its own shoots. Digging a small hole nearby, she piled several rounded stones from the stream in its bottom. Then she raked coals carefully from the edge of the fire and piled them over the stones. The small green bundles went on top of the stones and then the springborers slipped unprotestingly off her fingers to their final resting place on top of the bulbs. With the hole thus filled, Raunn placed a flat stone atop it and turned back to the fire.

The water was boiling so she raised the tripod a bit higher. The rigorbean pods were old and dried out from wintering over on the vine. She scraped the coarse hairs off the pods and then split them lengthwise: they cracked open easily. Carefully removing the poisonous beans, Raunn discarded them outside the camp. Then she put the pods into the pot and added the jura leaves. With these preparations complete, she awakened Aurial. The outworld woman groped her way into consciousness, denying its existence until her eyes were completely open. She did not move and, when Raunn asked how she felt, she only grunted in reply.

\*　　\*　　\*

Even lying completely still, every muscle of her body hurt. Moving was not to be thought of. Yet, she was hungry and very thirsty. Worst of all was the need to empty her bladder. Movement of some sort was essential but Aurial approached it cautiously: first a hand, then an arm. The pain was beyond anything in her experience. Each muscle felt as if it had been pummeled individually and had shrunk from the assault. Now stretching them out caused every fiber and cell to send emergency protests screaming up her nervous system. Nevertheless she persevered, flexing one by one all the under-used muscles that had been so badly overtaxed in one short day. Finally, she attempted to stand.

"Do you want some help?" Raunn asked.

"No. I can handle it," Aurial replied shortly.

"You look pretty sore. How do you feel?"

"Every part of my body is in pain," Aurial said. "Even my kneecaps. The soles of my feet feel as if I'm walking on spikes."

"The only consolation I can offer is that this is the worst it will be. Once you're moving again and get warmed up, you'll feel better."

"Gwynn always said that. I never believed her, either. Please don't talk about it." Aurial took a step and winced. Moving in a jerky, creaking fashion, she made her way into the trees and succeeded in relieving herself of one of the discomforts. Hobbling back to the fire, she found its warmth and cheer a small encouragement. Something smelled interesting. Unable to cope with anything beyond her own pain, she accepted it as a given that food was cooking. "Is that firstmeal?" she asked.

"Mmmm," Raunn said.

"What about the food in our packs?" she persisted.

"Yes, star food. It must be nourishing or there wouldn't be so many of you but it tastes like old fungus. I had quite enough of it in port, to say nothing of last night. This will taste much better and you need something hot in your stomach right now. Besides, until we get you into shape, it's going to take longer than I planned to get to Cliffmaster Citadel. We should save the supplies in our packs for an emergency."

Aurial swallowed. "I suppose you're right, but . . . well, what is it?"

"Good things," Raunn replied enthusiastically. "Roasted dumpling bulbs, steamed springborers, and a broth made of rigorbean pods and jura leaves. It's solid, sustaining and hot. It will fill your stomach and give you strength." In her anticipation of the meal ahead, she did not see the expression on Aurial's face.

"Where did you get it?"

"I went out while you were still asleep and found it all. The land provides—although it provides a lot more in some seasons than others. You just have to know what will feed you, what won't, and what will kill you if you're not careful. I brought it back here and cooked it." She lifted the flat stone off the hole. "It's ready. Crawl on over and get some."

"Very funny. It smells good," Aurial admitted. "But how do I know it won't kill me? I'm not a native, remember."

Raunn paused and her brow furrowed. "That's a good question. I don't know. But you had those shots before we left. Weren't they supposed to make it alright to eat the local food?"

Aurial conceded, "Among other things, yes, they were."

"Then what's the problem?" Raunn had the contents of the steaming cavity laid out and was ready to start eating.

Aurial hung back. "I've never eaten, mmm, live things before. The dumpling bulbs are just vegetables, but springborers? Aren't they, or weren't they, animals?"

Raunn grinned weakly. "Then you'll be eating real food for the first time. I'll wager that most people who live right down here at the bottom of a gravity well eat real food. Live things. Animals and plants and who knows what else. We have no choice, you see. But if you're going to impersonate one of us, you'll have to learn to eat it, too."

Aurial threw her a lethal look and filled her plate. "I can handle it," she said.

The dumpling bulbs came out of their wrappers smoking. Split open, their golden cores gave out a marvelous succulent aroma that had Aurial's stomach burbling in anticipation. She nibbled tentatively at one, then began eating in earnest while Raunn fished the rigorbean pods out of the pot and poured the herb broth into their cups.

The bean pods had softened and bleached from rusty brown to nearly white. "These don't have much flavor," Raunn explained, "but they are packed with vitamins and are very good for you. We cultivate them for bigger pods and smaller beans." Aurial, who had enjoyed the bulbs, tried the pods and found them acceptable, if not exciting. The borers, however, were another matter. She watched Raunn pick the rubbery body out of its shell with the point of her knife and blanched. Catching her expression, Raunn said casually, "You may not want to try too many new foods at once. Even people on Chennidur consider these an acquired taste."

"It's harder when something was just alive," Aurial explained. "It makes me feel like a predator."

"All the food was alive," Raunn responded pedantically. "Food is food. If you harvest a plant, you kill it and if you harvest an animal, you kill it. If we weren't supposed to kill to eat, we'd be able to live on sunlight and water."

Aurial gritted her teeth and picked up one of the spiky shells carefully. "Gwynn would eat it, no problem," she muttered almost to herself, and dug the meat out. Popping it into her mouth, before she could really look at it, she chewed brusquely. The borer was not as tough as it had appeared and had a mild nutty flavor, not all unpleasant. She was able to swallow it without mishap. To prove that her success was no fluke, she consumed two more, then concentrated on sipping the broth. It had cooled just enough to drink comfortably and filled her with a wonderful warmth that seemed to reach into her muscles and relax the tightness. By the time she finished it, Raunn was breaking up camp. It took them only moments to clean their dishes, douse the fire and pack up their things. Then it was time to start walking again—with a whole day of fresh air and exercise ahead.

## THE PUZZLE PALACE

Ten woke first. He lay for a while, disoriented, conscious of having dreamed himself in some other place. It was a warm and secure place and the comfort of it filled him with happiness. There was no wrong feeling in that place. No pain creature lurked there, gnawing on his leg. Instead it was filled with sweet smells and wonderful tastes that were all part of the knowledge that he belonged there. Best of all, he knew things in that place—his name, the names of his family, where he was. But this knowledge had slipped away when he wakened, drifting through the pores of his body, leaving him finally back in that terrible stone room where everything was wrong. The loss of both the understanding and that magical haven filled him with unbearable sadness. It left him alone and bereft of all that mattered.

The dream faded beyond his reach and Ten came more fully into consciousness. His throat was raw and felt as if it had been scoured with dry twigs. His tongue was thick and fuzzy. Ten stretched cautiously and discovered that, while he was in the healing sleep, he had soiled himself and his pants were stuck to his skin, stiff and stinking. He was mortified. Trying not to disturb Eleven, he struggled upward until he was sitting with his back propped against the stones. He tried to peel off the stained garment but lacked the strength to lift himself up and pull them away. The pain creature awakened in his leg and churned around, growling, but it did not bite.

He had no idea how long he had slept, could not even begin to think about it, but sensed that if he were this weak, it had to have been several days. The light was growing at the window: soon the door would open and the men would bring food. Eating could help to make him stronger; Medic had said so. Until then he merely sat weakly and observed the stone room. The atmosphere was stifling—close and fuggy with unpleasant smells, his own not the least of them. It was also crowded and that startled him. So many people. Ten did not even try to count them.

The people he recognized were still there but the new ones moved around and between them. These were different, more active and alert, yet their eyes still carried the same lost and bewildered expression as all the others. The ones who were not injured appeared to be engaged in the attempt to remember something that was gone as surely as the magical place of Ten's dream was gone.

Gradually he noticed one man whose movement in this room was purposeful rather than random. He appeared to be taller than Ten and slender but strong. His hair was an odd color, neither the white of childhood nor the black of maturity. It was like the Veil at dawn or mist in the hills. This unusual man moved purposefully among the injured occupants of the room, tending to their wounds and giving them sips of water from a cup. The guards took away the drinking vessels: why did he still have one? He was talking to people. Talking. Only by comparison did Ten notice how silent the room was. True, there were the sounds of bodies moving, the shuffling of feet, coughing and sneezing, the sounds of people using the noisome cans in the corners. But there was no hum of conversation, no arguments, no one talking to himself. Ten did not understand how he could not have noticed this before. The guards talked but the inmates were silent.

Ten watched the strange man intently as he continued his circuit of the room—waiting for him to reach Eleven's sleeping form. His attention waned; his eyes drifted. With determination, he pulled them back. He would not sleep, not even to go back to the wonderful place. It was important that he stay awake to make sure the man looked at Eleven. Ten's blanket covered him and he used it to try putting his thoughts in order. To his surprise, the thoughts came to him and it no longer felt as if he were slogging through the fields at Mudtime. Thinking felt more normal, although he had no idea what normal was. The thoughts he had pieced together and woven into memory with the blanket were still there. Most were random and unconnected but holding on to them kept him awake and lifted his spirits.

He still did not know who he was. He did not know why

he or any of the room's inmates were here. That information had resided in the part of his mind that had simply gone away. Pursuing these blank places only brought him quickly to a frustration so great he wanted to smash his head against the wall.

There was movement in front of him: the strange new man had made his way to their space on the floor. Ten looked up into eyes that were deep and dark, wild and yet serene. For a second he saw a third eye in the man's forehead but then he blinked and it was gone. Of all the people in the room, this man alone did not seem to be asking the single unanswerable question that preoccupied everyone else. "Who are you?" Ten asked, hoping that this one person, at least, would know. The man only shrugged and the corners of his mouth lifted in a faint smile. "I am Ten," he asserted, holding on to the one thing he could. The man fastened his eyes upon Ten's and became very still. Ten stopped breathing, held immobile like a merrain under a stickybush. Then the man's eyes blinked, breaking the link. "You are Astin," he said.

The name crashed on Ten, exploding with conflicting thoughts and emotions. The pervading happiness of the dream place mingled with the overwhelming terror of the wound on his leg. He was someone and no one at the same time. A shining goal and sense of accomplishment surged up against the desolate emptiness of the stone room. It was as if the name had unleashed every emotion he had ever experienced and they warred with one another, their battle churning up a nauseating fear and a terrible joy at the same time.

Astin. He clung to that name—his name, not just a number. How did the man know? Astin wanted to ask but the man had already turned his attention to Eleven and begun to check the dressings. He removed the bandages carefully, stopping when Eleven cried out in sleep, and found that the wounds were clean. Astin could see that they were no longer red and swollen and were covered by patches of skin that looked as fresh and fragile as newly-formed diktall wings. The strange man did not touch this and covered the wounds again with hands that were gentle and deft.

Before he could move on, Astin asked, "What is his name? I call him Eleven." The man fastened his hypnotic eyes on Eleven but after a few seconds, gave his head a faint shake. "He sleeps deeply. The name is too far down for me to read." He swung his eyes at Astin. "You too must sleep again. But food will come soon. Eat first. I will return. Others are more in need of help now." He rose with one smooth movement and continued his circuit of the room.

Eleven returned to consciousness that evening. Astin had eaten and slept and eaten again and felt stronger. He listened with concern while Eleven woke like a swimmer in spawning season, thrashing almost to the surface, then sinking again, coming closer with each attempt until he finally broke through the shining surface. With each approach, Eleven cried out in pain or anger before subsiding into silence, twitching and jerking then relaxing again. He opened his eyes as Astin was attempting to drip broth into his mouth. Eleven choked and retched while Astin held his head to one side so he would not suck the fluid into his lungs. For an instant they stared into one another's eyes and Astin could see the struggle as the man asked himself the question and tried ineffectually to make his mind give him the answer. Astin attempted a reassuring smile. "Don't try," he said. "It's gone. Think later, get stronger. You were very sick. Medic helped. You slept long. That's all. Don't talk. Just eat this."

Eleven must have been hungry because he obeyed, finishing the broth and the bread Astin soaked in it. Eating used up all his strength, however, for his eyes closed almost with the last bite and he returned to a healing sleep. Astin sighed: he would have to wait a while longer to find out the man's real name.

# CHAPTER 6

## TRAILHEAD

Surrein paced the length of the common room in the hostel at Trailhead, came to the end, pivoted and paced back. He had passed beyond mere anger some time ago and was now in a fury. His rage drove him into constant movement and without that release he felt as if he would explode. His thoughts swung in wild arcs like the arms of the windikins that farmers put in their fields to frighten away vermin. Control of the situation had been taken from him and Surrein was *always* in control. Worse, it had been taken by a drev, a mere servant, one of those who existed only to serve their masters. The tuupit had simply taken advantage of fortunate circumstances because he was not capable of outsmarting a troinom. The underranks didn't have real brains any more than they had a clan mark. The result, however, was that he had no choice but to remain here in this rustic trail house, a shelter little better than a tent, and wait.

Waiting was not usually a problem for him. Surrein prided himself on his patience, groomed it carefully, and used it to his advantage, whether it was to learn something he needed or to defeat an opponent. Waiting was an acceptable tactic when he was in control. This kind of waiting, while someone else mastered the situation, was different and he had no patience for it at all. It made him feel helpless. It was intolerable.

Also fueling his wrath was a small thing but one that demanded immediate attention. On the path from the relief house he had brushed up against a budding tendril of firevine and a red welt now striped his right cheek. Small blisters were rising painfully along its length and when they broke the itching would start. This early in the year the damage was not as bad as it would be during Abundance when the volatile oils in the vine's leaves were most potent. But then, in Abundance he would have seen the brilliant leaves and avoided the firevine's poisonous touch altogether. Surrein had called twice for his manservant to bring salve for the welt but the man had not responded. It was just like the little rockcrawler to disappear when his master needed him most; he had done it often enough before. When the drev finally showed up he would have his usual excuse, but that would not prevent Surrein from giving him a few welts of his own to remember the lapse by.

He knew the man was hiding, of course, just as he knew that they were hiding Torrian on the Rock. They had her shut away somewhere in that enormous fortress, somewhere known only to the family, no doubt. That was what he would do in their place. The tuupit's great lie about a contagious illness had forced him to leave the Clan citadel and before he could return they would have cleansed her of the stardust. It was not a complicated plan, but then it did not have to be. Although Surrein understood their intention only too well, he could not counter it without endangering his position as her betrothed by violating the law. He was immobilized.

Denying the stalemate with action, Surrein strode to the door, wrenched it open and moved outside where he had more room to pace. The clear air would also help him think. To his left, the trail curved around pasture fences on its way across the plateau to its terminus at the base of the Rock. On his right, it wound in switchbacks down the stony escarpment to a junction with the main road that went to Nandarri. He walked to the edge and looked over it to the trail's switchbacks. That was one way to break away from this intolerable situation. He could simply return to Nandarri and marshall his forces for another assault. It was a tempting alternative because it offered immediate action and the opportunity to remove himself from an impotent position in the game the intolerable tuupit was playing.

Beyond that gratification, however, it provided no advantage. By the time he returned, Torrian would be recovered and in charge, assisted by the tuupit. Any challenge to the betrothal would cause severe repercussions for him in Nandarri. At the very least he would have to admit the failure of a plan he had proposed and accept a rebuke. Far worse, he would lose his only opportunity to become part of a great clan, and next in line to be tansul. Under certain circumstances, betrothals could be broken: he was not secure yet. Surrein tugged at the thin braid on his shoulder as he thought.

Finally, he turned away from the edge and paced back in the direction of the Rock. Ahead of him, a bikkle scurried from under a bush and dashed across the path. Midway, it saw him and froze. Its camouflage was so complete that its jewel-bright scales stopped glittering and assumed the same drab blue color as the dirt. Even the beast's little round eye dulled and became no more animated than a pebble. Surrein stopped at the same instant and a narrow smile curved the corners of his mouth. Very slowly he removed a small throwing knife from its sheath in his boot and balanced it in his hand. With a quick flip of his wrist, the scene in the path changed as if by magic. The bikkle vanished and the knife shivered point down in the path where it had crouched. Surrein spat and allowed himself an oath. He was fast and his aim was deadly accurate but bikkles had incomparable reflexes.

Surrein retrieved the knife stealthily and then became immobile once again. Losing a contest of reflexes to a bikkle had not made him feel any better but bikkles were never alone, and he would have another opportunity to test his skills. He kept his eyes riveted on the bushes and a few moments later the bikkle's pod-mate burst from cover and made its run across the open space. Once again Surrein's hand flicked and this time the scene on the path ended differently. The throw was perfect, his aim flawless. The bikkle quivered in its death spasm, transfixed by the knife.

He watched the little animal die with enjoyment, gratified by even such a small triumph. When the final convulsion ceased and the bikkle relaxed in death, he waited for the piercing cry of its pod-mate as it felt their birth connection break. Surrein smiled again when it came.

Stooping, he pulled his knife from the limp body. Methodically, with no emotion, he eviscerated the small body as if seeking the answer to his dilemma in its blood, then cut the bikkle into pieces and strewed them across the path. When he was done, he wiped his knife on a tuft of dry grass and stood up. Turning his back on the grisly scene, he went looking for his manservant. A blister burst on his cheek and fluid ran down his face. Surrein did not notice. He was still smiling.

## THE PERIMETER

The two women shouldered their packs and Aurial cried out as the weight settled on her back. All the muscles in her upper body had stiffened overnight and they flared with pain as she stretched them. The first step was an insult of sharp blades on the soles of her swollen feet; the second was worse. She was convinced that she would never survive the morning and might not make it to the top of the next hill. She had said that she would manage, however, and so she ignored the pain and persevered, placing one foot in front of the other and not thinking beyond that.

Gradually, other things began to command her attention. Her databead told her that it was early in the season called Renewal, when the cold of the winter was giving way to warmer weather and a new cycle of growth. It did not tell her that shortly after dawn in this particular season the air was cold enough to be uncomfortable. She wore native clothing, of course, and it had seemed perfectly adequate on the shuttle. The carefully-fitted boots and woven stockings were fine, although tighter today than they had been. The loose trousers of native fiber were heavy but would have been warmer if they were not quite so baggy. The long-sleeved shirt and quilted over-tunic of the same material allowed drafts in at the neck and sleeves, causing her to shiver. Absurdly, Aurial wished for a nose warmer since the tip of her nose was freezing.

One foot in front of the other. Raunn seemed perfectly comfortable, Aurial noticed, but then she was used to this weather. She probably even thought it was warm. They started downhill and the change caused another set of muscles to register their displeasure. The muscles in the front of her thighs were sore to the touch and at the first downhill step she almost cried out in pain. Then the cold air started her nose running. She sniffed. A few steps later she sniffed again. She continued to sniff at increasingly regular intervals until a drip was imminent and she could not stand it any more. Having nothing else at hand, she used her sleeve as a handkerchief. Just as she did so, Raunn turned around and said, "It helps if you blow your nose every now and then." Aurial did not know what to say but her face must have expressed it adequately because Raunn added, "Look in your pockets for a square of cloth." Aurial hunted and eventually found a pocket fitted into the seams on each side of the tunic. There was indeed one square of cloth, which helped her nose. The pockets also kept her hands warm.

With the sniffing under control, she tried looking up instead of at the ground as they walked. She saw for the first time the beauty of early morning, and a morning on

Chennidur was spectacular. The Great Wheel, paling with each passing second, was a ghostly disc balanced on the horizon. In the sky opposite it the Veil streamed upward. Opaque white light poured across the hills, illuminating each branch and stalk of grass. Pockets of mist hovered in the valleys, soft and pearly, like cloud fragments that had been captured by the land. Groves of ridgepole trees stood up stiffly and a solitary klypt drooped its branches over the grass. Although the air was cold, it was so filled with scents and tastes that it seemed to her enriched.

Gradually it became easier for Aurial to put one foot in front of the other. By the time Raunn called their first rest stop, her body had warmed up enough to dispel some of the pain. As the aches that had restricted her movements loosened, she could breathe more freely. By mid-day she was still incredibly sore but better. At mid-meal they ate out of their packs. Raunn made faces at the taste but Aurial dined with excellent appetite, her food seasoned with the knowledge that her pack would be a little lighter when they started off again. The afternoon was mild and bright. A pleasantly warm wind blew from their left, bringing with it elusive scents of buds and sprouts and newly-turned soil. The journey continually presented Aurial with new and fascinating experiences. She had never before been so close to the various components of a complex ecology. Ignoring the databead, she asked questions about many of the things she saw and was impressed when Raunn answered all of them knowledgeably.

The afternoon wore on and the walking wore her out but they continued beyond the limits of her strength. She lost interest in the surroundings, stopped asking questions and grew irritable with Raunn. Finally, she could only focus on one step at a time, enduring until they could find a place to make camp for the night.

As the sun crept lower, they moved carefully across a hilltop, picking their way through closely-grown brush. Raunn stopped abruptly, then moved off at a sharp angle into the scrub to her right. Aurial registered dully what she had done and instructed her own feet to follow, but her body was close to exhaustion and the message never made it all the way down. Instead her legs kept moving like an automaton, taking her straight into a wide circular space that was clear except for a large bush near its center. She knew that she should skirt the clearing as Raunn had done. Yet it offered a much easier path than the one Raunn was bludgeoning through the brush.

Beyond thought, beyond caring, Aurial stepped into the clearing. When she was a few steps into it, a strong fruity scent erupted into the air. Almost the same instant Raunn barked for her to stop where she was. Aurial stumbled to a halt and Raunn strode to her side. "I told you," she said stiffly, "to follow me. Where were you going?"

"Across there," Aurial replied slowly. "It's easier." She looked at Raunn defensively. "Who needs to shove through scratchy brush when you can just walk in the open?"

Raunn gave her a disgusted look. "Watch," she replied simply. Picking up a rock, she threw it at the bush in the center of the clearing. When it struck the ground under the sturdy plant, its impact set off an instantaneous reaction among the branches, which shook visibly. A loud pattering sound followed. "If that rock was an animal," Raunn explained, "it would now be stuck firmly to the ground. Once it stopped thrashing around, trying to escape, the bush's roots would extrude themselves from the soil and embrace it, crushing its bones. After sucking out its life juices, the roots would draw the remains into a cavity where it would be digested. The stickybush eats efficiently. It leaves no traces of its prey to alarm any future meals and prevent them from approaching."

Aurial looked again. The ground beneath the bush was indeed suspiciously clean and the sap that glistened on it now looked sinister despite the enticing smell. "It's not big enough to hurt a person, is it?" she asked.

"Hurt? No, the stickybush, even one this large, couldn't hold an adult long enough for the roots to grab you. But you could waste a fair amount of time trying to get away and the sap it exudes is long-lasting. Everything you walked on for the next few days would stick to your boots. It's also caustic so after that the bottoms would fall off. Believe me, a stickybush may not be fatal to people but it's still easier just to walk around one, even if the underbrush scratches."

Feeling stupid, Aurial backed out of the clearing and followed Raunn around its circumference. They walked over and up and down some more. By dusk Aurial was staggering and her enemy, the demon of gravity, had control of her body once more. If only, she thought, they had started off on level ground: flat land would have been more forgiving of her offworld muscles. Scientifically she understood that people who lived at the bottom of a gravity well were accustomed to the pull from birth and moved against it as naturally as they moved through the atmosphere. Nevertheless, her own body insisted that this immutable force was a totally unacceptable burden and impossible to live under without hope of respite.

They stopped slightly earlier than on the previous evening because Aurial was incapable of continuing. Her fatigue was so great that she was dizzy and all her aches had returned to torment her body. Her feet were swollen and her hands were puffy. Yet Raunn was visibly unhappy at how little ground they had covered compared to how far they had to go. While Aurial sat in a stupor, Raunn put her remaining energy to good use setting up their camp and building a fire efficiently.

Then, snatching the gun from Aurial's pack, she stalked out of camp in search of dinner. After she had left, Aurial rested for a few moments but Raunn had given her orders that kept her from sinking into sleep. First, moving on hands and knees, she set out the ground sheets and sleeping sacks. Next she took the pot and hobbled over to a tiny rivulet of meltwater not large enough to warrant the name of stream. Another month or so into Renewal and it would be dried away, leaving not even a damp spot behind. She rested again while the pot filled. Then she picked it up, nearly undone by the effort, and carried it back to the fire. After that she lay down and waited for Raunn to return from harvesting their supper from the wilderness. She thought about the borers and hoped that there would be no similar surprises for tonight's meal. She was tempted to fill up with provisions from the packs but dismissed such an unworthy thought. She would eat the same food Raunn ate and without complaint.

## THE BELDAME

Rolfe spread his fingertips on the console and leaned against them as he reread the computer message hanging in front of him. He hummed atonally. This was an interesting development: As Aurial's control on the Beldame, it was his job to provide backup and support for her, to handle her requests and ensure that she had everything she needed to succeed at her first major assignment. So far there had been little to do. Now here was a scheduled message but it had not come through regular communication channels. Instead it was coded and had been transmitted directly to his own personal computer station.

She had probably gone around channels because she was requesting information unrelated to either the politics or religion of Chennidur. Instead she wanted to know about an upcoming labor shipment. On the first scan, the message had sounded irrelevant to her assignment but he knew that he should not leap to conclusions that could only too easily be incorrect. Some individual important to her mission on Chennidur could be in prison and awaiting shipment out. That was a logical scenario and one that Aurial would be absolutely correct to track. Not to mention perfectly aboveboard. Then why the secrecy? And why did the message contain a cryptic note asking him to handle this by himself?

He could do so, of course, quite easily. Because they were partners on this mission did not mean, however, that they were running the operation on their own. Both reported in to Itombe and she was, by her direct instructions, to be kept informed of all developments and any requests outside of the routine. Although defining routine was left pretty much to his own judgment, this was not a routine request by anyone's standards.

That left him suspended between Aurial's desire for secrecy and Itombe's directive for communication. Rolfe looked at the message a third time: it hadn't changed. To avoid speaking he used the command pad and sent the message to his private record bank where it would be encrypted and locked. Then he sat down to think. His left palm itched and he scratched it absently as he considered his loyalties. Itombe was the Old Lady's second in command and not someone to diddle about anything. She took her job and herself very seriously. Her sense of humor, if one had ever existed, was atrophied. That wasn't her fault, he knew: If he had grown up in the Old Lady's shadow, he probably would have ended up the same way. Itombe was a woman driven by her mother's demands and by her own need for perfection. Although a pleasant person, intelligent and entertaining, she was intolerant of any goals different from her own and was blind to lesser ambition. She made very few mistakes and followed the rules scrupulously. He knew of one incident when Itombe had deliberately disobeyed the Old Lady's instructions and, while she suffered the consequences of that choice, she had never regretted the decision.

Rolfe drummed his fingers on the console and stared at its controls without seeing them. Aurial was at the other end of the il Tarz family's somewhat lopsided tree. The youngest of the sisters, and younger than he, she possessed an energy and enthusiasm that he enjoyed. Although he was closer to Gwynn, another of the four sisters, by both age and inclination, he had helped Aurial to learn. She loved to listen to his stories of growing up in the Outback and he found her questions perceptive and demonstrative of a mind that could cut through irrelevancies to the core of an issue quickly.

His palm itched again and he smiled as he scratched it. That only happened when he was excited about something, and it had not itched often on the Beldame. He did not regret his decision to come, but had to admit that life here was not as exciting as it had been in the Outback. He was learning a great deal, growing in many ways and gaining whatever authority a man was allowed on the Beldame. Yet there were few opportunities on this sterile station for adrenalin to surge in response to a challenge and he missed that kind of action.

The Chennidur project intrigued him. He would have preferred taking on the assignment himself but the Old Lady had said he wasn't ready. Rolfe considered himself far more qualified than Aurial and he suspected that he would always hear the same answer. So he sat in an artificial asteroid manning the communications from Chennidur and getting his adventure second-hand. He would do a good job, the best, but he was not about to just follow the Old Lady's rules blindly, without thinking for himself. In the Outback, you didn't follow anything blindly. Besides, he had no great loyalty to the Old Lady; she had thrown him away before he was even born. He called her Mother when he was with the others because it was a mark of respect and expected by his sisters but his true mother had been a geologist. She had been perhaps a bit too single-minded in pursuit of her goal, perhaps not as practical as she might have been. But she had given birth to him and raised him as best she could and loved him. That was a mother in his eyes, not someone who contributed some genes to a laboratory event and then waved her hand either yes or no depending on the result.

He rubbed the palm of his left hand with the thumb of his right. It was time to start pulling out some information. He activated the computer's SEARCH function and directed it first to retrieve, analyze, categorize and report on all transactions connecting labor contractors and Chennidur. Next he disabled the NARRATOR function so the report would be visual only and directed it to FLAT SCREEN so that only he or someone standing directly behind him could read it. Quickly, he checked the area around his station. A few other workers monitored their computer terminals in pursuit of their own goals but most of the stations were empty. No one paid any attention to his activities. When he returned his attention to the computer it was waiting to report and he instructed it to proceed. The result was brief. Labor contractors began dealing with the Tulkan's regime about one STP after his assumption of power on Chennidur and the subsequent opening of trade with the Quadrant, in defiance of *shufri-nagai* and the unified opposition of the clans. The Tulkan's Chief of Council, a man named Verrer ni Rimmani san Derrith, dealt directly with the contractors and generally bid out a shipment contract among a group of them. The shipment went to the contractor with the best offer. In business terms, it was all open and straightforward. Even the labor contractors, as tough a group as you could find in the Quad markets, had no recorded complaints. That was in business terms.

Rolfe himself had no love for labor contractors and no respect for those who dealt with them. In his travels through the Outback after his father's death, he had several times bumped up against files of shambling blank-eyed human beings being shipped to what was euphemistically called the work site but which he thought of as their last stop. They looked as if their brains had been fried right out of their skulls and nothing was left but a body which, ordered to work, would do so like a machine until it was directed to stop or until it dropped. It made the hair on the back of his neck rise just to think about those specters.

Some defended the labor system as an efficient way of dealing with criminals and troublemakers, but in Rolfe's philosophy a culture's misfits should be dealt with by and within that culture. To ship them offworld for someone else to dispose of for profit was avoiding a basic responsibility. A culture that could simply dispose of its mistakes would never mature enough to fix them. When the M'Gwad Technocracy bought an asteroid cluster in the Kewei-i system solely for disposal of its toxic waste, the action had been brought before the Quad courts and ruled illegal. Was it different with people?

While Rolfe had no great sympathy for convicts who had committed serious crimes, he also knew that the contractors could not survive if all they had to buy and sell were criminals. It was therefore obvious that most of the people in those subhuman work groups were there because they disagreed with their government or believed in the wrong god or tried to protect an ecosystem that was being despoiled, or lost a war.

Rolfe had never been to a work site. Since the sites were closed and guarded, no one knew what really went on but what he had heard about the conditions was sickening. One assumed the eventual death of the laborers but there were other victims as well. A planet could be raped of its natural resources, species driven to extinction, semi-sentient creatures destroyed and no one would know. It was a system that focused only on results and ignored any costs not quantified in the project development budget.

Branching out from the business data, he instructed the computer to generate a background summary on each of the contractors who had done business with the Tulkan's Chief of Council. He followed that up with what little background information was available on the man named Verrer. After reading the biographies, he put them in the same secure file that held Aurial's request. Next, using the historical information as a database, he had the computer display the data records as a chart and extrapolate from them when the next labor shipment would take place. He compared it against the estimated STU date on the display calendar and saw that it was not far away. So, Aurial knew someone important was going to be included in that shipment. Now who could it be?

As Aurial's control on the mission, he tapped into the same databead, listened to the same language tapes, memorized faces of the same people and made sense of the same genealogical charts. He knew Chennidur as well as Aurial had when she shipped out, as well as anyone could who had never been there. Unlike Aurial, however, he also knew the Outback firsthand. He understood in his bones how things there were often not quite what they appeared to be. He understood how quickly events could move and shift, particularly when unexpected. Even stuck here on the Beldame, Rolfe could put that knowledge to use for her now. He made up a list of candidates for the crime of political dissent who were troinom or nayyat or influential for some other reason. He instructed the computer to compile a list of labor contractors currently buying up inventory in the quadrant and a second list of work sites with a labor contract out or on order.

When that information had been stored in his private record, he searched through the library network for briefing tapes on the labor market, its history, how it worked, where it could operate freely, where it was banned, major issues surrounding it, groups opposed to it and groups defending it—as much information as he could find. Then he wiped the screen, locked his station, walked down to the library to pick up the datastrip he had ordered. There was a lot to learn in a relatively short time. Before he was done, he would know more about this ugly little system than the contractors themselves.

# CHAPTER 7

## THE PUZZLE

When Eleven had first been brought in, Astin had seen death settling into the dark hollows around his eyes and waiting in the gauntness at the base of his neck. The presence of the Raveler in the room, close enough to lure a spirit, had caused him to reach out to the other and hold on. The pain of seeing another person hurt and then dumped on the floor like rubbish had moved him to expend his precious energy caring for another. Astin did not know any of this yet, nor was he aware that nursing the other man had given him a focus. Forcing his mind to concentrate and to be coherent enough to help had made him stronger. All Astin felt was a need to not be alone, to have the company of another person in the depersonalized world that was the stone room. He imagined that Eleven would be more like him than like the other vacant faces he saw. He had reached out for a friend and he held on to that friend, waiting for him to re-awaken.

His vigil was rewarded the following morning when Eleven came back into consciousness abruptly. Astin simply looked down and saw the man returning his gaze. Speech was beyond him so he said nothing and instead helped Eleven to sit up. He waited while the other man surveyed their small environment and absorbed what he saw. Eleven started to speak but his voice was cracked and hoarse. Clearing his throat, he tried again. "Where?" he asked. "What . . . place?"

Astin responded with a shake of his head and the little he knew. "More people keep coming in. Guards bring food and blankets. Days pass. That's all."

"Guards?"

Astin thought about the word he had used. Guards meant something about the place they were in. Guards were only in certain places. Another word came into his head. "Prison?"

"Prison," Eleven repeated. "Prison Puh Puzh." He stopped and shook his head.

Astin remembered how slow his thoughts had been at first, slow and painful. He waited: there was time. The door opened and the guards came in with firstmeal. He left Eleven propped against the wall and went to fetch food and drink for them both. In the press of people he saw the strange man again, waiting patiently for his allotment, but had no chance to talk to him. He took the simple fare back to Eleven and helped him to eat and drink before taking any himself. It gratified him to see how the food seemed to fill out the man's slack skin and bring a shine of alertness to his eyes. He watched while Eleven went through the same phases he had already experienced, trying to attach names to familiar objects and place what was happening to him in some understandable context. Astin did not interrupt the process, feeling intuitively that it would be better if the man experienced it for himself.

When Eleven looked intently at him, however, he spoke again. "Astin. My name is Astin. Don't know your name. I call you Eleven."

Eleven nodded soberly, his eyes searching his surroundings for some hint of his real name and finding nothing. All that day he became stronger in small increments, as if he were working at accumulating life force. Eleven spent the hours looking around the room, watching and collecting information as Astin had. He ate all the food brought to him and could have consumed more, but he would not accept any from Astin's ration. Although too weak to crawl to one of the corners, Eleven was already so befouled that it hardly mattered.

Astin watched as emotions flickered across the man's face, wanting to help but not knowing what to do. Astin watched the room also for the strange man whose pale hair floated above the other heads, but the constantly-moving crowd kept them separated. Like Astin's memory and so many other things in the stone cage, the odd one was always just beyond reach. Astin could have sought him out but it would have meant leaving Eleven alone and he would not do that. He felt, without conscious thought, that his energy was helping Eleven to mend and he would not remove that contact except to fetch food and attend to his own biological needs.

That night, however, there was no meal to carry. The guards brought only the blankets and then left quickly, as though apprehensive of what empty stomachs would do to the normally docile inmates. Astin was frightened. This was the first change in the routine that he had experienced since coming to the room, except for Medic's visit. That had been a good thing but the growing hunger in his gut was not good, nor would the lack of food help Eleven. There was no alternative, however, and when darkness took over the room, the two men wrapped their blankets around themselves, curled as close together as two bikkles in a pod and slept.

The next morning *everything* changed. The guards entered well before daylight had dropped through the windows to begin a new day. There were more of them than usual and they carried no food or water. Instead they roused the sleeping prisoners with bellowed commands and prodded them onto their feet with kicks and blows. Astin barely had time to help Eleven rise before one of the uniformed tormentors seized his shoulder and shoved him toward the egress. He staggered, but Eleven steadied him. When all were standing, the guards herded the mass of confused and frightened people through the door. Holding on to one another, Astin and Eleven shuffled out of the bleak chamber that had been their entire world into a dark hall leading to the unknown.

The two men were pushed into a rough line along with the rest of the filthy stinking inmates and marched between featureless walls. The serpentine group came to a corner, turned and followed an identical hall to another corner. This happened several times, the crowd jostling and moving faster with each turn, like livestock heading into the chute. Finally, they spilled into a large room and stopped in confusion. The doors were closed behind them. Astin paused, his heart pounding with fear and exertion, anticipating a new assault. For a few moments, however, it was quiet and he looked past the guards to the new quarters. He saw strange devices that he did not recognize but which made him feel uneasy. Other men, whom he could only describe as not-Guards, stood off to one side watching the prisoners in a critical fashion. They wore unusual one-piece garments that covered their bodies like a white skin.

The guards grouped the prisoners in a ragged circle, then ordered them to remove their clothing and drop it on the floor. Most of the inmates followed the instructions readily but some had to be helped. Astin saw the pale-haired man assisting someone, his naked body shining despite its dirt. Astin and Eleven helped each other to pry off pants which were stuck to their flesh and slip the stiff clothing past their wounds. Astin, at least, was glad to rid himself of the filthy garments. He looked down at his body and was shocked to find it emaciated, with flesh hanging from the bones and his ribs showing clearly. He shivered slightly in the cool air and waited once again.

One of the white-clad men approached them pushing a little cart filled with cups. As the person neared, he became aware of two things: that it was a woman and that he had a great thirst. Suddenly, the dryness of his throat was intolerable and he grasped a cup eagerly as soon as the cart came within reach. Swallowing the contents in one cool draft, he tasted only a mild, pleasant flavor like that of herbal tea. He wanted more but the woman made certain that each prisoner got only one cup.

The empty vessels were dropped on top of the clothing and then guards moved them once again, this time to a smaller room with smooth shining floor and walls. As they pushed into it, Astin spotted drains in the floor, although there was no water anywhere. Once again the door closed and he waited nervously with the others for the next inexplicable event to occur.

He did not have to wait long. A sharp cramp sliced through his abdomen, followed immediately by another. Then his stomach twisted and heaved. He moaned and wrapped his arms protectively around his belly but soon he, and everyone else in the room, was retching. In moments the room was unbelievably foul as people vomited on one another and themselves. At the same time their bowels loosened and voided involuntarily and they crouched in the filth, helplessly enduring additional misery. Finally, when Astin's body had evacuated what little nourishment had been in the digestive system, the cramps loosened and released him. Astin continued to gag as he breathed in the miasma of smells. A spasm of retching possessed him, driving the breath from his lungs.

When he could breathe again, a noise attracted his attention. Astin looked upward. Nozzles extruded from the walls and began to spray warm water. He stood up and raised his face to the shower joyfully, letting it wash the appalling mess from his body. The water stopped, then was replaced by a fine blue rain that was smooth and slippery on his skin. When Astin rubbed at it tentatively, the fluid foamed and lathered. A word came to him. Soap. It was soap. Relieved, Astin began to wash himself vigorously. Eleven followed his example and others imitated them until the room was filled with soapy figures scrubbing themselves and one another in a simple rite of cleanliness. The rain of blue soap stopped and warm water returned, rinsing their bodies and sluicing the grime of countless days down the drains.

When they were clean the water stopped and a door opened, but it was not the wide door by which they had entered. It was narrow and would admit only one person at a time. Astin eyed it warily. Too much was happening too quickly and with no explanation. People began filing through the portal one at a time and eventually, despite his misgivings, it was his turn. He put Eleven behind him protectively and stepped through. A guard on the opposite side immediately clamped a sticky blindfold over his eyes and told him to keep walking. Astin hesitated and the guard pushed him forward. He walked, shuffling uncertainly in the darkness, and attempted to pry the covering from his eyes as he did so. In a few steps he felt something warm on his naked skin that was replaced with something cool a few steps later. A guard's hand stopped him and the covering came away from his eyes. Astin found himself back with the others in the first room they had entered but everyone looked different.

Astin turned to stare at Eleven behind him and then raised a hand to his head. Like Eleven's, it was smooth and shining, and totally hairless. He looked at Eleven's body and then down at his own. Except for eyebrows and lashes, all body hair had disappeared, and a fine white ash powdered his skin where the hair had been. This change was so weird and startling that his mind would not encompass it. First, the strange people took the food from inside his body and they stripped the hair from outside. What would come next?

Surrounded by the guards once again, the group stood, anxious but passive, while the white-garbed people approached. Moving from one prisoner to another, these not-guards looked into eyes, ears and mouths. Then they ran odd little boxes up and down close to the prisoners' bodies. Astin remembered the box Medic had used and was somewhat reassured. Medic had been kind. He had helped. When each prisoner had been inspected, the white-garbed people marked that individual's chest above the breastbone. Astin tried to rub his mark off but could not.

When each prisoner bore a sign, the guards herded them into yet another room, this one the most frightening of all. It was lined with shiny metal cylinders standing along the walls. Each cylinder was cracked in half lengthwise and opened as though to allow entry. Astin did not like the look of the tubes at all and his heart began to pound with fright. He grasped Eleven's arm tightly. Eleven looked at him curiously but did not share his fear. The white suits entered and began leading the prisoners to the cylinders one by one. Astin watched as each naked, vulnerable body leaned back into the container and then appeared to fall asleep while remaining upright.

When his turn came, Astin pulled away from the white-suit's soft grip and turned in a panic to run but a guard was right behind him. With the guard on one side and the white-suit on the other, Astin could not resist and he was pulled toward a waiting tube. Stiff with fear, he leaned back and a small puff of gas blew in his face. He was asleep before he could wonder what it was.

When the bodies were all loaded, the guards left and the techs moved busily from one cylinder to another. They primed chemical feeds, adjusted muscle stimulators, fitted language tutor caps and set thermosensors. Well trained and experienced in their jobs, they wasted neither time nor motion in processing the shipment. By day's end, all the cylinders were occupied, operational and ready to load. The tech supervisor made one final check and then ordered the loading dock doors opened.

As the Port lights brightened, a cargo loader began ferrying the cylinders to a waiting shuttle. The driver's breath puffed visibly in the cool night air as he went about his work with practiced precision. He paid no particular attention to the nature of his cargo: it was all just a night's work.

## THE PERIMETER

Raunn balanced the ugly techish weapon the way the Tarraquis had taught her, aimed and squeezed the firing button. The durric jerked up and back off its perch on a dead tree branch and fell into the scrub behind it without a sound. The little herd pivoted immediately to flee into the klypt grove. Before they vanished she was able to get off a second shot and another durric dropped in mid-leap, its forelimb stretched out to grasp a branch it would never reach. Raunn regarded the gun with surprised respect, knowing well that even Rushain could not have taken more than one without two blowguns and a bearer to load. She recovered the first little body easily; it had not fallen far. To find the second one, however, she had to poke and prod through the darkening brush. Carrying her game by their long hind limbs, she headed toward the winking orange light of the campfire. On the way back, she searched for a patch of januga's pipe to season the meat but the herb hid in sheltered spots and it was too dark in the undergrowth for her to make out the stems.

When she reached camp, everything had been done according to her instructions and the water was hot. The outworld woman was soft but she tried hard. Taking the utility knife from her belt, and wishing heartily for her own hunting blade, Raunn beheaded, gutted and skinned the durrics quickly. She removed the offal, being careful not to touch the reproductive and excretory organs, and buried all the viscera outside of camp. Then she washed her hands carefully in the tiny stream and returned to work. Butchering the meat with her knife, she selected the choice pieces and tossed them into the pot along with a few left-over jura leaves. Next she spitted the rest of the meat on sweet wood and propped the spits against the tripod so that the meat hung over the coals. In the firelight she saw Aurial's face, drawn and green, staring at her. With a quick glance at the bloody meat, the starwoman asked in a small tight voice, "Did you just—kill—that?"

"Of course," Raunn replied testily. "The butcher shops close early out here."

"But . . ." Aurial began. "But . . . they . . ."

Raunn sighed. Education was one thing; she was confident she could teach Aurial anything about Chennidur that she needed to know. Overcoming squeamishness and childhood fears was something totally different. "Don't think of it as what it used to be," she said levelly. "Think of it as food. Right now that is just dinner and in a few minutes it will smell pretty good. Once you've rested for a bit your stomach's going to start reminding you of how much work you did today. If your stomach and the meat get to the same point at the same time, you'll have no trouble eating your share."

Doing her best to hold back a smile, Raunn returned to the cooking fire. Aurial's squeamishness would be amusing, she thought, but it reminded her too much of Torrian's prissy attitudes for comfort. The starwoman at least had an excuse: she had been raised on artificial foods grown indoors without benefit of sunlight or rain or good strong soil. Raunn could not imagine what such a place would be like but she did understand how it accounted for Aurial's weak muscles and lack of stamina. On Chennidur all life was interconnected: It was only too easy to see how one species lived off another and then became food for a third. Without this natural interdependency all species would starve and there was no room on the food chain for luxuries such as an aversion to good meat. Even Torrian, who had never in her life come nearer than the kitchen to a freshly-killed animal, had a good appetite for savory meat, preferably served with a fine sauce. The starwoman would have to overcome her delicate sensibilities or risk getting very hungry in her time on Chennidur.

Seizing one of the skewers, Raunn handed it to Aurial. If raw meat was unfamiliar, the best way to grow accustomed to it was to deal with it first hand—find out that it didn't bite, so to speak. She was gratified when Aurial accepted the skewer despite her wrinkled nose and followed Raunn's lead in turning it slowly over a pocket of coals. "You're stronger than Torrian," she commented in a matter-of-fact tone.

"Who's Torrian?" Aurial asked, sounding grateful for something that would take her mind off what she was doing.

"My sister. Older sister, in fact."

"And why am I stronger than she is?"

"You work at overcoming the things that bother you. She avoids them."

"Oh. Does she not like raw meat either?"

"Raw meat, cleanly butchered and ready for the pot does not bother her at all. Watching someone kill and dress game, as you did, would make her nearly ill. She would not have touched it after that." *But then she wouldn't have to,* Raunn thought, *when there were always servants to do it for her.*

Aurial turned her skewer over. "So she doesn't hunt the way you do?" she asked.

"No," Raunn replied. "She's not much for any kind of blood sports, even to put food on the table. When she does hunt, only as a social activity, mind you, someone else takes care of the messy game for her."

"What about the cooking part?" Aurial continued. "Does she enjoy preparing food?"

"She can cook. Torrian can do just about any of the work involved in running a clan fortress. That's so she'll make a better vellide when she has a citadel of her own to manage. But her idea of a meal is something that's presented to her, fully prepared, on a clean plate." Raunn paused and turned her durric over so it wouldn't char. Then she added, "I don't think she's ever slept on the ground either."

"It doesn't sound like you and your sister have very much in common," Aurial noted.

"We don't. Turn your meat again; it's burning. That's better. Torrian and I usually saw goodness in different things and neither of us had much respect for the things the other one liked. We're like Tring and Trill in the old stonefather stories." Caught up in memories, she missed the blank look on Aurial's face at the reference. "When we were little, we quarreled a lot. She liked to order me around, as if commanding the servants wasn't enough. We never spent much time together after she moved out of the children's rooms."

There was a pause in which they listened to the sound of fat spattering in the fire and wind whispering through the trees. Then Aurial said softly, "It seems as if you didn't like her much."

"Like her? No, I guess not. But you don't look at it that way when you're young, do you? She was my sister and part of my family. Just there, you know. But everything's different now. I don't want to talk about Torrian any more."

Raunn poked at the meat with her finger and then declared it done. They ate in silence and she tactfully did not comment on how quickly Aurial consumed the formerly repulsive fare. Then the starwoman rolled into her blanket and sank quickly into a restless sleep.

The fire consumed the scraps of their dinner, hissing and spitting as it relished bits of fat and marrow. The air had cooled enough to remind Raunn that Icelock was not long past and she pulled her blanket over her shoulders. Overhead the Veil had withdrawn, leaving the sky a soft black punctuated here and there with stars. The rim of the Great Wheel was rising with Smallmoon ranging just ahead of it. Raunn searched the sky greedily, exploring the scattered constellations for something she did not understand and had never found but which continued to draw her. She did not find it this night either. With a sigh she pulled her gaze back to the world she knew only too well.

Watching her companion sleep, Raunn mused that Chennidur demanded that its people meet it on its own terms. The starwoman was trying, despite her own physical weakness, to do the best she could on the land's terms. Raunn respected that but was still driven by her own impatience to move farther and faster. So many things were happening that shouldn't be and so many more were not happening but should. Yet here she was, sitting on a hill under the stars far away from them all. How could she help Merradrix or her father or Torrian or even Antikoby, by trudging uphill and down like' a burrky following the tail of the one in front? She snapped a stick in two irritably and tossed it into the fire. She knew that what they were doing was the only logical approach, thoroughly discussed in advance. Still, Raunn would have been far happier confronting the Council and handing some vague but powerful ultimatum to Verrer. The urgency of it all was hanging in front of her, tormenting her with the need for action that she could not take. Instead she put one step after another and hated every one.

She broke another stick with a sharp crack and Aurial twitched in her sleep. That was one thing in her favor, Raunn thought, the starwoman would help, had already helped. "Leave Merradrix to me," she had said and Raunn knew that she had no choice. She couldn't do anything, but knowing that didn't stop her from wanting to. She was filled with frustration—forced into virtual immobility when she was possessed by the drive to make things happen quickly. Perhaps, she admitted to herself, it was just as well. This was the same compulsion that had propelled her into the Tarraquis. Perhaps there was a reason why she was sitting on a cold and distant hill under the tranquil stars instead of rushing headlong into more trouble.

She removed the pot from the tripod and set it on the coals to keep warm. The thick broth would make a quick nourishing breakfast and the remaining meat would keep them going on the trail. When the fire was banked she composed herself to pray, knowing that the ritual would dampen her frustration and allow her to sleep. She felt a pang of guilt when she realized how long it had been since she had fulfilled her prayer obligations. She may have taken an irreverent tone about the True Word in the Port but that was only a facade. Inside she was still a Follower who had all her life answered the Call to Prayer twice a day. That had not changed until she donned the black camouflage of the Tarraquis and went out into Nandarri with Merradrix. The thought of him, of his strength and the way his eyes looked when he smiled, made her miss him so badly that it felt like an ache inside her. The thought of his body on hers, the strength and weight of him caused another ache. Truly her spirit was in sore need of prayer this night.

Raunn spent a long time at her devotions, seeking not only patience but guidance and understanding as well. The Kohrable had always structured her life for her and directed her onto the right paths. It would not fail her now.

## THE ROCK

"When do you think he'll return, sri-nothi?"

Torrian, staring out the window of the Moon Tower, replied without turning. "Tomorrow. No later. He will have calculated precisely the time of recovery from the choking cough. Surrein leaves nothing to chance."

Maitris stopped folding the bedding and looked at her lady's stiff back. "What will you do?"

Torrian's voice drifted back with the breeze. "I do not know." Maitris shivered. Where was the competent, often arrogant, woman who knew as much as anyone about the running of a great house? This new Torrian moved with unsettling speed from dreamy indecision to clear thought, the promise of action and then back again. Maitris was worried. From what she knew of Surrein, as well as from what Torrian had told her, this was no time for dreaminess. He was too dangerous for such indulgence.

Then, suddenly galvanized, Torrian turned and her dorchari swirled around what was now a painfully thin figure. The glint had returned to her eye and her chin was firm, her mouth determined. "What I do know is that I cannot wait until tomorrow. For anything. Now is when I have the freedom—and the ability—to move. It's time to go down from the tower, Maitris. I cannot hide up here any longer."

Maitris dropped the bedding. There would be plenty of time to come back up here and pack. One step behind her mistress, she sped out of the room and down the spiral staircase, right hand sliding along the inner wall for balance. At the bottom, Torrian stopped for a moment to catch her breath, slightly dizzy from the spiral journey and still not fully recovered from her ordeal.

"Where are we going, sri-nothi?" Maitris asked in the momentary interval. She hoped that the su-vellide was on her way to summon the tuupit so that, together, they could create a barricade against Surrein's assault. That was what she would have done.

The answer disappointed her. "To the only person who can help me right now. We go to the vellide, my mother."

As Maitris hurried along behind Torrian, her worries grew. What help would the vellide be? Did she think her mother had improved while she was in Nandarri? She had neither seen the vellide since returning to the Rock nor been aware enough to know what was said of her. What would happen when she found out? Worse, what would happen next? She could not imagine. Still, at least they were moving: Torrian was coming back to herself.

Retracing the path Antikoby had taken many nights before, they made their way out of the old wing and into the new, then up to the vellide's chambers. By the time they arrived at their destination Maitris had a stitch in her side, but there was no time to catch her breath before the door opened and they were ushered within. A chambermaid took them immediately from the anteroom to the inner apartment where Torrian's mother sat by a bright window having her hair combed. The room was flooded with sunlight and filled with flowers forced by the gardeners all year long for the vellide's chambers. Plants grew in pots on the floor, cut flowers were arranged in vases on tables, sprays drooped from moss cups on the wall and vines curled from hidden sources. Like all the flowers of Chennidur, these had no scent but Rutin-Xian had always loved the colors, the shapes and the sheer abundance of their display. The flowers still glowed exuberantly but the vellide no longer had an eye for them.

Torrian swept to her mother and sank on the rug at her feet. Maitris sought a place by the wall with the chambermaids where she would be out of view, as was proper, yet readily available if needed. From her spot behind a vase of rugas blossoms she could see clearly and hear everything. She tried to memorize every word so that she could report to Antikoby later on what had occurred.

The su-vellide seized her mother's hand in both of hers and held onto it as if it were a lifeline on the precipice. The vellide looked down at her with an unfocused expression that Antikoby would have recognized, and smiled faintly. A green dorchari hung slackly on her, like the leaves of a wilted plant. She said nothing. "Mother, let me explain," Torrian began, as if an accounting had been demanded. "I wanted to do well. I tried so hard, even though Father was often gone and even when he was home, seemed to be somewhere else. I kept the house as you trained me: everything ran smoothly, the accounts balanced, there was always a meal for Father when he wanted one. He could bring home any number of people at the last minute and be proud of how well they were entertained.

"But it was lonely. There were only the servants and Father and he entertained members of the council who were all old, dull political types. There were other people of my station in Nandarri, some I knew and thought were friends, but they never accepted my invitations to the house and never invited me to theirs. I saw no one and there was nowhere to go except the market and the temple. After a while I was bored: I hated it. Then an invitation came for me; it was for dinner at Uncle Verrer's house. Father agreed, of course, and it was a marvelous evening. There they all were, the young people who had been so invisible, and we had *such* a good time. After that I was invited everywhere, always to the proper homes and always by the best families." She paused and looked out the sunny window as if seeking her next words in the view beyond.

"Things are different in the city, Mother. Nandarri is alive, full of new and different ways. Some of them come from the Port and, well . . ." Her voice drifted softly. Maitris could tell that she was losing herself in her memories again. Then Torrian rushed on, responding to a protest that the vellide had not made. "I know that techish things are forbidden. I know what the Kohrable says. But I saw such amazements. People cured of disease by medicines we don't have. Lights brighter than any we know how to make. Pictures of fabulous places so far from here we can't even see the light of their stars. Foods that don't need special cooking and are twice as nourishing. Little boxes that give off enough heat to warm a whole house in Icelock.

"When I saw those things, I began to understand what

the Tulkan wants, why he opened up trade. When I thought of what those things could do for us here I was bedazzled. There seemed no end to the ways our lives could improve, to the ways in which we could learn. In my enchantment I forgot that other, more dangerous things could come from the stars. The Kohrable says, 'When the pasture gates are open, the herd may come out or the predator may go in.' I never understood that before, but the stardust came in the gates, Mother, and no predator was ever so cruel. They all urged me to try it, my new friends. 'It's harmless,' they said. 'It's just for fun.' They made it sound like another marvel and I was too naive, too backwards to understand."

Still the vellide made no reply. Torrian pulled on her mother's hand and beseeched her with her eyes. "I was always so good, Mother. You know how hard I worked to make you proud of me. I did what you said, what Father said, what the nayya said. Just this once, far away from everyone, I wanted to be different. I wanted to be bold, to do something risky, to not first think what was right and proper. So I did. And the stardust was everything they said it was. Exhilarating, exciting, overwhelming. After I tried it once, I wanted it again and then again. And it was always there.

"But the stardust was also everything they said it was not. It was dangerous: like a skri it bit into me and would not let go. After a while it was all I wanted and I thought of nothing else. I learned the importance of the laws against pollution of the body in the most painful fashion. Were it not for Raunn's common sense and the servants' loyalty, I would still be dreaming in Nandarri."

Torrian stopped her monologue, looking for some sign that her mother had heard her confession. For a moment there was nothing. The vellide Rutin-Xian continued to stare out the window while her maid combed her long hair, dark and lustrous with age. The only sound in the room was the rhythmic susurrus of the comb and the crackle of static at the end of each stroke. Then, slowly, the vellide raised her hand, dismissing her maid. Even from across the room, Maitris could see the glistening trail of tears on her cheek. Rutin-Xian looked down at her daughter and gave a tremulous smile.

That was all the encouragement Torrian needed. "But that's not all, Mother," she rushed on. "That's not even the worst. One of the new friends that I made in Nandarri was a man from a distant family with the name Surrein ni Varskal san Cannestur. He was attentive, polite, charming. And he seemed to like me because of *me*. He made me feel like the most important, the most beautiful woman in all the world. I was quite . . . infatuated. Captivated.

"Surrein already held Uncle Verrer's approval and he courted Father with even more diligence than he pursued me. His charm was successful there, too: we both saw what we wanted to see and looked no deeper into his character. What a fatal blindness. When Father told me that Surrein had requested a betrothal, I was happier than I had ever been. The stardust helped, of course, and Surrein always had stardust for me. So it was done—in proper form and with all correctness. Uncle Verrer attended the ceremony. Only afterward did I begin to see what Surrein really was, what he is. And it is too late. The betrothal cannot be undone. I shall pay for my foolishness for the rest of my life."

Maitris knew that what she said was not what she meant: underneath that contrition lay a plea for help. The vellide's forgiveness was important but not half as necessary as her intervention. Silence lay on the room once again. A rugas blossom dropped to the tabletop with a soft sound and the lightened stem sprang upright, nodding slightly. The vellide cleared her throat. "Such terrible things," she said to her daughter. "You must be strong." Her voice trailed off like a breeze in the treetops. She turned to look out the window once again.

Torrian gave a cry of astonishment. "Mother!" she protested. "Is that all you can say? I need your advice. I need your help. Surrein was tricked into leaving but he will be back here tomorrow. He will try to suck me into his power again. You must keep him away. Make him go away. You must." Maitris heard in Torrian's voice and saw in her expression an echo of the demanding adolescent she had once been. Although far too old for such behavior, she was frightened and beleaguered and seeking help from a source that had always been ready to help her.

The vellide looked down at her daughter again and repeated, "You must be strong." Then she withdrew her hand from Torrian's grip and looked away. Rutin-Xian was no longer there for anyone. She had retreated into the little dark room in her mind, behind a series of locked and barred doors, that was the only place where she could bear to exist. Torrian rose abruptly and turned toward Maitris but her eyes were blank with shock. She took a step, tripped on the rug and staggered, then recovered her balance. Gathering herself, she straightened up and marched toward the door, looking neither at Maitris nor at any of the chambermaids. Maitris detached herself from her position by the wall, took up her place, and followed Torrian out of the room. She wondered once again what would come next.

# CHAPTER 8

## THE PERIMETER

The next day was cooler and a thick overcast slid under the Veil, weakening the sun's early warmth. The pattern in the clouds, like that of a sandbar under shallow water, presaged bad weather, or so Raunn said over firstmeal. "There'll be rain within a day," she declared.

Aurial looked up and muttered an obscenity under her breath. As if things weren't bad enough, she thought. Although exhausted, she had not slept well, sliding into a light doze and then pulling back out of it to feel again the ache of her muscles and the discomfort of the hard ground. Tired and crabby, she was now facing another endless day of hiking that was unpleasant enough when she was dry. Rain was all she needed. "What do we do then, when it rains?" she asked, trying to keep the irritation from her voice and failing.

"Haven't had much experience with rain either, have you?" Raunn poked at her. "Just imagine, water falling out of the sky. Uncontrolled." She shook her head. "We get wet. And we keep on walking. At this time of year it usually doesn't rain hard enough to force us into shelter. Don't worry, you won't melt."

Stung by her tone, Aurial replied, "I know that. Even if I don't know much about the outdoors."

"You and Torrian. Let's go."

"I'm not your sheffing sister," Aurial retorted. "Whatever problem you have with her, don't take it out on me."

Raunn gave her a hard look. "If we walk faster, we might reach Perimeter House by mid-day tomorrow. If the rain holds off, we could make it until camp tonight without getting wet. Those two ifs are all we can look forward to." It was as far as she was prepared to go toward an apology. "And, by the way," she added, "no troinom uses language like that. Ever. Not even in Chenni."

Aurial did not reply and they set off in a lowering mood of repressed anger. Perhaps because of the stimulus they moved faster and Aurial was surprised to find her body responding to the demands she placed on it. That meant she was gaining strength after all and it did quite a lot to lift her spirits. She saw for the first time the possibility of defeating the demon gravity.

Raising her eyes, she took notice again of their surroundings, examining with curiosity the plants and trees, even the ground they walked on. The brown dirt of the hills was gradually turning to a more orange-colored soil. It appeared to be weathered from the stratified fingers of sedimentary rock that jutted out of the hillsides with increasing frequency. The rock was friable and soft, as if the pressure that changed it from sand to stone had been released before the process was complete. This gave the dirt of the trail a coarse and crumbly texture. Aurial wanted to know more about the rocks but was reluctant to break into Raunn's silence. Around mid-day, her stomach began to make its emptiness felt but Raunn continued to stalk single-mindedly ahead. Aurial sighed and told her gut to stop complaining as she followed her companion's stiff back downhill.

They reached the bottom of one slope and were picking their way carefully through the small overgrown valley before the next uphill stretch when Raunn suddenly stopped with one foot in mid-air. Aurial, thoughts of the stickybush fresh in her mind, halted immediately. She waited patiently for a moment until Raunn waved her up. "What is it?" she asked in a whisper. In lieu of reply, Raunn bent down and picked up a stick, then pushed some of the brush aside so that Aurial could see the obstacle clearly. The only thing visible was a disgusting lump of grayish matter oozing a viscous fluid. It was about the size of a melon but possessed of un-vegetable bumps and angles that made it appear to be only a small portion of something much larger. Mostly, it looked like a scrap of carrion from a decomposing animal and it radiated a smell unlike anything that she had ever experienced. A cloud of small flying creatures buzzed and hummed in circles above it.

Aurial grimaced. "Is it dangerous?" she asked.

"Not to us," Raunn responded. "Hold still and watch." Newly wary of seemingly innocuous things, Aurial kept her eyes fixed on the inanimate lump. The flying insects, which had been disturbed by the women's approach, returned to their focus. They spiralled in toward the lump until several of them landed on its repulsive surface. In typical insect fashion, they walked aimlessly about, searching for the right place to stop and bite. The lump's surface rippled with a movement so quick it was difficult to follow and an insect disappeared. There was another twitch and another insect vanished. As others continued to circle and land, the process was repeated. Aurial queried, "Is it a plant or an animal?"

"Oh, it's an animal. We call it the death catcher." Raunn nudged it with her toe, sending the insects buzzing off again. "One this size lures and eats the insects that breed in carrion. Bigger ones consume large beetles, and real giants can take on merrains and bikkles. But that's about as big as they get and the larger ones are rare."

"So they never grow big enough to eat, well, people?"

Raunn laughed. "Oh no. Never. There are stonefather tales, mind you, of death catchers big enough to swallow a child. But they're just stories that grownups tell to keep children from wandering off by themselves."

Aurial thought about it. "I suppose one that big would give off a smell so powerful that not even a child could stumble on it by accident. Or can they move fast?"

Raunn looked at her with a considering eye. "Death catchers can move, but not quickly. Mostly they just sit in one place and wait for meals to come to them. Look." She poked the animal with her stick and levered it up onto its side. Beneath the carrion camouflage it revealed itself as a living creature. Ringing its circumference was a fringe of sensitive antennae. Behind that, two rows of jointed legs waved sluggishly. Raunn lowered the creature and immediately it settled into immobility, assuming its disguise as a hunk of rotting meat. "They don't move fast," she continued. "With practically no enemies they don't have to move fast. But they usually avoid open ground." She paused.

"Cheyte, my brother, put a little one in Torrian's bed once as a joke. He and Rushain made a bet on whether it would eat one of her toes before she woke up. Then they argued about whether flies or toes would taste better to a death catcher. Rushain bet Cheyte that she wouldn't scream when her feet touched it."

"Who won the bets?"

"Nobody won the first one. They covered up the smell with perfume but she touched the thing with her foot as soon as she got into bed. Torrian didn't scream but she got out of bed real fast and she almost vomited before the chambermaid removed it. Then Torrian made Maitris throw out the sheets and the mattress, too. Said you could never get the smell out. Cheyte always did have an odd sense of humor." She broke the stick in two pieces and threw it away.

Aurial could not resist. "Would you have vomited if you had found it in your bed?"

Raunn grinned. "No. But I probably would have yelled pretty good. Cheyte would never have done something like that to me, though, because he knew that I would have found an even better way to get back at him. Torrian was an easy mark. She never fought back." She looked up at the position of the sun. "Let's move downwind and have lunch. We've made good progress so far and I want to keep going until just about sunset."

They set a fast pace and were rewarded when the rain

held off. The sky was just beginning to darken when a fine mist filled the air, forming droplets on their hair and settling damply on their clothing. Raunn looked carefully about for shelter, but the hills offered little protection and the valleys would fill with runoff once the storm began. They came upon an old ridgepole grove halfway up one slope and Raunn spotted a tree that had toppled but jammed in the branches of its neighbor before falling more than half way. They stopped beneath it and pulled the groundsheets from the packs. Draping the water-proof cloths over the tree trunk, they weighted them on either side with stones, forming a makeshift tent. Working quickly, they collected dry branches and kindling from the grove and started a fire at the mouth of the tent. Once again they made a meal from the supplies in their packs and stared out at the dripping darkness as they chewed.

Aurial watched the fire and marveled at its ability to hold attention with its shifting play of shape and color. She was equally fascinated with the mystery of how the flames could give comfort, radiate warmth, hold the darkness out and fear away, all at once. Her experience of open fires was nil, although she was certain that it would expand a great deal before she went back up the well again. Fires were among the many new and sometimes primitive forces that she was encountering for the first time. It was ironic that she was learning much from someone who would be considered an ignorant Outback noble by the self-satisfied and often condescending inhabitants of the Beldame. Until a short time ago, Aurial herself had shared those narrow convictions. Now she was pleasantly surprised to find herself appreciating strengths in the other woman that would have gone unnoticed before.

It was more of a surprise, and a far less pleasant one, that on Chennidur the il Tarz name, her sophisticated background and technological knowledge were not only useless but a liability. Here, Aurial had everything to learn; was ignorant of what to eat or where to walk; needed protection to keep from stepping blindly into harm or worse. Chennidur was literally a world of things to learn, but she needed the wit to listen and the humility to follow. Watching the rise and fall of the flames, listening to the crackle of the wood as it was consumed, she began to understand that this was the first and most important of all the lessons. This was at the heart of what her mother had sent her out to discover.

A knot in one of the logs popped as it burned, startling Raunn. She had been sunk in a reverie of her own as she stared into the wet darkness. She turned: inside the makeshift tent it was cheerful and a bit warmer than the dank night outside. The fire's protective glow encased the two of them, creating an intimate atmosphere that banished at least some of the reserve and barriers of distrust between them. Tendrils of smoke curled around the tent's peak, twisting and roiling before slipping out the end. Raunn, who had been thinking of her own family, ravaged by the warfare of politics, asked, "How big is your family? I mean your brothers and sisters. Not the whole Trading Family."

Aurial, thinking as she had been of the Beldame, answered easily. "I have four sisters, all older than I am. Also, they're talented and extremely intelligent. Itombe, she's the oldest, is beautiful, too. I mean, more than pretty, beautiful in a classic way. Just standing next to you, being herself, she makes you feel awkward and childish. Not that she would ever consciously do anything to make anyone feel inadequate. Itombe is strong but she doesn't hurt people."

"She sounds like a wonderful person. And a wonderful sister." Raunn's voice sounded wistful.

"Yes, she is. But because she's so much older, I have never been able to spend much time with her. By the time I was grown enough to be more than just a pest, she was already working in the family business. Now she's always busy with important work. Someday when Mother, well, when Mother dies, Itombe will take over."

Raunn replied, "That's a heavy pack to carry over a long trail."

Aurial smiled. "It certainly is. And I'm glad I'm not carrying it." She rubbed one shoulder reflexively where the strap of her pack had cut into it. "When it comes to something like that, I'm glad I'm not the oldest. Itombe's path has always been marked out for her. She's tough though, and she'll do very well at it." Aurial noticed that she could see her breath. The temperature was dropping as the rain became heavier.

"In a way, that was true for me also," Raunn said, taking up another carbohydrate bar. "Of course, Torrian was exactly the right kind of personality to be the oldest daughter. She always did all the things that troinom girls are supposed to do. I was never really sure, mind you, whether she enjoyed doing those things or whether she did them just for the praise and rewards that came with being a dutiful daughter."

"What kinds of things are troinom girls supposed to do?" Aurial asked. That information was tucked in the databead but she wanted to draw Raunn out, to keep her talking.

"Well, a su-vellide—that's the oldest daughter—like Torrian, learns to run a large household because she may marry into one or inherit her family's citadel. Not actually do any of the work, you understand. Troinom women never get their hands dirty and Torrian couldn't stand to break any of her carefully-tended nails. But she learned to run everything, from the pantries to the carding rooms. She went through the Rock with our mother, the vellide, learning each function and how it should be managed. Torrian is diligent, I have to give her that, and she is a lot more patient than I am. She put those traits to good use until she had learned as much as any vellide should to run her own clan house. All along she was praised for doing exactly what she should and for following the rules of the Kohrable. She did enjoy that." Raunn's voice held more than a trace of scorn.

"Most people enjoy being praised and rewarded," replied Aurial drily. "Will Torrian really have her own clan citadel to run some day?"

"Of course!" Raunn's expression was incredulous, as if everyone should know something so basic, even a star-woman. "She is a su-vellide and grew up expecting to be married off in a clan alliance. And now . . . the Rock . . .

she'll inherit it all. So Torrian did absolutely the right thing. But how she could stay cooped up in a stuffy storeroom, counting bolts of cloth on a beautiful day or supervising soapmaking in the heat of Abundance was always more than I could understand."

Aurial drew her knees to her chest and wrapped her arms around them. That kept her warmer. It was as if each raindrop threw off an infinitesimal chill. "And what were you doing?" she inquired mildly, "while your sister was being biddable and boring?"

Raunn replied with an unconscious pride, "I followed my brothers outdoors. They taught me to hunt and track, to dress game and cook over an open fire. I learned which plants were edible and which were poisonous, and how that can change with the seasons or the manner of cooking. When I could drop a stone merrain with one dart, they gave me a blowgun of my own. I learned to keep up: I learned not to complain. Tough things. Real survival skills."

"And was that a good thing for you to do?" Aurial's voice was quiet and a little detached. "Were you praised and rewarded, too?"

This time Raunn's look was openly scornful. "There was only so much of that to go around and Torrian got the girls' share. My behavior was much too independent for my mother's taste, not to mention the nayya's interpretation of a woman's proper duties. Like you, I was allowed more freedom because I was younger and someone else was already doing what needed to be done. I paid for it, though."

Aurial pulled her blanket around her shoulders and tried not to shiver. "How?"

"It's simple: I never really grew up. Even after I moved up out of the nursery, they all talked about me as if I were a child. 'Let her run around now,' they'd say. 'She'll settle down better later on if she gets rid of some of that energy now.' As if energy is carefully measured out when we are born and we carry that fixed amount around in a box for the rest of our lives. Use it up too soon and, pouf! it's all gone."

"It sounds like you're complaining about being allowed your freedom."

Raunn picked up some sticks from their sheltered woodpile and placed them on the fire. It snapped and blazed up, brightening the tent and making it somewhat warmer. "I'm not complaining. At least I got to do what I really enjoyed and I knew that someday I would have to make it up. No troinom gets to avoid responsibilities forever."

"Wouldn't you have liked some of that praise for yourself?" Aurial persisted.

Raunn shrugged. "There was no way I was going to hunt in that field."

It was quiet for a moment except for the dull pop of raindrops and the fire's hum. A log burned through and fell into the coals with a thump. Sparks whirled upward and winked out in the rain. Then Aurial commented, "Sometimes there are different kinds of survival skills. Maybe Torrian was learning her own variety. From her perspective, she may have been doing the tough things while you were only playing."

Raunn looked her full in the eyes and the expression on her face was unreadable. "That's exactly what she used to say." Then she rolled up in her blanket and turned her back on Aurial.

# THE ROCK

The nayya perched on his high seat and regarded Torrian. She held his gaze as best she could when his eyes were hidden behind the gauzy veil that dropped from his twisted headdress. The veil was the mark of his office, always present in public as the veil is always present in the sky during the day. The silken cords of the headdress that held the veil represented the multiple nature of the Chenni-ad, weaving a circle as timeless as the deity.

As a boy, her brother Cheyte had harbored an irreverent theory that the nayyat were interchangeable. He said that, hidden from the eyes of the world behind their veils they moved from temple to fortress to citadel to city on their own business. In each place, they took the name of whomever was supposed to be the resident nayya and then passed it along to the next visitor. She had giggled about it as they tried to match names with the mouths and chins that were all of any nayya's face they could ever see. Chetye's theory had long since been abandoned but sometimes she still wondered.

Torrian sighed inaudibly as she waited for this nayya, Nusrat-Geb, who had been in service to the Followers on the Rock for many seasons, to make up his mind. It was not an issue of whether he would speak to her: he had no choice about that. But there was speaking and there was speaking. She had not sought him out only to be dismissed with platitudes and quotations from the Kohrable and a ritual or two to perform in the temple. She needed Nusrat-Geb to commit himself to helping her with his influence, his intellect, and his physical body if required. Like all nayyat, Nusrat-Geb had memorized the Kohrable as well as the index of the many volumes of commentary during his training. Now he pondered the wisdom of the Kohrable and reviewed pertinent teachings behind his veil while she twisted on the horns of the dilemma she had created for herself. The betrothal had been made well and properly; it had also been completed with her consent. The only hope she had of breaking it lay in the dubious character of the man himself.

Involuntarily she thought of things that she would rather not remember, things that she had certainly preferred not to see in the first place. Surrein's servants came to mind first. They all treated him with proper deference and obeyed his orders immediately. They did so, however, not with the respect due his rank or even with the plodding passivity sometimes seen in drevs when they disliked or disapproved of their masters. No, Surrein's servants jumped to do his bidding out of fear, and with good reason. The face of his manservant rose up before her, with its one-eyed squint. Surrein had taken out the other eye with his whip before reaching his majority. She knew because he had bragged of his skill to her—but only after the marriage contract had been signed. She thought of his words, spoken in a cold whisper in the darkness of the carriage, while they waited for the driver to boost his considerable bulk upwards. As the man heaved himself onto the seat and the whisper went on, the hair had risen on the back of her neck.

She remembered the day they had attended the skri hunt at Uncle Verrer's estate and how Surrein's mount had shied, nearly unseating him. He had belabored the animal so brutally that the other hunters had protested the punishment as unsportsmanlike. Surrein had ceased then, but only from embarrassment. It was not just the action that had chilled her, but the unemotional way in which he had gone about it. Later there had been rumors about the beast having to be destroyed but she had been flying on the dust then and paid it no attention.

The dust. Surrein had brought her the dust and this is what it had brought her to. The blame was clearly his. She thought of him beating her in the same fashion with his face an inscrutable mask while his arm rose and fell mechanically. Her stomach turned. He would do it, she had no doubt. And enjoy it.

The nayya stirred and Torrian's attention returned from its wandering. The man did not speak, however, but rose from the study platform, his clothes giving off the smell of rennish, and walked to the bookcase on the far side of the room. There he selected several volumes of accepted interpretations of the Kohrable's tenets and returned to the platform. In an unhurried fashion he began turning pages, seeking the passages which were pertinent to the issue placed before him. Torrian waited: she was patient and willing to give him all the time he needed to find a way out of her marriage contract. She could feel Surrein's breath on her cheek, however, and knew that all the time the nayya needed might not exist.

The dry rasp of turning pages punctuated by an occasional clearing of Nusrat-Geb's throat were the only sounds in the room. Sunlight from the window on her left slid sideways and began to move up the wall. If Nusrat-Geb failed, who could she turn to next? With her brothers gone, only Raunn was left and she, as usual, was absent. Trust Raunn to disappear when she was needed. Trust Raunn to make herself scarce when there was work to be done. Trust Raunn to be irresponsible and unreliable. Torrian sniffed angrily. Raunn had always snubbed her chin at duty, the running of the household, her responsibilities as a troinom woman. Instead she had slipped out, up into the rocks or down into the hills, pretending to be a boy. Torrian did not doubt that she had played at that as well, leaving the unpleasant parts for Cheyte and Rushain to handle. They must not have minded since they not only allowed her to come with them but encouraged it. Leaving me behind, she thought bitterly.

Always they went off for their day of fun outside while I was left to count and measure, supervise and instruct. As if that were enough, as if I never wanted any fun. Well, she consoled herself, at least I could see my duty and I did it properly. I ran the house on Cheffra Street as it should be run—as it hadn't been run since Cheyte died and mother came back here for good. When Raunn tried it, her thoughts continued, it was too much for her and she ran away. She's probably on her way back here right now and making up some good reason why she shouldn't be where she was supposed to be. Torrian resolutely refused to see the reason why Raunn had come to Nandarri at all.

The nayya Nusrat-Geb put down one volume and slowly took up another. Still he did not address Torrian and gave no indication of his thoughts. What if Raunn was on her way to the Rock? Would she be any help against Surrein? Torrian did not see how but even her sister's company would be some support. Of course, there were always the underranks. They were loyal but, in the face of Surrein's force and his position as her betrothed, there was little that they would be able to do on her behalf. That was why the nayya's help was so important. He would have the force of the True Word behind him and that would be enough to hold Surrein at bay right now. After that, she would have a platform on which to stand in her attempt to break the betrothal contract.

Moving at the same methodical pace, the nayya put down the second volume and took up the last one. Torrian hoped that meant he was approaching a decision. By now the sunlight was nearly gone and the time for evening Call to Prayer was approaching. He would have to do something soon. Still, he turned the pages with slow deliberation. Torrian's thoughts turned to her mother: there was another puzzle. The vellide had always been the center of Torrian's life, pushing, teaching, leading, explaining. While the tansul was away on business of the estate or involved in politics in Nandarri, Rutin-Xian was the driving force on the Rock. Everyone deferred to her and Torrian, as the su-vellide, had spent more time with her than anyone else. This was as unchangeable as the Rock itself. No one, including the vellide, had ever thought that this would alter.

The loss of her sons had done it. Now the matriarch was gone and in her place was a weeping husk with no interest in the Rock or anyone on it. Also gone, according to the gossip Maitris had picked up from the chambermaids, were her appetite and her ability to get a good night's sleep. Torrian had not believed it, or at least had believed that she could break through this chrysalis of grief and free her mother again. The shock of her mother's appearance and manner, her indifference to the betrothal was still with her. The ally she had counted on was not there and in her place—what?

With a thud, the nayya disposed of the third book and sat up to face her again. Torrian held her breath. Would the True Word support her or leave her to the fate she had so unwisely created? The gauze veil moved in, then out as the nayya Nusrat-Geb spoke his decision. "Sri-nothi Torrian-Xian, eldest daughter of the san Derrith family and su-vellide of Clan Cliffmaster, I have heard your request. I searched all portions of the Kohrable that apply to your situation in any way. I reviewed the interpretations of the Kohrable and any relevant cases discussed in the appropriate comments. Daughter of the True Word, be strong. I have found nothing that can help you."

"Nothing? In all those words, nothing at all?" Torrian was aghast. "In the wisdom of generations there is nothing to help my cause?"

"Only this. Your betrothed, later your husband, must create the grounds for your suit by actions of his own that are deleterious to your mind, your faith or your person. Your fears and apprehensions about possible cruelty based on actions toward others, particularly those of the under-ranks, are not sufficient cause for annulment of the betrothal, sri-nothi. When, or if, he behaves in such a way toward you personally or toward what children you may have, you can press your suit for a setting-aside of the marriage contract. There are clear precedents for such an action and you are well-protected by the Kohrable in such an event."

Nusrat-Geb paused and Torrian waited for more words that she did not want to hear. "I must add," he continued, "that such actions on his part must be witnessed by one troinom male or two females to be valid as evidence. And may I say, sri-nothi, that I hope most sincerely that your fears are groundless."

Torrian stared at him, her face frozen into a mask. "Do you mean, nayya Nusrat-Geb," she queried in a voice oddly calm, "that once he has beaten me or injured me in the presence of another of our rank, I have grounds against him, but not until? Do I hear you clearly?"

"Yes, sri-nothi. That is exactly what I said."

"And what if I do not wish to be injured? What if I do not want to wait until I am missing an eye or until a limb is broken? What if I do not wish to endure being beaten in private until I can arrange to have a witness present in our bedchamber?"

The nayya leaned forward and placed both hands on the stack of books before him, as if for reassurance. "Then I would advise you to determine those things that anger your betrothed and avoid them. The Kohrable says, 'For a wife's world is in her husband and a husband's world is in his wife. Let her take strength from him, while he learn endurance from her. As the Chenni-ad are interwined, so also are the man and woman who are joined in marriage.' Since this man is to be your world, learn him well and seek not to arouse his anger against you. Thus will you avoid your fears, sri-nothi."

Torrian stared at him. "Perhaps," she said, almost under her breath, "I must seek out the Inayyam himself."

"If you can find him," Nusrat-Geb replied. "For the Inayyam is as the wind, which is never seen but can destroy stone."

She did not reply: what was the point? Moving stiffly, Torrian rose to her feet, turned her back on the nayya and left the room. As the door closed, the nayya Nusrat-Geb whispered, "Walk softly in this marriage, sri-nothi Torrian, for your own sake."

# CHENNIDUR

Locked in their chemical sleep, the clean and polished bodies of Astin, Merradrix and the Shaman were loaded into orbital shuttles. They were handled carefully, out of consideration for the fragile mechanisms which controlled life support in the cylinders. In every other respect, the cargo was treated as simple merchandise, no different than bales of cloth or logs of wood. Once loaded, the shuttle made its curving journey up to the orbiting freighter and waited nearby, floating patiently in the darkness. When the cargo was offloaded, the shuttle went down for another load of silver cylinders.

One by one the shining containers were locked into the freighter's hold and hooked to the life-support system, which activated the auto-electrodes that would stimulate the muscles of the sleeping bodies to keep them from atrophying. This mechanism would also strengthen the new laborers for the hard work awaiting them at the labor site. Then a language tutor was activated so that, no matter what the planet of origin, all the workers would understand the commands of the guards who controlled them. Finally, monitors were linked to the master computer.

The entire process was accompanied by the most matter-of-fact sounds: the hum of robot arms, the terse directions of workmen talking on comlinks, the bump of metal against metal, the click of switches. When the loading was completed, the hold housed more than a hundred prisoners but it was totally silent. There were no confused screams or moans of anguish. No one cried for loss of the home that hung in silver and brown splendor beneath them but would soon vanish forever. No prayers echoed from the metal bulkhead. No songs or chants comforted the occupants of the cylinders. There was only silence. The blank faces of the monitors reflected a row of emergency lights that stretched the length of the hold.

The sleeping travelers felt the vibrations that migrated through the ship when the engines turned on. The faint tug as the freighter left Chennidur's orbit went unnoticed. Isolated from their world, from each other, from humanity, they began the journey that would take them from everything they had ever known into places they had never imagined. Beyond the reach of the True Word and its rigid culture, beyond the weaving of the enigmatic Chenni-ad, they would awaken into lives simpler and far more rigorous than the ones they left behind.

They would endure conditions to make the daily lives of the underranks on Chennidur seem like great luxury. They would work as no troinom had ever commanded them to work. They would obey orders with an alacrity heretofore unknown. They would experience desperation deeper than anything they could comprehend. And all the while they would fight just to stay alive on a world that wanted to kill them. For all, save two, there would be no return.

# CHAPTER 9

## PERIMETER HOUSE

Aurial did not know what she had been expecting Perimeter House to look like but the structure above them was not it. If she had been picturing a massive stone fortress, what she saw instead was definitely a house, even though it was large and made of huge planks cut from single logs. It was set into the hillside in such a way that it seemed to be as natural an outgrowth as the trees and rocks which framed it. A wide porch ran around the first floor, sheltering the entrance and giving the house a look of comfort and ease. Gables pushed out from the second floor and above the broad roof four great stone chimneys rose. Only one of these, toward the rear of the house, was smoking. While Aurial took it all in, Raunn gave a satisfied sigh. "Well, there it is," she said, "Perimeter House. If I'd known it was this close, I would have pushed for it last night instead of making camp. We would have been more comfortable and slept a lot better, that's for sure."

*Now she tells me*, Aurial muttered to herself. But still, she was looking forward to resting, if briefly, in relatively civilized surroundings. It was still raining, although not as hard as it had the night before, and she was wet and cold. The house looked as if it wanted to take them in and shelter them and she was eager to oblige.

"We've arrived just in time for mid-meal," Raunn added. "Come on. I can use some hot food."

"Are you sure," Aurial asked, "that the staff won't think that it's odd, our popping up like this out of nowhere?"

"Of course they will!" Raunn was back to being superior and her tone was patronizing. "And they'll talk about it forever among themselves. The underranks like nothing better than good juicy gossip about their betters."

"But if they ask too many questions . . ."

"They won't ask any questions, Aurial. They wouldn't dare. I'll simply tell them what we planned—that we were camping and got lost. Then we'll eat a couple of good meals, pack up more food, appropriate a couple of burrkies and head out again. We'll be at the Rock in another day and by the time my uncle's family comes out here during Abundance it will be old news."

Aurial gave her a cynical eye, resisting being put back in the role of dumb student. "How about a bath?" she asked flippantly.

Raunn laughed. "You'll get a bath like you've never had before. Certainly not floating up there in the middle of nothing. We can both use one. Let's go."

With a far lighter spirit, Aurial followed both Raunn and the smell of cooking up the hill and onto the welcoming porch.

Their brief visit went much as Raunn had predicted. They entered the house with a royal flourish and Aurial observed carefully how Raunn played her role. She, herself, was presented as Aurial ni Nashaum san Asherith of the Stargazer Clan, "a friend from Nandarri." Raunn explained next to nothing else, leaving the astonished household to draw their own conclusions about what the two troinom women were doing wandering around the Perimeter in a cold rain. As predicted, the staff immediately set about providing for the troinoms' needs. First came food. Raunn reassured the flustered cook that what he had prepared for mid-meal would be adequate and no special

delicacies were required. For the moment, the two sri-
nothi were satisfied to dine simply, on the same fare as the
staff.

There was no question, however, of eating in the kitchen
with drevs. Raunn was adamant. "We have to maintain
our status," she declared. "The staff expects it. They would
be shocked if we did not." So they sat instead at one end
of a huge table that ran almost the length of an enormous
dining room. The white plaster ceiling above them was
beamed at the rooftree and sectioned crosswise with rough-
cut logs. A new fire burned across the room in a hearth
large enough for five full-grown men to stand in upright
but it did not dispel the room's chill of disuse. Aurial
found the food before her tasty and satisfying, although
Raunn complained about it being insipid. They were both
happy for the moment to be indoors and warm and pleasantly full.

Raunn then ordered that the bath house be fired up.
Her instructions were given in the same casual fashion as
all her orders but Aurial could tell by the expression of the
servant she addressed that this was a large undertaking. It
was also a great inconvenience; the stiffness of his face
confirmed that. Raunn, however, did not notice either his
expression or his manner and did not care and so it was
done.

While they waited for the bathhouse to be made ready,
Aurial contemplated the interaction between Raunn and
the servants and how the staff reacted to the troinoms. To
her eyes, the house staff was much more than just inquisi-
tive, they were practically coming out of their skins with
curiosity. Raunn ignored their reactions, their speculations
and their attitudes but Aurial watched them surreptitiously
and listened carefully, while trying not to show more
interest than would be expected of a clan woman. The
servants speculated wildly about everything from her identity to how the sri-nothi Raunn had gotten from Nandarri
to the Perimeter faster than was possible, and on foot.
Although they never asked a question of her or Raunn
outright, the servants were experts at obtaining information indirectly. In the course of waiting upon the troinom

ladies, they would drop an occasional open-ended comment that invited the sri-nothi to expand upon it or to
correct an erroneous assumption. Having been well-schooled
by Itombe in the art of hearing much but giving little,
Aurial educated herself by observing this game while maintaining her reserve. Raunn was, as usual, oblivious to it.

On the other hand, and less entertaining for Aurial,
were her own speculations on a culture that rendered the
underclass so powerless. Although well schooled in the
myriad patterns of different cultures, Aurial had always
lived on the Beldame, a self-contained world which supported only those who could contribute to the success and
profitability of the Family enterprises. There were, to be
sure, many machines which made their lives simpler and
better as servants did for the troinom. Yet Aurial found it
different to have a machine ministering to her needs: that
was the function for which it had been created and the
reason for its existence. People were another matter. The
people on the Beldame held different levels of responsibility and authority, based on their qualifications and depth
of experience. The lowest of them was expected to learn
and grow or be dismissed. That left Aurial with no experience of being waited upon as a superior being by another
person. She was appalled at how Raunn treated the
underranks as if they were no more than domesticated
animals. It also made her acutely aware of how great the
difference was between learning about something and ex-
periencing it for herself. *Score another point for Mother*,
she thought wryly.

Raunn led the way to the bath house, a separate structure built partly into the hill behind the house. "We both
could use a long soak in a very hot tub," she told Aurial.
"It will loosen up the sore muscles. We'll have a massage
afterward, too." Aurial hadn't been aware that Raunn had
any sore muscles but it all sounded welcome to her. "Fortunately," Raunn continued, "there's a woman here who is
trained properly to give massages. In many households,
only the men have this privilege and therefore only male
servants are trained to provide it. That would leave us
out." Aurial, who ached in every part of her anatomy that

moved and several that didn't, was grateful to Raunn's uncle for his generosity.

Inside, the bath house was simple, lined with dark and fragrant klypt wood. It contained one large room in the center of which were two vast tubs, made of the same wood as the walls, with rocks stacked three quarters of the way up the sides. The atmosphere was very warm and humid. In an anteroom on the left a fire leaped in a stone pit like a restive animal while four metal pots swung on a rod above the flames. Each had a lip for pouring into a wooden aqueduct that extended into the main room and tilted toward the tub on the left. That one was steaming, proof that it was nearly ready for them to enter. As they walked toward it, the servants tipped the last of the metal pots forward so that its hot contents sluiced down the aqueduct and into the tub.

Raunn led the way into a matching anteroom on the right where they undressed and hung their clothing on pegs. Aurial looked around for some sort of robe but Raunn simply stepped back into the main room without benefit of cover. Not accustomed to walking naked in front of men, Aurial shot a quick glance toward the fire pit and was relieved to see that the menservants in charge of heating the water had left. Two drev women bustled about, preparing the bath for its troinom occupants. Like Raunn, Aurial stepped over to a row of buckets lined up on a wooden bench and waited. One of the servants began immediately to wash her from the hair down with a soft cloth and some kind of soap.

Aurial had washed herself since she was old enough to do so and was uncomfortable having another person perform such an intimate service for her. Raunn, however, stood *contrapposto* with her eyes closed, in a posture of sublime relaxation. Taking the cue from her, Aurial swallowed her embarrassment and did the same. The soap was rinsed by the simple expedient of tilting a bucket of bracingly hot water over their heads. When they had finished spluttering and wiping the water from their eyes, the attendants wrapped their hair in warm towels.

They stepped into the still tub and Aurial leaped out

before getting her knees wet: the water was hotter than anything she had ever experienced before. Slowly, she dipped her feet and then, when they had adjusted to the heat, slipped her legs in by the inch. Raunn, already seated in the water so that it was up to her neck, smiled her patronizing smile. "You look like a plucked turch trying to avoid the soup pot," she said. "It's not as hot as all that."

"That's a matter of opinion," Aurial replied testily. "And of what you're used to."

"Why, don't you have a bath house at your clan holding?" Raunn inquired in mock-innocent tones.

"Certainly," Aurial replied playfully, "but we prefer the water a bit cooler. My father, the tansul, says that overly hot water congests the brain."

"I've heard that said," Raunn replied sweetly. "But my uncle believes that hot water relaxes both the body and the mind." She closed her eyes and tilted her head back so that the bath attendant could care for her hair. Aurial's servant approached and took charge, removing the towel from her hair and combing it out gently. Next she worked an herbal softener into it, massaging Aurial's scalp thoroughly as well. Then she combed the hair out again, spreading it so that it could dry more quickly.

By now the hot water was a sensual delight: it had relaxed all of Aurial's sore and knotted muscles and warmed the core of her bones. It also relieved her, if only for a few moments, of the presence of the demon gravity. She allowed her arms to float on the surface and her feet to drift playfully upwards. Delighting in the water's warm support, she cleared her mind of concern and was content to simply be.

She was drifting off to sleep when Raunn declared that it was time to get out. "If you stay in too long, you'll cook, just like a turch," she said. "I'm accustomed to the hotter water so I'll stay here while you get your massage." Reluctantly, Aurial hauled herself out of the water and found that the demon had been waiting for her and was now heavier than ever. Her limbs weighed twice as much as they had before and her bones felt flexible. The servant helped her out of the tub and dried her off. Aurial lifted arms and feet to assist her efforts, feeling ridiculous all the while. Then the woman directed that Aurial should lie down on the wooden platform, which had been cleared of its buckets and covered with soft cloth.

The massage was another sensual pleasure as the masseuse's strong fingers worked out all the sore places. When the woman had finished by rubbing a fragrant oil into the skin, Aurial felt as if she had been granted a new body. She was also more tired than she had ever been in her life—and hungry again. Raunn rose, dripping, from the tub like an elemental water spirit. "There will be clean clothes in the anteroom," she said, "and I have ordered that dinner be served in our rooms. I think we both could use some rest and some time to ourselves. If you need anything, just pull the cord by the bed and a servant will come. I'll see you at firstmeal."

Aurial donned a clean red dorchari that smelled of fresh air and sunlight, then allowed the servant to escort her to her room. She was grateful for the time to rest but needed privacy more to send a long message to Rolfe. She was behind on her status reports and wanted to patch into the Port computer to see if Rolfe had loaded down to it the information she had requested. She also wanted to describe some of the local flora and fauna so that he could evaluate possible commercial value. She thought that, with a bit of genetic restructuring there could be opportunities for profit. There was so much to do—if she could only stay awake long enough.

# THE ROCK

Antikoby knew that today, when the quarantine expired, Surrein would return. Antikoby knew it. Torrian knew it. Yet the su-vellide had still not summoned him. He locked his hands and stared out into his office, a room as gloomy as his mood. Last night's rain continued to fall, drizzling in half-hearted fashion from a sky the color of the blue-grey rock on which the fortress was built. He considered.

Maitris had told him about the su-vellide's disastrous interviews with her mother and the nayya. Since Torrian had received no assistance from either, the next logical step, he thought, was for her to turn to the tuupit. If she did not seek his counsel, which was unlikely, than surely she would wish to command him to rally the household in support. Her own experience with him since her return should have given her some confidence in his ability to offer more than simple obedience. Had she wit and strength enough to overcome her prejudices, she would have done so. He had been wrong, and just as well, for then she might also have perceived how much he had done unsupervised by any troinom and how much he now controlled the Rock. He wanted her to believe that she was in charge here as her mother had been. That left him with only one thing to do, the thing that he wished to avoid, which was to go to her.

Delaying the inevitable, he stared out the windows at the courtyard where a gardener was preparing huge stone pots for the rennish rhizomes that would soon be planted. The gardener looked cold, his shoulders were hunched, the hood on his quilted jacket was up and fastened tightly at the neck. The man's hands were blue, though whether from the cold or from the mud, Antikoby could not tell. He did not envy the gardener the discomfort of his work but longed with a sudden pang for its simplicity. At that moment the kind of job that required no thought was immensely alluring to him. To take on a task and work hard until it was completed was a satisfying thing to do. The soil the man worked with was wet and cold and heavy but it was also benign. It would not turn on the gardener or fight to undo his efforts. The gardener did not have to worry about defending himself against it.

Shaking his head against such self-pity, Antikoby stood and walked to the door. He had work of his own sort to do and it could not wait for his dreaming any more than preparing the soil would wait upon the turn of seasons. He reached out to grasp the door lever but it turned on its own before his fingers touched it. He stepped back quickly as the door swung open to admit Maitris, flushed and excited. "Tuupit, the su-vellide summons you to her chambers. Your presence is required immediately," she said importantly. Then, in a lower, somewhat conspiratorial tone she added, "I think she's finally ready to talk with you about that one to whom she is betrothed." Antikoby nodded and followed her out of the room.

Entering the su-vellide's apartment for the first time since he had abducted her, he found the rooms much changed. Although the furnishings were the same and the day was certainly not bright, the apartment had a more open air to it. The dark, secretive hush and foul smells were gone. Servants bustled about, doing the wishes of the su-vellide. Maitris ushered him into a reception room where he waited by a window, contemplating the dots of rain that appeared on it as if by magic before merging into drops that trailed slowly downward. The rain made him think abruptly of Raunn and how she would come in on a day such as this, cheeks red with the rawness of the air and eyes glowing from the excitement of whatever chase she had been on. He wondered where she was now—whether she was incarcerated in the depths of the Puzzle Palace, shut away from the outdoors that she loved so much.

Torrian entered and once again he pulled himself back from daydreams to the unpleasant business at hand. The woman he saw before him had also changed. The su-vellide was now alert, well-groomed and in full possession of both her position and her mother's authority. Her ordeal was still evident, however, in the shadows under her eyes and the hollows of her cheekbones. It was not his place to speak first so he waited while Torrian sat and arranged herself. She looked straight ahead. He assumed that she was feeling under pressure for she broached the subject immediately.

"You know that I was accompanied here by the sri-noth Surrein ni Varskal san Cannestur."

"Yes, sri-nothi," he said. Maitris would have informed her mistress of the man's expulsion from the Rock on grounds of quarantine. It was hardly a secret.

"What you do not know," she continued, "is that during my stay in Nandarri a contract of betrothal was completed between the sri-noth Surrein and myself. Since that took place, I have—altered my opinion of the man to whom I am betrothed. The reason why is not important here."

Antikoby demurred gently. "I have spoken to Surrein ni Varskal san Cannestur, sri-nothi," he said simply. While Torrian could not know the details of that conversation, she must be aware that the man's character showed clearly. To elaborate, however, would be impertinent.

"I see." She looked up at him, seeing Antikoby for the first time since she had entered the room. "I see. Tuupit, he must not return here. I do not wish to see him again until I go to Nandarri for the wedding." She paused and added, almost as an afterthought, "I wish that you had sent him there when you declared the quarantine."

"I did," he replied. "But he and his party went no further than Trailhead. I could not have the guard 'escort' him further without offering grave discourtesy. The quarantine did not require him to go as far as Nandarri."

"I thought as much," Torrian said. "Surrein does only what he wishes. With him even at Trailhead, I am afraid."

Antikoby nodded, encouraged by her frankness, and risked a direct question. "You fear the dust, sri-nothi? Would it still tempt you if he were to offer it?"

Her look sharpened. "Tempt me? I think not. He controls the dust and anyone who is subject to it. But Surrein would never be that open. No, he would be all bows and smiles and demonstrations of affection but somehow I would find myself back in the drug's grip without ever knowing how or when it happened. That is why I do not want him to climb the Rock again."

"Keeping him physically out would be simple, sri-nothi. The Rock is impregnable, as you well know, and the household guard would simply prevent him from returning."

"Which would send him back to Nandarri and to my kinsman, Verrer, in a rage. Then pressure would be put on the tansul, who labors under far too much of a burden already."

"Your pardon, sir-nothi, but such an insult could cause him to withdraw from the betrothal contract instead," Antikoby offered. "Then you would be free of him completely."

Torrian smiled thinly. "I think not, tuupit, although another man might act so. No, there will be no breach of contract on their side. And I cannot afford to provoke them, or him, with such direct action. You were devious on my behalf before, tuupit. Now I must be devious to protect myself."

Antikoby regarded her with the subservient attitude expected of him and wondered if she was aware of how freely she had been speaking or whether the fear had been speaking for her. Or perhaps she simply needed to talk. The troinom often spoke before their servants as if the underranks were incapable of understanding what they said. He decided to risk another question. "You said 'they,' sri-nothi, not 'him.' To whom did you refer?"

She lowered her gaze so that once again she was staring at the opposite wall. "I refer to my kinsman, Verrer, and his minions. They planned this trap, then used Surrein as a more-than-willing tool, to spring it. And I, like some ignorant blue-dirt farm girl, walked right into it."

Like any well-trained servant, Antikoby knew when to listen, when to talk and when to forget—or at least to present the appearance of doing so. It was always wise to distract a troinom who was being indiscreet before he or she regained composure. "There are two clear choices, sri-nothi," he said calmly. "To allow him back on the Rock and guard you as best we can, or to force his return to Nandarri and accept the consequences. He cannot stay forever at Trailhead nor can we continue to manufacture excuses."

"I must decide, I know," Torrian said. "And soon. I am surprised he is not already attempting the climb."

"He and his party are nearly at the base," Antikoby

affirmed. "There is very little time: the guards are waiting for instructions."

Again she looked up at him and her surprised expression said clearly that it had never occurred to her that one of the underranks could understand her problem and put contingency orders in place. "Then I shall decide," she replied.

"There is one more choice," Antikoby offered with trepidation. "Verrer has been ruthless; perhaps it is time for us to be brutal as well." Torrian did not react and he pushed on, "An accident would be simple to arrange. It would have the double effect of removing the sri-noth Surrein as a threat and confounding the sri-noth Verrer's plans."

Torrian shook her head slowly and, he thought, with reluctance. "It sounds like such a simple solution," she replied. "Unfortunately the disadvantage to removing a known threat is having to look for the unknown one that follows. The Rock is not a prize they will let go easily. If we can find a way to hold Surrein at bay, we can neutralize him for a while and keep Verrer from thinking up any new mischief. If Surrein is killed, Verrer will only find another way of getting his hands on the Rock."

Antikoby thought back to the previous night when he and Tarshionit had raised and evaluated all the options. The tapit of security was a valuable resource and Antikoby knew that the tansul would have had him here for this discussion. But then, the tanzl was accustomed to thinking about security in ways that the suv would not. Antikoby had the advantage of understanding both perspectives. "It is difficult to keep a man away from where he wants to be," he offered. "It is much easier to make him no longer wish to be there."

Torrian looked at him again with a faint trace of humor in her eyes. "Are you suggesting, tuupit, that I should allow him back and then behave in such an insufferable fashion that he removes himself from my presence?"

Antikoby coughed discreetly to hide a smile. He could not imagine Torrian, the obedient daughter, acting so. "From what you have said, sri-nothi, your behavior would have to be an outrage for him to take offense. No, I had in mind something that would make his presence on the Rock pointless because you are not accessible to him. If he cannot intimidate you, influence you, or even talk to you, why should he remain?"

"Why, indeed? And how do you propose to accomplish this?"

"By using the laws against him, as we did with the quarantine, sri-nothi. He could not argue with *shufri-nagai* then and he will not be able to argue with it now. You can go to the nayya and explain that your recent illness has caused you to understand the need to focus your life on the True Word before your marriage."

Relief showed on Torrian's face. "A vigil," she said. "He cannot deny me that; no nayya would discourage such a sacred undertaking. I could do the Vigil of the Heartspring."

"It would mean a great sacrifice on your part," Antikoby said. "Secluding yourself in the Chasm of the Heartspring for that long will not be easy."

"No, tuupit, it will not. But once there I would see only the nayya. The way to my retreat would be barred by *shufri-nagai* to anyone but the nayya."

"I would add a guard as well," he replied. "*Shufri-nagai* alone might not be enough to hold him this time. Once he is calm again, he will think."

Torrian's face tightened at the thought of Surrein's anger but she continued. "And what he will think is how pointless it would be to remain here when he could be in Nandarri preparing for the wedding and enjoying himself before marriage season arrives."

"If your plan goes well, sri-nothi, he will leave the Rock the next day," Antikoby concluded.

"If he does not, tuupit," Torrian added, "you must prevent him from doing any harm. You are under my orders to do so. Is that understood?"

"Perfectly, sri-nothi."

"Excellent. You are excused, tuupit. I have much to do before I undertake this vigil. The wedding plans must proceed without me for a while and that means giving everyone their orders so that work can continue in my absence."

"Thank you, sri-nothi. I shall assist in all possible ways."

"Of course, tuupit."

## THE BELDAME

Rolfe had retired with an engrossing book—he preferred the type he could hold—and a glass of Carrian azzinth when the comstation in his room chimed. Recalled to duty at an inconvenient hour, he sighed. Setting down both liquor and literature, he rose and went to his room monitor. The secure program he had set in place to oversee the data channels had gone quietly about its business, matching information with time schedules, checking activities, analyzing whole crystals of data, while he relaxed. Now that process was complete and the system was alerting him that a sequence of events he had anticipated was about to begin.

The electronic spy notified him that a shipment of over one hundred bodies in chemsleep capsules had been shuttled from the Port on Chennidur to an orbiting freighter. Within two Standard Temporal Days, that freighter would warp out of orbit and head for its destination. The program identified that location as Base Station 10011A-21Z of Dependable Work Forces, IncGM4Qb. The body that had once been named Merradrix and now bore an unknown company code was part of that shipment. The capsule in which he slept was going from here to there and stopping for a while: that was all the program could tell him.

Rolfe was not disappointed. Programs had their limits and were best at working with straightforward information that was readily available. After that, when things got complicated, it was time to bring in the hard staff. Rolfe knew his way around computers and data sources and, like the programs, could handle tasks that were complex as long as they were unsophisticated. He didn't live, the way a fully-augmented specialist did, with his head in the circuits. Nor did he want to.

Fortunately, some of the best specs in the Quad worked on the Beldame and someone was always on call to help a field team with system probes. The smooth taste of azzinth lingered on his tongue as he called up the comcode for access to a probe specialist. When that came up, he added the security sequence required to authorize project time. There was a pause while the on-call spec was brought online. Rolfe rubbed his palm while he waited. Within seconds, the image of a head was floating in front of his monitor.

The woman did not appear either tired or annoyed, despite the hour. Rolfe reminded himself that hours, days, even STUs, meant nothing inside Q-nets and feed channels. The disorientation that came from adjusting quickly from machine time to human time showed around her eyes, however. He took the jackhead through the problem and outlined the questions he needed her to answer. She did not move but he could tell by her dilated pupils that every word he said was being recorded in her G-base exactly as he said it. It was one of the advantages of being augmented.

When he stopped speaking, she began asking questions. He provided the name and limited physical description that Aurial had transmitted and the probable destination. Beyond that, he had no details for her to use in locating his company code. "That's not much to go on," she commented flatly.

"I know," he responded, "but it's all I have. If this were easy, I wouldn't need hard staff. I could do it myself. But I requested someone who could navigate around links and through bases and they assigned you."

"Got it," the woman replied. "She pays me for the tough ones, right? I'll face right in and start tracking. You'll hear back from me as soon as I have an answer, one way or another, and not until."

"Thanks," Rolfe said. "I appreciate the help. And good luck."

One corner of the woman's mouth twitched upwards. "There's no luck in the links," she quipped and then her image disappeared.

Rolfe imagined her consciousness speeding off, zig-zagging through the microscopic and incredibly complex connections that united the Beldame's computer system with others throughout the Quadrant and shuddered. While that journey, conducted at unimaginable speed, was happening her body remained here. It would be nourished, exercised, cleaned and otherwise maintained by life-support machines in the OOBLS department until her conscious mind returned to take control. That kind of existence was not his idea of either work or play. What he wanted to do was a great deal more basic: locate the work site and then go there himself to snatch this man back from the grasp of a slave master masquerading as a labor contractor. He also wanted to feel ground under his feet again, sunlight on his face and fresh air in his lungs.

Returning to his comfortable contoured chair, Rolfe sipped the azzinth and stared at his book, seeing nothing. He set it aside and scratched his itching palm. Tonight he would run through the authorizations, approvals and other obstacles that lay between him and a bit of adventure dirtside. Then he would figure out how to clear through them one by one. With the Old Lady preoccupied by the negotiations for the religious project, it might be easier to get through her or around her right now. Perhaps tomorrow he would speak to Gwynn and see what she could offer in the way of assistance. If he managed things right, he could have a good time with this project after all.

# CHAPTER 10

## THE PERIMETER

A tentative hand roused Aurial from a sleep deeper than any she could remember. Getting out of the warm, soft, comfortable bed was unthinkable and only the thought of how much was yet to be done pulled her upright. The servant dressed her in trail clothes that were newly cleaned and pressed, then braided and pinned her hair to keep it neat on the next leg of the journey. By the time Aurial entered the enormous dining room Raunn was leaving, "to look over the burrkies." Aurial had reservations about burrkies, but did not let them keep her from eating an excellent breakfast.

With a last piece of fresh-baked roll in her hand, she went out to locate Raunn and found her with one of the servants standing next to several large animals. The beasts were sturdy, with short fur that was splotched in varying shades of grey and wedge-shaped heads that loomed well over Raunn. Their broad faces had large eyes and ears that seemed able to rotate 360 degrees. A thick tail spiraled in a coil against their rumps and two smaller coils were tucked against the neck, just behind the jowls. These appendages gave the beasts a menacing appearance but, to Aurial's relief, the burrkies appeared extremely docile.

Raunn and the servant selected four of the animals and then, when he ordered their tack, she began to argue. Deferentially, but firmly, he insisted on accompanying them to the Rock. Raunn, in her most uncompromising tone, refused. The groom was persistent—he almost seemed afraid to let them proceed alone—and the argument could have gone on for some time but Raunn ended it by simply ordering him to take the rest of the animals back to the paddock and not return. The servant was not happy with this decision but could not contradict a direct order.

Aurial swallowed the last bite of roll and approached the burrkies. Raunn stroked the neck of the one nearest her and said, "Nice, aren't they? My uncle is famous for the burrkies he breeds. We'll each ride one and put our supplies on the other two. Not that we'll need much: it's only a day to the Rock from here."

"What was the fight all about?" Aurial asked, wanting to find out if there was anything she should know.

"Oh, that old merrain wanted to come with us, 'for our protection.' As if we needed protection. The servants all think we're still children that need nannies and grooms to make sure we don't fall down and get a cut. Most women do want a man to take care of them, mind you, but I'm not like most women. Are you ready?"

Servants saddled the burrkies with crisp efficiency and loaded the pack that had been brought out from the house. Aurial, who would have been only too glad to have animals carrying her pack when she was walking, asked, "If we don't need that many supplies, why take four animals? Surely one burrky could carry what we need."

"Strictly speaking," Raunn replied, "that's true. But burrkies are dwads—they only travel in groups of two or multiples of two. The third animal would just stand there and watch the others go. If he tried to go with them, they would drive him away."

"Oh. I see." Aurial looked at the saddle dubiously. "I don't know how to ride," she confessed in a voice pitched so that the servants would not hear. "There's not much call for riding where I come from."

Raunn threw a supercilious look her way. "Nothing to it," she said. "Just climb up, sit down, and ride. There's no fancy stuff with burrkies; they almost never go faster than a walk and are steady as the hills."

"Then why not just keep walking ourselves?" Aurial heard herself say with disbelief. If walking was a better alternative, then she must be more frightened of getting up on that thing than she realized.

"Because the burrkies walk faster than we do. They are also very surefooted and the trail from here to the Rock has sections that are, well, difficult."

Aurial thought again. "What if I fall off?" she asked in a small voice.

Raunn sighed. "I'll help you up and the burrky will wait until you get back on. He may be only an animal but you can trust him to do his job. He's good at it and he doesn't want you to fall off. It's not hard, believe me."

Aurial swallowed. "I'm ready," she said.

"Good."

Following Raunn's instructions, she scrambled into the saddle and jammed her feet into cup-like stirrups. A moment of panic followed when she realized how high off the ground she was. Then Raunn mounted and they set out, the two pack animals following without lead ropes. There was another flurry of fear when her mount started to move and Aurial felt out of control. She gripped the reins with clenched hands until the burrky's rocking gait and steady stride reassured her that she was not going to be pitched off at any moment. At that point she was able to take her eyes away from the animal's head and look around. *This is better*, she thought. *Now he's doing all the work.* By then they were on the far side of the hill and out of sight of Perimeter House. Ahead of them were yet more hills, bigger ones, and Aurial was suddenly glad to be off her feet.

The morning passed to the rhythm of the animals' hooves on the trail. A flight of migrating puffers sailing overhead and catching the sunlight on their diaphanous airbags was the most exciting thing that happened. The sun climbed higher and the day warmed. After the rainstorm's chill, the mild air was a pleasure in itself. The warmth brought a drifting of scents, some sweet, some pungent, with the smell of fertile soil underlying them all.

Around mid-day they stopped on a hilltop for a brief lunch. As the two women ate, the four burrkies placidly stripped bark from a ring of klypt trees. The view around them was clear and unbroken but for the next line of hills. "All this space," Aurial remarked. "All this space and no one lives here."

"Do you think that's good or bad?" Raunn asked between bites.

"I'm not sure. Part of me, the logical scientific part, thinks that it's all a waste. Every inch of the Beldame is used in some way: it has to be. So that part thinks empty land should be 'put to a good use,' and made productive in some way. But the rest of me is refreshed by all this wilderness and finds it beautiful. It is sufficient as it is and whole in itself. People and farms and roads and even ports would blight it. They would destroy the wilderness and turn it into usefulness. Here there's enough room for things to not need to be useful. I'm not saying this very well."

"Well enough," Raunn replied. "It's the spell of the Perimeter. In some ways the Rock is like the way you describe the Beldame. It's full of people doing practical, necessary things and space is used, sometimes in many ways. There, I'm always surrounded by people, too. That's why I like to come out here and feel the wild freedom. It gets into your soul like rennish smoke in your veins. Belonging to the wilderness is a rare joy that doesn't last."

"I feel like it will last forever," Aurial said.

"Only in your memory," Raunn said. "Besides, it's not completely empty. The Rugollah are largely invisible but they do live here."

"Why do they keep to themselves?" Aurial asked.

Raunn looked at the ground and then said in a low voice, "For one thing, they're *shirz*, non-Followers. They have some primitive religious beliefs of their own."

She made the words "their own" sound disgusting. "That means they're also *parostri*, separate forever from all who know and follow the True Word."

Aurial was surprised by the emotion in Raunn's voice. "Is that a problem for them?" she pursued.

Raunn shook her head. "We have attempted to teach them the True Word, sometimes forcibly. They resisted and a few of those who refused to accept the True Word were executed. The Rugollah retreated deeper into the hills after that, preferring to cling to their heathen ideas. If they stay to themselves, they avoid trouble."

"What are their beliefs?"

Raunn looked scandalized, as if Aurial had asked whether they committed ritual incest. "I don't know. No one does. And I have never seen one of the Rugollah myself. All I know is what any troinom knows about them."

*Which means it's probably all apocryphal and mostly wrong*, Aurial thought. She knew that it was time to drop the subject, however, before Raunn became haughty, which also meant less communicative. All she said was, "I see." The thought came to her, however, that most likely a conversation with one of the elusive Rugollah about the Followers would have sounded much the same.

They packed up the remains of their mid-meal, pulled the burrkies from their feast of klypt bark and mounted. The terrain quickly grew steeper and rockier. Brown sedimentary rock was still very much present but now fragments of a dark igneous rock were scattered randomly through it. It looked as if a platform of the older, harder stone had been submerged for eons while silt drifted slowly down and settled on top of it. Then at some less distant time, before the sediment had been fully compressed into stone, the ancient sea had been uplifted. Now the soft brownstone was eroding and exposing the hard blue-grey bedrock beneath.

The older, denser stone weathered along relatively straight fracture lines and broke off into nearly cubical chunks. The past season's freezing and thawing had broken off fresh chunks that rolled down the hillside and scattered randomly across the path. The combination of soft round pebbles and hard angular chunks was treacherous and the travelers found it dangerously easy to slide on the steeper slopes. Their mounts picked their way carefully up and down, finding few level spots where they could move more quickly than a plodding walk. When the slopes became steeper and more treacherous, the burrkies fastened on to tree trunks with their prehensile tails and jowl trunks for better stability. The boles of the trees alongside these stretches of the trail were shiny and smooth, testifying to their long use as anchors for the large beasts. Even so, the burrkies covered the distance much faster than the two women, encumbered by their packs, would have been able to do on foot.

By the time they stopped for the evening, the towers of Cliffmaster citadel were visible, rearing up from behind the line of hills on the horizon. At least, Raunn said they were: to Aurial the silhouette of the hills appeared no different than it had on previous nights. Not wishing to earn another scornful look from her companion, however, she kept her doubts to herself. Experienced now about the camp, Aurial set to work while Raunn went out scouting. Their packs were crammed with food from the kitchens of Perimeter House and there was no need for hunting, but Raunn's fierce independence drove her out, "Just to look around." Aurial began to object, preferring food that had already been cooked to a degree that hid its origins. Thinking better of her protest, she kept silent and went about her tasks.

After her first day in the saddle another whole set of muscles was manifesting displeasure. Upon dismounting, her knees had buckled and she had to hold onto the stirrup to keep from falling. Her buttocks were sore, her thighs were quivering. With Raunn out of the camp, she could favor her aches and not be concerned about keeping up a brave front. She shot a look at the authors of her discomfort, who had their large heads buried in clumps of old grass, nibbling bright circles of new growth. They were certainly inoffensive enough and she had lost her fear of them. Still, it would not be easy climbing back into the high saddle tomorrow.

Aurial was unpacking a couple of meat pies and relishing their savory aroma when she heard a rumble and felt the dirt vibrate beneath her feet. At first the noise meant nothing but Raunn had taught her the importance of being alert and observant in the wild. She listened carefully, noting the direction before the rumble diminished and was followed by a few random thuds. Aurial was filled with apprehension. Setting the pies down, she made her way quickly in the direction of the rumble. It did not take her long to reach the rockslide.

One of the outcrops of crumbly rock had given way, leaving a raw scar and a ragged pile of stone and dirt with a cloud of brown dust swirling above it. A groan directed her to where Raunn lay, partially buried by the dirt. The animal she was hunting had escaped but its mad scramble up the rock had sprung a trap for the hunter. Raunn did not move.

Aurial stared stupidly at the scene for one frozen second, trying to make sense out of it, while dust drifted past her face. Then she climbed carefully over the loose dirt to where Raunn lay and began pulling it away with her hands. Working as fast as she could, she scooped rubble and heaved it downhill, heedless of where rocks landed or how far they rolled. When she had freed Raunn's unconscious body, she stopped, chest heaving for breath, and looked about in momentary panic for a medic. She had always been surrounded by top medical staff on the Beldame and had never needed to know more about medicine than how to call for their help. Now she was alone, dirtside, in the wilderness with her guide and companion in need of help that she could not give.

First aid. Gwynn had insisted that she take a basic course in first aid before going out into the field. She fell back on that sparse training and found that she had more questions than answers. Raunn was unconscious, almost certainly concussed and possibly suffering internal injuries. Should she leave her here or get her back to camp? Was she in shock? Should she be kept warm? What should come first?

Aurial decided to risk moving Raunn and then had to

confront the fact that the dead weight was too much for her to manipulate. That left trying to care for her here and waiting until she woke. Or should she try to move the camp here so that she could watch the burrkies? Either way, she would have to go to the camp for a blanket and return as quickly as possible. She stood, anguished by indecision, when a quiet voice spoke over her shoulder, sending a frisson of shock up her nerves.

"Help is needed. Yes?"

Aurial wheeled with her hands raised defensively, aware too late of how vulnerable she was. Before her stood a tall wiry man, his skin hardened and crossed with fine lines like a cracked brown glaze. He had a thick crop of hair that might have been grey but was more like no color at all. His eyes were as dark and deep as interstellar space. One hand gripped a coarse fiber bag. The other hand was held, palm up, open and empty. "Help is needed. Yes?" he repeated. "I help."

He spoke Chenni but his accent was nearly as bad as hers. She peered at him through narrowed eyes. She had not been paying attention to her surroundings but, even so, he had come up on her very quietly, as though he were part of the land. He appeared old enough for his hair to be darkening into old age but instead it was the indeterminate color of cobwebs. There was something in his eyes that was different, although she could not pin down what it was. And if he spoke Chenni as a second language, as she did, then he had to be one of the Rugollah. But he offered help and she would have to take a chance. "Yes. I need help. Our camp is over there—not far. Help me to carry her, please."

The man smiled and handed her the pack, casually, as he had held it. Aurial took it and found its apparent lightness deceptive. She grabbed it quickly with her other hand to prevent it from hitting the ground. The Rugollah gathered Raunn up gently, cushioning her head against his chest. With surefooted care he bore his burden to their camp as if he already knew the way. Aurial followed, trying to keep the bag from either dragging on the ground or bumping painfully into her legs.

She was surprised to see the fire burning brightly: she felt as if she had been away long enough for the flames to have subsided into embers. The Rugollah set Raunn down and wrapped her in a blanket. He pulled the pack to his side and began to go through it. While he rummaged, Aurial took one of the cloths that had wrapped the meat pies and moistened it in water she had set to heat what seemed like hours ago. She began to wash the dirt from Raunn's face, cleansing the cuts and scrapes with great care. The warm water must have helped because Raunn's eyes flickered partially open and she mumbled, "What? Hurt. Tunser." Then her eyes fluttered and rolled upward, the lids closed and she returned to oblivion. Aurial wiped her forehead again and rinsed the cloth. When the Rugollah finished taking his supplies from the pack and set to work, Aurial stopped her ministrations to watch what he was doing. She was curious but she also wanted to make sure he did not do anything dangerous. How she would tell if something was dangerous she did not know.

The Rugollah's actions seemed innocuous enough. He took leaves from his pack and ground them in a device that looked like a handmill. He put the grounds into a cup and added liquid from a small bottle, then set the mixture aside. Noting the cuts and abrasions that Aurial had cleaned off, he went over Raunn's body carefully, testing for broken limbs and internal injuries. Finally he sat back on his heels. "She lucky is," he said. "Head only hurt." Ointment from the pack went on the skin wounds, soothing the angry flesh. He cradled Raunn's head in his left arm and dribbled a little of the mixture into her mouth. Most ran out and he put the cup aside. "Wait must," he explained, then added enigmatically, "One comes."

The Rugollah wrapped Raunn warmly and left her. He sat calmly by the fire, saying nothing and appearing to be completely at rest. Aurial studied him briefly and then returned to the pack with the food in it. She removed the pies and offered one to the Rugollah. He accepted it gravely, held it up to his face and smelled it. His large hands broke it in half easily and he sniffed the inside, then poked it with one finger. "Meat?" he inquired.

"Meat, yes," Aurial affirmed. "Meat and vegetables." She took a bite of her own pie and watched him while she chewed. The Rugollah bit into the pie tentatively, then bit again with enthusiasm. Several bites later the pie was gone and he smiled. "Good," he said. Aurial was full but she pulled more food out of the pack and gave it to him. He consumed whatever she gave him after examining it first. She was refastening the pack when he stood up. "One comes," he said again.

She turned to face the direction in which he was looking and saw another of his kind emerge from the darkness. This one looked and was dressed very much the same. He ignored Aurial and went directly to where Raunn lay. The two Rugollah conferred rapidly in their own tongue and the new one knelt by Raunn's side. Aurial had the distinct impression that the new arrival had been called and that the first one had simply been waiting for him. Curious.

The new arrival carried no pack but had a small pouch slung on a strap over one shoulder. He took a minute object from the pouch, tipped Raunn's head back, opened her mouth and placed the object on her tongue. Then he returned her to her blanket and waited. Aurial stayed close by Raunn, watching her protectively.

Soon Raunn began to twitch and jerk. Aurial was alarmed and turned to the Rugollah in protest but the one she had fed gestured her to be still. Feeling helpless, she subsided. Raunn opened her eyes. "Aurial?" she called faintly, and then with more force, "Aurial!"

Aurial responded immediately. "It's alright," she said. "You were caught in a rockslide and hurt. These men came to help. I think they're Rugollah."

Raunn looked up and saw the two men. Her eyes flashed wildly from one to the other. "Rugollah? Don't let them do anything to me, Aurial."

"I won't," Aurial assured her. "They don't seem to want to hurt us."

"Unclean," Raunn said. "They are *parostri*. Non-believers. Keep them away from me."

Aurial didn't know how she could do that if she wanted

to and she definitely didn't want to. Right now she needed all the help she could get and so did Raunn, even if she didn't know it. She wasn't quite sure how to respond to Raunn's command but before she had to, Raunn's eyes closed abruptly. She looked at the Rugollah.

"Sleeps now," the first one said. "Rest needed."

Aurial couldn't argue with that. She pulled her blanket and groundcloth out of the pack and spread them out. Both the Rugollah settled quietly together on the other side of the fire with their heads tilted toward one another, as though they were talking even though neither made a sound. Curious. The familiar weight of exhaustion fell on Aurial but she was uneasy about going to sleep with them in the camp. Then she realized that it would be even harder to sleep if they left and she had to watch Raunn by herself. One of them looked up, caught her eye and held her gaze. Fatigue overwhelmed her. She slept.

# THE ROCK

Surrein hauled himself up the last ledge and onto the entry terrace of the Rock. He was in excellent condition, with a lean well-muscled body, but he had thrown himself at the long climb and the Rock had taken its toll. He wiped sweat from his forehead with one sleeve and sucked painful breaths into his lungs. Two of his fingers were bleeding and his arms were scraped. *When the Rock belongs to me*, Surrein thought, *I will put an end to this barbarous ascent and devise an easier way up from the plateau.*

Being forced to scramble up rocks, ladders and crevices for the second time in less than a moon's passage had put him in a foul mood. Worse, even though he had signaled from the base, no one waited here to greet him: the entry terrace was bare. Where was the vellide, the su-vellide who was his betrothed, the tuupit, or even a kitchen servant with water to wash his filthy hands and beer to drink? The last time he had scaled the Rock an obligatory party had welcomed him at the top. Of course, Torrian had been with him then. A Patrol curse slipped from his lips: swearing was one of several offworld vices he had come to appreciate.

A scratching sound at his back told him that his manservant had finally reached the top. Surrein paid no attention as the drev dodged past his master and hastened on quivering legs to arrange for refreshments and the hauling up of their luggage. Sauntering across the terrace to the stairs up to the next level, Surrein sat down on one step and leaned back against the wall. He would go no further until there was a proper reception.

With his right knee bent and his arm resting casually on it, with his head tipped back and his dark eyes looking nonchalantly out from beneath long lashes, he presented the ideal picture of aristocratic refinement. It was impossible to tell that, beneath his cool facade, he was seething at the blatant disrespect demonstrated toward him by those who should have been exceeding one another in their attempts to please him. A furry yellow tarmit made its way along the opposite wall of the steps and settled into a ball. It began waiting patiently for small insects to emerge from between the stones so that it could scoop them up with its long, sticky tongue. Surrein watched it with eyes that barely flickered but that would have blasted the beast to a charred wreck if they could have vented his fury.

Footsteps clattered across the terrace above him and he thought, *At last, and long past time. But they will pay. Oh, yes, I will see to that.* He stood with a smile on his lips that showed no hint of its origin in anticipation of revenge. A passing observer would have seen only a man rising from a short rest to greet his hosts with all the courtesy of his breeding. The smile died when Surrein saw that Torrian was not one of those who had come to welcome him. Neither was the vellide present. There were servants, of course, bearing the water and beer needed for his refreshment. Instead of his betrothed, however, there was only the impertinent tuupit.

Once again Surrein locked eyes with Antikoby and asked the question that was of the greatest importance to him. "Where is Torrian? Why is she not here to greet me? She must be recovered by now."

"Indeed, yes, sri-noth," the tuupit responded. "The su-vellide Torrian is recovered from her illness, although she is not yet strong. She is grateful for your patience and begs your forgiveness for her absence. She hopes that you will understand her need for rest. She awaits you in the small audience chamber and asks that you meet with her there as soon as you are restored from the climb."

Surrein drew in a long breath that pinched his nose to a sharp point. Torrian's request was selfish and spoiled but he was prepared to ignore such childish behavior now: she would learn better manners later. He sensed something else going on here, however, and he didn't like it at all. Being surprised was unacceptable because it meant that he was not in control of the situation. This surprise darkened his mood further but he did not allow that to show by so much as a grimace. "Tell your mistress that I shall be with her as soon as I can make myself presentable."

The insufferable tuupit hesitated for a moment, then, recalling his duty, turned and left. Surrein washed his hands, oblivious to the sting of soap on his lacerated fingers, and took several long swallows of an excellent beer without tasting it. A servant brushed dirt and rock dust from his back and he was ready to follow the one whose job it was to take him to the su-vellide.

In the small audience chamber, which would have held fifty people easily, Surrein found only three waiting for him: the tuupit, Torrian and a nayya. Strange. Why here? Why the nayya? He wanted to embrace Torrian and dominate her physically, rouse her with his presence, remind her that soon she would be subject to his wishes. But the formality of the room and the cold stare of the nayya prevented him. Instead he greeted her with a courtesy even the nayya could not have faulted. She returned his greeting in the same way. Cold. She did not seem to want to touch him. The arrogant whore. She hadn't always been cold; he wondered what had turned her fire to ice.

Then she told him. She opened her spoiled mouth and words came out. After the first two sentences he closed his ears so that the words bounced from his skull and fell to the floor. All unknowing, her mouth kept opening and closing, her words went on and the nayya broke in to add his opinion, the way they always did. The words echoed up at him from the floor: *vigil, isolated, Chasm of the Heartspring, great sacrifice, preparation for marriage, sacred rite*. It was all burrky droppings. Rawfin lies. Lies and deception. Anger blurred his vision. He wanted to strike Torrian, knock her down and hit her until she begged for a mercy she didn't deserve. His hands clenched reflexively but he shivered and gained control of himself before they could act on his desires. Control—he needed to be in control.

Summoning up the charm that was his mask, his social disguise, Surrein held out his hands affectionately. Torrian, who could not hold back without seeming withdrawn, placed her hands in his. He smiled. It was important not to let them see how strong he was: if they knew they would try to destroy him out of fear. "Of course," he said, "if this vigil is what you need then it is what you must do." It was perfect: what he said and how he looked. All was perfect. His cheeks and lips felt hard and smooth, like smiling stone. He squeezed Torrian's hands. "How could I keep you from your duty to the True Word? It would be unthinkable." He squeezed harder: Torrian must know his strength that she dare not defy it again. "I shall place you in the capable hands of nayya Nusrat-Geb for the duration of the vigil but I will be with you each moment of that time in spirit."

She was looking at him now and he could see her eyes widen in pain, see from the set of her face that she was gritting her teeth. "Now, if you will excuse me, sri-nothi, I would like to retire to my rooms so that I may consider how best to prepare for our union while you are secluded in the Chasm of the Heartspring." Her eyes grew larger and he knew that he had hit upon it: she wanted him to stay or to go. What was it? He could remain here or he could leave—which did she want? It was important to know so that he could prevent her from controlling his actions. No one would ever do that again.

Speaking had made him feel better, more in charge of what was happening. Whatever it was they wanted—and he had no doubt that the ubiquitous tuupit and the nayya were part of it—he must do the opposite. Or better yet, something they could not possibly have anticipated. The best thing he could do now would be to leave them dangling, not knowing what he had decided. The nayya was saying something but he ignored the man's silly words. Freshening his smile, he gave Torrian's hands a final squeeze and was gratified to see her face stiffen. With a slight bow toward the su-vellide, he turned to leave.

Then the tuupit stepped forward and spoke. Without altering his stride or acknowledging the man's presence, Surrein lashed out with his right hand and caught him across the nose. There was a gratifying crunch and blood spattered in an arc, spraying the floor and Surrein, but the troinom paid no attention. He turned to Torrian once again and said in an off-hand tone, "You must discipline your servants, sri-nothi. They have grown lax in the absence of their su-vellide." Her face was pale, her eyes wide, but she did not reply. The nayya started to say something and raised one hand in protest but then subsided. Weak. All the nayyat were weak. Surrein strode to the door, his every move conveying aristocratic strength and grace, and left the room.

## THE BELDAME

The food in the commissary was excellent and Rolfe applied himself to a large lunch, knowing as he ate that he would have to sweat it off later in the gym. The workouts were the price he paid for keeping old habits. When working his way around the Outback worlds, he had burned up a lot of energy, generated an enormous appetite and eaten huge meals. The appetite had come with him to the Beldame but not the hard physical labor. He was thinking about adding to his gym routine when someone sat down on the other side of the table. He looked up, nodded, and returned his attention to his meal.

"Ahem," the woman said. "May I have a moment of your time?"

Startled, he took a closer look and recognized the augmented specialist who was tracing the labor shipment. This was the first time he had seen her in the flesh. "Your pardon," he said, "I was not expecting to meet you here and my mind was elsewhere."

She placed a cup of coffee on the table; it looked lonely next to his crowded tray. "I know," the jackhead replied, then added, "but I have the information you need."

"That was fast," he commented. "Is that all you're eating?"

She shrugged. "My job doesn't require a lot of calories, if you know what I mean. And it only seems fast to someone like you. Once you're faced in, you work at system speed and human time is like plate tectonics compared to that. Actually, it might have taken longer but we caught a break on the sort. Most of the shipment went to Veyik IV, as you predicted. A much smaller group, only ten or so, was sent in the opposite direction. There's a system called BG-x3 on the charts but known as Big Green in the Quad markets. Ever hear of it?"

Rolfe nodded. There were stories about Big Green but he had learned a long time ago not to believe most of what he heard. His work had never taken him anywhere near it.

"Well," she continued, "for some reason this group is going out to Big Green and your boy is one of them. Only three of the ten originated on Chennidur so pinpointing him was easy. The company holding the contract is still Dependable Workforces and his shipment number is Q3*CH/104-696. The ship is under warp drive now and will drop into realspace near BG-x3 in about 20 STDs. It's under lease to us and I have the registration number, drive plan, contract and all other appropriate data queued for transmission to your personal file. That's all there is, except that I need your print on this to approve the chargeback." She extended a charge key across the table.

Rolfe pressed his thumb to the key. "Who bought the contract?"

She took a swallow of her coffee and grimaced as it burned her mouth. "Oh, yes. The buyer is the Acre Company Lt4QInc. They had the successful bid on exploration rights for Big Green. Acre specializes in metals and mining so the workers will most likely be used to clear the jungle for open pit mines. They might also hunt up whatever other resources Big Green can contribute to the company's profits. Your target and the others in his group probably have some particular skill that will help with that. Whatever it is, I hope he's good at it."

"He may never have to find out," Rolfe replied, and immediately regretted having said even that much. The Old Lady had a way of finding out about a project and then jumping in. If she didn't like what she saw, the project died. If she was enthusiastic about it, she would involve herself. Unfortunately, her enthusiasms were almost as dangerous as her criticisms: once she got into a project, she made sure it was done her way, even if that wasn't always the right way.

On the other hand, the Old Lady was probably all wrapped up in the religious project he'd heard about. The top-dome church exec soon to arrive on the Beldame should keep her safely out of the way. He considered telling the jackhead to keep it quiet but decided that such a comment might be the fastest way to raise his visibility. He would have to gamble that, like most heavily-augmented types, she was more involved with the system than with people and would forget his comment in moments. To his relief, the specialist was not at all curious and simply sipped her coffee while he finished his lunch.

Back at his workstation, he accessed the information she had transmitted and factored it in to his analysis. Next, he plotted a course from Chennidur to the BG-x3 system and then a second course from the Beldame to BG-x3. It was tight. There was no way he could get to Big Green at the same time as the shipment. His target, Merradrix, would simply have to survive on his own until Rolfe arrived. Before that could happen, though, Rolfe needed to get the necessary approvals. Heading up the list was the requisition for his passage out and that of his backup operative. Then came three fares from BG-x3 to Chennidur and the return passage for Rolfe and the backup. Next came a requisition for the backup operative. There was the considerable cost of buying out Merradrix's labor contract. He would also need cash on hand for bribes and other expenses. His own time was not a problem because he could charge it to the project but the other costs required hard money in advance and it all added up.

He leaned back in his chair and steepled his hands in front of him, trying to decide what would be the simplest way to get what he wanted. His monitor chimed, signaling incoming data. Quickly he sat up again and scanned the display, relieved to see that the message was Aurial's overdue report. He read through it once briefly and then again carefully, for detail. Although the report was in Family code, Aurial's personality still managed to come through and he smiled as he thought of her trekking around dirtside. She would find out readily enough how difficult things could be when the il Tarz name was of no importance. He had to admit, however, that she was keeping her eyes open on the way. The stickybush she described had no obvious commercial value that he could see but the death catcher was another story entirely. With some modification, it could have very profitable applications in waste disposal. In addition, the more crowded inner worlds were always looking for more efficient ways to dispose of dead bodies. He would write his suggestions into the project report and, if Aurial's mission was a success, they would commission samples for genetic analysis.

The primary mission was, in fact, going as well as could be expected while she befriended the troinom woman and learned as much as possible. He coded a reply to let Aurial know that he was following through on the labor shipment issue. Before sending it off, he added a request for more frequent reports to reinforce the importance of maintaining close contact with the Beldame and transmitting all information, even if it seemed not relevant.

That completed, he began calling up the forms for the numerous requisitions he would need for the trip to Big Green and filling in the data. As he did so, an archaic joke crossed his mind: "The longest journey begins with a single piece of paper." Nothing had changed, really, but the medium.

# CHAPTER 11

## The Perimeter

Raunn awoke feeling disoriented and off-balance. She
lay for a moment with her eyes closed, listening to the odd
messages her body was sending, and wondering what had
happened. Her head hurt and she felt bruised and sore, as
if it she been beaten all over. A wave of dizziness swept
over her and a series of disconnected images that made no
sense appeared against her eyelids. A man with hair the
color of the Veil. Rocks falling. A cup of fluid. Hands
reaching toward her. The rump of a fleeing tunser. An odd
face peering into hers. Aurial's eyes, large with worry.
Fingers grasping something she could not see. The images
filled her with unfocused anxiety. Alarmed, Raunn opened
her eyes and saw only the camp, with the kettle on the fire
and Aurial sitting nearby, eating.

The sun, glowing high and white behind the Veil, showed
that morning was well underway. They were late; they
should have been on the trail long since if they were going
to make it to the Rock by day's end. She sat up abruptly,
incurring a wave of dizziness, and cradled her head in her
hands until the vertigo passed. Aurial scooted over to her

200

side. She was chewing on a pittari pastry and a string of green marmalade was stuck to her chin. "How are you feeling?" the outworld woman asked. Her voice sounded distant, detached from the place Raunn occupied.

"I'm fine," Raunn replied, denying reality. "Wipe your chin. Why should I feel any differently?"

"You were hit on the head by a rock, that's why. Don't you remember? You went out to chase some poor animal. It got away but it must have kicked up a rockslide when it escaped and the slide got you. You've been unconscious most of the time until now."

The disconnected images began to make sense. "When did this happen? How long have I been out?"

"Since last night. You woke up and talked to me but I don't think you really knew what you were doing or saying. You gave me a good scare."

Last night. They hadn't lost as much time as she'd thought: it could have been much worse. Maybe, if they moved fast, they'd still be able to make it. Eagerness to be done with this overlong journey surged through her and she wanted to be back home on the Rock. To lose an entire day to her own stupidity, to her own willful desire to hunt when food was not needed, was unbearable. The prospect of another night on the trail was unthinkable. "Then we can still get to the Rock today," she said, rising, "but we have to get started now."

"What?" Aurial exclaimed. "You can't go anywhere today."

"Why not?" Raunn asked, one hand to her forehead. "I told you, I feel fine."

"You're not well yet, that's why, and you're supposed to rest until at least tomorrow. That's what he said."

Raunn, on her feet now, looked down at Aurial. "Who said that? There's no one else here; what are you talking about?"

Aurial rose and faced her. "Him. The Rugollah. Don't you remember anything?"

Hair the color of the Veil. An odd face. The pictures told her what she did not want to know. "There was a Rugollah here? In camp? Last night?"

Aurial sighed. "Yes, of course. There were two of them,

actually, and a good thing, too. I don't know what I would
have done without their help."

A shiver of fear started at the base of Raunn's neck. The
Rugollah, the people of mystery, *shirz*. They had been
here last night while she was unconscious. They had talked
to Aurial. They had helped. Helped. Her voice was sharp
when she asked, "What did they do?"

"Well," Aurial considered. "The first one came and
carried you from the slide back to the camp. He checked
you over and mixed a drink out of some herbs but you
were out of it and couldn't drink anything. So he just
waited for someone he seemed to be expecting and ate a
great deal of the food they packed for us at Perimeter
House. Another Rugollah came along right on schedule
with a different sort of medicine, a tablet, that he fed you.
It seemed to relax you and relieve the pain. You got better
after that. They were gone when I woke up but they left
this drink for you to take if you were not feeling well."

Raunn didn't know what to say. Her throat was frozen.
A *shirz* had touched her, put some foul substance in her
mouth, while she had been helpless to prevent it. *Shufri-
nagai* specifically proscribed pollution of the body and
many of the allegories in the books of commentary told
how those who transgressed atoned for it in complex ways.
"And I knew nothing of this?" she croaked.

Aurial's response was slow. "You woke up once and saw
them, recognized them." She looked down. "You didn't
want me to let them touch you or do anything to you."
Then she lifted her eyes and her voice was challenging.
"But I had no choice. Was I supposed to let you die? I
know very little about medicine, even for my own people,
much less yours. They knew what they were doing: they
wanted to help. So I let them, because I couldn't do it
myself. The best thing that could happen, I thought, was
that you would get well enough to be angry with me. And
I was willing to risk that. I'm sorry, but I couldn't send
them away and then just hope you wouldn't die."

"It's not as simple as that," Raunn said tightly. "For a
Follower of the True Word, even contact with a *shirz* is
forbidden. Allowing one to touch you, much less introduce

some foreign substance into your body, is unspeakable. I shall have to pay for this, not you."

Aurial kicked a pebble with her foot in exasperation. "But I'm not a Follower, doesn't that make me *shirz*, too? What's the difference between associating with me and with a Rugollah. What's the difference between the medicine Dr. La gave you at the port and what the Rugollah gave you last night? They both worked. You're better. Nothing at the Port made you this upset. Why are you so angry now? It doesn't make sense."

Raunn was about to protest the comparison but the words stopped in her throat. She thought as quickly as she could with her head thick and dizzy. The starwoman was right. There was no difference, yet there was an enormous difference. It lay in how she felt about outworlders and about Rugollah. There was something there, something important that she would have to think about. But she would do that later on. Not now. She glanced up and saw that the sun had not stood still while she was arguing like a silly drev. "You're right," she said. "I can't explain. We can talk about it later. Right now we have to get started." She brushed Aurial's protests aside and began to pull their things together. After a long moment's hesitation, Aurial gave up her attempts to dissuade her and took over.

For all her fierce determination, however, Raunn was happy to lean against her burrky and let Aurial do most of the work. Once they were underway she had to admit that, while riding was better than walking, the burrky's placid, deliberate stride was not helping her headache or a decidedly queasy stomach. She gritted her teeth and pressed on, determined to make it to the Rock with enough time left to climb it before sundown. How she was going to do the climb when she couldn't even ride comfortably was a question Raunn could not answer so she put it aside. She would be feeling better by then. She must.

At the top of the next hill Cliffmaster citadel came into full view and they stopped so that Aurial could see their destination. Even from a distance, the Rock loomed massively. Its impregnable position atop sheer cliffs was immediately apparent. Aurial observed the setting carefully and said, "Well, it's a good climb, alright. Can it be approached from behind?"

Raunn replied, "No. Remember the map that your machine at the Port created? We're on the plateau that drops off over there." She swept her hand to the left. "The plateau ends here in a peninsula with the Rock on the tip. It's not isolated—it would take a chasm between the peninsula and the rest of the plateau for that—but the position is so strong that no one has ever tried to assault it."

"So far," Aurial replied enigmatically and urged her mount forward.

It was an easy ride across the plateau and Raunn knew that they were observed from the time they left the hilltop. The guards would not be able to tell who they were but all riders were watched carefully. She led the way around by the Trailhead hostel so that they could drop their packs and leave the extra burrkies for the servants to handle. Ordinarily she would have left their mounts as well and walked to the base of the cliff but she was not quite up to that right now. Raunn had expected Trailhead to be as clean, well-stocked and organized as always, but instead found evidence that someone had used it not long ago. She wondered who the visitors could have been and whether they had been coming or going.

When the animals were stabled, the two women entered the hostel and refreshed themselves. Aurial ate but Raunn could not and found even the sight of food unpleasant. This disturbed her. She could understand the dizziness and headache: such symptoms were only to be expected after a blow to the head. The nausea seemed out of place and the image of fingers holding something to her mouth persisted. The Rugollah had given her something and she did not know what it was. Raunn had left the cup of liquid in camp. She wondered if it would have made her feel better or worse. Rising abruptly, she went outside and found the path to the relief house. On the way, she noticed a clump of firevine growing near the path. She made a mental note to send a servant to cut it back before the warmth of Abundance made it virulent.

When they reached the base of the cliff, Raunn looked

up eagerly but the distance between her and home loomed impossibly high. Despite her determination to get well, she did not feel any better. She braced herself to make the effort: all it took was one step after another and then she would be home. The sun was lowering. There was no time for hesitation or it would be dark before they reached the top.

Aurial noticed her vacillation. "Are you sure you're ready for this, Raunn? It's a long climb. There must be some way they could haul you up to the top instead."

Raunn flashed her a pained look. "I haven't been winched up the cliff since I was old enough to walk and I'm not going to do it now. It's bad enough that I show up here when I'm supposed to be in Nandarri, that I'll have to explain to Mother what happened. When I arrive at the top, it will be on my own two feet."

Aurial let her annoyance show. "And what am I supposed to do when you collapse halfway up? Carry you the rest of the way on my back? I'll have all I can do to make it to the top myself."

"If something happens," Raunn said waspishly, "you just keep going and send someone down for me. Now, let's get started or we'll be climbing in the dark and that's dangerous even for experienced people." She took one step and then turned to Aurial. "I'll go first so I can tell you what to expect." Raunn took a deep breath, ordered her stomach to stay in its place, and started up. Aurial shrugged and followed her.

At first the climb was easy, as always. The path stepped up over enormous blocks of stone that had fallen from the heights and been worked into an irregular staircase. After this domesticated talus slope, the way became more vertical, angling up through a gaping crack in the cliff. This brought them to a ledge no more than three feet wide that continued steeply upward. Aurial took the climb slowly and carefully, as was only wise for someone who had never scaled the cliff before. Raunn called down what to expect and did not hurry the outworlder. For once, Raunn herself was glad of the slow pace and did not protest when Aurial stopped to rest.

There was not time to rest long, however, and few
places in which to do it. They made their way steadily
upward, past the first ladder of thick iron bolted into the
stone and through the chute which, luckily, was only
damp instead of running with water. Raunn showed Aurial
how to lean in to the cliff face when the trail narrowed and
there was a sheer drop at their backs. She was gratified to
see the outworlder take the slide with no trouble, hauling
herself hand-over-hand up the metal rod that provided the
only hold on sharply-slanted, featureless rock.

When they reached the midway, a flat shelf wide enough
for several people to sit on, Raunn sank down gratefully.
Her stomach was in turmoil and a second later she leaned
over the edge to vomit bile. Aurial did not attempt to help
her through the bout of illness but shrank back against the
cliff instead. Raunn was glad to be left alone in her misery.
When it was over, they sat quietly for a moment before
Aurial said in a worried tone, "Are you ready to go on?"

Raunn nodded. "I can handle it. We haven't much time
left." They started upwards once again. Three of the seven
ladders were ahead of them and the path was no easier
between midway and the top. The climb became a gruel-
ing race against fading light. Aurial, tiring rapidly, began
to flag and Raunn urged her on with words of encouragement. It was a steady climb with screaming muscles, burning lungs and aching sides opposing the ever-present danger
of the cliff.

When finally they flung themselves over the top, the
Veil was gone and only a faint glow clung to the horizon.
The Eyestar burned steadily overhead. Both women lay on
the entry terrace with heaving sides, gulping air. They
were incapable of moving and, for long moments, were oblivious to their surroundings. Then Raunn heard footsteps
clattering to a stop nearby and knew that the welcoming
party had arrived. She was mortified to be found thus,
incapacitated by a climb that she usually surmounted with
a shout of laughter. Rolling over, she propped herself on
one elbow to see a small group waiting respectfully a short
distance away.

In the forefront was Antikoby, expressions of worry,

relief, anxiety, and happiness chasing themselves quickly across his features. There was Maitris, her sister's maid, with towels in her hands. Behind them were other servants, bearing the traditional water and beer. And off to the side, another man, a stranger. No, not a stranger. She had seen him before in Nandarri. He stepped forward now, brushing Antikoby aside. "Sri-nothi!" he exclaimed, his handsome face set in lines of concern. "What a surprise to see you here. Why did you not flash a message from Nandarri so that we could prepare for your arrival?" He reached out and took her hand in an attempt to help her rise. She resisted the pull.

Looking around the man's body, Raunn addressed Antikoby. "Fetch the infirmarer to my chambers," she ordered. "I am not well." She was going to include a summons for the nayya, but the intense interest of the man beside her made her hold back.

"Yes, sri-nothi," Antikoby responded. He spoke to the servant with the water, took the bowl from him, and watched as the man sped away up the stairs to the second terrace.

The pull on Raunn's hand became insistent. The man leaned down and wrapped his arm around her. "Let me help you, Raunn. Surely you remember me. I am Surrein, soon to be your brother." He was strong and the slimness of his body was deceptive. Surrein pulled her to her feet and then, taking most of her weight upon himself, propelled her forward with ease. A servant hastened to take her other arm but Surrein dismissed him with a sharp twitch of his head.

Raunn, grateful not to have to be in charge any longer, leaned into his strength. She protested once, softly, turning back toward Aurial. "My friend . . ." she said.

"The tuupit will take care of her," Surrein said firmly. "I will look to your recovery personally." Tightening his grip, he took her up the stairs toward the warm glowing lights of her home.

# THE HEARTSPRING

Although the nayya had gone long ago, Torrian thought she could still hear the diminishing echo of his footsteps. She was alone: alone with her thoughts, with the dismal prospect of a marriage to Surrein, with her fear that the bedrock of Clan Cliffmaster was being undermined from beneath, with her anger. Her only companion was the Heartspring: cold, remote and silent.

As she listened to the indifferent dripping of water she reflected on how she had begun this retreat only as an escape from Surrein despite the nayya's instruction that approaching so sacred a task without proper dedication was sacrilegious. She had felt no compunctions at the outset and she felt no guilt now. All of Torrian's life the True Word had been the central point of her existence. Certainly the underranks were more devout, the troinom more reserved, but that was simply the way of life and did not affect the foundation of faith common to both classes. When her appeals to the nayya had been denied, however, that foundation had been destroyed.

How could she be faithless to a religion that had betrayed her faith and delivered her to a madman? What wrong could there be in using *shufri-nagai*, the True Word and Nusrat-Gegg for her own purposes? Without belief in the woven voices of the Chenni-ad, without acceptance of the laws, her life contained an immense vacancy and the only thing big enough and strong enough to fill that emptiness was anger.

So anger had possessed her and filled her thoughts. There was anger at herself for her many failings, anger at Nusrat-Geb for hiding in the Kohrable and abandoning her, anger at Surrein for deceiving her, anger at her mother for withdrawing from a family that needed her.

Torrian had carried the weight of that rage with her into the cavern of the Heartspring and now it sustained her. She clung to it as the one thing that would save her from drowning once again in the sea of duty. She had always done what she was told to do, placing responsibility and obligation above all, certainly above her own desires. She had followed the rules, done as she was told and been a good girl. Where had it gotten her? The one burst of rebellion in which she had indulged had only made things worse. It left her betrothed to a willing pawn of the enemies of her world, a man who would hurt her for his own pleasure. She was trapped and no one would come to her aid but an outworlder and a tuupit. Pathetic.

She would have been better off running from her duty the way Raunn had, or hiding from it as her mother was doing now. Even being killed in an accident like Cheyte and Rushain would be better, she reasoned, than living a hopeless life. Had her brothers only lived, she would not now be heir to the Rock and enmeshed in the coils of politics. *Surrein would not be here.* The thought went through her with a shock that jolted her out of the self-pity in which she was wallowing. Of course. How could she have missed it? Surrein did not want her, Torrian, except as a trophy and a symbol of his success. His orders from the Tulkan were to control Clan Cliffmaster and its fortress. Her brothers had been killed not only because they opposed the Tulkan's regime and were a threat to his rule but because they were an obstacle. The Tulkan had set a clever trap where she was both the bait and the victim.

Torrian looked around her wildly but saw only darkness and the rock walls flickering in lantern light. The walls kept Surrein out but they also kept her in. What to do? Should she stay here where she was safe and follow the plan she had worked out with Antikoby or should she flout *shufri-nagai* a second time and abandon the vigil? And if she did, could she fight Surrein? Was she stronger than he?

No, it was time to be calm and think. The Tulkan was far ahead of her in his planning and being impetuous would do her and the clan no good now. Better by far to stay here and create a counter-strategy. Even so, Torrian admitted to herself that she was unlikely to find any new answers and now she was more confused than ever. What to do? She was trapped in this cavern for a world of days, with only the liturgy of a forsaken religion to relieve her mind of its burdens. Worse, she had only two books to ameliorate the boredom of unending darkness and solitude: the Kohrable and the Book of Vigils. What to do?

Torrian knew that, first, she had to calm herself and free her mind to think clearly. Long attendance at the temple, had taught that the observance of ritual would help. Even if, before, she had always believed, she had not always been attentive; perhaps belief was not necessary and the ritual itself was sufficient. She turned to the Book of Vigils and found that the first rite began with a pair of chants. She worked her way through the chants methodically and then came to a period of meditation.

Torrian sighed. Meditation had never been easy for her. It seemed that others could clear their minds of thought with ease and listen to the contrapuntal voices of the Chenni-ad within. For her, the demands of the household had intruded. Even though the Rock was not her responsibility, she had gotten so wound up in its problems and needs that they were impossible to banish, even to make way for a greater voice. Meditation was no easier now. She felt pummelled and bruised within from all the emotions that shoved their way back and forth in her mind, demanding attention.

> *"Listen to the Heartspring,*
> *Hear its call.*
> *For it speaks with the voices of the Chenni-ad.*
> *Open yourself to its words,*
> *For the spirits speak through the waters.*
> *Deliver yourself to its music*
> *For it sings of tranquility . . ."*

*The spring is quiet,* she protested to herself and closed the book. Then she closed her eyes as well and listened. The cavern was silent; no voices spoke to her. *Why can't I ever do these things right?* she thought in frustration. But she kept her eyes closed and remained still. Gradually, sounds made themselves known to her. The noises were small, unobtrusive. They were so small as to be easily overwhelmed by something as great as a footstep or a spoken word. Torrian had been in the cavern of the Heartspring many times before, but always with others. She had rarely been properly reverent in its presence and never quiet. Now that she had stilled herself, she could hear the Heartspring's small simple voice.

Foremost was the constant trickle of water in the basin, delicate and serene. Punctuating this was an occasional, arrhythmic drip from the damp stone walls, each drop a musical tone of a different pitch. She could also hear the brazier, allowed to her because of the duration of her retreat, hissing with a susurrant companionship. The pulse of her heartbeat, heard with her inner ear, melded with the other sounds and connected her to them. She kept as still as possible lest any noise louder than breathing obscure the voices of the cavern. At the same time, she was filled with their music, lacking room for anything else. This slight chorus, as varied and yet interwined as the Chenni-ad, drove away the self-pity and the anger that plagued her. It carried her out of herself, making her one with the rock and the water. She drifted off.

When finally Torrian returned to herself, she felt as though she had been elsewhere for a long time. How long, she could not tell. In the tenebrosity of the cavern, alleviated only by the glow of the brazier and the flicker of a single lantern, the passage of time was not easily marked. She noted, however, that the brazier had burned well down and needed replenishing. When she did so, her body responded reluctantly, as though conspiring with her mind to remain in that state of peaceful otherness. Torrian became aware of stiffness, of being sore where hard stone had pushed through the mat, of being cold.

Shivering, she pulled a stoniver-wool sweater on and piled charcoal into the brazier, stirring it so that it would catch properly. She added oil to the lantern and raised the flame. Then Torrian picked up the Book of Vigils from where it had dropped on the mat and turned to the post-meditation instructions. It prescribed a short path of exercise designed to return her body and mind to a unified state, and then food. The exercises went quickly and helped to warm her. Torrian was not particularly hungry, but she took the time to prepare a hot meal and brew a mug of tea suffused with strengthening herbs.

The sweater, the hot food and the exercise combined to hold the cavern's damp chill away. Taking the lantern, she rose and climbed down into the small side-cavern that held a bucket for a latrine. It was darker there and Torrian was glad to return to the comfort of the Heartspring.

She took a relaxed position on the mat, placed the lantern beside her and picked up the Kohrable. The nayya had directed her to read at least one major section a day, her days marked only by Nusrat-Geb's visit. Completing this portion of the vigil would take her through all of the Kohrable. It was not what she wanted but it was better than being harried about the cavern by her own emotions. Torrian turned to the first section, Beginning, and read the first verse: Worldbirth.

> *"Out of the timeless dark,*
> *Out of the vastness of time,*
> *Came the Chen-i-ad who bore first light."*

*Light*, Torrian thought. It would be a long time before she saw the sun's light again, a long time alone here in the darkness at the heart of the Rock. Suddenly the cavern was no longer a sanctuary protecting her from the influence of a madman. Instead the weight of the bedrock pressed down and blackness oozed from the stone, crowding the lantern's small light into a feeble ball. Torrian shook her head against the illusion and lowered her eyes to the page.

> *"The light brought forth the world.*
> *The world was one with the darkness and the light.*
> *All time was around it but time was not upon it.*
> *It was completed."*

*Despondency surrounds me*, Torrian thought. When she looked into her future, it was difficult to see a way through the shadows cast by Surrein and the Tulkan. If her mind felt battered, it was because she had cast it in many directions, seeking a way out of her trap, and always it had collided with the obdurate stone of duty.

She realized then that anger was only one of the companions she had brought with her. Fear was the other. Foremost was the fear of being the means by which Clan Cliffmaster was defeated and brought to obedience by the Tulkan. Then there was the fear of wasting her life in a marriage where her husband was also her jailer. Another fear, more visceral, was the dread of bodily injury. And deep inside her, as hot as the coals in her brazier, burned the fear that she had been deemed dispensable by her father, the one who should have been protecting her most strongly.

*I must hold these thoughts at bay as the lantern keeps the darkness away*, she told herself. *Fear weighs upon me like the rock. But I will not be defeated.* She turned her eyes back to the page and resumed reading.

"*Yet was the world barren;*
*Divided into light and shadow, heat and cold, night and day.*
*Without life it was unfinished, as a rough gem or an unbaked loaf.*
*Without life it waited, having no purpose and no motion.*"

That was exactly how she felt: purposeless and without a center. Torrian stared into the flame of the lantern. The Kohrable was speaking to her as the Heartspring had. Despite her anger, she must listen. She continued to read.

## THE BELDAME

Itombe looked up as Rolfe entered the antechamber to Nashaum's office. She smiled and then turned to sort through the information on her security-recessed and encrypted datastation. Rolfe cleared his throat. "The, uh . . . Mother summoned me," he said in his best Family tones.

"Yes, I know," Itombe replied, still scanning data. "She channeled the order through me."

"I think she wanted to discuss my request for personnel retrieval on BG-x3," he prompted. "She, the order, said I was to come immediately."

"Of course," Itombe said. "Oh, here it is. Good." She looked up at him again, this time with her full regard. "Unfortunately, her attentions have been diverted elsewhere."

"I know," Rolfe replied. "That's why the order surprised me. I did not think that my request was important enough to divert her from her negotiations."

Itombe smiled. "She's in there," she said, tipping her head to the right, "in conference. The Third High Pompidor of the Church of Elvis the King is discussing their plans to put a graceland on Jaddon 16."

Rolfe whistled soundlessly. "Sounds like a big commission. Do the plans include a monastery?"

"Yes. There will be living space for 300 arens and a convent to house the same number of sillas. This graceland will service over twenty systems in that arm of the quadrant so it has to be big. Constructing the living accommodations for pilgrims alone will be an enormous project. Mother is negotiating the arrangements now and I know she'll make her point."

"Is there some special point she needs to make?" Rolfe asked, pretending an ignorance of the business that was no longer accurate. Since his sisters automatically saw men as subordinates, he was sometimes able to use their perceptions to his own advantage and learn a great deal by asking ingenuous questions.

"Well, they want to barter. They're asking for a discount on the passenger charges in return for the King's blessing on Family ships. It may come as something of a surprise to the High Pompidor that we're more interested in profit margins than in the King's blessing but, as I said, Mother will make the point. You know how she is about religion."

"Actually," Rolfe replied, "I only know how she is about organized religion."

Itombe conceded the point with a twitch of her lips. "When your request came up, she asked me to take care of the 'personnel retrieval' issue. She agrees with your trip justification that returning a person of value to one of the troinom class on Chennidur could create an obligation worth the cost incurred in retrieval. So do I: that's easy. The only issue in my mind is, who's going to go? You started the assignment as Aurial's control here, and you should finish it while someone else goes to BG-x3. You're already briefed and in contact with Aurial on the surface. Keeping you on the project is more efficient than having to brief a new control and bring her up to speed while you go. You understand that?"

"Of course." Rolfe kept his sigh to himself.

"I would have thought that there was no way Mother would agree to let you off the Beldame in mid-project. But she says that you need some time dirtside and you'll be more effective there than here. That's where I disagree but when Mother says that she knows, I don't argue—so you've got your ticket down. Wasnohe can take over as control on the Chennidur project."

Rolfe could feel the elation bubbling up inside him but he kept it from showing. It would never do to let one of the il Tarz women see that he did not think the Beldame was the center of the universe. Now was the time to balance the dispensation he was getting with good business sense. "Thank you. There will be no cause to regret this decision. I will speak to Wasnohe immediately and arrange for her briefing session. When that's done I will take her through all the messages that have been sent since and open up some of the areas of thinking I've been exploring. When I ship out, she'll be as on top of the project as I've been. And I'll make myself available for consultation on shipboard until we warp out. The project will be as covered as I can make it."

Itombe nodded, reassured but not convinced. "Good. I

have Wasnohe's official instructions here ready for her. You can get started immediately."

Rolfe turned and let his smile break through as he left the room. He knew that, dispensation or not, he had no room to munger up the job on Big Green without Itombe landing on him like an asteroid. But that was alright because he didn't intend to munger up anything. He'd show them that he was better at being an operative than a glorified jackhead spouting business jargon as if it really meant something. Then, when the job was done and this man Merradrix was safely in custody, Rolfe planned to have some fun before coming back. Somewhere down the well he should be able to find a woman or two willing to get good and sweaty with him without anybody thinking about attachments or relationships. It would be all the more fun because the entire Beldame would not hear about it before the next duty shift.

He rubbed the palm of his hand with his thumb. The fun was about to begin, but first he had some serious work to do. He strode purposefully down the corridor with an energy that had been missing for a long time.

# CHAPTER 12

## THE ROCK

Moving slowly and very painfully, Aurial made her way to the first terrace. Opaque morning light glowed through the Veil and a warm wind swept across the Rock, bringing with it exciting scents. The great holding's myriad everyday activities swept and bustled around her. Oblivious to the beautiful day and the exciting surroundings, Aurial concentrated her attention on commanding her body to do what she wanted it to do. Yesterday's hard climb had pulled muscles all over—particularly the quadriceps running down the front of her thighs—again. Walking up steps was painful; walking down was very nearly impossible. Aurial was grateful that the skirts she wore reached only to her calf and were not long enough to entangle her feet. That freed her hands so she could cling to walls and railings to aid in her arduous progress.

Having achieved the heights so laboriously, she persevered for several reasons, the most obvious of which being that she wanted to see the view. Aurial also had a perverse desire to look down at the ascent she had made the day before. In addition, she was fed up with the treachery of her body, which seemed to take every opportunity to remind her of its weaknesses. She had felt herself growing stronger on the trip and been proud of it, only to have the climb humble her one more time. Now she was determined to master her recalcitrant muscles.

Wakening late, Aurial had breakfasted on a firstmeal brought to her room by a maid obviously experienced at serving visiting troinom ladies. The briskly efficient woman had helped her to bathe and dress, then directed her toward the terraces. Aurial had met no one else so far in her progress and was thankful for it.

She thought, with mixed feelings, of her arrival the night before. Lying spent on the stone, she had looked up to find herself regarded by a handsome face marked by a broad brow, strong chin and eyes filled with character. Displaying the deference of one of the underranks toward a troinom, the man had helped her to stand, only to have his efforts foiled when her knees buckled and gave way. Without hesitation he had caught her up, as if she weighed no more than the clothing she wore, and carried her. From the terrace to the house, up steps and down numerous corridors all the way to her chamber, his heart had beat strongly against her cheek. Then he had left her to the attentions of the maid. If he had spoken, she did not remember it.

Aurial stopped and pressed her hand against a stone wall. She was mortified at collapsing, at being helpless as a child before such a man. Yet she also felt an electric thrill at the memory of how he had carried her. It was a sensation quite different from anything she had ever felt before and she was not sure what to make of it. *Just keep moving,* she thought, pushing away from the rough stones and continuing her slow journey.

Reaching the wall of the first terrace, she shaded her eyes against the high white sky and looked out to a spectacular view. Fields, pastures and orchards patterned the plateau, breaking it up into geometric shapes of assorted sizes and colors. Between the cultivated areas, rows of trees served as windbreaks, their branches furred with the bright colors of new leaves budding. Beyond the rim of the plateau, rows of hills stretched toward the horizon, fading into blue-grey distance. Somewhere out there was Nandarri and the Port, her link to the Beldame and her family, but Aurial could not see either.

With a swirl of shrieks and giggles, a flock of drev children swarmed down the stairs to play on the terrace. Their shocks of white hair bobbed as they ran. Seeing a strange woman, they veered away to the far end, close to where two great winches were locked into place and barrels and boxes made good hiding places for their game.

Aurial was about to turn back toward the view when she saw a small party of servants approaching. In the forefront were two laborers, each carrying a bag of tools, and a woman in the dress of maid with a sack swinging from one hand. Two large men in plain drev uniforms followed them. The group went to the first winch. From its arm, an open platform swung over the dizzying drop on the other side of the wall. The laborers hefted their tools onto the platform, then vaulted the railing and landed on the planks with practiced ease. The maid thumped the sack down onto the boards between them and stepped back. Working methodically, the two uniformed men manned the winch, unlocked it and lowered the platform at a smooth steady pace. The maid leaned over the railing and watched until the passengers were safely down. Then she turned and came toward Aurial.

Aurial accepted her greeting with the impassive expression she had seen Raunn use and nodded permission to speak. "Greetings of the day, sri-nothi," the woman said. "My name is Maitris and I am the personal maid of the su-vellide Torrian. I have come at the bidding of her sister to see how you are feeling and whether you are in need of any assistance."

Suppressing a grimace, Aurial replied, "I want only a new set of muscles to replace the ones that were insulted by the climb last night. How is Raunn today? Is she feeling better?"

"She is much recovered but the infirmarer has given her a sleeping draft and ordered her to stay in her bed until tomorrow." Maitris cocked her head to one side pertly. "I can take you to her later if you would like. First, however, I can have the infirmarer give you a powder that will relieve the pain you feel." She smiled. "Many people suffer thus after their first time up the cliff. It is to be expected. Would you like to do that now?"

"Yes, I would. But . . ." Aurial's voice trailed off as she saw on the terrace above them the profile of the man who had taken charge of her the previous night. "Tell me, Maitris, who is that man?" she asked instead.

Maitris turned for a brief look. "That is Antikoby. He is Tuupit of the Rock." Her voice conveyed both respect and warmth.

Tuupit. The databead told her that he was the overseer and administrator of the citadel, foreman of all the servants. Although a drev, he was responsible for running the holding smoothly and profitably for its troinom owners. He was high among the underranks; not troinom, but not blue-dirt either. This fleeting snobbish thought told Aurial that she was fitting more into her role than she had planned; yet not so far that she could not see how handsome he was.

There was a scream from one of the children and an argument broke out among the others. Antikoby turned in their direction, alert to trouble. Aurial and Maitris also looked toward the cause of the tumult. The children were gathered by the winch that had lowered the laborers to the plateau. "He's frozen," one of them declared. "You dared him and now he's frozen."

"He didn't have to do it," another defended himself.

"Yes, he did. You dared him. It's your fault."

Their voices broke into flying allegations. "He's not even to midway."

"He's going to fall."

"No, he's not. He'll make it."

"You shouldn't have."

"It's not my fault!"

"You knew he was too little."

"Nobody ever falls."

"He's going to diiiieee!"

The last one was a wail of panic from the smallest child.

Antikoby braced himself with one hand and leaped the rail, landing on the lower terrace. He was running as soon as his feet touched the stone and it took him only seconds to reach the winch. "How far down is he?" the tuupit demanded.

"Halfway to the midway ledge and frozen," said the first boy. "He's not moving at all, just hanging on."

By now others were running toward the winch but Antikoby did not hesitate. Grasping the thick rope, he swung himself over and disappeared. Aurial stood still, feeling that unfamiliar tingle again.

Maitris attempted to reassure her. "It is nothing, sri-nothi, Antikoby will bring the child back."

Aurial affected a neutral tone of voice: troinom did not demonstrate concern over the fate of servants, not even children. "Does this happen often?"

"Often enough. The winch ropes come up the sheerest part of the cliff, as you can see. The midway ledge runs across the length of the cliff, there, but a notch cut into it allows the rope and the cargo to pass through. The older children dare one another to climb down the rope, swing across the gap to the ledge and then climb the trail up again."

"Is this allowed?" Aurial asked in a voice that did not reveal how appalled she was.

"No, sri-nothi," Maitris answered. "It is forbidden because it is so dangerous but they do it anyway. Sometimes, like now, a child looks down and freezes. You can see him there, past where the rock bumps out, just hanging on. It's a reaction to the fear of falling. He stops thinking and clings to the rope with desperate strength. Antikoby will talk to him until he can let go and then bring him up safely. The child will be punished later."

"Of course. How unusual." Aurial mouthed the vapid troinom words automatically but she actually found the scene fascinating. Children broke the rules on the Beldame, too, and sometimes had to be rescued from the consequences of their foolishness but it seemed far more mundane. Nothing she had seen on the Beldame was ever quite so thrilling.

Observers were lined up along the rail by the winches and Aurial wanted to join them but instead maintained her distance to demonstrate the reserve of her position. Besides, she could see well enough where she was. Antikoby slid down the rope smoothly and with as little effort as if he were in freefall. He reached the child and, as Maitris had predicted, began talking to him. She could tell by the cries of encouragement from the crowd that things were going well. Long moments passed while he attempted to penetrate the fugue of fear that possessed the boy. Finally he was able to reach down and grasp the child's arm. The boy transferred his death grip to Antikoby, who lifted him so that he could cling to the Tuupit's chest. The boy wrapped his arms around the man's neck and scissored thin legs around the tuupit's waist.

Then Antikoby began to climb, walking up the cliff while pulling hand-over-hand on the rope. He reached the top and his head rose above the railing. The boy's face appeared next, as white as his hair and his eyes were large with fear. Antikoby swung over the railing and then stood, simply holding the child and reassuring him until the boy relaxed his grip and slipped to his feet. He was taken in hand immediately by an old woman who visibly checked her urge to scold him and instead marched him through the crowd and off the terrace.

Aurial was entranced. The tuupit's mastery of the situation, his awesome strength in executing the rescue, his warmth in reassuring the child all combined to make a powerful impression on her. Silently she watched Antikoby move through from the admiring crowd. "You all have work to do," he murmured to them. "Be about it now. This was not an entertainment." He turned toward Aurial and for a second she caught his eye. Then he strode across the terrace and up the stairs.

"If you are ready, sri-nothi," Maitris said quietly, "we can proceed to the infirmarer's chambers."

"What? Oh, yes, of course," Aurial replied, aware that she sounded witless. Maitris led her up the stairs to the next terrace and then up more painful stairs until they reached the massive lower wall of the citadel. They walked slowly to accommodate Aurial's stiff muscles. Once inside, they threaded their way through rooms, down halls and around corners until Aurial was thoroughly lost. She felt as though she could wander for days through the labyrinthine structure without finding her way out again. Finally, in the far corner of the building, they reached rooms that smelled pungently of herbs.

The infirmarer was a man past the fullness of life. He was thin, with coarse wrinkled skin and long dark hair that was pulled back severely and tied at the nape of his neck. His demeanor was dour yet, when he looked at them, his eyes were deep and full of humor. Maitris described the problem to him and immediately he lifted a covered crock off a shelf that was crowded with similar vessels. He scooped a heaping spoonful of dark powder from the crock and dropped it into a mug. Lifting a kettle from where it steamed over a low fire, he poured the mug nearly full and stirred. From a decanter filled with thick green fluid he added a dollop to the mug. Then he stirred some more.

"Drink this, sri-nothi," he said finally, handing the mug to Aurial. "This will numb the pain in your muscles and speed them toward recovery."

*So would a hit of betacaine*, she thought, accepting the flagon gingerly. Aurial sniffed the steam rising from the liquid and was surprised to find the scent pleasant and familiar, if somewhat sharp. She sipped. It was hot but went down easily. She sipped again. "It's a mixture of herbs, sri-nothi," the man explained helpfully, as if she had requested a list of ingredients. "Each has its own healing properties and together they are quite powerful. The water is from the Heartspring, of course, and the pittari syrup is just for sweetening." He proceeded to list each of the herbs that had gone into the drink along with its restorative powers. When he finished, the mug was empty and Aurial felt warm and very relaxed. Her muscles had loosened their painful knots. In fact, they seemed barely able to hold her up. She put one hand to her head.

Immediately the infirmarer took her arm. "You are tired," he said. "The mixture often has that effect, sri-nothi. If you would like to rest, there is a couch in the next room."

With him on one side and Maitris on the other, she was steered toward a mattress covered with a soft blanket. Aurial collapsed onto it and was asleep before Maitris could remove her shoes.

## THE ROCK

Surrein staggered drunkenly into the room, slamming the door behind him. Inside, he fell to his knees, then slumped to one side on the floor. With an effort, he wrenched his body over until he was lying on his back, arms by his sides and legs out straight. Then his entire form began to vibrate. Surrein's face contorted into a mask that was a parody of its normal appearance, with jaws clenched and eyes bulging. His hands knotted into fists, his buttocks tightened and his heels drummed on the floor. The seizure, like a paroxysm of anger, went on for long silent moments.

Then, abruptly, the convulsion ceased, Surrein's legs fell awkwardly apart and his head rolled heavily to the right. Now the man seemed drained of life. His eyes closed. A trickle of saliva slid from one corner of his mouth and rolled down his cheek. He did not move, not even to blink, and his respiration was nearly imperceptible. To all appearances he was dead and the simulacrum of a corpse remained on the rug, immobile, for a long time. Not so much as a finger twitched.

Finally his torso jerked in a brief spasm that rippled outward into his limbs until it ended in the tips of his fingers and toes. It was almost as if, having been drained of life, his body's reflexes now responded to vitality returning. Electrical impulses raced along the neurons and jumped the synapses, causing the empty host to twitch in reaction. Surrein drew in a long, irregular breath and opened his eyes.

He knew immediately that it had been bad. He always felt odd after an attack—lightheaded, dizzy, as if his body did not quite fit. This time was worse. Spots of light danced in front of his eyes. His throat and tongue were dry. His stomach felt as if it had turned inside out. All these symptoms meant that he had been away for a long time.

Surrein hated the possessions for what they did to him, for the way they made him feel. Always it took time before he could once more fit inside the skin, stiffen the bones and command the muscles. Most especially he resented the loss of control the seizures imposed upon him. Thus when Surrein felt the onset of an attack, he sought solitude so there were no witnesses to observe his weakness and he never knew, upon awakening, where he was or what he had done.

Moving stiffly, he propped himself up on one elbow. A wave of dizziness surged through him and he waited for the vertigo to pass. Surrein lived with anger; it was always present in him at varying levels. To a large degree, anger drove him, motivated him, made him what he was. Anger was his friend, his constant and closest companion. He cherished it and nurtured it but he kept it carefully under control for this one reason. When it swelled into fury and rage, he knew that it would possess him in an inevitable progression that he dreaded.

When fury took him, it drove out everything else; drove his very consciousness from his body. Where he went during these possessions he did not know, but it was a terrible place, filled with nightmare visions of monstrous faces, and ominous landscapes swept by cold wind. In this hideous dream country, he was always small and weak, at the mercy of huge figures that loomed up out of nothing and menaced him with leering mouths and swollen, grasping hands. There, his lack of control was complete, he was at the mercy of the monsters and he shivered in the cold without hope.

Yet, even as he struggled to put the images of the nightmare country out of his mind, Surrein knew that the period of possession was necessary: it cleansed him and restored his dominion over himself. While the fury built, it drove him to do foolish things, such as striking the tuupit in front of Torrian, that jeopardized what he had been directed to accomplish. Now he could be cool and clear-headed once again, able to deal competently with the challenges before him.

Surrein pushed himself up against another wave of dizziness, so that he was seated with his knees raised. He rested his head on his knees until the lightheadedness receded, then looked around to see where his flight for solitude had taken him. He was in the Clan Chapel. The room was empty and appeared to have been so for some time. He breathed a cynical prayer of thanks for the good fortune that had brought him to this place where the seizure would be unobserved. The chapel would also answer another of his needs: he had a consuming thirst and there was always water on the nayya's table. Fortunately, he had fallen on the strip of rug between the first row of chairs and the table so he did not have to move far to assuage his thirst.

Using a chair for support, he pulled himself up, paused while the room whirled and steadied, then lurched over to the table. It was a solid piece and did not move when he virtually fell against it. After another moment he was able to let go of the table's edge and reach for the pitcher of water. The ritual cups were at the other side of the room so he ignored them and simply drank from the ewer. The first draught was a relief as it washed away the unbearable dryness in his mouth and throat. Drinking again, more slowly, Surrein could taste the water's slight mineral tang and feel the tingle of its effervescence on his tongue. *How appropriate,* he thought, *that the water which revives me is from the heartspring of my quarry.*

After a third drink, he put the pitcher down and turned to the row of chairs. He slumped into one and flexed his limbs until they responded properly. Restored, although still weak, he looked around at the chapel once more. What he saw twisted a smile onto his lips. The nayya's table glittered with the finest ritual implements: the bowl, the burner, the pitcher and the bookstand were all wrought

of silver inlaid with syddian. From the tooled leather
covers of the chanting books to the polished lamps on the
walls, the chapel sang of prosperity. In every aspect, it
was a display of pious wealth that nearly took his breath
away.

Surrein thought of the chapel in his own clan holding on
the bleak fells to the west. The Kohrable, an ancient scroll
attached to wooden rods, had never been replaced with a
handsome new book bound between ornamented covers
like the one that lay before him. The other implements on
the nayya's table at home were hand-wrought but of simple materials and mismatched design. He considered the
fine kristopresh ritual cups glowing on their tray and could
feel in his fingers the battered metal cups used in the
chapel at Fellsdown. And the water . . .

The heartspring at Fellsdown had begun to falter when
Surrein reached his maturity. It was no longer clear and
plentiful like the water he had just drunk. Now it was slow
and unpredictable; its output brackish and its purity questionable. The Cannestur family had kept the secret of the
spring's depletion so far but the lie could not be continued
indefinitely. It was only a matter of time until the
heartspring of Clan Fellskeeper failed and then the Clan,
lacking the supply of uncontaminated water that flowed at
the core of every clan, would break up. Without a Clan
Fellskeeper, Surrein would lack a holding and be without
position. As a "poor relation" he would have no place in
the society of Nandarri and no claim to marry into an
established clan. Even worse would be the eyes of his
friends and associates as those who had previously welcomed him now found no place for a Cannestur in their
circle of "acceptable" people. *I might as well be bluedirt*,
he thought with bitterness.

In the core of his being, Surrein knew that the situation
was his fault and that knowledge goaded his ambitions.
Sometimes, when he was emerging from the nightmare
country of the seizures, he saw his uncle's body plummet,
heard his final scream. Sometimes. But not this time.
Surrein put that image firmly out of his mind. The
heartspring was drying up and with it would go the Clan's

grace and the blessings of the Chenni-ad. He had to protect himself against that eventuality—make a place for himself that did not depend on an uncontrollable trickle of water. Then, when the inevitable happened, he would be secure elsewhere and untouchable.

When Verrer had approached him with his offer hidden beneath a smooth smile and easy manner it had taken all Surrein's self control to prevent his face from reflecting the elation he felt. He had accepted that offer, worked very hard and been clever. Now the reward was here, virtually in his grasp. He gazed once again at the chapel's fittings, appreciating the richness of colors and textures, savoring the opulence. This was what he strove for. Once he and Torrian were wed, all this would belong to him.

Surrein was not stupid: he knew that Verrer would continue to direct his actions and use him as a political pawn. He had no objections. Let Verrer concern himself with such things. While the Tulkan's Chief of Council was consolidating his own power and wealth, Surrein would be enjoying himself. Here on the Rock and in the family's superb house on Cheffra Street, he would be able to indulge his tastes freely. The Tulkan would be no hindrance, not with Verrer to persuade him otherwise. And Torrian, reluctant as she might be now, would return from the bonding period trained to his will. He would enjoy both the training and the delights that would follow.

Surrounded by the sight and scent of the faith that suffused every aspect of life on Chennidur, Surrein considered how little he cared for either religion or politics. He was quite skilled, however, at wearing the mask that granted him social acceptance in both areas. He could pretend to hold a particular point of view and even debate it heatedly. Proficient at all the rituals, he could execute them flawlessly without the obligations of commitment and morality that were attached. As long as everyone saw the mask and believed that it was the man, he was free to pursue his own desires and do whatever he liked. He was aloof from everyone else, superior, completely in control.

His hand caressed the carved and polished arm of the chair. In a few moments he would go back out into the house's stone halls. Right now, though, he was feeling particularly lucid and he would take advantage of that understanding to make the decisions that had seemed so difficult before. To stay or to go—those were his choices. If he stayed, he could not influence Torrian without violating *shufri-nagai*, which would cause the mask to slip. He could attempt to build an alliance with the younger sister, Raunn, but that seemed a profitless occupation. It did not matter whether Raunn, who was by all reports irresponsible, liked him or shared Torrian's newfound distaste. She could not be used to reach her sister on his behalf and had no influence with the Tulkan. The other woman, Aurial, was not part of the game at all.

If he returned to Nandarri, on the other hand, he could consolidate his position with Verrer and the Tulkan. In Torrian's absence, someone had to arrange the details of the wedding and doing so would create the mask of the dutiful new son. At the same time, he could make sure that all such details suited him. Then there was the pressing need to engage a location for the bonding vigil that was appropriate for what he had in mind.

Most important of all was the psychological contest. While he remained on the Rock, he would be the insistent swain from whose embrace the clan daughter ran away. Absent, he became the betrothed who awaited his bride eagerly and counted the days until the beginning of the wedding season.

Surrein weighed both sides and found the return to Nandarri more important by far. Yes, the seizures were unpleasant but they did have their uses. He rose from the chair and turned toward the chapel door. It was time to go.

## BIG GREEN

The inhabitants of the metal cylinders slumbered on in their chemical prison. They never saw the rough orbital sorting station loom out of the blackness nor felt the freighter dock. They had no knowledge of the robot arms that detached the mechanisms of the cylinders and removed them from their mechanical berths. There was no sense of loss when all but ten of the cylinders were reloaded onto a larger transport that soon decoupled and warped away on a separate journey. Nor did the remaining ten suffer pangs of fear when they were taken to a second transport and placed among the hundreds of cylinders already in place.

Their dreamless slumber continued after the sorting station vanished behind them and their ship sped toward a destination beyond anything they could have visualized in their nightmares. This trip, like the first half of the journey, was long and uneventful. Although labor transports were fast, the distances they covered were great. Time could be tamed but not conquered.

The chemicals dripping into the veins of the human cargo were nearly gone when the ship dropped back into realspace near the system of a fat yellow sun. Two planets circled this star, each nearly the same size but of different colors. The outer planet was brown and arid, the patterns of its continents plain to the naked eye, even from such a distance. The second world was obscured by swirling cloud patterns that allowed few glimpses of its surface. It was above the equator of this world that the freighter locked into a parking orbit.

After a while, shuttles rose from beneath the clouds like fish leaping from a silvery sea. They circled the freighter then docked long enough to load before seeking the safety of the cloudy ocean once more.

On the surface of a planet once again, the cylinders were taken to a decanting room by robot attendants. There, a mechanical doctor monitored the life signs of the occupants, administering medical attention when it was required. Its primary task, however, was to wake up each sleeping figure with an injection of another chemical, crudely nicknamed Jolt, which stimulated the metabolisms of the cargo and brought them back to a conscious state. It also jolted their brains, which had healed slowly during the long voyage, and returned them to a state close to functional. This particular robot medic dispensed a dose that was stronger than usual under the direct programming of the labor supervisor, who was tired of attempting to get good work out of hulks he considered brainless zombies. In a few cases, the extra dosage proved too great a stimulant and the prisoners made an abrupt transition from near-death to the real thing. Those bodies were placed in stasis for use as organ banks.

Astin, Merradrix and the shaman all survived resuscitation. When Astin awoke and saw that he was still encased in the coldsleep capsule, a look of horror swept over his face. Moving as quickly as he could, which seemed to him as slow as a death catcher, he pulled himself up and out of the container that he equated with pain and fear. Around him, people of all sizes, shapes and colors were doing the same. A prisoner from a world which buried its dead would have thought that it looked like a breakout in a graveyard.

Although there were great differences in appearance among the prisoners, all were naked, all were hairless and all wore the confused look that had brought the archaic word zombie to the labor supervisor's mind. They were also larger and stronger than when they had entered the cylinders. The labor contractor's art had been refined over time and through experience. During the long journey, muscles would atrophy, causing workers to be weak and useless, unless they were exercised electrically. When done properly, this conditioning could actually go beyond maintaining a body's existing state and improve upon it. Thus the bodies that stood on the floor of the decanting room were as unfamiliar to their owners as the faces around them.

Moving stiffly, with jerky steps they pulled themselves away from the cylinders and staggered toward the end of the room. The robots did not aid them in this process but the laborers did not need assistance: their sole goal was to escape from the vicinity of the capsules. Along with the others, Astin pointed himself at the door and the light which glowed beyond it. He walked, each stride smoother, more controlled than the one before it, straight at that door, knowing that he would be himself again, whole and strong, once he was on the other side.

The first of the laborers pushed his way through and light streamed over the ones who followed, bringing with it a strange and powerful smell. It was rich and full, a mingling of scents more than a single aroma. It was the odor of growth, the exhalation of lush vegetation, the tang of life in abundance. He sniffed the intriguing scent eagerly, seeking to fill his lungs with it as if it were an elixir that brought the new life he sought.

In the next room were the screws. Astin did not know yet that they were guards like the ones in the stone room. He could see that they were all big, regardless of sex, powerful and hard. Each carried a weapon and seemed familiar with its use. Instinctively, he tried to avoid them but they would not be evaded. They waded in to the flood of laborers and began separating them, herding the columns of prisoners like frightened animals, toward more doors that lined one wall of the room. Astin ducked around the huge arms and thick, callused hands in an attempt to get to one of the doors without being prodded. In this room, the smell was more intense. Now and again he felt odd blasts of heat that began and ended abruptly. He did not like this and became apprehensive that something evil, something deadly, was in the room with him.

He knew that he had to get out, but the next time a burst of heat caught him, he stopped, frightened. Surrounded as he was by naked bodies all surging and pushing in their own attempts to get away from the screws, standing still was impossible. The crowd pulled him closer and closer to one of the doors. Finally a big hand landed on his back, shoved, and propelled him through.

The heat waited for him on the other side. The force of it was like a blow that would have pushed him backwards except for the inexorable forward motion of the bodies around him. Astin was propelled toward a table where other screws waited behind stacks of folded clothing. One of them thrust a bundle of red cloth at him and he clutched it to his chest reflexively. On the far side of the table, another group of the guards acted as a barricade, bringing the crowd to a standstill. One of them barked out harsh orders in a language he did not recognize but understood nonetheless. "Put the clothes on!" the man commanded.

Astin followed this order with alacrity, eager to cover his nakedness. He donned a brief loincloth first and then stepped into a one-piece garment that was too big for him. It covered him from neck to wrists and ankles and was far too much to wear in the heat. Fastening it was like sealing himself inside an oven but when he tried to loosen it, the screw raised one hand menacingly. Astin noticed that the guard wore much the same kind of clothing but in white.

Once the jumpsuit was on, he was pushed onto a kind of platform that blinked once. Within seconds high boots were thrust at him with socks rolled inside. It was torture to encase his feet in cloth and leather but the screws were not to be denied and, since they also wore the boots, Astin did not even try to argue. He was sweating before he was fully dressed. Once the boots were fastened, however, the screws ceased to bother him and went among the crowd forcing others to get dressed.

Astin, frightened and confused, looked around to see the prisoners all crowded beneath the peaked roof of a large structure that resembled an enormous tent. Except for a roof, the structure was open to the air, to brilliant sunlight and to a wall of vivid, incredible green. The smell of growth and life was overpowering. Astin no longer had to seek to fill his lungs with it; the scent penetrated the cells of his skin. It was invasive. It was inescapable. It was the smell of Big Green.

When all the prisoners were dressed in their red uniforms, a man mounted one of the tables and called for their attention. An immediate hush spread over the crowd. "Pull your brains together and listen here!" the guard shouted. "I'm Kappin Trenk and I'm going to tell you how to survive on this mungering furnace but I'm only going to say it once. I know some of you are just meat and haven't got enough brains left to understand what I'm saying but that's your problem. No one here is going to watch out for you. If you want to live, use whatever brains you have left and pay attention now."

He swept his arm around to indicate the wall of green outside the tent. "Out there is Big Green," he continued. "The techies call it BG-x3 but they've never been here. It's *dumaass*, jungle, and it goes all around the equator, which is as far as any of you is going to see. The jungle is all green or brown: there are no other colors. None. That's why we wear these uniforms. If you see white, that's one of us and you follow the screw's orders as fast as you can. If you see red, that's one of you; just keep working.

"These uniforms aren't comfortable. They're heavy and hot and you sweat so bad you want to rip them off. Scog it, we wouldn't wear them if we didn't have to. But we do and so do you. These suits are the only thing between your body and the *dumaass*. Lots of things live in the jungle and they're all hostile. Most of them would like to have some part of you for dinner. They'll crawl onto you and attach themselves to your skin any way they can. So you wear the reds and keep them fastened tight around wrists, neck and ankles. When you go out to work in the bush, you'll be issued a hat with a net that ties around your neck. It keeps the rain off and the creepies away. Wear it all the time. Get sloppy once and you're dead. The *dumaass* won't give you another chance."

He paused for a minute and looked around at the faces turned up to him. "There's more. Every day you'll get a blue pill with your rations. Take it. The chemicals in the pill replace what you'll sweat out when you're working. Two days without a pill and you'll keel over." The kappin put his hands on his hips. Astin could see sweat running down his face to join the dark circle at the neck of his whites. "It's steamy and dirty and awful out there. When you're in the bush, you'll work harder than you ever believed possible, I don't care where you come from. Some of you, the ones who can think, might get the sheffin idea that it's easier not to take the pill and just let the jungle have you. Well, forget about it. Miss your pill once and we'll jam it down your throat. Miss it a second time and we'll make you wish the jungle *had* gotten you.

"At the start of each day, you'll be issued tools to work with—axes, saws and chettys. They're all sharp but don't get any ideas about using them on the screws. All the guards carry these," he held up a rod about the length of Astin's forearm. "It's called a diz and it can give you a shock or short out your whole body. Either way it hurts a lot and you'll be out of action, maybe for good. It doesn't have to touch you to knock you down. Just in case you don't believe me, watch this." He gestured and one of the screws pulled a prisoner out of the crowd. Before the man could protest, the kappin pointed the diz at his chest. Immediately the man snapped backwards and dropped to the ground where he twitched spastically, his eyes bulging and mouth gaping. The kappin looked at them impassively. "That's it. Remember what I just told you, obey the screws and work as hard as you can and you'll do alright. You're never going to see your homeworld again so the faster you get used to this place, the better off you'll be. Now Zarjint Ota here is going to give you your orders. Whatever she says, whatever *any* one of us says, you *do* it. If you had gods before, forget them. *We*, the screws, are your gods now."

A woman his height and almost the same mass jumped up onto the table next to him. "We're going to hand out food," she said in a voice that would shrivel trees. "You don't feel like eating any of it because your stomachs have forgotten what they're for. But that don't matter 'cause you need food. You need it bad and if you don't get it, you'll die. Now, Big Green takes some gettin' used to so the idea of dyin' may not be so bad right now. But some important people spent a lot of money to get you here and now that you're here, they want you to work, not curl up and croak. So you eat. You eat *everything*. And the first rawfin worker who barfs gets to eat that too. You understand?" There was a low murmur among the prisoners around Astin. "Good," she continued. "The food is behind you, get to it."

Astin turned and was inching his way toward the tables when he saw, off to his right, a familiar face, one that was lined with pain but awake and aware. It was Eleven! Astin shoved his way through the mob of strangers toward the man he had nursed, hoping for a friendly look, some sign of recognition. At the sight of Astin, the man's guarded expression opened up slightly, as though it were a locked door breaching just enough to admit one person. Astin's heart leaped as he saw recognition in Eleven's face. Eleven knew him, seemed glad to see him, and that was the finest thing Astin could conceive of. Its importance was all out of proportion to the length and depth of the friendship. But having a friend, even one known briefly, was infinitely better than being alone among strangers on a world that was a nightmare.

The sudden thought of his home bent Astin over double, like a blow. A beating would have been easier to accept than the fact that he would never again see his parents, his sister, the hills around his home. Astin wrapped his arms around his middle as if to contain the pain and moaned.

Eleven's arm came around his shoulder and pulled him up. "Don't think about it," Eleven said. "Don't think about anything. Just do what they tell you."

Astin looked at him, amazed. Eleven was no longer the sick and disoriented prisoner he remembered. Instead Eleven was a man, older than he and bigger, with intelligent eyes and determination stamped on his face. "What?" he asked.

Eleven looked him full in the eyes and his gaze was as cold as the air around them was hot. "Those screws, they're the troinom here, boy," he answered. "Bad ones. Worst you've ever seen. And the troinom say, 'Eat.' Let's eat. You understand? Don't think about anything else."

The roles had been reversed: now Eleven was taking care of him. This did not upset Astin, in fact he welcomed it. He followed Eleven to the table and together they took up their food. Then they went of to one side to eat. "Take small bites," Eleven admonished him. "It's easier that way." Astin followed his advice but the first bite was the hardest. He choked on it and had to fight to keep from vomiting. The next bite was nearly as bad but he got that one down too. By the fourth or fifth, chewing and swallowing became easier, more mechanical. Their plates were clean before it seemed possible. Wiping his mouth with the back of one hand, Eleven looked at Astin. "You helped me, boy," he said. "I was hurt bad and you kept me together, kept me from dying. Some things I can't remember but that I won't forget. You stick by me here and I'll take care of you now."

Astin nodded. "Thanks. I'm going to need help. In that room, you were the eleventh prisoner brought in so I called you Eleven. What's your name?"

The man smiled. "My name is Merradrix," he said. "Blue dirt, from a farm south of Nandarri, and proud of it." Then he looked out at the green wall. "But whatever color the dirt is here, doesn't matter. It's just us and the screws—and the jungle. We're going to have to work hard to stay alive."

Zarjint Ota called out a command and they stood. The time for talking was over. Now it was time to meet the jungle of Big Green and engage the battle for survival.

# CHAPTER 13

## THE ROCK

Awareness returned to Aurial before she was willing to accept it. Lying still felt so good that she was reluctant even to raise an eyelid. So she didn't. Instead she inhaled the fragrance of the infirmary's herb-scented air, luxuriated in the soft warmth of the blanket covering her, listened to the drone of voices conversing in the next room. At first the voices were simply an indistinct rumble that rose and fell beyond the shell of her drowsiness but, as she wakened further, they gradually took on the shape of a dialogue. Without realizing that she was doing so, Aurial began to listen. The infirmarer's low voice said, "Do you really think Suv Torrian is keeping vigil out of devotion to the Word?"

"Who knows why troi'm do what they do," came the reply in the higher tones of the maid.

"It's just that now is the time she's supposed to be entertaining her intended, getting ready for wedding season, finding a place for the bonding period and other such concerns, not hiding inside the Rock all by herself."

"There are many ways of getting ready," replied Maitris,

with a depth of meaning in her voice. "And a woman may be concerned with things other than entertaining her intended."

The man tapped a spoon against a crock and there came the clink of the lid slipping into place. "That's for sure," the infirmarer agreed. "And from what I've heard of him, no amount of getting ready may be enough."

"And what is that gossip you've heard?" queried the woman lightly.

"All servants talk," he said bluntly. "His don't say much but their faces tell you more than an hour's worth of idle talk over a mug of beer. Besides, Vel Rutin's maids know the family and what they have to say is not good. No, not good at all."

Maitris snorted. "Well, you won't hear anything from me, for all that you ply me with your special herb tea and my favorite sweet buns. I know how to keep the suv's secrets for both of us. Well, alright, just a little more. And one last bun."

There was the sound of liquid pouring, then the infirmarer said, "Only one thing puzzles me. That's how the tanzl could have approved this match. He must know what the man is. And suv Torrian's his own daughter, his favorite, who always behaved just right and proper. If it was Raunn, now, you might say he'd done it to teach her a lesson the hard way. But Torrian—that just doesn't figure."

"Best watch your tongue, man," Maitris said firmly. "Questioning the tanzl won't make you popular with any of the marked ones. I won't say anything outside this room but don't go repeating talk like that to anyone else."

The infirmarer laughed. "They never pay attention to the gossip of servants and you know it. You just don't want to answer the question."

There was a moment of silence while they drank their tea. Aurial thought of the medicine she had swallowed and immediately a belch pushed its way up her esophagus. She tried to stifle it but only transformed it into a hiccup. The first hiccup gave way quickly to a second and then a third. She took deep, even breaths but could not control her diaphragm's spasms and soon the hiccups expanded into a noisy outburst. The door opened and both Maitris and the infirmarer entered. "I thought," he said, "that it was about time you woke up. Are you feeling better, sri-nothi?" he asked smoothly.

Aurial propped herself up and assessed the state of her body. It did feel less sore, and certainly more rested. Her muscles were also looser. It was still a long way from normal or even comfortable but she reassured the infirmarer that she did feel improved.

"That is good," Maitris offered. "The sri-nothi Raunn has asked that you attend upon her in her chambers as soon as possible. Will that be acceptable?"

"Perfectly," Aurial said as she rose. "Let us proceed there immediately."

The infirmarer stood aside for them to pass and then moved quickly to open the door to the hall. "I shall bring another draft to your chambers after last meal," he said. "It will help you sleep this evening and you will feel even better in the morning."

Aurial nodded her thanks and swept out of his rooms. She thought how different the servants' voices sounded when they were speaking together, with no troinom present. The conversation she had overheard was the real thing, equal speaking to equal. When they talked to or in the presence of a troinom, it was as though they became puppets. Their faces were empty of true emotion, their voices without sentiment. They were always guarded against displaying any thought or feeling that might not be acceptable to the troinom masters. Aurial wondered if those masters knew how they were patronized by their servants. Or knew what talk went on in their absence. Perhaps they did not care.

The walk to Raunn's apartments was longer than Aurial expected and she recognized none of the halls and chambers they passed through on the way. The size of this structure was daunting and finding one's way was made more difficult by the fact that there seemed to be no logical plan to its design. Aurial had the impression that rooms, apartments, whole wings had been added on haphazardly over centuries and that living in it was the only way to learn how to get around. The immensely complex Beldame seemed simple and well-organized by comparison.

Eventually they arrived and found Raunn awaiting them in a nest of pillows and quilts. A gleaming tray, holding a pitcher and a glass, rested on the covers next to her. A thick old book was splayed open beyond them. To Aurial's eyes she looked better: her skin was no longer waxen and the dark circles under her eyes were diminished. She greeted Aurial with a smile and waved her to a chair by the bed. "We are both of us more than a bit worn by the journey," she said. "Maitris tells me the infirmarer has dosed you with one of his potions, which must have made him very happy, and that you are feeling better. A few days of rest and several more draughts of his elixir and you'll forget you ever climbed up here."

"I don't think I'd go that far, but his medicine certainly did help," Aurial commented.

"He dosed me, too," Raunn went on, "and the nayya spent most of the morning praying over me and purifying me with draughts of water from the Heartspring. That means I'm cured in body and spirit but the two of them conspired to keep me in this bed until tomorrow, so here I stay. Unfortunately, there's too much going on here for me to languish as a proper troinom lady should." She turned her attention to Maitris, who was hovering by the bed. "Fetch the tuupit Antikoby," she ordered. "I must speak with him as well."

Maitris left swiftly and Raunn waited for the door to close before she asked, "What have you heard in your wandering about the place? Anything that sounds strange?"

Aurial shook her head. "I'm not sure what 'strange' means," she said. At the same time, she wondered exactly what was going on. Ruann was not usually this chatty, even when she was relaxed, and although she was wrapped in comfort she looked and sounded distinctly nervous. *Perhaps*, Aurial thought, *it has to do with the mysterious "he" that the infirmarer mentioned.* Whatever the cause was, she would have to find out and then make it work in favor of her job here. It was time to listen carefully and make a full report tonight.

"No," Ruann replied. "How would you? Just tell me what you've seen and heard so far today and then I'll fill you in on what I've learned. I need to sort through what's going on and then come up with some way of fixing it."

The best way into the situation was straight on, so Aurial told her what had transpired on the terrace and then communicated the gist of the conversation in the infirmary, as objectively as she could. When she was finished, Raunn shook her head. "Not much there, but it does confirm what I've heard. Antikoby should be able to fill in the rest, if my suspicions are correct."

"What is going on?" Aurial asked. "Where is your sister and who is *he*?"

Raunn resettled herself among the pillows and straightened the covers. The pitcher tottered and then righted itself. *This is going to be a long story*, Aurial thought. "I went to Nandarri," Raunn began, "because word had arrived that Torrian was unwell and needed help. It was my turn to be dutiful clan-daughter: I'd evaded it long enough. So Chewtti packed my trunks and off we all went to the city. It was quite exciting, actually: I was being treated as an adult for the first time. Nandarri is always interesting and, for a change, I was going to be in charge of Torrian.

"Once we arrived at the house on Cheffra Street, I found that things were not quite as I had believed them to be. Torrian was not ill, she was flying on the stardust and so badly in its hold that having her stay in Nandarri was out of the question. My father, the tansul, who should by rights have sent her home long ago, was deeply involved in political concerns and barely noticed what was happening. In fact, he seemed not to be aware that Torrian was anything but ill and even when I told him about the problem, he would not deal with it. Instead he instructed me to do what I thought necessary and went back to the Council chamber.

"His reaction was strange but I didn't have much time to worry about it. I thought he was just unable to admit that his cherished older daughter had violated *shufri-nagai* and polluted her own body. I was shocked myself. That kind of behavior, as you may have guessed, was out of character for her. For once the goody-goody slipped up and did something she wasn't supposed to. If it hadn't been such a serious mistake, I might have actually enjoyed it.

"I did what needed to be done and made all the arrangements to send Torrian back here. The only thing I did not do was tell the truth in the mirror-relay message I sent to the Rock. I was afraid someone would intercept it and, even though it was in code, I didn't want to risk anyone else finding out about her addiction. I guess I was squeamish about that, too. I didn't know that it was common information among her friends." Raunn stopped, poured water from the pitcher into the glass and drank. Aurial kept silent and Raunn continued her monologue.

"But something else had happened in Nandarri before I arrived, something that should have been public knowledge but somehow was not. Something that should have been a cause for joy and celebration but that was not even acknowledged. Something that should have been communicated to the vellide, my mother, immediately, but had been kept from her instead. That little something was my sister's betrothal." Raunn stopped speaking again and her gaze slipped past Aurial's shoulder to stare at empty air.

"Torrian's betrothal?" Aurial asked, startled. More questions tumbled out of her. "You mean, she was engaged to marry someone while she was addicted to the dust? Who? Did he know about the dust? What happened when she came here? I'm astonished."

Raunn brought her gaze back to Aurial. "*You're* astonished," she exclaimed. "You can imagine how I felt when I was told. What made it worse is that *he* is the one who told me. Not my father. Not even Torrian—so far as she could talk about anything by then. Not even Maitris, who might ordinarily have dropped a word or two. They both wanted to avoid the whole thing, so they did. I was arranging Torrian's journey home when he—Surrein ni Varskal san Cannestur by name and family—arrived one evening and requested a few moments with me. I didn't know who he was. I mean, I had never met him even socially. He is of the Fellskeeper Clan and their citadel is far from Nandarri.

"I invited him in, of course, and he made himself comfortable immediately, as if he had been in the house often before. He had done exactly that, but I had no way of knowing and thought his familiarity offputting. Surrein was quite charming in a practiced, somewhat superficial way. I did not like it much but I thought that, perhaps, such manners were the fashion in Nandarri. Or maybe it was the effect of the outworlders. Having little experience either with the city or with young men, I tried not to be judgmental. Then he told me that he knew Torrian was returning to the Rock. I was taken aback: only members of the house knew that and the servants had been ordered not to speak of it.

"What he said next was even more astonishing. He wanted to accompany her. As her betrothed, he said, it was his right. His *right*, mind you. For a moment, I was speechless as I tried to understand what this stranger was saying. It was obvious that he must be lying. Had he been speaking the truth, I would have heard of it long before. My father was away that evening and, since I could not consult with him, I did the only thing possible. I dismissed Surrein and his petition both. I was also rude to him when I sent him away. The next day, Torrian set off on her journey to the Rock. Alone."

"That seems pretty straightforward," Aurial said. "There are worse things than being rude, especially when the other person is arrogant and lying besides."

"The problem is," Ruann replied, "that he wasn't lying. When my father returned, I confronted him. He was evasive, not at all his usual self, but when I insisted, he admitted that the betrothal had taken place. Not in public, with both families all around and feasting afterwards but slyly, with just the few people absolutely necessary—and Verrer. When I heard that *he* was there, my heart dropped."

"He is your father's cousin," Aurial commented evenly. "It would seem normal for him to be present at such an occasion."

"Verrer may be my father's cousin," Ruann countered, "but he is the enemy of the family and the Clan. He serves the Tulkan."

"Yes, I know," Aurial stated, "he is Chief of Council. Because your father fights the Tulkan's policies, does that mean he cannot invite his relative to a betrothal?"

Raunn's voice grew bitter. "My father is a good man. He is clean and noble and a strong Follower. But he lives in a world of his own making. He knows how things should be and, if they are not so, he convinces himself that they are. He simply sees what he prefers to see and turns a blind eye to what really is. He thinks that my mother is grieving and cannot admit that she is lost in her grief, perhaps beyond recovery. He thinks my brothers died in accidents and refuses to acknowledge that accidents can be arranged. He thought that Torrian was ill because he could not accept the alternative. What he thinks about my disappearance from Nandarri, I do not know.

"He fights the Tulkan's policies with determination but cannot admit to himself what Verrer's place is in the government. That made Verrer a willing weapon in the Tulkan's hands, a man who would turn against a cousin who would defend him until the Great Wheel fell and sliced Chennidur in two. Whatever he proposed to my father about this betrothal, it is false. And now I believe that it is dangerous as well."

"Why?" Aurial asked. "If Torrian is safe here, surely we can protect her. The Rock can be held against any attacker: you said so yourself."

Raunn gave her a hard look. "I was thinking of attacks from without. Torrian is here, but she is not safe. Her betrothed, Surrein of the slippery charm and dangerous smile, is here as well. The adversary is within."

"He came while we were in the Perimeter?"

"No. He came with her. Surrein and his party must have intercepted Torrian's outside of Nandarri and he accompanied her to the Rock. The guards would have defended her to the death against an enemy. They had no defenses against a lover. He has been here ever since."

Aurial was silent for a moment, thinking over this information. "What does he look like?" she queried, wondering if he had been among those on the terrace in the morning.

"You've seen him already," Raunn replied. "He's the man who came to my assistance last night when we reached the first terrace."

Thinking hard, Aurial tried to pull the man's image from her memory but exhaustion had kept her from any kind of clear observation at the moment. She shook her head. "I don't remember. By the time we reached the top, I could barely keep my eyes open, much less notice anyone in particular."

"I understand completely," Raunn replied. "But don't worry, you'll have plenty of other chances to watch him. Like at last meal tonight and evening Call to Prayer. I'm sure he will take the opportunity to escort the vellide to the temple—doing his duty in the absence of her husband and sons. It will solidify his position with the family. Just watch out for him."

Aurial nodded. "There's something going on here, that's for sure and it sounds like he's in the middle of it. I'll keep my eyes and ears open and let you know what comes up. But you still haven't told me where Torrian is."

Before Raunn could respond, the door opened and the tuupit Antikoby entered. He approached the bed and stood quietly at its foot as he waited to be addressed. Aurial took the opportunity to study this man whom she found attractive and disturbing. The tuupit of fortress Cliffmaster was tall and held himself straight with a proud posture. His large frame was filled out with the kind of muscle that Aurial had only begun to recognize and appreciate. His hair was dark, nearly black, and it capped a face marked with the kind of lines that come from responsibility and concern. His eyes conveyed a quick intelligence and his mouth was strong. Aurial sensed depths in him that Raunn and the other troinom barely guessed at and might not be capable of perceiving in any drev, regardless of position.

Raunn addressed him directly. "Antikoby, the sri-nothi Aurial was just asking where the su-vellide Torrian is. Tell her."

Antikoby turned his penetrating eyes on Aurial and replied in an even voice, "The su-vellide Torrian is secluded in the cavern of the Heartspring, observing a vigil in preparation for her marriage." His voice was deep and rich. Aurial felt the little tingle again.

"That seems odd, does it not?" Raunn commented to Aurial. "I would have expected her to be directing an army of seamstresses, bakers, maids and other servants in the preparations for the wedding." She turned her attention back to the tuupit. "Where will the married couple live during the bonding period?"

"I do not know, sri-nothi," Antikoby replied. "It has not been decided."

"Just as what day of the wedding season they will be married on has not yet been decided. Is that correct?"

"Yes, sri-nothi. It is so." Antikoby's gaze was steady but reserved. He was not hiding anything, but neither was he offering it. Aurial decided that he was feeling Raunn out before committing himself.

Raunn did not make him wait long. "Stop being the perfect tuupit and tell me what is going on here, Antikoby. My mother is not—dependable—my sister is in seclusion and my father is in Nandarri. I need to know what has been going on here in my absence and the only person who can tell me is you."

The tuupit regarded his mistress with that steady gaze for what seemed like minutes and then turned it on Aurial. Raunn replied to his unspoken comment. "The sri-nothi Aurial can be trusted. Now speak."

He did. He began with the arrival of Torrian and Surrein and related events as they had transpired, without embroidery or judgment. The story was appalling. It confirmed everything that Raunn had told her but added whole layers of complexity to the relationship between Surrein and Torrian. Antikoby himself had behaved, as far as Aurial could tell, in exemplary fashion. He had done what needed to be done and made the best of what must have been a very difficult time. Yet she detected an occasional hesitancy in his narrative that led her to wonder if he was hiding something. She set that aside and focused on the main issue which, at this point, seemed to be what to do with Surrein.

"So," Raunn summarized when he had finished, "Surrein is still here and my sister is hiding from him. He might have left as you anticipated but then we showed up quite unexpectedly, providing him with another audience to charm and bully. Well, he won't find me as gullible as my sister." Her voice was hard and angry.

"Be careful, Raunn," Aurial warned. "He sounds unstable. That makes him unpredictable and he may be truly dangerous. But he's betrothed to your sister for a reason. He's here for a reason. We have to find out what those reasons are." Aurial watched the other woman's mind race and decided to take a risk. "Antikoby," she said, "you've been dealing with all this for a while now. What do you think he wants?"

"What he wants and what he thinks he wants are different things," the tuupit replied. Again he paused, as if uncertain of what to say and he appeared uncomfortable. Aurial realized that she was forcing him to step out of his role as servant and join them in discussing the machinations of the troinom. That meant setting the pretense aside and speaking openly. It also meant stating an opinion rather than merely following orders and for one of the underranks to state what he thought of a troinom was a dangerous thing to do.

Then something shifted in his eyes and she knew that he had made the decision to answer honestly. "I have spoken to the sri-noth several times and I believe that he is twisted inside. It is unlikely that he is planning any of this himself: he can't think that straight. So others must be using him."

"What do they want from him?" Aurial asked.

Raunn replied. "Wed to Torrian, he becomes the heir to the Rock. That puts him in a powerful position. It also makes him a very wealthy man. Those are both strong incentives." She looked at Antikoby. "Do you think he cares for the su-vellide?"

The tuupit shook his head. "Sri-noth Surrein cares only for himself."

"She cannot feel love for him," Raunn continued, "otherwise, why would she be hiding from him before they are wed?"

"The su-vellide told me that she changed her opinion of him after the betrothal. She did not say why. But he had something to do with introducing her to the stardust and she fears the dust."

Raunn recoiled into her pillows. She was shaken and it was clear that she had not considered another troinom to be the source of the drug.

Aurial tried another angle. "Antikoby, is Surrein doing this out of his own greed and ambition?"

Again the man shook his head. "That is hard to know. He may think that this was his idea but others may have put the thoughts into his head and made them possible."

"Of course," Raunn added. "The Fellskeeper Clan is small and their citadel is far from Nandarri." She nodded toward the book. "I looked them up. They have not had true wealth in two generations and participate little in the government. They do not own a home in Nandarri and do not pay the water tax. Surrein would never have been included on the list of potential husbands for Torrian, much less placed at the top of it."

"So someone else is behind all this," Aurial commented.

"Exactly. And who might that be?" Raunn asked in a deceptively mild tone. "Who was at the betrothal, Antikoby? Do you know? Who would gain if the Rock and Clan Cliffmaster were on the side of the Tulkan?"

The tuupit looked uncomfortable again but he replied immediately. "The su-vellide told me that the tansul's cousin Verrer was in attendance at the betrothal."

"Verrer. What a surprise. How like him to take advantage of the opportunity. What do you think, Aurial?"

"I think that we must be very careful. Antikoby, does anyone outside the Rock know that we are here?"

Antikoby responded. "When the sri-nothi Raunn appeared last night from—wherever you have been, I composed a message to the tansul, and held it until the sri-nothi approved it for transmission."

"Good," Aurial said. She looked at Raunn and continued. "I would recommend not sending it. I understand that you wish to relieve your father's anxieties but the security of the Clan is more important." *And it won't hurt that man to sweat a little*, she thought. "If Verrer thinks that the Patrol still has you bottled up inside the Port, he is at a disadvantage. I can't think immediately how to use it, but something will come up. In the meantime, we have more leeway to act."

"I agree," Raunn added. "Let's not rush into anything. Torrian is safely tucked away in her damp sanctuary and Surrein has no support here other than his servants. Aurial, I want you to watch him this evening and learn as much as you can without bringing yourself to his attentions. Antikoby, tell the message tower to get ready. I'm going to write a query to the tansul from my mother asking for information about Surrein. The Kohrable says, 'A fool walks naked before his enemy but a wise man clothes himself in knowledge.' Right now he knows more about us than we do about him. You may go."

Antikoby turned and left the room. Aurial noticed that Raunn had never thought to ask him to sit. "And what are you going to do after that?" she asked.

Raunn grinned and patted the sheets. "I'm going to stay here, out of the way and wait and think. Now, why don't you just take your aching body back out there. As soon as I appear tomorrow, he'll be hanging around me, trying to learn whatever he can. I need you to help me handle him. Maitris will get you whatever you need."

Aurial decided that she was right, hauled herself onto her feet and went out. She had an important message of her own to send off in a somewhat different direction.

## BIG GREEN

The shaman pulled back on his end of the saw one last time and then stepped away from the huge bole of the tree as it began to tip. The tree leaned, balanced on a shred of uncut wood and bark, then plummeted. It tore its way through the upper canopy of leaves, pulling the intertwined branches of other trees with it, then roared downward through the understory. When it hit the ground, its impact nearly knocked the work crew off their feet and the crash echoed in their ears long after a cloud of leaves, twigs and dust had settled.

The tree had been huge. Although not the biggest tree in the *dumaass*, it had possessed stature and the dignity of centuries. Now it was just a big log. Dead wood. The enormous hole its fall left in the canopy allowed sunlight to drop heavily through and onto the floor of the jungle, increasing the heat. The shade-loving plants of the jungle floor cringed visibly and curled up in defense. A ring of brown wormlike creatures wriggled up from under the plants and shimmied into the *dumaass* away from the sunlight. Something larger shimmied across the shaman's foot as it sought escape.

A lifter cranked its way across the clearing to the fallen tree. As soon as it stopped a crew jumped off like red parasites leaving a host animal, and began lopping off the branches of the crown. Myriad flyers, small and green, swarmed out of the falling branches and teemed around the work crew, trying to get through their clothes. The crew flailed wildly until the flyers abandoned their efforts and retreated into the jungle. Then the crew resumed work and in a short time only the tree's naked trunk was left. The lifter's operator positioned its huge pincers so that they could grasp it firmly. Straining against the weight, the lifter raised the tree trunk off the ground and carried it to the edge of the clearing. With another, smaller crash, the trunk fell onto a pile of similar logs.

The shaman had not paused to watch all of this: there was no leisure on Big Green for such observation. He and his partner on the two-man felling team had already gone on to the next tree and begun the cut with their axes. All the shaman knew as he worked was that each tree to fall continued the destruction of the *dumaass* and he was a part of it. A dark ache of wrongness coiled in his chest and grew larger with each tree killed, each stream blocked, each gash made in the ground, and every day that passed. It was physically painful for him to participate in what he knew to be the murder of a living system but his only choice was not viable. Protest and rebellion meant death. While the fact of dying did not bother him, was in fact preferable to what he was doing, he must live to accomplish what his path had brought him here to do.

He continued to chop and pale chips flew out of the cut with each rhythmic stroke, like tiny birds escaping from the tree before it fell. Lumbering back across the clearing, the lifter moved slowly as its engine stuttered, revived, then faltered again. Finally it choked and died, causing the shaman to smile grimly as he worked. The lifter would have to be fixed and while it was out of action for repairs, the clearing of the *dumaass* would be delayed.

Any equipment failure was a small victory for the shaman and these triumphs occurred frequently. Manpower was important on Big Green because of the unreliability of any kind of machinery. The screws blamed most of it on fluctuations in the planet's magnetic field. They also accused the heat, the rain and the stupidity of the laborers for the problems. Only the shaman understood why the techish equipment failed and would continue to break down despite a powerful device the Project leaders had erected in the base and other elaborate precautions. He kept this information to himself, however, holding it secret lest the screws learn something that would assist them in perpetrating their outrage on the world they contemptuously called Big Green.

A whistle blew. The shaman and his partner put down their axes and walked toward the water cart. The climate necessitated breaks for replenishing the liquid they sweated away every moment that they worked. The breaks also gave them the opportunity to conserve their strength against the debilitating heat and smothering humidity. The shaman was strong in the way of his people, who lived on and with the land. Strength to cope with the rigors of their lives began developing in childhood and was as much a part of the People as their knowledge of the land. Although far stronger than the Silent Ones around him, he had never experienced such backbreaking toil. In the Living Hills, work was done as necessary for the maintenance of life and the observance of ritual. Work as the focus and meaning of existence was unknown to him.

There was a touch on his shoulder and the shaman turned quickly to see Astin with Merradrix close by, as always. These two had come with him from the Provider, had been with him in the same dank prison and they were as close to friends as someone not of the People could be. When they sought him out and asked his name, he had not been able to tell them that a shaman had no name. He could not even tell them what a shaman was but had simply given them the title instead.

"That was a big one you just took down, Shaman," Merradrix said, gulping water.

The shaman nodded. "It was a great tree," he responded. "Old and wise. We killed it but it did not give its spirit to us. Nothing on this world has given its spirit. And rightly so when the gift would only be wasted."

Astin looked around the clearing, water running down his chin. "What does that mean?" he asked uneasily.

Merradrix interjected, "Nothing. It's heresy. None of the stuff he says is part of the True Word. If trees had spirits, it would say so in the Kohrable."

Astin shook his head stubbornly. "He knows things. About all of this. He knows because he's closer to it." He looked at the shaman again. "What does it mean?"

"It means," the shaman replied, "that we are not of this world and it does not want us. We are its enemy."

They drank again in silence, each man recalling the "accidents" they had seen in their short time on Big Green. Then there were the stories told by the screws and the other prisoners. There was no denying that the *dumaass* was dangerous.

"What should we do?" Astin queried.

They were speaking Chenni and the shaman's partner was shut out. He moved away from them uneasily.

"Do?" Merradrix scorned. "Just keep on working. Eat, drink, sleep and work, that's all. Do anything else and the screws'll fix you."

The shaman ignored him and nodded his head toward the green wall of the *dumaass*. "It's alive and it knows what we're doing to it," he said quietly. "Respect it and walk carefully."

"Of course it's alive," Merradrix responded stubbornly. "Trees only grow when they're alive; everybody knows that."

Shaking his head sadly, the shaman replied, "Not just the trees, not just the *dumaass*, all of it. Slow it may be, and cautious, but it can feel pain. And it is aware." He gestured dismissively toward his partner, who paid no attention to the talk. "The others won't listen," he added, "and the screws shouldn't know. I tell only you."

Before either of the men could reply, the whistle blew again. At the same time the shaman was struck a blow on one shoulder that knocked the cup from his hand. "None of that!" a screw roared behind him. "No gibberin'. No talking." He gestured with his diz. "Get back to work before I drop you."

Merradrix turned away, his eyes hard, as he tried to accommodate what he had just heard with what he had always been taught and with his strong need to survive. Astin surveyed the *dumaass* grimly on the way back to their station, looking at it with new eyes.

The shaman's partner grunted and fell in beside him as they returned to their half-cut tree. A few more strokes and they could take up the saw again. Abruptly, it began to rain. In the jungle it rained frequently and, because the sky was usually hidden by the trees, unpredictably. In the clearing it would have been possible to see the storm approach but work left no time for looking up. All the laborers knew was that the rain started and then it stopped. They were wet from sweat and then wetter from rain, but the work went on.

The shaman's red work suit slicked down to his skin and water dripped from the brim of his hat. He despised the hat and the suit, at the same time valuing the protection they gave. Always, but especially when it was raining, he wanted to strip off the suffocating garment and lie naked on the ground. He was sure that, skin to soil, patiently adjusting his time frame to the longer rhythms of the planet, he could learn how to communicate with the great bio-intelligence that his Allsight now sensed only vaguely.

In the Living Hills, he was a part of the Provider's consciousness. It flowed by and through him like the wind stirring the grasses. He was constantly aware of all the elements of nature. The shaman did not need to look up to see if the sun was strong against the accursed Veil any more than he needed to feel his pulse to know that his heart beat. It was no more necessary to listen to the wind foretell the weather than to ask his stomach whether he was hungry. In oneness with the world lay both knowledge and understanding. To him, and to all the People, the Provider was not a place or a thing, but a creature that was respected, cherished, feared, protected. His Allsight told him that it was as conscious of them as they were of it.

He could feel a similar consciousness here but because he had not been born into it, that awareness was separate from him, alien and hostile. He kept the suit on because he knew, better than any of the Silent Ones around him, the increasing anger of this bio-consciousness. Life and death were a natural part of its experience and so it was slow to feel the destruction that had been visited upon it by the humans. Trees grew and trees fell but devastation eventually became felt and then pain could not be ignored.

Why, he wondered, did the bio-consciousness not strike out at its persecutors with all its power and eradicate them? Could it be that it perceived them as a natural plague? Or that it did not understand the nature of its enemy? Or had it simply not turned its full attention to the source of its pain? If he could tune his Allsight to its rhythm, talk to it, teach it . . . He stopped swinging and stood as still as a tree, immobilized by the enormity of the thought. His partner also stopped, puzzled, and at the same time afraid that one of the screws would see them malingering and point his diz.

The shaman knew now what he had to do, what he had been brought here to accomplish. The realization was enormous, as huge as the task itself, and frightening. At the same time it was liberating. Now that the path was clear, he could give himself up to it. The only problem was in finding the freedom to walk the path. For a prisoner, nothing was simple or easy. He had much thinking to do yet before he could proceed. And yet . . . He smiled.

At the day's end, as the work crews were herded back to the base for a disinfectant spray, dry clothes and a meal, Astin and Merradrix approached him again. They exchanged a quick glance and then Astin spoke. "We talked it over," he said in Chenni with a furtive look at the other prisoners, "and we agreed to follow your—what you said. How can we help?"

The shaman regarded them sadly. "You cannot help," he replied. "This world is as blind and deaf to you as you are to it and as you were to the Provider, which you call Chennidur. To be safe, anticipate the unexpected. Think of everything in the *dumaass* as aware and watching you. Walk in stealth."

Merradrix nodded once. "I hear you. This isn't Chennidur. Maybe the True Word doesn't apply here. The animals are all different, the plants try to trap you and every one of them wants a piece of us to eat."

"Even the suit doesn't keep them from biting you," Astin added. "They crawl and fly and hop. The creepies are nasty and they're everywhere but I can understand that. What I can't figure is how the trees and plants will hurt us."

The shaman stretched his hand across a gap as wide as the galaxy and grasped Astin's arm. "There are no animals on Big Green," he said.

## THE ROCK

The daystart meeting was over, the staff dispersed to their various duties, but Antikoby remained alone in his office. He stared at the wall and tried to sort out his confusing, conflicting emotions. He had been the tuupit of

Clan Cliffmaster for five years and was accustomed to running the day-to-day activities of a complex holding. For him, as for every other tuupit, however, true control lay always with a troinom. That troinom, whether tansul, vellide or a son of the clan, ordered, reviewed and supervised everything that he and his staff did. Troinom were thinkers and the underranks were workers. Troinom commanded and underranks obeyed. That was the way of it.

Some tuupits were more competent than others. Some toinom were better thinkers than others. A strong tuupit might chafe under weak clan leadership, as Antikoby had himself when vel Rutin sank into her grief, but that dissatisfaction was never voiced to anyone, not even another tuupit. The order of things was accepted and understood by all involved. The underranks knew their place and kept to it. How could it be otherwise, when the structure of the world was written in the True Word, documented by the Kohrable? And was this way of life not reinforced in the commentaries of generations of nayyat?

And yet he *had* stepped out of his place. True, he had not wanted to, but instead done only what he had felt was necessary to deal with a difficult situation in the absence of any troinom to command him. True, he had told vel Rutin of the circumstances and given her ample opportunity to accept the responsibility that was hers by law, right and custom. But in the end, he had done it, and then continued to do it because continuing was necessary. After a while, however, Antikoby had become aware that he was enjoying the power of command, no matter how reluctantly he assumed it or how circumspectly he wielded it. That was not a complete surprise: a tuupit had some power of his own after all, even if it was only to direct other servants. Still, he had been able to describe himself as a tool that had functioned without a guiding hand until the tool's proper master took control again. Not until Raunn's return had he known that he was fooling himself.

Then, for the first time, he understood that he did not want to relinquish the power.

Antikoby's head dropped into his hands and he rubbed his eyes with the tips of his fingers. It was easy to feel

again the twinge of reluctance that had surprised him
when Torrian was restored to health. At that point, however, he had not been in control of the Rock for very long
and was still fearful. Then, too quickly, the su-vellide had
retreated to her cave and left him once again on his own.
Left him to match wits with the unpredictable Surrein.
Relied on him to save the Rock.

He snorted quietly. What arrogance. What pride. What
foolishness. How could he, an unmarked servant with no
spark of troinom intelligence between his ears and no flare
of troinom command in his spirit, dare to match wits with
any of his betters? How could a drev presume to accomplish what his master could not do?

This delusion and the temptation that accompanied it
were, he knew, the work of the Raveler. Only a being who
existed solely to destroy the woven might of the Chenni-ad
could have created such a situation and placed him in it.
He could imagine the Raveler watching as the tuupit
struggled and laughing his cosmic laugh.

Antikoby tried to see himself from the perspective of
the Raveler, who was a doubter, a mischief maker, a
mocker of all that was sacred. How well this tuupit fit into
his schemes: a jumped-up servant who played at being a
master, who rejected proper subservience and set himself
in opposition to a troinom, who dressed himself in bor-
rowed power and then refused to take it off. The final fillip
to the joke, the twist to make the Raveler roar, was that
the pathetic servant actually thought he was succeeding.

This vision of himself was so degrading that Antikoby
could not bear to lift his head for fear that he would see his
own reflection in the window and be unable to look himself in the eyes. Squirming in a distorted mixture of self-
pity and self-loathing, he could not imagine going on. But
the sounds of the clan holding proceeding through its daily
routine penetrated his sanctuary. His heart, after all, kept
on beating. The sun continued on its course, shielded by
the attendant Veil. The floor remained solid and did not
open up to admit him. He was forced at last to take his
head from his hands and confront the day.

Dust motes floated serenely in a ray of morning light.

Antikoby forced himself to look through the window to where the gardener's stone pots waited in the sunlight, stolidly incubating their clutch of rootstalk cuttings. There was no guarantee that those cuttings would sprout but neither the gardener, nor the rhizomes, nor the pots questioned their role. If they simply accepted their place in the seasonal drama, doing their part in it, could he not do the same? The rootstalks did not worry about failing the gardener. Nor did they shrink from the gardener's plans, but continued in their attempts to put forth shoots. The most pitiful thing of all, he decided, was a tuupit who worried about what the Raveler thought of him.

Antikoby pushed himself out of his chair and went out to do his job. Whether the troinom punished him or the Chenni-ad scorned him, he would not think about it until later. Now he had to work with Raunn, who seemed perfectly willing to take over the reins of power, ignorant of the very thought that he had ever held them. Whether she was capable of what needed to be done was still unknown, nevertheless he must turn all decisions over to her. Raunn had never shown either a desire or an aptitude for the responsibilities of her rank, preferring to play instead. To all young things there came a time of maturing and adult duties. Perhaps this was Raunn's time to grow up.

There was, of course, still another concern: the role of the mysterious woman who had accompanied Raunn, unannounced, to the Rock. He had many questions about she of the curious accent and eccentric ways, who did not quite fit as she should. *It's as if*, he thought, *she does not know her place as a troi'm*. She displayed an odd hesitancy that marked her in many small and nearly imperceptible ways as different.

*Except for the look.* He knew that look and had expected a summons by now. While it was her right and pleasure to command his service, the sri-nothi Aurial was oddly diffident. Most troi'm women would have added to that first sparkle of interest a second that said, equally plainly, "Later." From this one, this Aurial, there was nothing.

Antikoby was not ignorant of his appearance. He had been summoned to the beds of many guests and knew he would have to perform sexually on other occasions in the future. He was proud of his ability to satisfy the fine ladies, even as he despised those same ladies for demanding such service from the underranks. Not all the troinom women who smiled in his direction were young or beautiful. Some were not even clean. Yet, while they could pick and choose, amusing themselves among the drevs, he had no alternative but to do as he was bid, and with enthusiasm. *The troinom command, the underranks obey,* he repeated to himself. Why, then, did this troi'm not assume her rights?

Antikoby was far more concerned about whether this hesitance indicated that the woman could be trusted. Raunn obviously trusted her and spoke freely in her presence but Raunn's judgment was not always the best. Still, it was far from his place to question his mistress or to second-guess her. Raunn was now in charge. He only had to concern himself with following her orders. There must be an end to his delusions of power and authority, planning and strategy. There must be no more hanging back, no more reluctance. Still, Antikoby had the nagging feeling that, for him, there could be no return to the man he had been before. The experience of being truly in command had marked him indelibly. It was as if he now bore a clan mark on his soul, invisible to all others but inescapable to him. *Would anyone ever see that mark?* he wondered. *What would happen if they did?*

# CHAPTER 14

## THE ROCK

When the morning Call to Prayer was concluded, Aurial rose from her seat gratefully. The sun had barely risen when she had entered the chapel and now it was broad morning outside. Although the service was an opportunity for her to watch and learn, she had found it a trial to sit through the entire thing without fidgeting. First the rennish smoke stung her eyes and gave her a headache that pounded just behind her temples. Then the prayers, the chants, the singing went on interminably. In addition to which, she was starving and her stomach had rumbled embarrassingly through the last two chants.

She had forced herself to sit serenely next to Raunn when she was itching to get away and wondered why she was so on edge. Aurial was well aware that this behavior was both unprofessional and atypical, patience being one of her strong points. Now that the service was finally over, she could barely wait to get free of the dark temple with its press of bodies and wisps of rennish smoke snaking around the rafters.

Raunn leaned imperceptibly toward her. "See," she whispered, "He's doing just what I thought. You might think it was his own mother he was escorting."

Aurial followed her glance to where Surrein was solicitously assisting the Vellide from her chair. "When we're outside," she commented, "let's try to talk with him. He was not at dinner last night."

Raunn nodded her assent and they took their places in the aisle behind the vellide as she moved toward the door. They stepped through into the courtyard and Aurial shielded her eyes against the brightness of the sun. The morning was incandescent with an unusual lambent light. The colors of the courtyard and of people's clothing were extraordinarily vivid. Raunn also noticed a change and lifted her head inquiringly, one hand raised against the glare. "What is it?" Aurial asked. "Something's changed."

"Yes, that's true," Raunn replied, with worry in her voice. "It's the Veil: it's much too thin, particularly for this time of year. 'Thinning' happens sometimes during High Cold or Ice Lock, but it's not a problem then because everyone stays inside, anyway. It's nearly planting season now and most of the servants are in the fields, preparing them for the crops. This will throw everything off."

Aurial looked at the courtyard with fresh eyes and saw that the sunlight was clearer, more direct, than she had seen it before. Sharp lines drew distinct boundaries between light and shadow. Shapes rendered soft by the diffused light that normally filtered through the Veil's opaque screen were now hard-edged. The sensation reminded her of stepping from Mother's carpeted chamber on the Beldame, lit by gentle recessed lights, into the bright corridor with its harsh functional illumination.

A quick databead access confirmed what she remembered from the briefing: the Veil screened more than light rays. It also protected the surface of Chennidur from a form of radiation harmful to humans. Yet the sunlight, deadly as it was, felt so warm and relaxing that she wanted to bask in it. "Does this mean," she asked, "that we have to stay indoors all day?"

A deep masculine voice replied, "Yes, sri-nothi, it does." Antikoby had approached them while she had been focused on input from the databead. The tuupit continued, speaking this time to Raunn. "I was about to confirm that order with you, sri-nothi, so that I may order the workers in from the fields and pastures."

"Yes, of course, Antikoby," she responded. "To do otherwise would endanger lives."

He nodded his assent and went about his duties. Aurial's eyes followed his broad back as it moved away. She turned to see Raunn watching her with a smile twitching one corner of her mouth. "It is time for firstmeal," the other woman said. "You must be famished." As if in agreement, Aurial's stomach growled again and she could feel herself blushing. "Don't be embarrassed because your stomach reveals its hunger," Raunn commented. "Rennish often has that effect, particularly on those who are not accustomed to it as we are. In the dining room you shall have plenty to eat."

They crossed the flagstones and entered the main body of the house, going from the courtyard's sunny warmth to a cool, stone-shaded hall. Inside, the smell of food caused her to forget everything but filling her stomach as soon as possible. Although she had partaken of a perfectly adequate dinner the previous night, she felt as if she had not eaten in years. Surrein was already in the dining room, ensuring that the vellide was comfortably seated and in possession of everything she required. Raunn introduced him to Aurial, who attempted to ignore her ravening hunger long enough to be polite. Surrein gave a slight bow and then commented, "Aurial. An unusual name, is it not?"

"Yes," she said. "It is so different that I sometimes find it annoying." *Keep it simple*, she thought to herself. *Elaborate explanations are treacherous.*

"And a strange accent, as well," he added. "I don't believe I have ever heard it before. It is quite charming." He smiled but his eyes said that he was familiar with that accent and knew exactly from where it originated.

There was nothing Aurial could say in response so she simply acknowledged the "compliment" with a smile of her own. Before Surrein could pursue his comments, she was extricated from the conversation by Raunn's call to the table. They seated themselves at one end of a long dining table that could easily accommodate five times their number and the servants entered with food and drink.

Aurial accepted portions of almost everything from maids carrying platters piled with an assortment of breakfast dishes, but was particularly drawn to spicy and salty foods. Conversation during the meal was desultory, which suited her because it allowed her to eat without interruption. She consumed an immoderate number of slender, highly-seasoned sausages and practically an entire bowl of a thick dark sauce into which small cakes were dipped. When the meal was over, she had managed to assuage her hunger yet rose from the table filled more with energy than with food.

"I was going to show Aurial around the Rock today," Raunn commented, wiping her lips with a creamy napkin, "seeing as this is her first visit. I was hoping that you would accompany us, Surrein. Thanks to the thinning, we shall have to confine our excursion to the inside but there is still a great deal to see."

His reply was polite. "I thank you for the invitation, but regret that I must decline. Although I have seen only a small portion of this wonderful estate, I must prepare for my return to Nandarri tomorrow. Since my betrothed is engrossed in her sacred vigil, it falls upon me to make the plans for our wedding and the bonding period to follow. Although this is normally the bride's task, I undertake it joyfully. Torrian asked this sacrifice of me so that she would be free to prepare herself mentally and spiritually for our union."

Raunn was visibly surprised by his statement and it took her a long moment to find a suitable reply. "Surely your servants can pack on their own and what other preparation is required? This is your last day of leisure before you begin attending to your duties in Nandarri; why not spend it with us?"

"Were it not for the thinning, madam, I would leave today but now I have time to draw up lists, consult with the nayya, think through what is needed. When I reach

Nandarri, I will be ready. I would like nothing further than to devote my last day here to my future sister and her charming friend but it cannot be so. Since I plan to leave quite early in the morning, I shall take my leave of you all this evening. Now, I beg you to excuse me so that I may go about my business."

"C-c-certainly," Raunn stammered. "If I may be of any assistance, please let me know."

Surrein bowed and left the room. When he was gone, Raunn looked at Aurial in amazement. "Well, do you believe that?"

"It was quite a surprise," Aurial affirmed. "What now?"

"I don't really know. Let's take my mother back to her rooms and then I'll show you around, as I had planned. After that, I guess we'll think of something."

Together they helped the vellide to her feet and walked with her, very slowly, to her rooms. This was the first real opportunity Aurial had had to observe Rutin-Xian—the absentee matriarch of Clan Cliffmaster—closely, and she noted the symptoms mentioned previously by Raunn. The listlessness, the dull eyes and expressionless face, the disinterest in anything or anyone around her, all were clearly present. She felt that the vellide's infirmity was important to her work on Chennidur but she was not sure how. Rather than spending time on the problem, Aurial set a mental flag and went on.

The tour was, as she had expected it to be, confusing. Aurial was more than eager to follow Raunn up and down stairs, through rooms and wings, to the tops of towers and the bottoms of cellars. In fact, she was so filled with energy that any itinerary less strenuous would have driven her crazy. Nonetheless, she was lost after the first few rooms. The Rock was every bit as impressive as Raunn had painted it and more complex than anyone not raised here could ever appreciate. *They're so worried about invasion,* she thought, *but if a conqueror did succeed, all they would have to do is hide. They could conduct a very effective guerilla war from the inside.*

There was so much to see that they did not stop for midmeal, picking up fruit and rolls on their way through the kitchens instead. Aurial tried to keep her appetite in check and ignore the savory meal being prepared. Beset by an outrageous thirst that was the logical consequence of her morning indulgence, she did pause long enough for a huge drink of water. Lowering the cup, she saw Raunn treating her to a superior smile. "After all the *taki* and *zegwan* sauce you ate, you should want the whole pitcher. It's a good thing we don't eat *jirrifish* for firstmeal or we would have had to carry you out." The troinom woman regarded the water jug thoughtfully. "Did you drink a lot of water from the Heartspring yesterday?" she asked.

"Why, no," Aurial replied. "Should I have?"

"Yes. After the time we spent in the Perimeter drinking contaminated water, it's important that you flush all the toxins out of your system as soon as possible." She sniffed the fluid in the jug and shook her head. "This is just from the cistern. When you return to your room, have the maid bring you a big pitcher of Heartspring water and drink it all. Even if you feel waterlogged, keep drinking."

"Why is the Heartspring water pure while stream water, or cistern water, is not?" she asked. "This tastes fine." She took another drink.

"Taste has nothing to do with it. Water in the streams picks up toxins from the soil it runs through as well as the plants that grow in and around it. Rainwater is cleaner but still carries traces of poison. Only the Heartsprings are unadulterated because they are a gift from Mchul, the Maker in the Chenni-ad, and come from the world's core. That is why they are so important, why they are the heart of every clan. Without its Heartspring, a clan would have no reason to exist. Without its cleansing powers, troinom and underranks alike would die." A line creased her forehead. "Didn't you know that?"

Aurial shook her head. Revealing the presence of the techish databead would have been counterproductive so she improvised a reply. "Before I came here, I was briefed, taught all about Chennidur, and I thought there was so much to learn I could never remember it all. Now I'm aware all the time of just how little I know. Don't worry, I'll drink 'til I slosh but tell me one more thing before we keep going. Is everything on Chennidur poisonous to humans?"

Raunn's answer came readily. "In one way or another, yes. That's why a large part of the Kohrable deals with the selection and preparation of food. It's a matter of life or death to know which parts of foods are safe and which are not, what has to be cooked before it is edible and in what fashion, which substances are so toxic that even traces left on your fingers can kill. That's why the laws against the pollution of the body are the most important and strictly enforced. I will send a copy of the Kohrable to your room so that you may read the laws yourself.

"Chennidur may be the gift of the Chenni-ad and the most beautiful planet outside of the Great Wheel but it is always testing us. Only the worthy may live here; the careless and ignorant are culled."

Aurial slipped in another query. "And these poisons affect both troinom and underranks in the same way?"

"Oh yes. Just the same. Now the Rugollah, they're supposed to be different. Some say they can live in unfiltered sunlight and eat things raw that would kill us when cooked, but then, what do you expect of *shirz?*" Her voice had the same disgusted tone that it had held the last time she spoke of the Rugollah.

They took their fruit and rolls and continued exploring the great maze of the Rock. The only place they could not go was the Cavern of the Heartspring, where Torrian was secluded. After a while, however, the beautiful carvings and elegant architecture, the intricate tapestries and finely-crafted furniture, all began to look the same. Finally Aurial was left with a single overriding impression of emptiness. No matter how rich or how ancient the rooms, they were nearly all vacant, echoing, and suffused with the slightly musty smell of disuse.

Hesitantly, she mentioned this to Raunn and the other woman nodded in reluctant agreement. "Long ago, when wars were common and a safe place to live was of the greatest importance, all of Clan Cliffmaster lived here and it was filled with people. Our history teaches that when the first conciliator came to power and waged his peace, this way of life changed. Not all at once, mind you, but a little bit at a time, allowing people to come out of their fortresses. Cities grew and the troinom built fashionable homes in Nandarri, near the conciliator's palace. They paid water tax to the temples so that people could live away from the Heartsprings and thus created a new social milieu. It was so enjoyable, they added summer estates in the country and built homes in other places that were, as the nayya would say, 'conducive to pleasurable entertainment.'

"My great-uncle Chazzin and his family lived here until his sons received their clan marks. Then he built his house in the Perimeter and moved there with his wife and all their children. Once, the buildings of the Rock were filled with the tanzul's family and the vellide's family for many generations. Now only my sister and I remain: my brothers died before their betrothals were arranged."

The Rock reminded Aurial of a hive creature, cultivated on Dur-Iss, that built and lived in calcareous mounds of great size and amazing complexity. When it was time to harvest the mound, keepers would gas it, killing off all but the dominant breeding pair. These two survivors remained to occupy a tiny portion of the convoluted structure until the keepers removed them to begin another hive. Here on Chennidur, history had killed off the human hive, and progress.

They continued the tour until midafternoon when Aurial's burst of energy departed abruptly and completely. Her enjoyment went with it and she found herself standing in a vacant room surrounded by old furniture, faded artwork and dust. Feeling silly, she said, "I'm tired," in a voice as flat and colorless as the carpet. To her relief, Raunn did not argue with or ridicule her but merely nodded, as if she had been expecting this to happen.

"We'll go back to your room, then," Raunn replied. "It's not close, though, and if you feel too tired to walk all the way, just say so. I'll call a servant to carry you."

That prospect was so repellent that Aurial rejected it immediately. Instead, she slogged on through corridors and halls, down staircases and up again, dragging her feet one laborious step after another until finally she recognized the door to her rooms.

Raunn and the maid put her to bed with a pitcher of Heartspring water to assuage a thirst that had an energy of its own. Then they went away and Aurial was glad to be alone with her thoughts. By now, they were circling in her head like a fleet of transports orbiting the Beldame but she could not make them connect in any way that made sense. The smell of rennish on her clothing brought to mind the smoke's odd effects on her body. There was a similarity between the way she had reacted to it and the behavioral patterns produced by other substances she had studied—substances that had nothing to do with religious rituals or spiritual experiences. She leaned back against the pillows and remembered the unease she had experienced when confronting the vellide's absent face and vacant eyes. She still could not shake the idea that the illness of Raunn's mother was important in some way. Aurial took another drink of the bubbly Heartspring water with its pungent taste and considered an ecosystem so toxic to the species at the top of the food chain—and only that species—that all food and drink must be monitored carefully. She recalled the meticulous way in which Raunn had cooked and dressed game on the trail, how painstakingly she had disposed of certain parts of the animals.

The trail brought to mind the Rugollah, another enigma. Here was what appeared to be not only a totally separate race but another species of sentient beings. They also lived on Chennidur but could not be said to share the planet with the troinom and the underranks. Instead they lived an existence that might as well be on another world. They occupied the same position on the food chain but what was poison to the humans was nourishing to them.

The bright day faded, taking with it that light's wonderful, deadly warmth. She wondered if the Veil would be back in its accustomed place at sunrise tomorrow, and that led her to ponder the question of what caused the meteorological phenomenon to appear at the beginning of each day and then vanish at sunset when it was no longer needed. There was a reason for that, and it had to be an interesting one. She tapped the databead but, once again, it told her nothing that she did not already know.

There had to be a way of fitting all these disconnected facts into their proper places and of making some sense from what seemed a muddle. If she could only find that key, it might help her to accomplish the mission that was her goal on Chennidur. Obscure now, that key would be blindingly obvious once glimpsed. All she had to do was find it. Aurial wanted that more than anything else. Well, almost anything. First, she had to get to the privy before all the water she had drunk caused her to explode.

Being too tired to move made it difficult for her to pull herself up from the bed and cross the room. Fortunately, the nearest privy was outside in the hall, a distance she could handle. Aurial nearly collapsed onto the seat and the relief of emptying her bladder was so great she could feel it all the way down to her toes. Unfortunately the parts most directly involved stung and her urine was a dark shade she had never seen before. *Toxins*, she thought, *it's the poison burning its way out*.

She staggered back to her room and crawled into bed again. If she could not sort out the puzzle right now, she could make her regular report to the Beldame. It was late—again. This time, however, she would have some very specific questions to ask in order to obtain the information she needed and the databead lacked. It was also time, she thought, to patch a call through to the Portmaster. Some things could best be attended to from resources closer to the Rock than the other side of the Quadrant. With any luck, the information she obtained would fill gaps and reveal the key. Aurial took out her transmitter and tried to decide where to begin.


# BIG GREEN

Astin's leg ached but he didn't know whether it was due to the humidity or the work or something on this Wordless

planet that he didn't understand. He had discovered that
when his leg ached, things happened and they weren't
ever good. The last time, a tree had fallen wrong and
crushed three workers. The time before that, a screw had
been pulled, screaming, above the understory by a thick
green tentacle. The man had never been seen again. Neither had the animal that took him, although it must have
been large. Astin was uneasy and on edge.

It was nearly the end of the day. The air was steaming
from the most recent rain and smelled even more potent
than usual. Astin was soaked, the reds clinging with sodden weight to his body, dragging at it. He ignored the
irritation and continued to hack at a thick, stubborn vine
draped from the branches of an understory tree. The
vine's interwoven loops shielded the tree from the cutting
team's axes. Astin wondered, as he did frequently, what
this clearing of the *dumaass* was for. The laborers had
been told nothing and he could not imagine what the good
of it was. According to Merradrix, who had been bred to
the farm, the soil was not fertile enough to support agriculture, and pastureland would soon be overgrown. He
took another breath of the air, so rich it seemed to have a
life of its own, and shivered.

Astin was almost through the vine when something long
and sinuous slid downwards from the leafy understory
toward him. He froze. The creature, as thick as his arm,
was the same vivid green as its surroundings, mottled with
brown markings that camouflaged it perfectly. It looked
like nothing Astin had ever seen before, having no legs
and no wings. The alien look and motion of it both repelled and fascinated him. He could not believe what he
was seeing but he knew that he must look hard enough,
and concentrate on what he was seeing, so that he could
figure it out.

The front part of the thing lifted and swayed toward
him. Repulsive, it had no eyes and no discernible face, but
it knew he was there. It knew him and it wanted him.
Astin told himself to step away from it but his legs were
rooted. The thing's head moved to one side and his moved
with it, as though they were connected. Then the faceless

thing dehisced: a dark line drew itself across the green face and widened into a split. The gap grew broader and wider until it was the size of Astin's head. He watched the gaping orifice expand as it approached, staring into its blackness as if it were the gate through which he could escape Big Green. The blind and hungry head swung close enough so that he could see tiny fine hairs growing on its surface. Then a gleaming arc scythed in front of him, there was a singing in the air, and the creature flew in two pieces. Its head spun to the ground at his feet.

"Watch it, boy," Merradrix barked, grabbing his arm and pulling him backward. "That thing wasn't looking for a kiss."

Astin looked up to see the creature's bottom section, dripping a clear fluid, shrivel back into the tangle of vine. He searched amid the leaf clutter on the ground for the top part but it had vanished. Only a chunk of vine lay on the leaves. *How could it move?* he wondered. *It was dead, where did it go?*

"Snap out of it," Merradrix ordered. "Get back to work before the screw notices anything. And sharpen your wits."

Astin shook himself and looked at his partner. "Thanks," he said, then hefted the axe and took a swing. Together, he and Merradrix worked their way through to the tree trunk before the guard whistled to mark the end of day. When the signal came, they stacked their tools in the carrier under the watchful eyes of heavily armed screws, and formed up for the march back to the barracks.

Merradrix fell in beside him, dripping wet as they all were and stinking of sweat and jungle. Blotches of fungus marked his neck. He leaned toward Astin and risked, in Chenni, "What happened there?"

Astin scanned their surroundings nervously. "Don't know," he replied. "Something odd." The guard looked in their direction and they retreated into silence, not daring to speak at all during the march back to the barracks. The long hike through dense air that became only fractionally cooler as darkness dropped, required all their breath and whatever energy remained to them.

During the night meal they sought out Shaman, who

was sitting by himself as usual. His partner on the felling team usually disappeared into the mass of workers as soon as he could. They sat next to him and began methodically consuming the food, a grey sludge studded with chunks of a substance that might once have been meat. "What do you feel?" Astin asked in Chenni, confident that Shaman would also have felt the odd sense of impending action.

Shaman calmly spooned the sludge into his mouth as though it were real food. "There is something," he said. "It's building, coming closer. I can't tell when or how. But soon."

"Never mind that," Merradrix said roughly. "Just tell us *what* it is."

"What must happen, will happen," Shaman replied. "The *dumaass* learns in its slow way. It draws to itself what it needs. It becomes aware of us. That is what you feel."

Merradrix and Astin looked at one another, confused and uncertain. "What do you mean?" Astin asked. "How could the jungle learn?"

"As I told you," Shaman replied patiently, "the *dumaass* is alive. You think of it as many living things all in one place but that is only partly so. There is more. All those single fast-moving lives are part of a bigger entity, slow to move or think, but unified. This awareness includes all the small lives but is greater."

Merradrix scratched at his chin, scraping off a patch of fungus. "Are you saying," he asked skeptically, "that the *dumaass* is conscious?"

"Yes," Shaman replied, "yes, that is the word. The jungle knows what happens to it, what we are doing to it."

"How do you know this?" Astin asked sharply.

Shaman shrugged. "Some I feel and some I think. How much of what I think is correct I am not sure. I, too, am learning."

"You said 'what we are doing to it,' " Merradrix said thoughtfully. "Cutting it down cannot be good for it."

"We are hurting it, aren't we?" Astin queried intently. "But how much? The *dumaass* is so enormous, what can cause it pain?"

"I do not know," Shaman answered. "Perhaps the *dumaass* feels some pain all the time as a normal part of life. Trees die for many reasons. Floods and lightning, fires and wind all cause damage even though they are normal occurrences. Perhaps the jungle experienced this 'project' in such a way at first but now it is different."

"Now we're dangerous," Merradrix said flatly.

"And the *dumaass* is fighting back," Astin added, the image of the blind head and black mouth fresh in his eyes. He began to say something else but was interrupted by a bark of orders from two screws pushing laborers out of the way. Silence, sullen and resentful, fell across the area where the gathered prisoners ate and rested. The screws usually left them alone during meals and talking was tolerated. The screws intruded, generating fear among men accustomed to whatever security lay in routine.

Astin looked up to see the white-garbed legs of the men stop in front of them. He rose, as did Merradrix and Shaman. Around them, the other prisoners drew away, leaving them isolated with the guards. One of the screws consulted a portable comlink in his right hand. "You from Chennidur, right?!" he demanded of Shaman.

"Yes, that is so," Shaman conceded, then added, "Sir."

"You, too?" the man asked Astin.

"Yes, sir," Astin replied, "and so is he." Whatever happened, they would do it together.

"Why?" Merradrix asked in a hostile voice.

"Shut your mouth, troublemaker," the second screw barked with his hand raised. "We ask the questions. You answer. Got that?"

"Yes, sir," Merradrix said.

"Any of you from the city?" the first man asked.

All three of the prisoners shook their heads. "Good," the screw said. "Records say you know about hunting, tracking, things like that. That so?"

"Yes, sir," they said in unison.

"You ever hunt in the forest?"

"Yes, sir."

"Good. Tomorrow morning, I'll be waiting by the gate when the work detail goes out. You find me first thing, understand? Make me go looking and you'll be very sorry. We've got a special project for you."

"Doing what, sir?" Astin asked, ducking as the second screw raised his fist again.

The first man raised his hand and blocked the punch. He smiled beatifically at the three. "We're going out there," he said. The screws turned and left. Even when the door had closed behind them, talk remained muted. The prisoners who had been close to the three Chennidur natives moved away. A murmur sprang up nearby and made its round of the group quickly. When it was done, Astin, Shaman and Merradrix were shut out, as though they did not exist. The screws' attention had made them dangerous and they were going into the jungle. They were dead men.

Astin looked around them at the empty faces of their fellow laborers, who were now strangers. "I don't like this," he said. He rubbed the scar on his leg to relieve the ache, which had become stronger.

"Which?" Merradrix asked. "Them?" His eyes swept the other prisoners contemptuously. "Or that?" he gestured toward the jungle.

"All of it," Astin replied. "Why are they sending us out there? What does it mean?" A small shrill voice in the back of his mind gibbered, *It means we're all going to die.* He silenced it.

"The *dumaass* draws what it needs," Shaman repeated in a remote tone. His eyes were open wide but unfocused and he appeared to be away somewhere. "It is closer than I thought." He came back into himself and looked at the other two. "You must remember one thing," he said. "When I find the right place, I will know. Then you must kill the screws, and quickly."

A cold spot grew in Astin's stomach and the sludge churned around it. He hated the screws, some worse than others, but he had never killed anyone. Killing violated the tenets of the True Word and, besides, he did not know if he could. And if they succeeded in the murders, what then? They could not return to the barracks or the project,

yet escaping into the *dumaass* was impossible. It would
kill them. *We're all . . .*

Merradrix's deep voice interrupted his thoughts. "Just
like that? Unarmed? Kill screws who would love an excuse
to splatter us just for the fun of it?"

Shaman was undaunted. "When the time comes, a way
will be found. You must believe. But when I tell you, kill
them. Do you understand?"

Astin nodded solemnly and heard his voice say, "I hear
you. We will take care of it somehow." He felt drawn to
say it, to support Shaman, but he did not know why.

"Good," Shaman said. "There is nothing more important than this. Nothing. It will change everything."

"What do you mean 'the right place'? What kind of
place?" Astin pursued.

Shaman shook his head. "I cannot tell you now. I do not
yet see it clearly myself. When it happens, you will understand. I know this is difficult, but you must trust me."

"Why not?" Merradrix said. "I could use something to
trust in this place."

Astin said nothing and continued to rub his leg. He was
frightened even as he was drawn to Shaman's words. He
could see in the other man's eyes that this journey they
were about to undertake was a part of what was pulling
him now. It was all connected to the feeling of something
happening and when it did, everything would be different.
Whether it would be better or worse he did not know.
Would this trip be like the one he took for the Tarraquis,
running for them to support the True Word? If so, then he
could be at least as courageous as he had been then.

There was a stirring around them. Mealtime was over
and the laborers were being herded into the barracks for
their anti-fungal spray and a hard sleep. He stood up as
eagerly as his drained body and aching muscles would
allow. This was the best time of the day, when work was
over, the sun was down and there were luxuries to anticipate. The spray offered relief from constant irritation in
the folds of the skin caused by the fungus as it took root
and spread. The dry heat of the barracks was heaven after
the steambath of a day in the *dumaass*. Sleep was oblivion,

dark and deep as a drug. But best of all, he got to take off the red worksuit.

## THE HEARTSPRING

It was on the tenth day of Torrian's vigil that the rock began speaking to her. The sound started gradually, at a level so low that it was nearly beyond perception. In her solitude she had become accustomed to the small noises of the chamber because they helped to channel her thinking and were a form of company. She knew all of those sounds and their variations well. This was different. It was a barely-audible groaning, so deep that she felt the faint vibrations in her bones. Gradually formless noise took on shape. The pitch rose into an audible range. Tone and modulation developed. At some point, Torrian could not say when, she became aware of the changes and began to listen.

Even then, she thought the sound resulted from great shifts in the bedrock beneath her. So much time passed between modifications to the sound that any other explanation never occurred to her. Later Torrian would reflect that stone has its own time-frame, infinitely slower and more enduring than that of living creatures. Then she would marvel at the effort required to alter such a medium so that it synchronized with the ephemeral nature of a single human.

The ten days of solitude, contemplation and study had brought Torrian to a previously unknown state of mind. It was a quiet place, serene and harmonic. Lacking any need for hurry, her actions were deliberate and methodical. As the sole inhabitant of the cavern, she was able to attend to her requirements as they made themselves known. With a bastion of stone between her and all those who would help or hurt, she could detach herself from the turbulent emotions generated by other people and explore the core of her own being. Her thoughts ranged over the years of her childhood and cast themselves forward into alternate courses for the future.

Torrian spent much time considering how she had never accepted herself or considered herself adequate. Compared to Rushain, who was the confident eldest son, or Cheyte, the prankster who could take nothing seriously, or Raunn, the spoiled hoyden, she had felt herself drab and without character. Lacking any idea of what she wanted for herself, afraid of being nothing, she had become instead what everyone else wanted her to be.

Out of this, Torrian fabricated the persona of the good daughter. She was diligent and industrious about household duties, devout and attentive to religious responsibilities. She was respectful to her parents, adult relatives, and the nayyat. She even treated the underranks and domestic animals with care and regard for their well-being. Yet, while praise came her way, she never felt as if she deserved it. The accolades did not satisfy, directed as they were to the dutiful Clan Daughter everyone saw, and not to Torrian, who hid inside. She was invisible.

Once ensconced in the well-shaped identity of the good Clan Daughter, however, she had found it to be much like the clickbug's purloined shell. It fit, at least for a while, and it was secure, but she could not leave it for fear of exposing her most vulnerable parts. When she had finally cast off the shell, unwisely and for the worst reason, that vulnerability had undone her by drawing Verrer and Surrein to the prize.

*I was dutiful,* she thought, *and I was praised and accepted for doing only what was expected of me. No one knew who I was at all.* The rock shivered under her. *I didn't know who I was, either. Maybe I still don't.* The stone quivered again and ripples ringed out from the edges of the heartspring, marring its pure stillness. *Surrein doesn't want me except as entertainment, a diversion. My mother is no longer interested in me, only in nurturing her own misery. My father . . .* Her throat swelled and she moved quickly away from that thought. Then she continued her anguished exploration. *But why is that surprising? If I don't know who I am, how are they supposed to?*

The vibration began again, shuddering upward through her bones, into her teeth, and finally reaching her ears. "Whoooooooo," it said. There was a pause and then the sound came again, still deep but audible. "Whoooaaarreyoooouuu?"

Torrian froze. The voice, if it could be called that, was an intrusion beyond her experience. It excluded anything the nayya had said to prepare her for the vigil. It was unreal, unbelievable. Her eyes, long accustomed to limited light, probed the dark crannies and fissures around her for the source of the voice. Even as she searched, she knew that it had come from no one place, but rather from the stone surrounding her. Her mind raced, trying but failing to provide explanations and rational theories for what she had heard. Yet, perhaps because of the effects of the vigil, she was not afraid.

The voice came again, higher pitched this time and with the words distinguished. "Whoooooo aaaarreee yoooouuu?"

Her mouth was dry but Torrian felt compelled to answer the question. "I, I am Torrian," she replied and her voice sounded thin and insubstantial. She could barely hear it herself and it died before reaching the walls around her.

"Whooooo?" came the question again. The sound of it filled the chamber completely, booming from the stone.

Torrian tried again. Taking a deep breath, as in preparation for one of the exercises in the Kohrable, she centered herself and said in an upstanding voice, "I am Torrian ni Obradi san Derrith. Eldest daughter of Clan Cliffmaster. Child of Rutin-Xian ni Pejjin san Obradi, vellide of the clan and Krane ni Srinnioth san Derrith, tansul of the clan. Affianced wife of Surrein ni Varskal san Cannestur of the Clan Fellskeeper." She reached for something else to say and realized with a sinking heart that she had defined herself but only in terms of other people.

"Aaaaaahhhhhhh."

Torrian waited for another question but there was silence. *What was this thing?* she wondered. *What was happening to her?* She recalled, suddenly, Maitris's stories about being frightened as a child by the rocks making noises. Torrian had discounted those stories as born from fear and superstition of the underranks. Now she wondered. Could Maitris have heard something like this? Would an ignorant, illiterate drev be worthy audience for something so extraordinary? Had others heard it but been afraid to speak? The voice came again. "Whhhaatt aaare yooouu?"

This question was so unusual she hardly knew how to answer it. What was she? Or was the whole problem that she did not know? Torrian attempted an answer. "I am troinom. Female. Frightened." *Why did I say that?* she wondered. *I am not frightened—not of this. Of what, then?*

"Aaaaahhhhhh." There was silence again.

Had this happened to others? People went on vigils all the time. Claims of hearing voices in the wind, the water, the sound of rustling leaves or waving grass were common and Torrian could understand them. But no one claimed to have been spoken to by a voice big enough for all of Chennidur. Who would be so arrogant as to claim the attention of an entire world? Surely such immense pride could not be countenanced.

"Whhyyyyyy?" the voice asked.

Why what? It must refer to her last statement. *Why am I frightened?* The words came from Torrian spontaneously and tumbled from her lips before she could weigh their meaning or measure their import. "I am alone. I do not know who I am or what I want. Once I was strong but now I feel confused and weak. The man I am to marry is cruel and takes pleasure in inflicting pain. I am afraid of pain. I do not know what to do so I am hiding here. So pathetic. I am afraid of it all."

"Aaaahhhhhh." Then it was over. The voice, the vibrations, an undefinable presence that had been unnoticed until it disappeared—all were gone. Torrian let out a breath she had been unaware of holding. Could it truly have been the voice of Chennidur that she heard? Or the Chenni-ad. She thought of the deity's multiple, intertwined nature. In Worldbirth, Aahks was the Planner, who turned the world, bringing night and day, the seasons, time itself, to the world from out of the timeless dark. Perhaps Aahks had spoken to her. But why? And what should she do about it?

It occurred to her that there was nothing she could do. Who would believe her if she spoke? Was that why no one else had ever reported such a thing? After long contemplation, she decided that silence was her best choice. She would remain here to complete the vigil. Whatever had happened, was happening here, she needed to see it through. Torrian consulted the Book of Vigils. It told her what her body was already saying: it was time to move and return circulation to her limbs. First, however, she must attend to another need. She rose stiffly and stretched, then went into the side cavern to visit the privy.

# CHAPTER 15

## THE ROCK

A warm wind from the south rushed past Raunn, drawing the night sky closer, making it restless. Above her the Great Wheel blazed, a glittering disc poised on one end, hanging close enough to touch. The few scattered stars spun off by the Wheel, blazed defiantly in isolated splendor. Raunn tilted her head. The Eyestar burned alone, surrounded by a nimbus of utter blackness. Its role in the heavens demanded that it remain solitary, for how could it watch and report to the Chenni-ad on the world's affairs unless it remained aloof from the company of other stars? Smallmoon surged up in the east, its full azure face beaming blue light onto the starwalk where Raunn stood.

As always when she was up here alone with them, the stars beckoned to Raunn, calling her with a compelling voice of cold fire. As a child she had climbed this pinnacle to stare at them while they seared their way into her soul. The stars aroused in her a formless longing, an ache of ineffable desire that sometimes grew beyond bearing. Now she confronted them and felt, as always, alone, and unutterably homesick. There was no explaining this feeling;

she was, after all, in the middle of her home. She had never understood it any more than she had been able to deny or avoid it. Instead she sought it out, opened herself to it, yearning for a cold and mysterious companionship that she could not begin to comprehend.

There was a scuffling on the steps and Aurial pulled herself up onto the starwalk puffing from the climb. She drew in her breath and began to speak but Raunn forestalled her, holding up a hand for silence. Aurial looked startled and Raunn simply pointed skyward in explanation. Whatever the outworlder had been about to say went away as she took in the spectacle of the heavens. Both women stood in silence watching the stars until a new light rose from the south, transited the arc of the sky and merged with another bright spot riding close to the northern horizon. "A shuttle?" Raunn asked in a hushed voice.

"Probably," Aurial replied. "How could I have missed seeing all this when we were in the Perimeter?"

Raunn shrugged. "You were tired, it rained, I was hurt. There were other things to think about than watching the stars."

"Is that why you came up here? Just to watch the stars?"

"Yes," Raunn replied bluntly, feeling suddenly testy and uncommunicative. "I have always come to the starwalk to do this. They . . . the stars . . . Well, I just like it. Why are you up here?"

"I was looking for you and Maitris told me where you were."

Raunn resisted the intrusion to her privacy. "What do you want?"

"To talk about what to do next. Surrein is gone and I didn't learn much that will help us. We were both so taken by surprise and he left so quickly that we haven't decided where to go from here."

"No, we haven't. Nor have I received a reply to my message, although I really did not expect one so soon. I, I'm really not sure what to do next. On one hand, I have to make arrangements for my sister's procession to Nandarri and her needs for the wedding while she hides in the Heartspring. My mother must be made ready to go as well and there's her participation to think about. Not to mention my own. On the other hand, now I have to worry about what Surrein is doing while he's out of our sight, and what he's plotting with my uncle Verrer."

She paused. "Then, of course, there's also the Rock to run: someone has to give Antikoby his orders. He's been holding things together as best he can until now. That's what he *would* do, but even the best tuupit can't go on forever without a troinom to direct him."

"I thought running the Rock was the tuupit's job," Aurial inquired.

Raunn recognized it immediately as one of those oh-so-innocent questions that Aurial used when she wanted to make a point. The points were usually at Raunn's expense and she found them very annoying. "Yes, of course it is," Raunn replied, irritation in her voice. "But he still needs orders. Antikoby is an excellent tuupit but he's only a servant, a drev. You can't expect him to really think." She reminded herself that the starwoman did not understand the basic order of things because she had never lived with them. How could she comprehend the underlying nature of the underranks, how limited they truly were? She had not grown up commanding them, dealing with their slowness, their hesitance, their laziness. She could not appreciate how getting one of the servants to do something often felt like moving a large bag of wet sand from one place to another, that it could be more exhausting to make them do their duties properly than to do them oneself.

Aurial's next comment convinced Raunn that the outworlder was walking a narrow line between ignorance and insult—or the class structure was truly incomprehensible to her. "But you told me that Torrian and your mother ran the household, not you. Surely that means he knows what to do better than you."

Raunn's anger flared but she refused to rise to the bait. This was quite beyond the starwoman's experience, after all. "Trust me," she replied. "Without a troinom to give commands, any one of the underranks will falter, even Antikoby. It's true that he knows the routine of the household very well because he deals with it every day. Antikoby can even make small decisions because he's quite intelligent for one of his kind. But any major issue is simply more than he can deal with. It must have been very difficult for him with both Torrian and Mother ill and me off in Nandarri. I'm sure he was quite relieved when we turned up." *That should put an end to this silly discussion*, she thought. Then her vexation drove her to do a little baiting of her own.

"Since we're talking about Antikoby," Raunn continued, "I've seen how you look at him. Why haven't you called him to your room? It's not quite the season, but most women find that even more exciting." She was quite gratified to see a number of emotions pass quickly over Aurial's face, with consternation predominant.

"W-what do you mean?" the outworlder stammered.

"Oh, please don't play the innocent," Raunn goaded. "Antikoby is quite handsome and you *have* noticed it."

"Well, of course I have," Aurial protested. "I'm not blind."

"Well then, what's stopping you?" Raunn could see that Aurial was at a loss and she followed up her advantage mercilessly. "Or are you—inexperienced—at this sort of thing."

"I'm not sure what sort of thing you mean," Aurial retorted heatedly. "If you mean sex, I've had all the experience I want. If you mean pursuing an attraction that's not mutual, you're right. I have no experience in that at all. I would be taking advantage of my position and Mother taught us never to do that."

"Oh, but you're not up there now," Raunn said, gesturing toward the Great Wheel. "You're here and we do things differently on Chennidur. Aren't you the one who preached to me about right and wrong, or what's immoral, depending on where you are? If a troinom woman wants to amuse herself with a handsome servant, she summons him to her room and he comes. When he's there, he performs well. That's what the underranks are for—to serve us, to please us."

"And what if that troinom woman becomes pregnant? What happens then?"

Raunn was repulsed. "Pregnant?! What a disgusting idea! No troinom woman would become pregnant by a drev. Pleasure is one thing but keeping the lines of inheritance pure is quite another."

"So what does this troinom woman do to prevent it?" Aurial pushed. The discussion was becoming extremely interesting.

"Why, nothing. Drevs can't impregnate troinom; it's impossible. It wouldn't even occur to anyone—except an outworlder."

"You mean it's never happened even once?"

"Never. Not even in Stonefather tales."

It was time to let that issue drop. "What if the man doesn't want to be summoned? What if he's not interested in 'performing' for some woman he may not know or like?"

Raunn laughed at the very idea. "You keep thinking as though drevs have minds of their own. I've told you before that they follow orders and they don't dare ask questions. Their wishes—if they have any—are of no consequence. It doesn't matter whether you want breakfast in bed or something more substantial. You order; they do it."

"I don't think I can," Aurial said defiantly.

Her self-righteous attitude infuriated Raunn, pushing her beyond anything she might otherwise have said. "You are supposed to be a troinom lady. That means doing the things the sri-nothi Aurial would be expected to do. Is bedding a handsome man harder than eating cooked flesh?"

Aurial began to speak and then stopped. When she tried again, it was with less certainty than before. "Is this really what a troinom woman would do?"

"Yes," Raunn said bluntly.

"Couldn't I just do nothing?"

"You can do anything you like but if you want to be accepted as a troinom and avoid gossip, you'll follow through on this. Antikoby has noticed your interest and so has Maitris. You haven't been exactly subtle. Servants gossip, even though they can be punished severely for it, and gossip spreads. Seducing him is out of the question, of course. That's only for a man of your own rank."

"And how would the troinom lady go about this?" Aurial asked.

Raunn knew that she had won and backed down a little. "She would look thus at Antikoby, then gesture, so. She would say where and when. That's all that's required."

Aurial nodded and, in the full light of Smallmoon, Raunn could see that she was troubled but excited at the same time. It added sauce to her mischief making.

Then Aurial struck back with a soft question. "And have you had your share of the servants in your bed? Do you find the underranks exciting?"

Raunn sighed. "Sometimes. But I spent most of my time here on the Rock and I know all these servants too well to think of bedding any one of them. When I went to Nandarri, that was different. I knew the first time I saw Merradrix that I had to have him."

"And so you looked, so, and gestured, thus?"

"Basically, yes," Raunn replied simply. "He performed very well. So well that I wanted more and afterward he spoke of the Tarraquis and how he helped them sometimes. It was impudent of him and he risked a good deal by speaking at all, but I was all torn up inside with anger and fear and frustration. I wanted to do something and the Tarraquis showed me how."

"Do you miss him?"

"In the night, I miss his body, the pleasure he gave me. What else is there?"

"If all he meant to you was his body, then why were you so adamant that he be rescued?"

"Because he was helping me on the mission and he was my responsibility. A troinom takes care of the drevs under her authority. *Shufri-nagai* says that we may not abuse them or abandon them. The water of the Heartspring forms a bond and those who command must accept the responsibilities of that bond."

Aurial's eyes narrowed. "That may be part of it but that's not all of it. I saw the way you reacted and I heard real concern in your voice. Come on, what's the real reason?"

Raunn waited a long moment, reluctant to admit that

she was less sophisticated, less of a woman than she had just appeared. Finally she said, almost in a whisper, "He was my first."

Raunn expected a taunt or a joke from the starwoman but Aurial said nothing. The silence lengthened and then Raunn added, "And what of Merradrix? Do you know? Have you heard anything?"

"It's being taken care of," Aurial replied. "The person—Rolfe—who has gone to bring him back is the best."

"Who is Rolfe?" she asked. If Aurial knew his name, she thought, he could not be some faceless helper.

Aurial said simply, "He's my brother."

Raunn was startled: this was a surprise. "I didn't know you had any brothers at all," she said. "You have spoken only of sisters so I assumed your mother delivered girl babies."

Aurial laughed in a way that told Raunn there was a story worth hearing. "That's exactly right," she replied. "Mother didn't deliver boys, she only conceived them. Several of them in fact, although she never mentions it. She doesn't like men so she didn't want to carry male fetuses to term, much less give birth to them. Instead she farmed them out to surrogate mothers and paid them well to foster the boys. End of story for mother. We girls are not really sure how many brothers we have but we've been trying to track them down. Mother doesn't mind as long as they stay on the periphery of the business. Rolfe is the first of our 'finds' and so far it's worked out well."

Raunn tried to imagine a woman so careless of her sons that she gave them away, and could not. But then her mind, unbidden, presented her with the memory of her own mother, whose grief for Cheyte and Rushain had enclosed her in a shell that her daughters could not penetrate. She pushed the thought away. "What about your father—her consort—didn't he mind? All men want sons to raise and fight with."

Aurial laughed again and Raunn made a disgusted face; she hated it when the outworlder acted superior. Immediately Aurial apologized, while laughing even harder. "I'm sorry. I'm just trying to imagine it." She calmed down a bit and continued. "We all—boys and girls—have different fathers and mother has never had a consort. She wouldn't allow a man that much control over her. It's possible she's been in love but it's equally possible that she simply picked out a man whose genes were satisfactory for breeding and then stayed with him long enough to get pregnant. She could have done it artificially, of course, but that's not her style."

Raunn was even more appalled at this last statement. Artificially? How was it possible to conceive a child artificially? Part of her wanted to ask but another part found the outworld idea so contrary to the tenets of the True Word that it made her stomach churn. She asked another question quickly. "How many of you are there?"

"Well, five girls," Aurial said. "And we're more different than you might expect. Wasnohe is very dark, Gwynn is light and creamy. Itombe is a golden in-between and Tumi is nearer to a lovely bronze. Then there's me. I have this nondescript complexion of no particular color and hair the color of Perimeter dirt. I may not know who my father was but I'm sure he didn't contribute the kind of genes, lookswise, that my sisters got."

Raunn was both amused and perplexed. She had thought Aurial striking when she saw her for the first time in the Portmaster's office. If the woman really thought so little of her own looks, what did she see in the mirror? Did she not know that her "hair the color of dirt" was the same tone as burnished klypt wood? Her anger had dissipated, allowing her to say, "I have never seen your sisters so I can't compare, but you are certainly far from plain. My brothers . . ." She stopped that thought. It was harder to talk about them here than it had been in the Perimeter. Everywhere she looked was filled with memories that made it difficult to talk about them without tears and she did not want to cry in front of Aurial. She brought the conversation back from its side-path. "You said Merradrix was being taken care of, that your brother had gone to bring him back. When will you know?"

Aurial shrugged. "I don't know. Rolfe tracked him to the base station and discovered his code number. That told him where Merradrix had been sent and he has gone after the man personally. That's enough for me. I'll tell you as soon as I hear anything."

Raunn looked back up at the sky as if seeking her lover in the spangled darkness. Then she shivered. "I'm getting cold," she said. "Let's go down."

"In a minute," Aurial responded. "I have two questions I'd like to ask."

*What now?* Raunn thought, then resigned herself. If she wanted to go back inside she would have to just get it over with. "Just two? What are they?"

"First, why were you so angry with me? I'm sorry if I interrupted you but it didn't seem to bother you."

Raunn was startled; she had not expected to be confronted with her own ill-mannered behavior. She fumbled for an answer. "Because I . . . Because you . . ." She looked up at the stars again and found the answer there. "Because you own the stars," she blurted, "and I can't even touch them. What's the second question."

"Oh. Why do you call it Smallmoon when there is no Bigmoon? It's not logical."

At this question, it was Raunn's turn to laugh. "Oh, but it is. There used to be a Greatmoon. At least, according to legend, but the Raveler stole it to annoy the Chenni-ad. He hid it in a place where only he could find it, a place so clever that the Chenni-ad never thought to look there. But he outsmarted himself because it was soon clear that Chennidur was better off without it. When the Raveler saw that his mischief was undone, he hurried to fetch Greatmoon and return it to its place, only to discover that the hiding place was so safe and so clever, he could not remember where it was. So Greatmoon was never returned and we have only our beautiful blue Smallmoon to light the sky. Can we go in now?"

"Yes," Aurial replied. "I'm chilled, too."

# ORBIT

As the supply freighter came up on Big Green, Rolfe continued to juggle possibilities and alternatives. Since dropping into realspace, he had worked through countless scenarios and felt like he was ready for just about any-thing—or absolutely nothing. *Why don't I just give up and play this by ear?* he told himself. Disgusted, he forced his brain to stop working and relax. Strapped into the seat beside him, Autex stared mindlessly at the bulkhead, com-pletely relaxed. *But, then, relaxing is easy when you're an android,* Rolfe told himself. Autex looked perfectly hu-man, of course. The mechanical and augmented parts of him were tiny and imbedded far out of sight in synthetic bio-materials.

Rolfe had chosen an android for his back-up deliberately because the constructs could focus on the job to the exclu-sion of all else. Androids weren't great company but they had the advantage of never being distracted by human needs and failings. Their attention never drifted; they didn't have to relieve themselves at a critical moment; they weren't tempted by the most alluring of bodies; they never slept. Most importantly on a mission such as this one, they had no conscience.

Autex*259 was the best of the available free-lance androids programmed for security work. Rolfe had contracted with his M'Gwad handler and obtained passage out for them both, but not before acquiring black-market databeads on Big Green and Dependable Workforces. The 'bead sockets were the only augmentation he had, installed before his father had died, before he ever saw the Beldame. A socket was virtually essential to survival in the Outback and were now common throughout the Quad as well. As an opera-tive, though, Rolfe knew that an implanted comlink would be a useful addition, particularly on a mission such as this one. But that would have to wait until he returned to the Beldame. He remembered how Aurial had resisted having a socket installed for her mission and smiled. It was not easy to give up body room to a piece of hardware but one quickly forgot that objection in the greater efficiency—and improved odds for survival—they provided. She was probably just coming to appreciate the benefits now.

He had listened to the beads over and over again but did not feel that he knew any more now than he had known before. Dependable Workforces was indeed a straight front for men associated with the Ya-ku'z, the Quad's largest and most profitable criminal organization. It gave them a way of cleaning money acquired through illegitimate activities but was a profitable enterprise in its own right. The company's criminal ties gave him more leeway in his approach but also offered more risk. He could resort to force, if necessary, without fear of legal entanglements because Dependable Workforces would never press charges in the courts. Instead they would simply deal with the problem in their own way and Rolfe had no desire to end up dead or, worse, one of the slack-jawed workers on the line.

Worry would get him nowhere except stressed when he couldn't afford distraction. To divert himself, he tapped his console into the bridge's viewscreen and watched as the freighter approached Big Green. The silvery swirl of the planet's cloud cover obscured most of the broad green belt that girdled its middle. Big Green looked closed and mysterious, and Rolfe imagined that, once beneath those clouds, there would be no easy return. He shook his head. This was no time for daydreaming: he would have enough real problems without creating imaginary ones.

The 'bead on Big Green held more hearsay than fact, but that was to be expected. Only guards returned from BG-x3 and they would not be disposed to talk much about what they had experienced. The truly useful information on the 'bead had been what he could infer from the facts: the Project on Big Green was in trouble and it was growing worse. Any raw world was extremely hazardous but usually became less so as its developers learned more about the hazards and gained experience in avoiding them. On Big Green, the trend was going the other way. Both workers and screws were being injured and killed at a steadily increasing rate. The Project was falling behind schedule and no one knew why.

So here he was, about to drop onto a killer world where he would talk diplomatically with the toughest of the Quad's human refuse about retrieving one man who might be a hot commodity and who might still be alive. He smiled. It was far better than waking up to another boring day on the Beldame.

It took longer than he expected for the Call light on his console to indicate that it was time to disembark. When it finally blinked on, he released the seat harness and pushed himself up toward a hold bar. Supply freighters did not have expensive luxuries like artificial gravity. "Time to go," he said to Autex. The android did not waste energy on a reply. Single file, they floated their way toward the landing shuttle, pulling themselves from one hand-hold to another and bouncing through connecting passages. The shuttle was already filled with replacement guards, men and women who looked like the galaxy had chewed them up and spit them out. Rolfe had seen their like before, had sometimes wondered if he would end up the same way when the Outback was through with him. Now, when he looked at them, he could afford to shudder.

As they strapped themselves in, the captain entered the shuttle and clamped his shoes to the deck in front of Rolfe. He wasted no time on etiquette. "Once you're dirtside, you'll have one standard temporal week to get your business settled. It will take us that long to unload our cargo and then reload what they have for us down there. After that, on STD eleven, we warp out of orbit whether you two are on board or not. Don't think you can take your time and hold up my schedule because you're connected to the il Tarz. They don't own the ship and I don't play politics. If you want to warp out with me, be here. Otherwise wait for the next freighter; it's all the same to me. Understand?"

Rolfe gave a quick nod. "Yes, Captain, I understand completely."

"Good," the captain replied. "Enjoy the steam bath."

He gave a little mocking salute, then detached himself and pushed out.

"Nice man," Rolfe commented.

"Nice men run cruise ships," Autex commented.

Then the warning klaxon blared and it was time to drop.


Steambath. Rolfe had been in steam baths that were cooler and dryer than the tropics of BG-x3. He might have seen a jungle bigger and meaner than this one but, if he had, he could not recall it. His dismay must have been plain on his face because Kappin Trenk laughed at him. "What did you expect," the man said, "this ain't exactly a pleasure garden." No, Rolfe could not associate any kind of pleasure with this world. The air was so thick with heat, humidity and an incredible overpowering smell that it felt thick enough to hold in his hands. The atmosphere was so oppressive it encased him like an energy field. Moving, even talking, meant pushing against steady, enervating resistance. He could not imagine doing hard physical labor here. He could not imagine doing anything on Big Green but taking the first shuttle out.

Kappin Trenk laughed again. "We're in the shade, too. The cloud cover keeps direct sunlight down to scattered fast-moving patches but when one of those mungerers hits you, it's like being slammed by a tree."

Rolfe groped for some response. "Surely the living quarters are climate controlled so you get some relief," he said.

Trenk shook his head. "Quarters are dehumidified but that's it. Wringing the water out makes it feel cooler, though."

Rolfe was appalled at his own reaction. He had experienced extremes of heat and cold before. Physical comfort had never been important to him, and irritating environments were just a price to be paid for the challenge and excitement. Why, then, was this heat so overwhelming? Had his time on the Beldame softened him so much? Was he becoming accustomed to a controlled environment, a regulated schedule, dependable mealtimes with plenty of processed food? Was it that he now depended on all the comforts technology and engineering could provide? Or was it that he had simply never felt anything like this before and wanting to escape it was the only logical reaction?

He pulled his attention back to the kappin. "Why?" he asked. "There must be enough energy on a planet like this to fuel fully-controlled environmental units."

"Sure is," Trenk replied. "But with quarters at normal temperature, the transition to this would shock the body. Moving back and forth a few times a day would be tough and my screws couldn't work up to regs while they adjusted." He laughed in his throat. "Not to mention the rawfin hard time I'd have rousting them out of that nice, comfortable bunk and back to work in this. I'm running a project here, not a dinner club, see?"

"I see," Rolfe said. The logic made sense.

Trenk continued. "The only reason we dehumidify is to kill off the fungus. It grows on clothes, skin, anything it can, and real fast, too. Without dry air, we'd all be walking mold in two days. It keeps the creepies out, too."

"Creepies?" Rolfe had seen his share of life forms and was not repulsed by much of anything. But people were dying on Big Green and he needed all the facts he could get. The databead gave him no information on creepies.

"Yeah, that's what we call all the little scogs. They crawl, fly, climb, whatever it takes to get to humans. Sometimes they look like bugs or snakes but most of the time, you can't tell what they are."

"Are they dangerous?"

"*Everything* on Big Green is dangerous. No exceptions. Not that we give anything a chance to prove it's harmless before we goosh it. That's the rule: If it moves, goosh it. Follow that rule, and you can stay alive, too."

"I will do that, kappin. I certainly will." Rolfe liked this place less and less. The best thing he could do would be to buy out the target's contract and get back up onto the freighter before he encountered the creepies or any of their larger relatives. It was time to get started. "I have a small item of business to transact," he began, "and then I'll get out of your way as quickly as possible."

"Sure. The family didn't send one of its fine representatives here, with back-up, to see the *dumaass*. What are you after?"

"One person. A man. He was sent—um, shipped here by mistake and I've come to take him back."

Kappin Trenk shook his head. "Rawfin big mistake, comin' here. But the man signed a contract. He can't just walk out on it."

"Of course not," Rolfe replied smoothly. "I am authorized to pay Dependable Workforces the full value of his contract with them. Since he is already on the job, the company will get whatever labor he has provided free."

"Company don't see it that way," Trenk countered. "DW invests in its workers. There are the costs of recruitment, transportation, nourishment, and education to factor in. Man hasn't worked long enough to repay the company for those."

Rolfe smiled inwardly. Trenk didn't even know which man he meant, so how could he know how long the worker had been on the job?

"Surely not so great an amount," he replied. "We aren't talking about a scholarship to Gwad-Tak University, are we?"

"Scoggin close," Trenk said. "Big Green's a long way from anywhere and labor's not cheap these days."

"If compensation for those is required, I can pay it," Rolfe acquiesced, "within reason, of course." So far, so good. Everything was going according to script.

"Course. But you're causing me a lot of personal inconvenience." Trenk pulled out a cloth and wiped his face and neck. "I got to pull a man off a team, see, then replace him with someone else who doesn't know the job as well. Thing like this disrupts the whole work flow, if you know what I mean. And like I said, I've got a project to run. We're behind schedule as it is and this is gonna make it worse."

Rolfe wanted to laugh. If he could get away with the cost of the contract and a reasonable bribe, he would be able to wrap this one up nice and neat with lots of time left over for R&R. "I would be willing to offer something extra to offset your difficulties," he said calmly. "Again, within reason."

They negotiated a number until Trenk had what he wanted and Rolfe was satisfied. They both knew that one worker was dispensable anyway and that Dependable Workforces would probably never see any of the money. The captain nodded once. "Know the man's ID number?" he asked.

"Certainly," Rolfe said.

Trenk gestured toward a worn computer panel. "Speak it in here, then," he said.

Rolfe crossed the room. "Locate worker number Q3*C104-696," she said.

The computer garbled something indecipherable. *The heat's getting to the equipment,* Rolfe thought. Trenk, who had followed him across the room, reached out and shifted the computer's response to the monitor screen. They waited a few seconds and then a code scrolled across the screen. Trenk studied it, frowned. "You just ran out of luck," he said.

Rolfe knew it had been going too smoothly. "Why?" he asked, afraid what the answer would be.

"Man you want got sent out on a scouting detail. He's not here."

Rolfe breathed out in relief. This was just a delay, not a real glitch. "When is the detail due back?" he asked.

Trenk consulted the computer and found the answer. "Fifteen days, Big Green time," he replied.

Rolfe did not want to be held dirtside until the next freighter warped in. Not on Big Green. "Could we find him?" he queried.

"Yeah, guess you could," Trenk answered. "But I don't see what good that would do."

"If we, ah, rented a flyer, we," he nodded toward Autex, "could follow their planned course and put a sensor fix on their bio-indicators. A flyer must be faster than whatever ground equipment they're in."

"They're on foot," Trenk said cryptically.

"Even better," Rolfe continued. "We could overtake the scouting party and pick him up, then head back here."

"Won't work," Trenk said.

"Why not?" Rolfe asked, irritated with the man's laconic statements.

"For the same reason they're on foot," Trenk said. There was an undercurrent of anger in his voice. "Equipment doesn't work that far out in the *dumaass*. Flyer would die halfway out and dump you in the jungle. You don't know squat about survival out there. *Dumaass* would eat you for dinner—even with backup."

Rolfe wanted to slam the table in exasperation but he maintained his cool company facade. He wouldn't find a solution by losing his temper. "Why doesn't the equipment function?" he pursued.

"Don't know," Trenk commented. "It worked fine when the project started. Then machinery began malfunctioning all over. Project just about stopped until the company flew in a magnetic field regulator. That fixed things just fine—inside the regulator's range. Trouble is, the range only extends about two klicks. That covers this equipment," he nodded toward the computer, "and everything else in the main buildings. Once you get outside that range, machines go queer real fast."

"Sounds like you need more MFRs," Rolfe said.

"Scoggin' right." Trenk spat in the direction of the jungle. "But the company won't send 'em. They ship more workers instead, then tell me to stop whining and get to work." He shrugged. "That's my problem. Yours is that machines just won't fly as far as your man is walking."

"Then what do you suggest I do?" Rolfe asked in frustration.

Trenk gave a small smile. "Sit it out. When the patrol comes back, you take your man and go. If they aren't here in fifteen days, they aren't coming back at all. It's real simple."

*Yeah*, Rolfe thought cynically, *real simple*. He felt like hitting someone, preferably Trenk. His hands started to curl into fists and he forced them open again. Autex caught his eye and moved his head upward slightly. The construct was right. It was time to return to the freighter, regroup and make a plan. They could use the ship's sensors to locate the scouting party. The only alternative was to stay here sweating puddles and watch slave laborers cut down the jungle. At worst, they could come back down the well when the freighter left and wait dirtside for the next one. He decided.

"We'll wait," he said. "Back on the ship. We'll be down again before it goes."

Trenk nodded. "All the same to me. Least it's cool up there. Come back down any time. Bring me a cold beer." He smiled. "I'm not going anywhere real soon."

## THE HEARTSPRING

Soon the nayya would return on his regular visit. In the cavern, time flowed as smoothly and unmeasurably as the Heartspring, yet Torrian sensed the imminence of Nusrat-Geb's arrival. This awareness, a simple knowing, was increasingly familiar to her although she had never before experienced anything beyond the limits of the five senses. She was learning to trust the feeling, just as she had learned to stay warm in the damp cold of her stony sanctuary.

This time, when Nusrat-Geb left the cavern, she would leave with him. It was time for the su-vellide to reassume the responsibilities of her life. Torrian's few things, including the sweater she no longer needed, were folded neatly in the corner. The brazier was cold. Only her small lamp persevered in casting its brave circle of light. She would not have used that either, but for the fact that she could not read or write in the darkness.

The anger and fear that had come with her into seclusion were gone—or at least in abeyance. Torrian knew that both emotions would return on the outside, but it helped that Surrein was no longer on the Rock. Although he awaited her in Nandarri and the Marriage Season was not far distant, she had some time to adjust to new attitudes and practice new skills.

Still, leaving the cavern would be difficult. She had grown so accustomed to silence, darkness and isolation that she felt one with the Heartspring and the stone. Even the nayya's intermittent company had become an intrusion. Emerging once more into the bright whirlwind of life would be a challenge. Torrian studied the Kohrable that lay open on her lap. Its familiar passages, flowing in elegant calligraphy, did not hold her interest. Instead she scrutinized the tiny words that she herself had inscribed meticulously in the margins, words which recorded the message of the Voice that spoke from the stone.

Torrian's regimen of study and meditation had done much to prepare her for the conflicts and ordeals that awaited her outside her sanctuary. Her strongest ally, however, the best fortification of her spirit, was the voice of the stone. After all the time she had spent listening to it, speaking with it, even arguing with it, she still did not know if the stone had spoken or Aahks, the Chenni-ad's Planner aspect, or Chennidur itself. But the voice spoke directly to the emotions—self-doubt, fear and anger—that had consumed her and driven her into the cavern.

The voice had learned to modulate itself and articulate carefully so that she could understand it and converse with it. During many "discussions," she had learned much about the origin of her emotions and how to deal with them. Nothing could have been more precious to her at that point. Forgetting any of it was unthinkable, and Torrian had demanded pen and ink of Nusrat-Geb so that she could hold each word in her grasp. The Kohrable, the most sacred and inviolable of all books, was undoubtedly the correct place to inscribe these words, the place where they belonged. The nayya would be appalled at her desecration of the sanctified volume but Torrian knew that what she had done was right. The words spoken by the voice belonged there as much as any of the ancient tenets.

Gazing at the book on her lap, she read the phrase that carried the greatest meaning for her. "Do not fear, for then you draw to yourself that which you fear." She understood how her fear of not being anyone had caused her to become only what others expected. That in turn had drawn to her a man to whom she was nothing but a political pawn. Her fear had attracted a husband who wished to make her his own creature. Fear was Surrein's weapon, with which he sought to control her. Torrian understood this, but still she struggled with the concept of fear as a spiral that drew you ever deeper, held you ever tighter, and finally created an ending that might never have existed if you had not feared it in the first place.

How to break that spiral was Torrian's greatest concern, for she still feared Surrein and had no idea how to overcome that trepidation. Here in her stygian sanctuary, the fear had no dominion, but she knew that it waited for her above, in the daylight. She would have to walk carefully and guard her emotions to defend against the cold coil that wound itself around her stomach and squeezed until she could feel nothing else. When that happened, Surrein would be in control and the pain that she dreaded would occur. What to do? The words told her not to fear but they did not tell her how to break the spiral.

The pool of the Heartspring quivered and tiny ripples raced across its surface. The air thickened as though filled by an invisible presence. Torrian drew in her breath and held it without noticing. The Voice had come again to answer her question before she had even asked it. Quickly she assembled the writing implements and found a page in the Kohrable with clean margins. It was important that she miss nothing and remember everything.

"Woman," the voice said in its deep timbre. "The way to conquer fear is with laughter."

Laughter? Torrian was dismayed. How could she find anything humorous about Surrein or her marriage to him? And if she were to laugh at him . . . She shuddered. Surrein was too unstable to withstand that. It would infuriate him beyond all control and then he would lash out to punish the one who mocked him.

"Laugh at your fears themselves, not at those who frighten you. Laugh within your thoughts, where no one can hear or see. Laugh in your dreams." The voice stilled. Ripples diminished in the pool until it was once again perfectly still. The air cleared.

Torrian dipped pen to ink and began writing. The message had been brief; she would have no trouble putting it all down. She was totally unaware that she had not spoken a word; the voice had addressed her thoughts. The answer she asked for had been given and yet she felt as burdened as before. There was so much to remember, such a great deal to do and all of it to be juggled so that it came out right. It was like learning to make cloth. You had to place one hand just right on the frame and move the other in a certain rhythm. At the same time, your feet had to push down steadily on the pedals while you kept your back straight. It all seemed impossible at first and she had despaired of ever learning to do it right. But giving up was out of the question and so she had worked hard and eventually learned to do it well. It was all a matter of practice.

A door opened above her and Torrian could hear the nayya's steps scraping on the stone as he began his descent. She put away her Kohrable and the writing implements. Lifting the lamp, she rose. It was time to emerge.

# CHAPTER 16

## TRYST

It was done, and while Aurial's mind was still divided, her body was not confused at all. That afternoon, while they were making up lists of what would be needed for the wedding in Nandarri, Aurial had "invited" Antikoby to her room. In a matter-of-fact way, he had nodded his understanding and proceeded with the work. Later, when he had gone, Raunn smiled approval at her. So it was done: he would come to her room this evening when Smallmoon was at its zenith.

Having made the assignation, Aurial discovered to her surprise that her mental conflict remained unresolved. The logical half disapproved of coercing someone into having sexual relations and wanted to back out of the arrangement. There could be no question of real enthusiasm on Antikoby's part, which meant that he would not be her partner. Thus the tryst would be a kind of rape, a reinforcing of troinom power over a drev. As a male of the underranks, he could only follow orders. The whole idea violated her moral training and made the act repugnant to her.

The emotional half dismissed this argument as irrelevant and insignificant and was, in fact, awaiting nightfall eagerly. This part argued that Antikoby had not seemed reluctant. Such duty was expected of him and how could she be sure he did not enjoy it? She could not read his mind. Besides, she had no choice but to follow through if she was to be accepted as troinom. Distracted by fantasies of what the night would hold, she kept drifting from the task at hand, then forcing herself to pay attention, only to have her thoughts drift away again.

For the remainder of the day, her mind dueled between ration and passion. She was as ashamed of her lack of mental discipline as she was of her lust but she was also beyond the stage where she could deny her desire and force it back into its dusty container again. It simply wouldn't cooperate.

When the evening Call-to-Prayer was completed, and Rutin-Xian had retired to her chambers, Raunn followed Aurial to her room. The other woman was brimming over with helpful suggestions, with which Aurial surmised she was familiar only by hearsay. A hot bath sounded fine, however, and her maid was sent off to prepare it. Along with her suggestions, Raunn had brought a tunic that was the most beautiful thing Aurial had seen on Chennidur. Delicate, light, the color of Smallmoon at first rising, it was alluring, enchanting, not to be resisted. Aurial did refuse perfume, though, feeling it to be dishonest. Perhaps it simply highlighted the ambivalence of her feelings.

The bath relaxed her, the robe excited her. There were twinges in her stomach that changed, as the time passed, into a spreading warmth. Night darkened the sky. The room also was dark, lit only by a small lamp beside the bed. The air smelled faintly of the rejected perfume, as if Raunn had left the bottle uncorked somewhere, hidden so it could emit phantom wisps of scent undetected. The great structure quieted as the household noises ceased one by one until the creaks of the floorboards became as loud as a call to prayer. Smallmoon crept upward by imperceptible degrees.

Finally there came a tap at the door and Antikoby

entered, closing the door quietly behind him. He looked the same as he always did, and wore the same clothes, but he had bathed and the clothes were clean. He approached the bed, entering the circle of her lamp, and Aurial tried to read his face, his eyes. Her conflicted spirit sought to discover some expression that would remove the ambiguity of her emotions. Instead she found only a man, whose visage wore the guarded mask of the underranks.

She could think of nothing to say. Silently, she watched as his eyes explored the curves and shadows of her body under the azure wrap.

"You are beautiful," he said softly, as if it were acceptable for him to speak first in such a setting.

"Thank you," she replied, far more coolly than she felt. He was big and very masculine. Alone in this room with him, she could appreciate his strength and virility more than ever before. She was on fire, yet she could not surrender herself to him without being sure. "You don't have to," she fumbled, then began again. "If you would prefer not to do this, it is alright. You may leave if you wish." She stopped, embarrassed. What would he think of her, the troinom woman who did not know how to command?

Antikoby looked down at the woman, puzzled. He had served the pleasure of troinom women before, and done it well, yet none of them, not one, had ever given a second's thought to his feelings. Not one woman had ever treated him as anything but a means of gratifying her own desires. There had been soft words, endearing phrases, praise for his prowess. None of those words had ever offered him the choice that this strange sri-nothi had just spoken.

He was momentarily taken aback. Was she playing some kind of game with him? It would not be the first time. Troinom women often acted out with a servant fantasies that they would not admit to their husbands. He had become adept at reading what they really wanted from their posture, their tone of voice, the things they said and left unsaid. He could not read this one. She was eager for his body, that was clear: it had been obvious for days. Yet she also seemed reluctant, as if needing reassurance, that he was ardent, too. Well, if that was what she wanted, there was evidence enough. He would give her the assurance she craved.

For an instant, he was tempted to accept her offer, if only because he was not likely to have a real choice ever again and wondered what it would feel like. If she really meant what she said, he could just turn now and leave, return to his room. The temptation passed quickly. His rejection would hurt her and, in the long run, a drev always paid for hurting a troinom. In the short run, he was together with a beautiful woman who desired him, and his body's response was hard, undeniable. Antikoby had no real wish to turn away and seek his cold, solitary bed in despite of her. He smiled and said, using the intimate voice permitted in the bedroom, "I prefer to remain."

Removing his shirt, he sank down on the bed beside her. Antikoby slid the thin fabric of her robe to one side and caressed her right shoulder with his fingertips. Her skin quivered beneath his touch. "You are so strong," she murmured, reaching out to him.

His lips followed where his hand had been, tasting skin like some exotic spice. Moving over the curve of her breast, they found a nipple that was tight and rose to meet his kiss. Her fingers wound in the hair at the nape, slid down his neck and ran over the muscles of his shoulders. If she wanted his strength, he could give her that easily, and match her pleasure with his own.

He set about it with an eagerness that surprised him.

Their passions spent, Antikoby lay back, enjoying how the woman curled against him fitting into the arch of his arm. Some of the troinom relaxed in complete abandon after having their desires satisfied. Others rose immediately, as if donning their clothes armored them against their lust and allowed them to forget how they had submitted to it. This Aurial did neither, acting instead as a partner of his own rank would. She made him feel important, something no other troinom woman had ever done. He stroked her shoulder absently, enjoying the smoothness of her skin and attempting to define the ways in which she was different. From the moment he had first seen her stagger to the top of the Rock ... No, he thought with sudden comprehension, it was from the moment *she* had first seen *him*. That was the difference! She had looked at him as if he were a person, with a mind and a will, and not a thing that existed for her convenience.

Even now, half asleep, she gave herself up to his strength and made him her protector. It was an odd sensation that even the women of his rank could not evoke, since they knew as well as he the limits of any protection he could offer. She stirred, rubbed one hand across his chest, and murmured something. The words were muffled and he leaned in to her, asking her to repeat it. "Did you mind?" she asked.

Incredible. The three simple words astonished him. He kissed her head. "No," he replied. "I most certainly did not. It was wonderful." *Who was she?* he wondered. *Where had she truly come from? And was she what she claimed to be?*

Thinking he referred only to the sex, she smiled and slept again. Antikoby watched their shadows in the flickering lamplight and breathed in the faintly scented air as he thought. He had meant the coupling, and more besides. He was elated, yet he worried. Had he anything to fear from her? Did Raunn? The Clan Daughter trusted her, had revealed the secrets of the family to her. If Raunn trusted unwisely, there could be danger. Suv Torrian had learned this lesson too late and to her sorrow. But this woman, Aurial, was not Surrein. The strangeness she bore was like an aura, masking her true identity.

Antikoby, who was familiar with pretense and with masks thought he recognized in this woman another who had assumed an unfamiliar role. But what was she pretending to be? She was certainly a woman, he could bear witness to that. Turning carefully, so as not to wake her, he tugged the robe away from her left shoulder to expose the clan mark. It was one he had not seen before but that meant nothing: he could hardly claim to be an authority on clan marks. He rubbed it slightly with one finger, smiling ruefully when it did not rub off. Yet neither did it look exactly right.

Antikoby pulled the lamp closer so that its pool of light fell directly on the mark. He might not be able to identify every clan mark that existed, but he did know what a mark was supposed to look like and this one was not quite right. From a distance, it would have fooled anyone but close up, he could see faint differences. The mark did not penetrate the skin as it should have, but seemed instead to float on the top layer. Its color also was subtly wrong, being a flat black without the blue highlights that came from the nayya's sacred ink. He pulled the robe up again.

He was shaken. Aurial was not a troinom. She must, therefore be of the underranks but he could not accept that explanation either. Viscerally, he did not believe that any drev had either the intelligence or the courage to carry off such a deception. It would mean death if she were caught, and who would risk that? To what end?

If she was not of the troinom and not of the underranks, then . . . There was only one conclusion and it shook his composure. Aurial was a starwoman. His mind raced. Did Raunn know? What did it mean? What was she doing outside the Port? Should he do anything? Say anything? Warn Raunn? He was at a loss. The imposture explained all the little oddnesses he had seen and heard over the last few days. He had possessed a starwoman. What would the nayya say about that? And did it violate the law?

Antikoby pulled away from her without being aware that he did so. For long moments he stared into the darkness, thinking, but his thoughts were all jumbled and gave him no answers. Although he was repelled by the idea of contact with an alien female, at the same time it excited him. He wanted to taste her skin again. If he made love to her a second time, it would be as her partner in deception and there would be truth to the equality she had expressed before.

He looked down and saw her eyes, open, watching him. He did not know what to say, or whether to say anything at all. She saved him the trouble. "You know," she said.

A hundred responses rushed to his tongue but Antikoby rejected them all. "Yes," was all he said.

She turned on to her back and held his gaze. "You must tell no one," the woman said, and her voice sounded worried. It surprised him. Then it occurred to him with surprise that he held power over her.

"My duty is to serve the Clan, to protect the family," he replied, considering the power he had held, unwanted, and then given away with regret.

"I offer no danger to Clan or family," Aurial said.

"Does the sri-nothi Raunn know?" he asked.

"Yes, she does."

Antikoby's thoughts slowed and became focused once again. Awake, the starwoman was unaccountably less threatening than when asleep. "What do you want here?" he queried.

"To help," she said. "Only to help." She lifted one arm above her head, pulling her breast up. "What do *you* want?"

"Only this," he replied, and leaned close to taste the soft exotic skin.


## BIG GREEN

They were five days out from the Project site and still alive. Astin wasn't sure why. When he summoned the energy to reflect on it, his ideas were disturbing and he preferred not to think at all. The first two days they had spent just making their way through the *dumaass*, a back-breaking journey that required applying all their concentration to fighting the jungle and defending themselves against its defenses. After that, the days fell into the pattern they now followed, divided between chopping at the *dumaass*, walking and waiting. Nights were spent pursuing a shallow, fitful rest and keeping watch against attack.

The head of the exploration party was not the screw who had ordered them out but one of the small techish group known as scientists. This one had a special name, metallurgist, and was called Ferrin. On Chennidur, Astin had been taught to fear the menacing outworlders inhabiting the Port, but thought this one was more like a nayya than a monster. He was harmless, particularly when compared to the screws, and all his interest lay in the ground beneath them. He did no fearsome outworld things, although he did have techish instruments and used them to do his job. Mostly that job involved pulling long tubes of rock from out of the ground, placing them in an instrument like a box, and then looking at symbols that appeared on one side. Sometimes Ferrin knelt and dug in the dirt, then held another instrument over the cut before reading the symbols. As far as Astin could determine, these nonsensical activities were the only reason that the group was out in the jungle at all.

The two screws maintained security; that was their specialty and their menacing brutality offered no surprises. They never turned their backs on either the laborers or the *dumaass*, and maintaining that vigilance was no mean feat. One screw was always awake and on watch during the night. A weapon was always at hand.

Astin, Merradrix and Shaman had multiple roles, however. As bearers, they carried on their backs the equipment, food and shelter the little expedition required. As trackers, they found a way through the *dumaass* in the direction Ferrin indicated. When the jungle obstructed their progress, the three men hacked through it with long blades, making a path for the others. Their last, and perhaps most important function, Astin thought, was to serve as a kind of lightning rod. They tested any potentially dangerous situation, from crossing a treacherous stream to fighting off the more aggressive plants and animals. In fact, he, Shaman and Merradrix had been selected because they were the ones most likely to help the group survive, even if that meant dying in the process. Since only one laborer was really needed to clear away the jungle, two of them were expendable, their lives to be used up and thrown away when necessary.

During the day, they moved ahead under Ferrin's direction, and all three laborers worked at clearing a way through the jungle. Then Ferrin would call a halt and apply himself to his techish devices. While the scientist dug up rocks and talked to his profane instruments, the laborers rested as much as was possible under the eyes of screws and in a hostile environment. Astin and Merradrix wiped the sweat from their faces and peeled fungus from any exposed skin. Shaman sat quietly by himself, loose-limbed and unfocused, slipping deeper into one of his inexplicable trances at each break. Astin watched him, concerned and apprehensive. Shaman had said to kill the screws, but what about Ferrin? The scientist had done nothing to hurt them.

On Chennidur, he had known others of the underranks who would like nothing better than to kill a troi'm, any troi'm, given the opportunity and a chance to escape hideous punishment. Astin did not feel that way. The troi'm master of his family had never been a large presence in their lives. As long as they paid to him a majority of the profits from the craft-house, they were allowed to go about their business largely undisturbed. As a result, although he resented troi'm, he harbored no need to kill one who had caused him no harm.

They were resting now while Ferrin muttered to himself and then smacked his instrument with one hand. "Scoggin' planet," Astin heard him mutter. "First no long-range scan, then no flyers, now the portables aren't working right. Next, I'll be down to digging up rocks with a pick and tasting the samples for an analysis." He shook the instrument and its symbols blinked out, then reappeared. The scientist seemed satisfied with this information and rapidly became absorbed with his task. The screws were upright and alert, attempting to watch both the laborers and the *dumaass* with equal attention. They seemed almost more concerned about the workers, and well they might, Astin thought. They knew nothing of Shaman's strange plans but Merradrix with a blade in his hand was a threat to be considered at any time.

He rubbed the scar on his leg. It was aching again and not from fatigue. Their path had been clear this day and they had done little cutting. Shaman walked the point, as he always did now because the going was easier when he was out in front, as though he could see paths invisible to the others or as if the *dumaass* was making them. Astin didn't like to think about that either, but yesterday he had seen a branch pull back before Shaman could cut it away. Since then he had watched more carefully and noticed plants shrinking from their passage, vines curling upwards to give them room, underbrush parting before their feet. Merradrix saw these things, too; it showed on his face. The others were too caught up in their own concerns to pay any attention. All they knew was that this part of the jungle was not as thick or as difficult as what had come before and that was good.

They were also no longer being attacked by either plants or the animals Shaman said did not exist. The others thought this was another good sign, although the screws did not relax their vigilance. Astin, however, was worried. Shaman had said the *dumaass* was conscious, so why was it no longer treating them as the enemy? He could think of only one answer—that this was a trap. If so, then why was Shaman walking into it with his eyes closed? If the jungle was setting a trap, why did he tell them to kill the screws? What happened when the trap was sprung? The ache in his leg was getting worse and his worries increased along with it. There was nothing to do except keep moving forward and hope that the end, when it came, would be quick.

He had accepted the fact that he would die in this Wordless place and his spirit lost to the Raveler. It was irrelevant, then, whether death occurred at the hands of the screws or by assault from the *dumaass*. Either way, it would be a pointless death severing him from the grace of the True Word forever and rendering him *parostri*. A surge of homesickness engulfed him. He remembered how he had loved music and wanted to hear the blaikist at the drakshouse near Lower Chuktoo. There was no music on Big Green, no high bright sky, no Call to Prayer, no family. He would never find out how his sister, Esski, had reacted to his disappearance. All the things that were important to him at home on Chennidur were gone here and what he had left was a life that would be spent by others, used up without a second thought. Perhaps when the time came, killing the screws would be easy.

Merradrix passed him a bottle of water and he drank, holding the bottle with both hands. The fungus was creeping into all the nooks and crannies of his body, stiffening the joints so that his fingers were no longer flexible. Only the shower with its profane chemicals and the dry air of the barracks would kill the blight and, one way or another, they would not be returning there. If the screws did not kill them, and the *dumaass* let them live, the fungus would continue its inexorable growth, until it covered them completely and immobilized them.

Ferrin completed his work with the mineral sample and stored the data. "Time to go," he ordered, packing his instruments away. One of the screws waved a diz in their direction and Astin rose along with Merradrix. Shaman opened his eyes and looked straight at Astin. "Soon," he said, standing smoothly. Astin felt a chill even through the overpowering heat. They stooped to pick up their packs and continue the pointless journey.

## THE FREIGHTER

Rolfe drifted into the darkened cabin just as Autex scanned the last of the shuttle's technical diagrams and wiped the file from his monitor. Anchoring himself behind the android, he asked, "Well, did you find what you need? Can we do it?"

Autex blinked as he processed data and calculated the

odds. Then he turned to face his human employer. "Yes," he replied. "It's on the thin edge of probability but we can do it with a good chance of getting out alive."

"If everything goes right," Rolfe added.

"That is correct."

Rolfe reached over him and punched the console to bring up the cabin lights. "What are the odds?"

Autex gave him an inscrutable look. "It's never good to know the odds before you go in."

Rolfe chuckled. "Yes, I'm sure you're right about that."

"Actually," Autex continued, "the mechanical components of this project are far more stable than the human factors. I can rig up a magnetic field regulator in one of the shuttles without any great difficulty. It will occupy a lot of room in the cargo bay but that won't keep us from fitting another body in. When it's running, though, there will be a heavy drain on the power packs, and the shuttle will only make it through the one run."

"So," Rolfe finished, "we'll have to go in, grab the target and get out again fast, with no mistakes."

"That's right." Autex paused and cocked his head. He was jacked-in to the ship's computer and Rolfe could tell that data was downloading. It took only a second, then the android continued. "The larger question is whether the captain will grant us the use of his shuttle."

Rolfe smiled sardonically. "Oh, he'll agree to that—on his terms, of course."

"And those are?"

"He won't free up a shuttle until the cargo is nearly all loaded. That means we have to have the MFR ready to install the minute we board. After that, we have exactly one STD to run the pick-up. If we're not back, he warps out and charges my company for the cost of the shuttle *and* the MFR."

Autex nodded. "Does he insist that one of his crew pilot?"

"He offered but it's not required."

"That's good," Autex commented. "I don't like outsiders around when a job's going down. It cramps my style."

"Are you sure you can handle the shuttle on a run like this?" Rolfe asked.

Autex almost looked offended. "I'm certified to fly anything that goes up or down the well," he replied. "That's one of the reasons you hired me, remember?"

"I remember. Just checking. Let's get back to running the sensors over the grid so we can find our man."

Autex attempted a smile, but androids did not simulate human expressions well and his face contorted into a grimace. "That turned out to be the simplest part of the whole job. I've already found them."

Now it was Rolfe's turn to show disbelief. "So quickly? How do you know the sensors located the labor party and not a herd of animals?"

"The answers are actually connected," Autex replied. "It was so easy to find them precisely because there *are* no herds of animals. I scanned the jungle for hundreds of klicks around the base and the sensors picked up no animal life signs at all. None. It's all vegetation except for the humans at the labor site and the field party."

"Hmm." Rolfe was not sure how to react to this startling new information. "But the kappin said . . ."

"Yes," Autex interrupted, "I know what the kappin said. The sensors do not confirm whatever he's seeing, however. There are no animals in the *dumaass*."

"Did you scan any other locations, just to be sure?" Rolfe queried.

"Not yet, but I will. Something tells me, though, that the readings will all be the same."

"Android intuition?" Rolfe asked.

"Extrapolation," Autex replied with his usual straight face.

"Then the creepies the kappin talked about . . ."

"Must be plants," Autex continued. Then he touched the jack with one finger. "I tapped into the labor's site's computer through the link and read the personnel file. The camp has suffered 250 casualties since work started on the Project. Approximately one quarter of those were attributed to what might be described as 'accidents' or 'natural causes.' For example, a lifter failed and dropped its load of logs, crushing two men."

Rolfe shrugged. "It happens. Especially at labor sites."

"Certainly," Autex agreed. "But the cause of the other fatalities is listed as 'attacks by native predators.' There aren't many details but aggression by an ambient life form was involved in each case."

"So, 187 men were killed by predatory animals that don't exist."

"Exactly."

"Hmm." Rolfe rubbed his right palm with the thumb of his left hand. "Was there any other data you found of interest?"

"Yes, two things," Autex said. "The attacks did not begin until the project was well under way and labor crews had started clearing the jungle over the mineral deposits. Once the incidents began, they escalated continuously and at a compounded rate. Men have been dying in steadily increasing numbers, and that includes the guards as well as the laborers. You could, perhaps, explain that. But then, just a short while ago, the attacks began to diminish."

"What happened?"

"Reason is unknown. I cannot pin down any factor or combination of factors that would account for it."

"I wonder . . . Did the reduction in incidents occur before or after the target arrived on Big Green?"

Autex accessed the data and calculated dates instantaneously. "After."

"Un-huh. What's the second bit of interesting information?"

"You remember the kappin talking about how equipment didn't operate outside of the MFR's range?"

"Remember?" Rolfe responded. "That's why we're jury rigging a shuttle in the first place."

"Equipment repair records for the project duplicate the pattern. Machines of all types worked fine at the inception of the project. Then they began to malfunction and the failure rates are exponential. Now virtually nothing operates for even a few hours outside of MFR range."

"So the hardware failure rate has not shown the same drop-off as the incidence of attack."

"That is correct."

"Do you have any idea what all these things mean?"

"None whatever. I'm an android, not a hyperlink. What I do know is that we better move fast and not munger up. It seems there's more to worry about on Big Green than creepies."

"That's for sure. Can we rig the MFR ourselves?"

"Most of it. If we need assistance, I'm sure I can persuade one of the ship's mechanics to help."

Rolfe frowned. The cost of "persuasion" was going up at every step. He hoped his ready-credit balance would hold out. He didn't relish the idea of explaining to Itombe why he went over budget on his first field assignment. "Well," he said, "let's get going on that MFR. I want it ready to go fast. The more we do up front, the more time we'll have to deal with the unknowns down there."

"Do you have a plan for what happens once we're dirtside?" Autex asked. "We need to work the details out so that we both know what to do and when. There won't be any room for uncertainty."

"Of course I have a plan," Rolfe said. "It's pretty simple but, then, it doesn't have to be complicated. Let's do the MFR first, then we should have time to rehearse the snatch."

Autex released his seat harness and floated up to meet Rolfe. Together they swung out the door and headed for the cross-passage to Engineering.

# CHAPTER 17

## THE ROAD TO NANDARRI

Once Torrian emerged from her vigil, the wedding party assembled itself quickly and set off for Nandarri. It happened with a speed due largely to all the planning that Raunn had overseen in her sister's absence, aided by a staff of experienced servants. Because they were traveling to the clan's city house on Cheffra Street, they required little baggage—just supplies for the journey and the simple grey marriage robe that was Torrian's wedding garment. To ensure that all who were united during the Marriage Season did so as equals, with no ostentation, the Kohrable dictated what both participants would wear. The robe, which Raunn had modeled in her sister's absence, was folded carefully amid layers of heavy cloth and sweet herbs on one of the baggage burrkies. Packed with it was the heavily-embroidered ancestral wedding belt of Clan Cliffmaster.

They ate in the gritty hour before dawn and spent only a brief but obligatory moment at the morning Call to Prayer, then left so as to get an early start. Aurial discovered to her distaste that climbing down from the Rock was no easier than climbing up had been, except that it offended different muscles and took less time. Her old nemesis, the demon gravity, was waiting on the trail, eager to teach her the lesson that preventing yourself from coming down too quickly could be every bit as tiring as fighting to lift yourself higher. She was relieved to find a burrky train, escorted by servants and security men, waiting for them at the base. Aurial climbed with gratitude upon the broad, docile back of her mount and turned the work of traveling over to him.

The vellide's maid and Maitris, Torrian's woman, rode in the back of the small procession with the baggage animals and the rear guard. Raunn's woman, Chewtti, awaited them in Nandarri. Rutin-Xian took her place at the front with as little interest as if she were part of the burrky. Torrian edged her mount in just behind that of her mother while Aurial and Raunn rode together.

Moving sedately in the cool morning air, they crossed the plateau and passed the hospice buildings. Aurial watched the vellide as they went, noting in her the same lethargy, the same hopeless sadness. Rutin-Xian stayed in the saddle mechanically, but showed no interest in the journey and seemed nearly unaware of her surroundings. When one of her daughters addressed her, she spoke but was otherwise silent.

They came to the rim of the plateau and entered the switchback trail that led down to farmlands and the Nandarri road. It was a treacherous track, narrow and winding with steep slopes and numerous switchbacks. Despite the dangers of the terrain, the burrkies went about their business placidly, setting one foot in front of the other, taking the downslopes with ponderous precision. At hairpin turns in the trail, they reached almost languidly with their prehensile appendages, winding them around worn posts and anchoring themselves to swing around the curve. Aurial swallowed her nervousness and let the animals concentrate on their jobs with a minimum of interruption from her.

At the bottom, the trail skirted a compact village tucked against the base of the plateau. Although the citadel of the

Rock was self-contained, most of the holding's agriculture took place at this lower level. Fields were tilled, orchards pruned and animals tended by the village's "blue-dirt" farmers and their families. They occupied the lowest niche in the stratified social order of Chennidur, but were relatively free here from the scrutiny of their troinom masters. Only a few old people and young children gathered to watch the vellide and her entourage pass, however. The adults were all in the fields doing the heavy work of the planting season.

Once past the village, the trail leveled out and wound through vast fields and pastures, greening with new life. Here the burrkies picked up their pace a little and Aurial shifted her seat to match their gait. The day brightened with opaque sunlight so bright she had to shade her eyes when looking into the distance. Flights of puffers drifted over them, their airbags gleaming with iridescent colors. They called to one another with delicate, crystalline notes as they passed over on their migration toward the mountains.

Using the puffers to cover her curiosity, Aurial watched the other members of the party indirectly. Raunn was the same as always, although with normal high spirits tempered by the presence of her sister. It was Torrian who held the most interest for Aurial. After listening to Raunn's often-deprecatory depictions of her sister, Aurial had expected someone a bit prissy, somewhat smug, perhaps a little overbearing in the rightness of her role. Instead a pale quiet woman had emerged from the vigil and rode with them now in silence. Aurial could see that, unlike her mother, Torrian's inward stillness came from deep thought. Her mind seemed to be cast far from her family and the journey, occupied with things unrelated to either traveling or their destination. Her preoccupation made Aurial feel like an intruder.

She caught Raunn casting puzzled looks in her sister's direction. Periodically, the younger sister assayed comments or questions, to which Torrian responded politely but without enthusiasm. It was as if she were trying to distance herself from emotions and from involvement with her family. Aurial was reminded of another woman she had once seen serving tables in a drakshouse on a world far away from Chennidur. Young, new to the job, she had moved through a crowded room balancing a heavy tray full of glasses on her head. Concentrating all her attention on keeping the tray even and the glasses filled, she had been oblivious to the noise of the room, the jostling of diners and even rude comments from a table of youths baiting her into dropping her burden. Torrian's tray was invisible but, whatever it carried, she was working hard to keep anything from spilling.

They stopped for midmeal and Aurial watched in astonishment as the servants emptied baskets, spread cloths, uncorked bottles, and filled plates, setting out an elegant meal for the troinom ladies. It was done so smoothly and with such grace and expertise that she was tempted for a fleeting second to applaud their performance. Instead she applied herself with enthusiasm to the first outdoor meal she had actually enjoyed on Chennidur. After the early start and a morning spent breathing fresh air, her appetite was enormous. She ate immoderately until she was almost ashamed of herself. Since Raunn and Torrian also consumed hearty meals, however, she soon conquered her guilt.

During the warm drowsy afternoon, they passed from farmland into wooded hills steeper than those in the Perimeter, with many dark stone outcrops. Trees covered them all the way to the top, creating a forest that, even early in the season, was cool and mysterious. Aurial found herself gazing into its depths as if seeking a glimpse of something wondrous, the Rugollah, perhaps.

Periodically the shade of the forest gave way to rocky meadows that were tilted precipitously on the hillside. They emerged into one such grassy expanse, bright with sunlight and new grass, in time to hear a booming crash. Raunn stood in her stirrups and shaded her eyes as she searched the uphill terrain off to their right. "Come with me," she said under her breath. "I'll show you something you haven't seen before." They urged their mounts off the road and up toward a jutting stone outcrop. One of the rear guard broke out of the small caravan and followed them at a discreet distance.

Circling the outcrop, they approached what appeared to be a field strewn with blue-grey rocks, some of which bore a twiggy bush on top. Raunn stopped well away from them and Aurial strained to see what unusual thing had drawn them here. She was startled when two of the rocks rose on short legs and walked stiffly toward one another. Her perspective shifted then, transforming the stones into a herd of large animals, a few of which carried a single horn with multiple branches. "What are they?" she asked.

"Wild stonivers," Raunn replied. "Watch."

Aurial tapped the databead which, as usual, provided only sketchy information. Stonivers were large ruminant herbivores which mated on a biannual cycle. Although mating took place once every two seasons, only half the herd mated each season so there was some activity every year. The arrangement kept the size of the herd from becoming too large and also ensured that no one crop of newborns risked their survival on bad weather conditions. The databead gave her no information to explain the activity she was observing now.

As if on signal, the beasts stopped, shook their scraggly horns, and bellowed. For a four-second interval they froze, glaring at one another with rigid hostility. Then they broke their stances and rushed forward. Colliding with unrestrained force, their horns crashed together with a boom that echoed back raggedly from a distant line of trees. Unhurt by the collision, the two beasts sparred with seeming viciousness that actually was a struggle to disentangle their horns. Free of one another again, they shook their heads ominously and wheeled to return to their positions.

"Is this part of the mating ritual?" Aurial asked.

"If you mean, are these two males battling for the right to mate, the answer is no," Raunn replied. "These are two males fighting to be the champion in a mating group."

Aurial ran "champion" and "mating group" through the databead. It told her that certain species formed small mating groups existing independently within the larger herd. Each group consisted of an even number of females, a single fertile male, and an infertile champion. The champion protected the members of the group from attack and prevented females from stealing away to another group.

"Where is the male?" she asked, glad to have some information for a change.

"He's probably over there," Raunn replied, pointing toward several clustered furry bodies lying in the meadow somewhat apart from the herd. "The male is the small one; he's already been selected by the females. Once the champion is victorious, they can begin breeding."

"What happens to the loser? What does he get?"

"He gets to go off by himself until next year, when he tries again. The losers usually hang around the herd in a group of their own, though, and help to defend it against predators. Often, they charge hunting parties and can be quite dangerous. Hunting stonivers with any weapon but a blowgun is a sport for the courageous."

The champions rose and began another pass at one another, muscles bunching and straining under their grey hides. They seemed equally powerful and determined; Aurial could not tell which would win. "This kind of ritualized body contact is prevalent among many species," she commented. "But it's usually the males who engage in it. It seems to be an important way for them to find their place in the species order."

Raunn chuckled. "You're right. Even people do the same thing. Just think about all the ways men find to butt into and slam up against one another. Young men fight and play sports. Old men use power and politics. But it's all the same thing."

"Imagine measuring your worth by conflict and confrontation," Aurial said.

"I can't. The stonivers are better at delegating the roles, though. Fertile males may not be fighters, but they are potent. And just look at the females, keeping off to the side, waiting for this aggressive display to be done with so they can get down to the important business of replenishing the herd." She smiled. "Stonivers also understand that what helps the herd to survive is cooperation. After the breeding is over, the females lead the group to food and water, assist one another with birthing, even warn of predators. If they did not work together, the mating groups would fall apart; the herd would die." She plucked a stalk of grass and began to chew on the sweet inner growth.

Aurial hesitated, then took a shoot of her own. Nibbling it cautiously, she found the grass had a fresh taste. "Of course," she noted mildly, "animals aren't the only ones who use ritual. Humans cloak their natures in castes and politics, roles and ceremonies. Things always appear as different from what they really are." The animals clashed again and the boom of their meeting shivered the ground. She looked at Raunn with curiosity. "What do you think of these differences?"

If Raunn perceived the bait, she didn't rise to it. "I rather enjoy being out here in the wild, watching the real roles play out."

Aurial persisted. "The real problem comes when one sex is in power and becomes blind to any way of behaving but its own. It mandates that behavior as being the only acceptable one. I've seen that happen on several different systems, sometimes to great extremes. It always results in a radically unbalanced society driven by anger and frustration."

"What happens when men dominate?" Raunn asked.

"Then male behavior patterns are approved and normalized. To succeed, women must abandon nurturing, cooperative behavior and become aggressive and confrontational instead. It's hard to do and it never feels right even when they do it well. The alternative is to accept a submissive, powerless role."

"What about when women are in control? Frankly, I can't imagine that. Women don't like to be leaders."

Aurial smiled. "Tell that to my mother. There are matriarchal societies where women lead quite well but men are forced to sublimate their aggressions, or channel them into acceptable behaviors like sports or military activities. If they can't find a proper sense of themselves within the society at large, they become indecisive. Whichever gender takes on the behavior pattern of the other is often uncomfortable inside its skin."

Raunn threw her stalk of grass away. "What about the men who prefer to have sex with other men? Or women with women?" she asked. "Both are proscribed by the Kohrable and are subject to severe punishments, but they still happen."

Aurial hesitated for a moment. "That's different. It's behavior that appears deviant to others but is normal and comfortable to those involved. The only stress comes from outside forces like the Kohrable's proscription."

"You mean, left to themselves, they would be happy?"

"It happens."

Above them, the champions wrestled with locked horns. One pressed inexorably forward, pushing his opponent slowly to its knees. Stiff-legged and stiff-necked, the other fought back without quarter but was forced lower and lower until his forelegs buckled. Once his knees hit the turf and his neck bowed, it was over. The victor wrenched his horns free, raised his head and bellowed his conquest. Immediately the mating group pushed forward, surrounding him, and welcoming him to their ranks.

"Come on," Raunn said, taking up her reins. "The display is over and we have to catch up."

"Are we on schedule?" Aurial asked as she turned her mount around.

"So far. We'll stay tonight at the halfway house and be in Nandarri by mid-afternoon tomorrow. If we catch up." She urged her mount to a faster pace and headed downhill.

Aurial goaded her burrky until it broke into a reluctant, lumbering trot. She jounced in the saddle for a few paces, in increasing danger of losing her seat, then took the reins in her right hand and grasped the saddle front firmly with her left. Feeling somewhat more secure, she charged down after Raunn toward the road.

## CONTACT

Following his path toward the time of contact, Shaman led the way deeper into the *dumaass*. His Allsight was clear once again, almost as it had been back in the Living Hills. Through it he could see the path as though it were marked. While his Allsight focused most powerfully, his other senses were also fixed on the path, attempting to establish contact with the great amorphous intelligence that drew him to itself. With every fiber of his being absorbed in that communication, the other members of the exploration party had ceased to be quite real to him. Instead they existed in an encompassing dream that distracted him from the all-absorbing task.

He was changing in other ways as well. For Shaman, the heat was no longer unbearable and felt normal instead. The periodic downpours had become refreshing and welcome. The fugitive patches of sunlight that had once hammered his body, driving him to his knees, now energized it and gave it strength. Even the overpowering smell of the jungle was as familiar and comforting as his own body odor. Strips of greenish-grey fungus peeled from his hands, neck and face, dropping to the ground as he walked. The jungle cleared the way before him and Shaman followed the path, drawn by the compelling need to communicate with the mind of the *dumaass*.

The others followed him, aware that soon, now, it would be time. Meanwhile, he pushed his way through the growth of the understory, through rain, sun, and heat, increasingly eremitic and oblivious to anything else around him.

The scientist, Ferrin, called another stop. Shaman was so deep into the pull that he continued nearly out of sight before noticing that the others were no longer behind him. He forced himself to turn and go backward to where Astin and Merradrix squatted on the ground. Positioning himself next to them, he closed his eyes. The pull was clearer this way. He could feel it drawing him off to the right, more powerful than ever before. The place he sought was not far and on this day he would find the end of his strange path. He opened his eyes again and looked at his fellow prisoners. "Soon," he whispered in Chenni. "Very soon."

Astin looked disturbed and fastened his gaze on the ground so that the screws would not see his reaction but Merradrix tightened his grip on the hilt of his blade as if he were more than ready for a fight. "A diversion would help," he whispered back.

*Yes, of course.* Shaman recognized the logic of the suggestion immediately. A diversion would guarantee success and what better source for one could they have than the *dumaass*? He closed his eyes again and pictured a simple idea. Resisting the pull that sought to occupy his mind completely, he instead concentrated on the idea. Over and over he visualized that image while the scientist played with his rocks and the guards kept their uneasy vigil.

It was past mid-day and they took advantage of this break to eat from their provisions. Ferrin chewed absently as he watched the coring device bring up a cylindrical sample of Big Green's rocks and soil. His attention was on the machine, and he was as distracted as Shaman while he consumed his food. The screws talked while they ate. One of them gave his food a dubious sniff. "It's starting to turn," he commented sourly.

"Yep," said the other. "We'll have to start back soon or live off the *dumaass*."

"*You* live off the scogging jungle," replied the first. "I'd rather starve."

"Trouble is, we didn't expect them all to survive this long," said the first. "Rations are getting used up faster than they should."

"Well, that could change anytime. This easy going is making me nervous. *Dumaass* never acted this way before; don't know why it's acting this way now. Alls I know is that I don't trust it one mungering bit."

"Me either. It gives me the creeps. But something bad's going to happen before we hit the Project again, I just know it. I'll lay you odds."

The other man laughed harshly. "I never bet on anything I may not be alive to collect on. It's one of my personal rules."

Their voices washed over Shaman as he repeated his visualization to the rhythm of his breathing like a mantra of violence. His eyes were locked on the screws from under lowered lids but they were accustomed to him sitting quietly and paid him no attention.

Ferrin packed up his equipment again, signalling the end of the break, and they all struggled back to their feet. It began to rain with the surprising abruptness of the jungle and one of the screws swore as they were drenched. Shaman paid no heed. What difference if one was wet from perspiration, from rain, or from the humidity? Wet was wet. *Wet was healthy,* said the new part of him. *Rain brings growth.* He led the way into a green vault where the understory was thin and the canopy arched high overhead. The jungle's pull to the right strengthened and his spirits rose with each step. As if from a distance, he heard Ferrin protest that they were not traveling in the right direction. He ignored the comment and kept walking, willing the group to follow. Soon. It would be very soon.

Shaman was exhilarated when he found the clearing and led the way into it. The others filed into the open space behind him and then stopped in amazement. The clearing was large and roughly circular. The *dumaass* encircled it like a green wall but inside that circle, one thing was taller than the grass. At the clearing's center, a huge tree rose, one of the great, ancient creatures of Big Green. Its lowest branches spread out far above them and the tree's lofty crown seemed to touch the clouds. The rain ceased, leaving the tiny humans to wipe water from their eyes as they attempted to comprehend the age and size of the arboreal giant. The group had not walked far into the clearing and stood clustered against its edge, intimidated by the open sky and the awesome tree. This was the largest, natural open space anyone had encountered on Big Green. The cut made for the Project was larger, but this possessed a presence that the Project could never own. The vaulting cylinder, dominated by the tree and a surrounding ring of bright sky, commanded near reverence. Vibrations emanated from the tree in waves, running along Shaman's skin, raising the hairs on his arms and neck. These resonances, invisible and felt only by him, pervaded the clearing, confirming that this was indeed the place he had been seeking. Here, his path and that of Big Green came together. In this place he would escape the labor site forever and achieve his mission. This clearing held the meaning of his life. He would never leave it.

Shaman turned to Merradrix and said quietly, "Now."

Merradrix and Astin shook themselves free of the clearing's spell and turned toward the screws, who were standing together some distance from Ferrin and close to the *dumaass*. Although the screws could not have heard Shaman's comment, something, perhaps body language, alerted them. Dizzes raised, they faced the prisoners. Their faces were tight but showed relief at finally having an opponent they could see and fight. Absorbed by the movements of their enemy and the imminence of battle, they were blind to Shaman's diversion as it crept up behind them.

Two serpentine green shapes reached out from the jungle and slid through the grass. Silent and quick, they reached the screws quickly and then each one whipped around an ankle. The screws bellowed in fear and rage. Stabbing downward with their dizzes, they jammed the prods in until the vegetable attackers quivered and dropped off. More tendrils emerged from the *dumaass*, reaching for their prey, but now the men turned to face a more immediate danger. Astin and Merradrix stood at blade's length before them and the blades were moving. It took less than a second for sharp edges to strike unprotected throats and the screws went down in bubbling, bloody death. Astin and Merradrix stepped back from the throes of their captors, watching impassively as more creepers took possession of the twitching bodies. The fingers of the *dumaass* encircled the corpses, wrapping them in green shrouds, drawing them back into the jungle with eager sinuosity. Twin trails of red gleamed on the grass as the only proof that the men had ever existed.

Then it was over. Shaman released his breath. The obstructions were gone and nothing stood now between him and the end of his path. In the ring of sky overhead, the clouds swept away. Sunlight dropped into the clearing with brazen weight, increasing a heat already intolerable. It felt good to him. Shaman shaded his eyes as Astin and Merradrix approached him. "What about that one?" Merradrix asked in Chenni, gesturing with his bloody weapon toward Ferrin. The scientist stood frozen with shock and fear, staring at the spot in the *dumaass* where the bodies of the guards had disappeared. Slowly it registered that a weapon was being pointed at him and he turned as if drugged. Fear made his face a mask from which his eyes, wide with shock, stared out at them.

Shaman shrugged. "As long as he does not interfere, I do not care," he replied. "You may do with him as you wish."

"Interfere with what?" Astin asked suspiciously.

"With what I must do—what I was brought here to do," Shaman said evenly.

Merradrix persisted. "If he returns to the Project, he will draw the other screws down on us."

"If he returns to the Project," Shaman countered in the language of the labor camp, "he will die. All there will die."

"All?" asked Astin in protest. "The laborers are innocent."

"That is a distinction too fine for the jungle to make. Besides, it is the laborers who wield the weapons that injure the *dumaass*."

"What about us, then?" Merradrix queried. "What do we do?"

"Stay here until the process is complete. Then you may leave safely: the jungle will no longer be your enemy."

Merradrix grunted. Astin approached Shaman and stared into his face. "What process?" he asked. "Tell us."

Shaman nodded. At that moment, the sunlight vanished as suddenly as it had come. Ferrin sank to the ground as if the sun had been supporting him and, without its assistance, he could not remain on his feet. Shaman removed his net-covered hat and placed it on the ground. "You know the *dumaass* lives and is aware," he began. They nodded. "It has been attempting to understand the Project, which it perceived as a painful infestation, since work began. It has had great difficulty with this because the jungle is purely vegetable, there are no animals. The *dumaass* does not comprehend the idea of individual life.

"It has attempted to learn from the new creatures—that is why so many of the crews have vanished—but those 'creatures' could not hear the jungle, much less speak to it, and so they were useless. An interpreter was needed. That is why I was brought out of the Living Hills to Nandarri and from Chennidur to Big Green. I am to become the interpreter, who translates the language of animals into the language of the jungle."

"What will happen then?" Astin queried in a tight voice. "When the *dumaass* understands that we are all separate lives, what then?"

Shaman pulled off his shirt, folded the wet cloth and dropped it to the grass. "Then the *dumaass* will know the extent of its pain and how it is caused. It will know the greater pain to follow."

"And it will learn how to fight back," Merradrix interjected.

Shaman nodded. "Exactly so." He bent one knee and unfastened his right boot. "From me, the *dumaass* will learn about the individuality of the creatures which infest it—and the vulnerability. That is why you must not return to the Project. Once the jungle understands that it is being attacked, I believe that it will learn the need, and the means, for defense. It will rid itself of the infestation." He pulled his boot off, removed the sock and placed them beside his shirt.

"Then where shall we go?" Merradrix asked.

With a slight shrug, Shaman said, "North is probably best. If you walk north long enough, you will come to the edge of the *dumaass*, to a place where the climate is like that of the Provider. There you may live in more comfort than here." He shifted his weight to the other knee and began removing his left boot.

"But you will remain here," Astin stated. The shock he felt at seeing Shaman casually remove his protective clothing showed on his face.

"My body will, yes," Shaman replied. "My spirit will be one with the *dumaass* and so I will be with you as long as you are in the jungle." He placed his boot and sock by the first.

A sound like a hoarse croak came from behind them. Ferrin, who had been listening, cleared his throat and tried again. "You will die," he said. "The jungle will kill you."

"No," Shaman said, standing. "It will not." He removed his pants, folded them, and placed them on top of his shirt. His body was pale and wet but as hard as the trunk of a tree. There was not a shred of fungus anywhere on it and his skin looked improbably clean, as though he had just bathed.

"The animals," Ferrin said. "How can there be no animals? We have all seen them. They have attacked us and we killed them. There must be animals."

Shaman shook his head sadly. "No, the *dumaass* is vegetable life only but it is very versatile. All the 'animals' you have seen and killed were parts of trees or other plants that separated themselves from the plants in order to attack or abduct people. Because these segments must act as animals do on the Provider, they mimic animals in our eyes. It is possible that, if my interpretations are effective, the *dumaass* will decide that animals are a more efficient means of accomplishing certain things and try them."

He removed his loincloth and stretched, as if reaching out toward the sky that swirled high above them. Then he turned and walked toward the base of the great tree. The three men followed him silently. Speaking with them had lessened Shaman's concentration on the pull but now he gave himself up to it gratefully. He stopped when he stood between two enormous roots that thrust out of the trunk like a wall and plunged into the ground. It was darker here and the vibrations came up from the grass through his bare feet. The bulk of the roots raised the ground so that it was tilted upward toward the tree. He lay down on this incline with his head upward and the tree behind him. At once, the vibrations ran up into his skin and the grass quivered beneath him. The pull was irresistible now.

The three men sank down, cross-legged, around him and he pulled his attention back long enough to say, "You must stay with me until the transition is complete."

"How will we know when that is?" a voice said.

"You will know," he replied, then gave himself up to the *dumaass*. The vibrations increased and the grass began to eddy around him. He felt it snaking up, swirling over him and winding itself around him. Then awareness of his body faded and he comprehended a pattern in the vibrations. The jungle's voice was complex but infinitely fascinating. The clearing, the other men, his body, all disappeared as he began listening to the overmind of the *dumaass*.

# NANDARRI

Surrein stared into the flame of his small desk lamp, seemingly inattentive to his surroundings. The list of wedding tasks rested forgotten on the desk, a blot of ink darkening one corner where the pen dried slowly. It was late at night; the house was quiet and even the kitchen servant dozed on his cot. Surrein, unable to sleep, had put his restless energy to work on wedding plans but his thoughts were now far away from the room, even from Nandarri. Planning had become dreaming and he pictured the wealth and luxury that would be his when the wedding was done. As the Fellskeeper Clan had neither the means to own a city house in Nandarri nor the ability to pay water tax, he was staying in Verrer's home, surrounded by the very elegance he craved. The lavishness of the hospitality, the number of servants in livery who bustled about, the weighty furniture and precious appointments, all testified to a lifestyle that would be his in only a few days.

Once the marriage was complete, Surrein would be rewarded beyond anything he had anticipated before meeting Verrer. The future certainly exceeded the dreams of an impatient boy cooped up in the decrepit house that was Fellskeeper citadel. And it had all been so easy. First he had proved himself by removing the eldest son, Rushain. The young *su-tansul* had ridden, all unsuspecting, into ambush and bubbled his astonishment into the rain-swollen stream along with his life. Following up on that success, he had abducted Cheyte, so full of good humor and always ready for a joke. But the joke had been on him and Surrein had arranged it so well that no trace of the man would ever be found on Chennidur. How could it, when Cheyte was sweating his life away somewhere on the other side of what the starmen called the Quadrant. Surrein's ingenious plan had been sweetened by the bounty on Cheyte received in addition to his payment for the job.

Then Verrer had ordered Torrian removed and Surrein, thinking quickly, had proposed a match with the *su-vellide* instead. Supported by brilliant logic, he had made his case so well that Verrer could not deny the advantages the scheme offered him. It was then that Surrein had proved his cleverness and his value to the Tulkan's Chief of Council. It was then also that he had cemented his future, saving himself from the ignominy attached to a dying clan. That he had also saved the clan from oblivion was of no interest to him beyond how it affected his personal reputation.

Yes, once the wedding was over, everything would be different. There would be no more evasions, no more running away on Torrian's part. She was the bounty that came with the successful execution of this strategy and in the flickering lamplight Surrein considered how he would bend his new bride to his will. Torrian must learn quickly that her husband was the master of their relationship if Surrein was to turn the Cliffmaster Clan toward Verrer's interests and use the power of his position to further both their ambitions. She must not be allowed to think even for one moment that her clan, money or inheritance rendered her superior to him.

In the yellow flame he saw Torrian kneeling, her smooth

naked back to him, her hands tied somewhere above her. He, the lord of the citadel, waited, considering the most suitable way in which to discipline her. Surrein had indulged in this fantasy before and the method changed with his mood. Most often, he held a riding whip and thought calmly how long to use it and where. Just thinking about it now, caused his fingers to clench around an imaginary leather handle. A fine balance must be achieved, he knew, between the fear and pain that were the tools of domination and a brutality that would give her legitimate grounds for complaint under *shufri-nagai*.

Surrein was completely aware of what the law allowed and what it prohibited, but disregarded it as applicable only to others less clever and ambitious than he. He would violate *shufri-nagai* when and how it pleased him. Surrein was equally aware, however, that he must at all times present the appearance of observing the law or those same inferior others could gain control over him. His challenge was to master his wife in such fine increments that Torrian would be unaware when the line was crossed and, if she did notice, would lack the will or the strength of mind to protest. Afterward, when he was tired of the game, he would use the stardust to make her grovel. The process demanded an equipoise planned as carefully as the wedding itself.

Although he pictured the delectable scenario taking place in their secluded hideaway, Surrein knew that such open domination would come later, after long and patient training. The bonding period was a time for pleasure mixed with hints of discipline, expressions of tenderness reinforced with casual authority, gestures of devotion tinged with almost accidental pain.

He had made a single mistake in allowing his ardent suitor's mask to slip after their betrothal, a serious error which had caused Torrian to run from him. Fortunately, she had fled to the Rock, far from Nandarri and Verrer's unforgiving gaze. When she returned to Nandarri, Surrein would recover from that lapse. He would lull her into believing that he was not the hideous person of her stardust dreaming and that the marriage would be fine. He could use her fear, however, tapping into it and channelling it to make Torrian more pliable. Using the fear to manipulate her would turn the mistake to his advantage—another testimony to his cleverness.

Surrein smiled and his eyes glittered, reflecting the lamplight flame. The Tulkan and his right hand would have no reason to be dissatisfied: Within days, he, Surrein ni Varskal san Cannestur, would be lord of Citadel Cliffmaster—one could not count the ineffectual tansul or the sniveling vellide—and he would see to it that Torrian never caused a problem.

Blinking, Surrein shook away his reverie and returned to himself. It had grown late: Smallmoon, new and dim, was setting outside the window and the oil in the lamp was low. He took up the paper on his desk, folded it precisely, and set it aside to give to his mother or sister in the morning. Delighted at the renaissance of the clan's prospects, they had answered his summons to Nandarri promptly, eager to help arrange the wedding and smooth his entry into Clan Cliffmaster. When he was tansul they would, of course, move to the Rock along with the many other relations who could no longer survive at the Fellskeeper citadel. His family would fill the empty rooms—siblings, cousins, nieces and nephews, aunts and uncles . . . His uncle's face flickered before him but he banished the unwanted vision.

Surrein stretched to relieve muscles grown stiff from his hours at the desk and felt as he did another, more pleasurable, stiffness. It was not unusual to find himself filled with lust from his dreams of shaping Torrian to his own desires. If this was what mere contemplation could accomplish, then the reality would have an intensity beyond anything he had ever experienced. Caressing himself, Surrein felt with satisfaction the size and tumescence of his member. He remembered that Torrian had always been flying on the stardust when they had coupled and thus she had never been truly aware of her betrothed's virility. She would soon, he thought, have ample time in which to observe it, to entice it, and to serve it.

Impatiently, he pushed back his chair, rose and took up

the lamp. Soon was not now and, if Torrian was not here to serve his pleasure, others surely were. This was Verrer's house and it was well staffed with servants who understood how to please their troinom masters. He had sampled a few of the women already and found them to be delectable, but of a type. They protested and even struggled but he could always see in their eyes how much they wanted it, wanted him.

Closing the door behind him, Surrein moved quietly down the hall. He knew his way to the dormitory where the female servants slept and he wished to draw no attention. Once inside, he would simply select one by lamplight, wake her and order her to accompany him. Surely, the ones he had already taken had bragged to the others of his potency. That meant whoever he chose would follow him in wide-eyed silence down the dark halls to his chambers and he would savor the apprehension radiating from her at every step. Tonight Surrein knew what he wanted and it was important that he choose the woman well. Then he would fasten the door of his quarters firmly behind them.

# CHAPTER 18

## THE HOUSE ON CHEFFRA STREET

Aurial needed the Port computer. It was only moments away, through the streets of Nandarri, but as far out of her grasp as the freighters that rode in parking orbit. So in mid-afternoon of a warm, bright, vernal day, she sat in her room in the Cliffmaster house on Cheffra Street struggling to pull together disparate pieces of information. The room was lovely and elegant, filled with costly objects and comfortable furniture but not made for work of any kind. She was trying to accomplish something with no proper equipment, and no data feed, surrounded by distractions. She could just imagine her mother smiling.

Every time she started to concentrate, a teasing wind blew in through the window, filled with alluring scents and beckoning sounds. Perfume from the flowering tree in the courtyard mingled with the exotic scent of spicy cooking and the more humble smells of animals and wood smoke. Although the tumult of everyday commerce never intruded on distinguished Cheffra Street, the calling of street vendors and the rumble of wagons drifted to her over the rooftops. Scraps of music came from another room of the house, or perhaps from another house, lilting and full of life. The air itself was infused with a heady vitality, a headlong reawakening that had never been programmed into the life-support system of an artificial world without seasons. It called to her, enticing her from between walls, away from her task, into the promise of the day and the excitement of Nandarri.

Aurial sighed. If she was ever going to complete her work, she needed one of the antiseptic cells in the port, equipped with its standard datastation. There, she could engross herself in wrapping up loose strands and bits of information into a logical plan. Instead, she resolutely set thoughts of play aside and assembled her ideas.

There was so much to do it was frightening and the plan had to proceed in sequence if it was to work. She had to risk revealing part of her scheme to others and then persuade them to accept her ideas and to help her. She was forced to assume that the information she had requested from the Beldame would arrive on schedule and confirm her assumptions. With all those dependencies, the success of her mission was no sure thing. She sighed again. The only way to start was at the beginning. Summoning a maid, she sent for Raunn.

Within moments, the other woman swept into the room, a long pale-blue dorchari floating about her in an aura of uncharacteristic femininity. Noticing Aurial's raised eyebrow, she explained, somewhat defensively, "It is traditional garb for the women of Chennidur. Surely you have seen it before?"

"Of course," Aurial replied. "It's just unlike you, that's all. You usually wear clothing that's more . . . more . . ."

"More functional," Raunn supplied. "That's true. But I've decided that adopting a more conventional appearance would be wise while we're here in the city. I'm trying to be a proper sister and clan daughter, at least until the wedding."

Aurial smiled. "An astute decision," she said. "And that color looks very nice on you. Listen, you know I am here for reasons other than attending your sister's wedding and it's time for me to move ahead with my mission. Part of what I plan to do involves the vellide, your mother, and I'm going to need your help."

"My mother?" Raunn queried. "You've seen my mother. What could you possibly want of her?"

"To cure her," Aurial replied bluntly. "I think I know what's wrong with her and if my diagnosis is correct, Dr. La can cure it."

"Dr. La from the Port?"

Aurial nodded.

Raunn crossed her arms and fell silent. She thought for several moments and then asked, "What are you asking me to do?"

"Dr. La will come to this house tonight while everyone is at the evening Call to Prayer. I would like you to excuse your mother from attending the service and bring her to this room. You should remain here as well, to assure yourself that no violation of *shufri-nagai* occurs."

"And this will help you with your mission?" Raunn asked skeptically.

"Yes. Will you do it?"

Raunn nodded. "Of course I will. Do you think I want my mother to stay like this? You never knew her when . . . before, but she would not have wanted to live this way."

"Good. But I'm going to ask something more difficult of you afterward. We'll need the cooperation of the most trustworthy servant you know in this house."

"That would be Maitris, of course. She'll cooperate when I tell her to."

Aurial nodded. "When your mother is gone, Dr. La will sample your blood and that of Maitris." She saw the look on Raunn's face and added, "It won't hurt."

Raunn looked aghast at the starwoman. "*Sample* our blood?" she asked in revulsion. "You mean remove it from our bodies with your techish devices? Absolutely not! What a disgusting thought." Then she calmed herself and thought again for a few moments. Aurial remained still and listened to the music floating on the warm air. "What for?" Raunn challenged. "What are you planning to do with it?"

Aurial took a deep breath. "Test it. I have a theory

about the troinom and the underranks that explains a great
deal about Chennidur. If I'm correct, it will also help my
mission."

"But will it help Chennidur?" Raunn asked. "I won't
allow you to remove part of my body just to help your
mission, much less if it would hurt us."

"It will not harm Chennidur," Aurial reassured her,
wondering as she did so whether she was being truthful
and knowing that she had no idea what the final consequences might be.

"And this blood testing will tell you if you're right?"

"Yes."

"It will be the last thing you'll ask of me?"

"For now, yes. But there will probably be more later
on."

"Cure my mother," Raunn said, almost to herself. "What
next? Are you planning to save my sister, too? Make
Surrein disappear, perhaps?"

Aurial smiled.

As the Eyestar brightened in the evening sky, the Call
to Prayer drew the Cliffmaster household to separate temples. The troinom strolled to an imposing white stone
structure nearby and the underranks hastened to a small
and ordinary place of worship many blocks away. Aurial
remained behind and waited in the shadows by the porter's station near the main door. The porter, like the
kitchen staff, was still on duty and for him a short version
of the evening chants must suffice. She could hear the
man singing softly in a reedy tenor, chanting the familiar
words with a fervor she did not and could never understand.

As if drawn by his prayers, a dusklizard emerged from
its cranny in the wall and puffed out the air sacs under its
hind legs. Then, balancing on its tail, it rubbed its legs
together to produce a deep rhythmic thrumming that made
a counterpoint to the porter's melodic words. This odd
duet was interrupted by a soft knock at the door. The
porter ceased his song and responded to the summons
with a puzzled look on his face. At this time of the day, all
true Followers were either at their prayers or attending to

tasks so important they took precedence over ritual. Who, then, could be knocking at his door? When he opened it, a slight figure enveloped in a dark cloak with the hood well forward slipped through. Emerging from the shadows, Aurial nodded to the startled porter, releasing him to his prayers. She escorted Dr. La, who carried a large bag, across the courtyard. In the warm dusk, the tree's perfume was even more intense and it infused the air. Its sweetness almost made her dizzy.

Once in Aurial's room, the doctor slipped off the concealing garment and approached the two women who awaited her. The vellide was seated passively as always on the bed, holding her daughter's hand without apparent feeling. Raunn, perched beside her, was obviously apprehensive and clutched her mother's hand with nervous strength. The doctor nodded in her direction. "Sri-nothi Raunn," she acknowledged. Then she waited.

Raunn rose and took a step forward. "This is my mother, the vellide Rutin-Xian ni Pejjin san Obradi. Not long ago she was very much alive and filled with energy. She had ideas and plans, she fulfilled her duties and was an example to the entire clan. Since the death of my brothers, Rushain and Cheyte, the vellide has been as you see her now, quiet and still, as though the life has drained out of her. She cares nothing for her family, for the Clan or even for the True Word when once these things were the core of life to her. Aurial says you may be able to make her as she was and return the love of life to her spirit. Return her to her family." Her voice was hopeful, almost pleading.

Dr. La made a noncommittal sound. "I will see what I can do," she replied. Opening the bag, she busied herself with very techish medical equipment.

Raunn's eyes widened and she looked to Aurial who stepped in to allay her fears. "Perhaps, doctor," she said, "you could tell me what you are doing and I can help explain it to the sri-nothi Raunn. That way she can be certain we are not going to hurt her mother or violate *shufri-nagai* in any way."

Dr. La looked skeptical but then said, "Certainly." She began her examination with the simplest of procedures—

checking the vital signs of heartbeat, pulse, and temperature. Then she examined the vellide's ears, eyes, and mouth. These actions were the same things that a doctor of Chennidur would do and the familiarity allowed Raunn to relax a bit. For the more complex analyses, Dr. La relied on non-invasive scanning equipment that appeared formidable but remained a sedate and legitimate distance from the patient's body. Raunn was suspicious of these profane tools but, after watching carefully, concluded that they did not threaten her mother. Throughout the process, Dr. La talked in simple terms about what she was doing and Aurial "translated" any scientific concepts that were alien to Raunn in culturally acceptable terms.

When the examination was done, the doctor retreated to one corner of the room to consult in peace with her diagnostic computer. Aurial suspected that Dr. La was augmented but had the good sense not to demonstrate that capability here. She and Raunn waited nervously for the results, but the vellide sat as silent and remote as always, showing no interest in the present or in her own future.

Finally, Dr. La approached them. "It is as I suspected when you relayed the symptoms," she said to Aurial. Then she turned to Raunn, "I will explain. Your bodies—and ours as well—produce many different substances each day that help you go about your life. We call these substances by different names, many of them complex, but I will refer to them all simply as chemicals. These chemicals digest your food, give you energy, help you become pregnant, make you feel happy or sad, prepare you for sleep and wake you up again.

"Sometimes, for any number of reasons, the body either stops producing one of these chemicals or produces too much of it and this imbalance causes problems. The mind often affects the balance of chemicals and, in the vellide's case, I believe that the deaths of her sons brought about a mental state which shut down production of a particular one. The lack of this chemical created the condition you see her in now, a condition which we call depression. She will remain this way until the chemical imbalance is corrected."

"Can you cure her?" Raunn asked. "Can you make her body start producing the substance she needs again?"

Dr. La nodded. "Fortunately, I can. And doing so is relatively simple." She reached into the bag and removed a clear flat container which held a small dot. "This little patch here," she said, pointing to the dot, "is saturated with the chemical your mother requires. If I place it just under her skin, the substance will move from the dot into the vellide's system over a period of many days. This will stimulate her body to begin producing it regularly once more."

"How long will it take before she returns to being herself?" Raunn asked.

"Actually, only a very short time," the doctor replied. "You won't see much of a change for the next two days, but after that, the vellide will become more and more like herself.".

Raunn looked at the doctor and then at Aurial. "This is amazing," she said, with something resembling awe in her voice. "Because this 'chemical' is a substance natural to her body, there can be no question of pollution by alien drugs. Correct?"

"Correct."

She turned to Dr. La again. "No one can see the patch?" she asked anxiously.

The doctor nodded. "It will be absorbed by the body and leave no trace."

"Thus our enemies will not be able to see that star medicine has cured her. This is truly a gift from the Chenni-ad."

"From the Quad Market more likely," the doctor replied, but Aurial hushed her. She did not want to interfere with Raunn's enthusiasm. Once the vellide was cured, there would be time enough for her to make the point. "Shall we proceed?" she asked Raunn.

Raunn agreed eagerly and at the doctor's direction, she lifted her mother's hair away from the neck. Dr. La disinfected a small section of skin and then used the applicator to insert the patch just behind the right ear. She covered the tiny incision with a flesh-colored patch and the micro-operation was over in a few seconds. The vellide showed no signs of even noticing that something extraordinary had been done to her.

"I will return my mother, the vellide, to her rooms now," Raunn said, "and then come back with Maitris as we agreed. I will not be gone long." She helped her mother to her feet and the two women left. As Dr. La placed her equipment back in her bag, Aurial asked, "Were you able to complete the analyses that I requested?"

The doctor nodded. "I did, and the results were definitely interesting. You were parked in the right orbit, but I think you'll still be surprised by what I found."

"Then the rennish is a drug?"

"Not a narcotic, no, but it *is* a stimulant. Fortunately, it's not a strong one. Since you have been exposed to rennish smoke regularly, though, you must have noticed its effects—dizziness, a mild euphoria and temporary sense of well-being, increased awareness of detail, voracious appetite."

"The appetite is the worst," Aurial affirmed. "I'm hungry all the time and I'll be positively fat by the time I go up the well again. My sisters won't recognize me."

"We all make sacrifices in the line of duty," Dr. La replied drily. "And, of course, we can't ignore the body's craving for more or the mind's desire to experience it again. Incorporating this drug into religious ceremonies is ingenious. The stimulant heightens the impact of the dogma in the chants and reinforces the sense of elation which the True Word seeks to impart. The regular ceremonies with attendance mandatory create both the opportunity and the necessity for repeated exposure. Clever of the nayyat."

"Use of drugs in religious ceremonies is hardly unusual," Aurial observed.

"That's so," Dr. La replied. "There is a difference on Chennidur, however, a rather important one."

"Alright, I'm curious. What is it?"

"The rennish also has alexipharmic qualities that are

quite astonishing and far stronger than its properties as a stimulant."

Aurial was indeed startled. "Alexipharmic? You mean—it protects against poison?"

"Exactly. Don't you want to know which poison?"

Aurial shook her head. "With just about everything on Chennidur containing one form of poison or another, I don't have to. Half of the Kohrable deals with food, identifying which foodstuffs are safe and giving specific instructions on the proper ways to prepare them for consumption. Protecting against inadvertent poisoning occupies, of necessity, a great deal of time and effort here."

"Yes, and that's something I had not been truly aware of until your query came through. But your request made me curious and I picked up a variety of food samples from the marketplace. My equipment at the Port is neither new nor top of the line but I was able to identify a staggering variety of vegetable toxins alone. There are alkaloids, glycosides, oxalates, and phytotoxins as well as guelphasides, ionanines, and trumpilates."

Aurial made a face. "I'll bet you found even more interesting ones in meat and fowl."

"Ha," the doctor laughed grimly. "There you have double jeopardy. The vegetable toxins concentrate as they move up the food chain and are stored in the viscera, particularly the digestive and genital tracts. In any beast, these organs are usually lethal to consume. But in addition, certain animals secrete their own poisons—tetrodotoxins, ouabains, bufotoxins and even a rare ibokanine. There are, of course, substances that I can't identify easily but I'll keep working on it. Chennidur could keep an army of exobotanists, zoologists and ichthyologists busy isolating possible medical benefits of the poisons that exist here."

"That's fascinating," Aurial replied impatiently. "But what's the point?"

"The point," Dr. La replied emphatically, "the truly significant fact, is that rennish is a universal alexin. It doesn't just protect against one or two of these poisons: its alexipharmic qualities apply to all of them. That makes it an extraordinary substance and, as far as I know, quite unique."

"So continual breathing of the smoke has a prophylactic effect," Aurial said. "I'm sure the people of Chennidur are completely unaware of it. They only know about the water."

"The smoke works to keep levels of poison in the body from actually building up since it wouldn't be strong enough to actually reduce them," Dr. La continued. "I'm testing different concentrations to see whether a stronger dose could actively reduce the levels."

"What about in combination with Heartspring water?" Aurial asked.

"Yes. I tested that as well. The water itself is pure and it leaches the toxins out of the blood to be excreted, but it requires large amounts to work. Does that answer your question?"

Aurial should have been triumphant. She had obtained Raunn's cooperation and the first step in the plan had gone well. The second step was about to begin without difficulty. Dr. La's analyses had been completed and her own speculations had been confirmed. So why was she suddenly feeling irritable and edgy? Some of her theories, although pure speculation, had been vindicated but she felt flat instead of jubilant. "Yes, it does."

"But it raises another big one, doesn't it?"

Aurial hesitated. "If we both mean the same thing, yes."

"How can a species—even a sentient one—evolve on a planet that is biologically incompatible with its metabolism? If people cannot eat the food, whether animal or vegetable, they need without protecting themselves against being poisoned, how did they survive long enough to become sentient?"

"That's it," Aurial agreed. "That's what's been nagging at the back of my mind for days. Do you know of any other world where a similar circumstance exists?"

Dr. La grinned. "I'm glad I stayed a step ahead of you. My medical records show no such world in the entire Quadrant—where the species occurs naturally, that is. And it's only logical. The odds against a species surviving, much less evolving to the sentient level, in such a hostile environment are astronomical."

"How about when the species is introduced?" Aurial

followed up. Her head had begun to ache and she rubbed her temples to relieve it.

"Ah, there analogs do exist. I cross-checked my search parameters with the central medical data banks for the Quad but, without priority access, it will take a long time before I receive an answer. Longer than you need, perhaps."

Aurial agreed, but added, "I have authorized a parallel check into this line of inquiry directly through my resources on the Beldame. I expect a reply within a few days."

"You outrank me," Dr. La conceded with a shrug. "You must also then be checking on the logical extension of this line of inquiry."

"Yes, of course," Aurial replied. "But there may not be any answer to that one. At all. Anywhere. When you take into account how much exploration has gone on in the Outback sponsored by so many different groups, plus official reluctance to record some of those expeditions, we may never be able to confirm whether or how or when these people were introduced to Chennidur. That's why I need you to analyze the genetic structure of the two classes."

"Why both?" the doctor queried. "Wouldn't they have the same genetic origin?"

"The more I learn, the less likely that possibility becomes," Aurial replied. "The troinom and the underranks are completely different, even though they are similar in appearance and share a single culture. Did you know that no troinom can impregnate one of the underranks, or vice versa?"

"Just through rumor. I have heard the guards gossip but I never had any chance to verify it." She paused. "Remember, my charter is to treat the staff of the port and the crews of the freighters. It's not to conduct research into the genetic origins of people who are, shall we say, uncooperative."

"Well, this will be your chance to do some independent research," Aurial said. "Make the most of it. I need an answer before the fifth day of the Wedding Season."

Just then, Raunn returned with Maitris in tow. The

servant wore the usual bland, subservient mask typical of
the drevs and did not look directly at the strange woman
who shared the room with Aurial. When Raunn told her
maid what would transpire next, however, Maitris threw
her head back in fear. "You would have me violate *shufri-
nagai*, sri-nothi?" she asked.

Raunn replied, "No, Maitris, not truly. The law speaks
of what must not be put into the body. It does not address
the taking of any substance, including blood, from it. At
any rate, this is extremely important and I must order you
to do it."

Under direct order from a troinom, Maitris had no
choice but to do as she was told. Dr. La took the blood
samples cleanly and quickly, then scanned both women
with her equipment. It took only a short while during
which the maid remained rigid with fear. When the doctor
was done, Raunn said, "You will speak of this to no one,
Maitris. No one. Not even the nayya. Do you understand?"

Maitris nodded dumbly, unhappy but obedient. They
left the room together and Aurial escorted Dr. La back to
the main gate. By now, the evening services were over
and the household had returned to its normal activities. As
they passed under the flowering tree, Dr. La commented,
"With such a variety of naturally-occurring toxins readily
available, I wonder why the art of poisoning has not been
refined here as it has in some other cultures."

"I would imagine that *shufri-nagai* has a great deal to do
with it," Aurial replied.

"In what way?" the doctor asked.

"The penalty for murder on Chennidur is death," Aurial
said. "The penalty for murder by poison is worse. First the
nayyat excommunicate the killer from the Followers of the
True Word, stripping him of his religion. Then he is
marked as *parostri*, taken into the wilderness and abandoned. Even if he survived the religious and cultural
ostracism— worse than death for a Follower—his chances
of surviving by living off the land are not high. Eventually,
the weapon he used would kill him also."

"Oh," the doctor said. As they approached the porter's
kiosk, she asked, "How are you feeling right now?"

"Me?" Aurial countered in surprise. "I'm fine. Why?"

"I thought perhaps you might be not quite yourself right now. Somewhat cranky. Short-tempered maybe. Perhaps a headache."

Aurial stopped walking. "Yes. You're right. I'm edgy and my head hurts but I thought that was just from the worry about whether everything would go well."

Dr. La shook her head. "I would assume it has more to do with the fact that you missed the evening service and the dose of rennish smoke that goes with it. A few moments in the temple before you eat might settle you down."

Aurial was stunned. She had long accepted the idea of rennish smoke being addictive but had associated that fact only with the native population. Addiction was something that happened to Followers of the True Word after years of exposure. She, an outsider who had been breathing it for just days, considered herself immune. Now, she was faced with the physical symptoms that proved her vulnerable. It was not a feeling that she liked or a picture that she enjoyed. Aurial was more inclined to fight the addiction than give in to it but she understood that there would be plenty of time for that when the mission was complete. Here and now she needed a clear head and as few distractions as possible.

She parted from Dr. La outside the gate and slipped away to the temple. It was deserted but the doors were open and she made her way to the front, close to the table which held the rennish bowl. The smoke in the air had thinned so she took deep breaths, holding them as long as possible. Aurial stayed until the dragging ache behind her eyes diminished and she felt better. By that time she was also, predictably, ravenous.

It was completely dark and close to curfew when she hurried through the streets back to the Cliffmaster House. As she arrived during dinner when everyone was at the table, no one paid any attention when she returned alone. Aurial hoped that the meal was not over and food would still be on the table so that she could begin eating immediately. With any luck, there would be zegwan sauce. And no jirrifish.

## BIG GREEN

Rolfe watched Autex pilot the shuttle down, wishing that he could monitor what was going on behind the android's fixed eyes. Faced into the shuttle's navigation system, Autex was part of the craft, piloting it directly through LCM crystals, molecular wires and quantum-microcircuits. Occasionally the android's hands moved incredibly fast and with microscopic precision over the control board. Even when the hands sank into repose, the fingertips still twitched as if shadowing the flow of electricity he guided through the controls.

Rolfe shifted his gaze to the viewscreen as the shuttle emerged from the planet's cloud wrapper and Big Green's enormous verdant belt rushed toward them. He busied himself with the sensors, which first located their quarry and then informed him that the small group of humans had stopped conveniently at the bottom of a large circular clearing. A quick calculation told him the open space was big enough for the shuttle to land in and take off again. He smiled. This was great good fortune that would save them considerable time and increase the odds of success immensely. As the shuttle came closer, the bad news emerged —that the center of this clearing was occupied by an enormous tree. The sensors indicated the presence of a navigational problem before they began throwing off ghosts and false readings. Rolfe turned them away from the tree and the readings returned to normal immediately. Focused again on the arboreal giant, they gave off the same odd vibrations.

Rolfe didn't know what the readings meant, but he didn't like them at all. He turned the sensors away from the clearing and tried tracking around the tree rather than measuring it directly. All he learned was that the tree occupied the center of the effect, something he had already figured out. He wondered if this nebulous, unmeasurable condition was similar to the one that caused equipment on the Project to malfunction. If so, it cancelled out any other advantage they had. He rubbed the palm of his hand absently.

Although an excellent freestanding pilot, Rolfe did not possess the computer augmentation that would make him the navigational brain of the shuttle. He was glad that Autex had the job of piloting them into the clearing, around the mysterious tree, and onto the ground. The shuttle angled steeply downward and twisted into a tight spiral. Rolfe was pulled forward, his body straining at the net which held him into his seat. To stay in place, he wrapped his hands tightly around the thrust handles on the arm of his chair. His stomach lurched but he gritted his teeth and hung on until the shuttle's nose lifted and the craft settled with an absurd lightness to the ground. Rolfe released his breath with a whoosh, freed himself from the net and made his way quickly to the door. Autex disengaged himself from the interface and followed.

The hatch swung open and they were hit in the face by the heat and humidity of Big Green. Braced against its impact, Rolfe scanned the clearing quickly and located his quarry at the base of the enormous tree. At least, he assumed that one of the three men was his quarry, but he couldn't tell which one. Using the swing bar, he dropped from the hatch to the grass and walked quickly toward the small group. All three men watched him approach warily.

Two were armed with chettys and had the underfed, hollow-eyed look of laborers. Their expressions were hostile, as if he were intruding and had interrupted something important. The third man wore the uniform of a scientist and an expression of unutterable relief, as though Rolfe had come to rescue him from certain death. No one spoke. *Was this all that was left of the exploration team from the Project?* Rolfe wondered. *What was going on here?*

There was no time to solve mysteries. He stopped and said in the common tongue, "Is one of you named Merradrix?" The larger of the two laborers raised his chetty into a de-

fensive posture and nodded once, affirmatively. "Good,"
Rolfe said. "Get in the shuttle. We're taking you home."

"Home?" the man queried skeptically. "Back to the
Project?"

"No," Rolfe replied evenly. "Back to Chennidur. I was
sent to get you."

"Who sent you after me?" Merradrix challenged. "You
speak nonsense, man. Why would anyone come all this
way to bring back a bluedirt farmer?"

"I believe the name of the person who sent me is Raunn
ni Obradi san Derrith," Rolfe said. "And I didn't ask why.
Now get in the shuttle; we don't have much time."

Both laborers started at the name. They looked at one
another then, together, they gazed down at a low mound
of grass. "It is finished," the smaller man said. "It would
be all right for you to go now. This is a great gift, from the
Chenni-ad themselves. You must return."

Rolfe looked at the mound that was the focus of their
attention and then looked again, more closely. To his
astonishment, he saw that it was a man's body wrapped
and covered in grass. The shape of a body was plain
enough once you knew what to look for, but only a few
patches of skin on the soles of his feet testified to humanity. "What is this?" he asked guardedly, against his better
judgment.

The second laborer replied, "Shaman is now a part of
this world. He speaks to it and has become the translator
who will teach the spirit of Big Green about people,
animals, all creatures who are not plants."

"What do you mean, 'the spirit of Big Green'?" Rolfe
followed up, not certain he wanted to hear the answer.

Merradrix answered him. "Shaman told us that Big Green
is alive, conscious, as we are. But it did not understand us,
or the Project because there are no animals here. It only
understands about plants. When the Project injured it, the
spirit fought back by killing people and making the machines stop working."

The other man continued. "Shaman learned to speak to
Big Green's spirit and he knew he had to teach it how to
protect itself from those who made the Project. He came

here, to this clearing, to do that. He lay down and became part of Big Green. He will interpret the activities of humans for the spirit to comprehend."

Behind him, Rolfe heard Autex whisper, "Like a biological interface; a human augmenting a planet." Rolfe was fascinated but he ignored the comment and addressed Merradrix again. "If it is over, then we must leave quickly; there is no time to argue. Get in the shuttle."

The smaller man spoke to Merradrix again, "Shaman does not need us now. You can go home—go!"

Merradrix shook his head slowly, stubbornly. "And leave you here alone?" he asked. "How could I return to Chennidur knowing that I had abandoned you here? A troi'm woman met her responsibility to me and I will meet mine to you." He turned to Rolfe. "I go nowhere without Astin. Give the troi'm my thanks, but either he comes or I stay here."

"It's impossible; there's only room for one," Rolfe protested.

Merradrix said nothing and shook his head again. His mouth was set in a grim line and the knuckles of the hand that gripped the chetty were white.

Rolfe was about to argue when Autex spoke again in a low voice, "If I shut down and ride machine class, Astin can use my passage. It will cost you extra for my place in the hold, but we can do it." Rolfe weighed the alternatives and made a split-second decision. "Alright. Both of you. Drop the chettys and get in the shuttle, fast!"

The two men followed his instructions and were striding toward the hatch when the scientist gave up his silence. "What about me?" he challenged in a stricken voice. "Are you going to leave me here, alone, with *him*?"

Rolfe turned back to the man. "I can't help you," he stated.

"I won't stay here!" the scientist shouted, his voice rising to the edge of control. "You can't do this to me. They killed the guards and I can't go back to the Project; I'm coming with you." He took one step and Autex raised his light pistol. With almost theatrical gestures, the android released the safety and aimed his weapon at the man's chest. The scientist stopped, torn between his fear of the gun and a terror of being left behind.

"I can't take three," Rolfe said quietly. "It's impossible. I can't help you."

"I'll die here," the scientist said, his voice high and quavering. "This place will kill me."

"Perhaps not," Merradrix responded. "Shaman is translating. He said we would be spared."

"Spared for what? To be the only living human on this entire planet?"

*What?* Rolfe wondered. "Why can't you make your way back to the Project?" he asked. "It may be dangerous, but it's a chance. There are still people there. They didn't vanish while you were exploring the *dumaass.*"

"If what Shaman said is true," the scientist argued, "they won't be there for long. Big Green is going to destroy the Project and everyone working on it. I'll be alone."

*By Mavi's arms,* Rolfe thought. *We've got to get out of here. Now.* "I can't take you," he said finally. "If you try, Autex will kill you. When we get back on the ship, I will send a message to the company giving them your coordinates. That's all I can do."

"But the Project . . ." the scientist persisted.

"If the Project is destroyed," Rolfe replied, "they will send a team to investigate. You know that. The team will know where you are and come to get you. I give my word they will know where to find you." *I don't know how I'm going to get away with this,* he thought. *But I can't worry about it now.* "Get in and net down," he ordered the two men. "We're going up, now!" As Autex held the scientist off, Rolfe backed toward the shuttle.

The laborers scrambled in and fastened the netting around their seats with a little help from Rolfe. Autex sealed the hatch behind them and was already faced in when Rolfe got to the navigator's seat. The shuttle rose smoothly and then lurched. Rolfe checked the MFR's reading: it was low but it still had enough power to protect the craft while they lifted out. It strained slowly upward as though checked by a localized, intense gravitational pull. The tree.

Rolfe spared a quick glance out at the massive structure as it spiralled slowly past the forward port and saw nothing unusual. On the ground, by the tree's enormous bole, a dwindling figure stood. As he watched the shuttle rise the scientist resembled a solitary priest guarding the sanctuary of his thatched god.

The shuttle pulled past the crown of the tree and was instantly released from its invisible tether. Autex kicked in the secondary thrusters and took the ship up toward the cloud cover as fast as it would move. Above the clouds, the freighter waited in the blackness of space. Rolfe calculated again: they would make the rendezvous with little time to spare, but they would make it.

Rolfe pondered what he should do once they were back on board. Revealing that the Project's imminent destruction was pointless since no one would believe his story. Neither would anyone give credence to the idea of a human being interfacing with a living planet in order to teach it how to protect itself from development. He could do only what he had promised the scientist—make sure the company knew the man's location so they could rescue him. There was no guarantee, however, that they would choose to do so.

Merradrix broke the silence. "Must we travel back to Chennidur in a—in a cylinder?" he asked and his face showed a claustrophobic fear. His aversion to chemsleep was clear.

Rolfe shook his head. "You may if you wish," he replied. "Some people actually prefer to travel that way, but it is certainly not necessary."

"Good." Both men looked relieved. "I do not know how to address you properly," Merradrix continued, "On your world, are you troi'm, a sri-noth, or are you of the underranks?"

"Neither," Rolfe said. "But speak to me as you would speak to one of your own class. We will both be more comfortable that way."

Merradrix nodded. "That is also good. There is much I would ask you."

"I will tell you what I can," Rolfe commented. "And there is information I would ask of you, as well." It would, he thought, be an interesting trip back.

# CHAPTER 19

## THE HOUSE ON CHEFFRA STREET

It was several days before the tansul found the time to meet with Aurial. He made no excuses: he did not have to. She saw him around the house at meals and attending morning and evening services with the family. He was of medium height, slender and lacking in any physical presence. Antikoby was, she thought, far more imposing and impressive than this man. His face was so average as to be forgettable and rarely did any expression cross it. The single most memorable feature about the tansul was his hair. Thick and dark, with a tendency to shift actively about, it sat atop his head like a small furry animal perched on an uncertain roost. The mat of hair seemed to weigh him down so that his shoulders hunched over to accommodate its mass.

He did not look, Aurial thought, as she had imagined the tansul of Clan Cliffmaster would appear, although she was incapable of verbalizing that mental image. She would watch the tansul indirectly, and ask herself whether he looked like a man so out of touch with the world that he

would give his daughter in marriage to a psychopath. The
answer was always different.

Aurial rehearsed what she would say to him over and
over with no one but herself to listen. These were words
she could say to only one person on Chennidur and there
would be but one opportunity to speak them. Here, where
she needed Raunn's opinion and guidance most, she was
unable to seek either. The requested data had come through,
on time and in more detail than she had expected, but still
the acid of uncertainty etched at her confidence. When,
finally, the tansul granted her an audience, she feared
being both under-prepared and over-ready.

The meeting took place at night, in the hour after the
family dinner. She had anticipated this timing, as the tansul
was away in the council chambers from early morning until
just before the evening Call to Prayer. Each afternoon she
rested so as to be awake and alert when her opportunity
finally came. That night, he received her in an austere
chamber on the house's upper level. The blue light of
Smallmoon spilled through windows which faced the street,
an unusual feature in a house otherwise turned traditionally
inward, blocking the city's intrusion with solid walls and
sturdy doors. The room was lit by a single lamp. Its walls
were bare of decoration and the floor's hard tiles lacked
the forgiving softness of a rug. The only furniture in it was
a large table set up like a desk with one chair behind it.
On the right corner of the table lay a bound copy of the
Kohrable, old and ragged from use. The single chair was
placed behind the table so that its occupant had a direct
line of vision through the window to the great dome of the
temple. It was a spare room, revealing of the tansul's nature.

He was seated at the table when Aurial entered. He did
not invite her to do so; there was no seat to offer. She
stood before him, uncomfortably aware of being at a disadvantage and resenting him for placing her in that position.
It was up to the tansul to speak first and she waited
patiently for his attention, trying not to feel like an erring
servant called to account. Her emotions rose but Aurial
shook them off and pulled herself together. Not a word
had been spoken and already she was off-balance. She

could not give him that advantage. Finally, he looked up at her. "You are Aurial ni Nashaum san Asherith," he said. "An unusual name. It is not listed in the Book of Clans and I am unfamiliar with its history. Perhaps later you can inform me of your Clan's noble heritage. I am a busy man, however, and for now I must ask you to come to the point."

Aurial heard the warning implied in his words but was also relieved not to have to begin by answering difficult questions about her false identity. "I am here," she began, "to make a request of you. This is a presumptuous thing for a guest of the house to do but I beg you to hear me out."

The tansul nodded once and she knew that he expected to hear a request so trivial that he could deal with it quickly and return to his work. Aurial continued. "The conflict between the Tulkan's government and those who believe that Chennidur should sever all contact with the Quadrant's galactic markets is obvious to all. It is also common knowledge that you are of the faction which favors the return of Chennidur to a state of sacred isolation. There are advantages to both sides of this schism. I have come to present the advantages of trading with the Quadrant and to ask you to reconsider your position."

The tansul's face registered the beginning of a surprise that was suppressed immediately. Only a glitter in his eyes remained. "That is a remarkable request," he stated. "And coming from a woman, a young woman, of uncertain ancestry, it is even more amazing. But why do you speak to me of this? Yes, I oppose trade, but I am only one member of the Council and one with no particular power. Even if I were to agree with you, nothing would change."

"You have important contacts, Tansul," she replied, "and you may have more power than you know."

He paused a moment, thinking. During that short time, he remained completely still. "Who sent you?" he asked finally.

"No one," she replied. "I have come on my own initiative and acting out of my own beliefs."

"I do not accept that, young woman. We are not discussing your marriage or debating a point of commentary," he said in a flat voice. He might as well have been talking about the weather. "The issue of trading with the Quadrant is more than just opposing points of view. Belief in the sanctity of the True Word and the tenets of the Kohrable permeates everything that I think and do. It is who I am and I cannot change that any more than I can change my height or the color of my eyes."

"And I am not asking you to do so," Aurial countered. "I am asking you to change your political position."

"You are completely out of line," he said calmly. "And out of your depth. You are impertinent, young woman. By what boldness do you even broach this subject with me, much less make such an impudent request?"

"By the right of my beliefs," Aurial replied quickly, "which are as strong as yours. The Kohrable says that we must do what works for the good of the people and I believe that trade with the Quadrant benefits the majority of the people." She was very uneasy. He was not taking her seriously and there could be no real negotiation unless he accepted her as a credible opponent. The tansul gave a wintry smile. "You, who do not believe in the Kohrable dare to use the True Word in support of its enemy's cause? You have more audacity than I thought." A lock of hair flopped out of place and fell across one eye. He smoothed it back automatically.

Aurial reacted defensively. "How can you make such an accusation? We are all devoted Followers."

"If you were a Follower, young woman, if the True Word was your life as it is mine, you would not be here now. You would not be arguing this cause. You would be joining with those who seek to keep Chennidur holy. You would be defending your home and your faith against the insidious attack of profane technology." He stopped and his eyes narrowed. "But then, this is not your home is it?"

Aurial hesitated for a moment, confused and uncertain how to respond. "What do you mean?" she said.

"Oh, come now," he replied. "Let us not waste time arguing what we both know to be true. You have disguised yourself and that masquerade has fooled many—particularly those who see only what they expect. You have befriended my daughter, lied your way into my house and slept with my tuupit. But I am not a fool to be taken in so. Who are you?"

Aurial's mind raced. She had prepared herself for the necessity of disclosing her name. She could only maintain her cover if the tansul agreed to her request readily and it was apparent that he would not. To bring her strongest pieces into play, she had to reveal her identity as an offworld trader. She had not expected to be found out. It was no secret that she had slept with Antikoby and, if questioned, the tuupit would have had no choice but to answer his master truthfully. "You're right," she conceded. "Chennidur is not my home and I am not a Follower."

"That tells me what you are not," he said. "This I know already. I asked who you are."

"My name is Aurial il Tarz," she said briefly.

"Of the il Tarz Trading Family presumably," he added helpfully. She nodded and began to speak but he cut her off before she could continue. "This conversation is finished. I do not talk with the emissaries of my enemy."

"I am not your enemy," she interrupted him. "And you must listen to me because what I have to say affects you closely. If trade with the Quadrant stops, Chennidur will stagnate and your people will die without it. You cannot condemn those you say you love more than yourself to ignorance and death when the Quadrant's knowledge could help. There are medicines to cure diseases that kill your children now and others to help them to live better and longer. There are nutritious foods that could be adapted to Chennidur to keep anyone from going hungry. There are efficient ways of lighting your houses against the darkness and heating them against the cold. There are ways to improve transportation that would help your economy to grow. These are just a few of the many benefits trade offers to all the people of Chennidur."

"It is trade with the Quadrant that will kill us," he interjected. "It is killing us now. Our culture and our religion are two sides of one whole that was given to us by the Chenni-ad, divinely ordained when Chennidur was created. How we live, what we eat, when we pray, all connect us directly to the deity. The Quadrant has no respect for that. It denies those sacred traditions. Children die when the Chenni-ad have woven it so. Disease is a way of maintaining the balance of life. We can already heat and light our homes. We have roads and trade of our own. The Chenni-ad have given us all that we need and we require no 'better' methods from the Quadrant. You speak of the benefits of trade but you do not speak of the price. The price is the death of our culture from heathen thinking, techish devices, the seduction of wealth and the pollution of stardust. Chennidur needs none of those things."

Engrossed in their argument, neither the tansul nor Aurial heard the door of the room snick open. It did not swing far and admitted only a slim crack of hallway darkness, but that was adequate.

Aurial regrouped. There was no persuading this man. She could argue until they were both dead of exhaustion and he would not hear her. It was time to adopt a different approach, one that would force him to take her seriously. "You say that your culture was divinely ordained. The separation into troinom and underranks. The tenets of the Kohrable. The rules which govern what you eat and when you worship and how you live. Is that not so?"

"It is."

"What if that is not the truth?" she asked.

The tansul nearly smiled. "Don't be absurd. You change the subject to try and shake my faith."

"Listen to me. The Kohrable teaches you to listen, also to believe and obey. It does not teach you to question. Have you never asked yourself why so much of Chennidur is poisonous to your people? Have you ever wondered why rennish is so important? Did you never think it strange that troinom and underranks do not breed children upon one another? Were you never curious about who the Rugollah really are?"

He shook his head. "Never. Those things are not given to us to know. They exist: we accept them. The Chenni-ad know and we have faith in them. It is sufficient."

"Being from the stars," Aurial responded, "it *is* given to me to know and I *was* curious. What I found out was this.

Many years ago, generations beyond counting in your history, Chennidur existed without either troinom or underranks. It was a beautiful world with a great deal of promise and it was attractive to systems which needed room to expand or a place where they could live as they wished. A group seeking religious freedom bought development rights for Chennidur and set about establishing a colony. There must not have been many of them or they could not afford more than one vessel because just one ship is listed in the records. It was chartered to deliver its passengers and then go on to another assignment, but it never left Chennidur. We can assume that it either crashed or suffered a malfunction that forced the crew to land before the parking orbit decayed. Communications being what they were in those days, a rescue mission to an Outback world would have been out of the question."

The tansul lifted one eyebrow. "I'm sure you think this is fascinating but, as I said, I am a busy man. Please get to the point." A strand of hair slid out of place but he ignored it.

"The facts tell us little more, but we do know that the passengers were Hidaljians, probably one of the radical sects for which that planet is famous. The crew, on the other hand, were technicians and teamsters from the Nordref system. Both races are human but they are of a different strain, which makes them genetically incompatible.

"Imagine the situation. The Hidaljians begin establishing a colony and discover that Chennidur is toxic. Making the colony viable will not be as easy as they had planned. If it is to succeed, then everyone, including the crew of the disabled ship, must devote themselves completely to its survival. Work cannot be divided between establishing the colony and repairing the ship, but the crew's attentions are on restoring their vessel. They are not interested in the colony; they only want to get back up the well and home again.

"So the Hidaljians outnumber the Nordreffians and they take drastic measures. The ship is destroyed and all things 'techish' are banned. The Nordreffian crew, whose technical skills are now useless, are strong and accustomed to work. They become the servants of the Hidaljians, who control survival on Chennidur, and the class system begins. Discoveries are made, probably the hard way, as to what is most and least toxic and how to eat without being poisoned. There are codified and rules added that solidify the new aristocracy's hold on power. The importance of these rules to the colony's survival is so great that they are incorporated into the Hidaljians' pervasive religion.

"The rest develops over time except for one especially interesting point. Before the ship and its equipment were destroyed, the Nordreffians must have carried out some preliminary work on a science we call ecoforming. They altered a few of the critical components of Chennidur's original structure to make the planet viable for alien life forms. The Veil is the most obvious example of this. It exists at or just above the tropopause, which is the top of the cloud layer, and revolves around the planet following the path of the sun. Its job is to screen harmful radiation out of the sunlight so it disappears at night when it is no longer needed. Quite ingenious, really. Another example is the fabled Greatmoon, which may have been removed.

"In short, Tansul, what you believe to be a divine gift was really the result of an accident."

The tansul, who had listened with cynical patience to Aurial's recitation, said, "That is a fascinating story, young woman, a wonderful tale. But it has nothing to do with you or me or trade with the Quadrant."

"Oh, you're wrong about that," Aurial countered. "They are very much related. Because if you continue your opposition to the Tulkan's trade policies, this story will become public knowledge. Once it is on people's lips it's in their minds, too, and the doubt it causes will begin destroying the faith you hold so dear. When that happens, neither your fervor nor your dedication will be able to call it back."

"A dramatic picture," he conceded, "but completely unconvincing. Why do you not go out tomorrow into the marketplace and preach this heresy? See how many people listen. See how many give credence to your apostasy before the Followers tear you apart."

Aurial smiled. "I have no desire to be a martyr," she said. "There are many ways of spreading information discreetly and indirectly. I only have to give the word for it to happen. My presence, in the market or even on Chennidur, is not required."

The tansul rested his elbows on the arms of the chair and steepled his hands in front of him. "And you really think I find this threat so compelling that it will force me to change the beliefs of a lifetime and withdraw my opposition?"

"Yes," Aurial replied. "Because no one who holds power relinquishes it voluntarily, not for himself and not for the next generation. Your sons are dead but you have the children your daughters will bear to consider. You would not wish the new children of Clan Cliffmaster to be anything less than what you are today."

She approached the table and stood so close that its edge cut across her hips. "Think about it, Tansul. Once the underranks begin to suspect that their subservience is not the will of the Chenni-ad, once they understand that abuse by their troinom masters is not an inescapable destiny, do you think they will go on as always? Do you think they will do nothing? You may have no history of slave uprisings on Chennidur to educate you as to what happens then, but I can show you the histories of a hundred systems and they tell a very bloody story. Usually the masters win the first time but it's only a temporary victory. The repressed class never rests, never stops, never relents until they have achieved their freedom and the higher the price their masters pay, the better."

The tansul's face remained expressionless but it was frozen. Aurial could see him thinking and that meant he was, for the first time, taking her seriously. "Keep in mind," she added quietly, "that the outcome changes when the underranks are armed with techish weapons that give them a tactical advantage." He looked startled and she knew she had reached him. Aurial stepped back from the table and slipped her hands into the voluminous pockets of her *dorchari*. Then she waited. The silence lengthened. Unnoticed at the other end of the room, the door inched quietly inward, opening a gap the size of a man's hand.

Finally, the tansul spoke. "You present a convincing

argument," he said briefly. "The welfare of my people is truly more important to me than my own life. But I simply do not have the ability to change the current situation that you think I have. Supposing I compromised my principles and reversed my position, the opposition would go on, the Tarraquis would continue their raids, the nayyat would preach adherence to tradition. And my sacrifice would not prevent you from unleashing your upheaval."

"If the tansul of Clan Cliffmaster simply altered his position in the Council, no, nothing would change," Aurial agreed. "But you are more than that, are you not? It seems we both have secrets. It is the Inayyam whose position is important here and you are the Inayyam."

"I? How interesting. What makes you believe that?" he asked.

"Torrian's betrothal," she replied.

Another errant lock lost its place and the tansul tucked it back in place. Then he folded his hands. "What has one to do with the other?"

"Protection. To keep your secret, you must maintain the outward appearance of being a weak and ineffectual member of the council, opposed to the Tulkan but lacking any real influence. Verrer, more than anyone else, had to believe in that guise. When he proposed the match, possibly as a test, you had two choices. If you rejected his offer, and whatever blandishments were attached to it, you would have drawn attention to yourself, thereby jeopardizing your role. If you accepted, you kept your cover intact but allowed an agent of your enemy to penetrate your clan and your stronghold. You also condemned your daughter to life with a psychopath.

"It was a difficult decision. After all, even the ineffectual tansul could have reasonably opposed such a questionable son-in-law. But you preferred to avoid conflict and made the safe choice. It was the only decision the Inayyam could make, but it cost you a great deal."

"You are a very dangerous woman," he said quietly.

"Only if we do not reach an agreement," she countered. They were at a critical juncture. The tansul had given her his full attention and granted credibility but he also perceived the threat she posed as real. His reaction was unpredictable. He could begin serious negotiation or he could attempt to neutralize the threat.

One corner of his mouth twitched upward in a way that reminded Aurial of Surrein. The expression chilled her. "Let me be certain that I understand your proposal," he began. "If I alter my position in the Council and withdraw my support for the Tarraquis—my full support—then you will go away and all will continue as before. If I do not agree to your demands and continue my unqualified opposition to the Tulkan's policies, you will set in motion a plan to undermine the True Word and create an insurrection that will bring Chennidur to its knees. Is that a correct statement?"

"It is a bit simplistic, but correct," Aurial said.

"And you can carry out your threat with a single command? 'By speaking one word' I think is what you said."

"Yes."

"Then all I have to do is prevent you from ever saying that word, or any other word, ever again. In this house, I command. My orders are carried out without hesitation. I have but to speak my one word and you cease to be a problem, outworlder. Everything continues as before and this conversation may as well never have happened. It is the best, the safest, choice for me by far."

"Certainly," Aurial replied. "If you can do it."

"And what is to stop me, outworlder? You?"

"Two things." Aurial willed her heart to beat at a normal pace but it defied her. "Like you, Tansul, I am a member of a large family and I have a job to do. Should I disappear, my family will come looking for me. They are aware of my work and will continue it. They will also seek justice, formally or otherwise, against anyone who harms me. All you would buy is time and you would pay a heavy price for it in the end."

His lips twitched again. "Time can be extremely valuable," he said simply. Behind the expressionless mask of his face, Aurial could see him evaluating alternatives and selecting options like a high-speed processor. As a citizen of the Quadrant, she thought, he would have been augmented six different ways.

"The second reason," she continued, "is this." She drew her nerve pistol out of the *dorchari's* voluminous pocket, pointed it directly at him, and steadied it with her other hand. The tansul's eyes widened in surprise. Aurial hoped that the quaver she felt in her stomach would not reach into her voice. "With this," she said evenly, "I can stun you, which renders you momentarily harmless but still dangerous, or I can kill you, which removes support for the Tarraquis permanently. Either way you say nothing and I simply walk out the front gate."

"The curfew . . ." he began.

"Is my friend," she interrupted. "I'm an outworlder, a starwoman, and an il Tarz. The first Patrol I encounter will escort me safely back to the Port and consider themselves honored to do so." Her heart pounded and her pulse raced. Aurial had never aimed a weapon at another person before.

"You came prepared," he conceded.

"Of course. Does the Kohrable not say, 'For then he looked upon the Raveler but feared not, for he knew the Raveler's mind as his own'?"

"The question then becomes, can I call out faster than you can fire," he said. "Once I alert my guards, you have a very short time to escape and find a Patrol before they catch you and kill you."

Aurial was about to reply when a low voice from the far end of the room interrupted them both. "Stop this." Although startled, Aurial resisted the compulsion to look, keeping her eyes and the muzzle of the weapon trained on the tansul. The corner of her eye tracked a figure in a dark *dorchari* as it crossed the room slowly and entered the pool of light around the desk. Aurial moved slightly to her left so that she could keep both people in her sights. The figure turned and Aurial saw, to her great surprise, the vellide.

"Stop," the woman repeated. "This is a waste of time and it solves nothing." She looked at Aurial and said in a kindly voice, "Put your weapon down, child, there is no need for violence here." Aurial ignored her and the muzzle of the gun did not waver. "As you wish. It does not matter." The vellide turned to her husband, on whose face an expression had finally surfaced. He was frankly astonished.

"Are you not glad to see me, my husband?"

"You are a gift of the Chenni-ad," he said with emotion in his voice. "It has been so difficult alone. I did what I thought best, but without your wisdom I lacked certainty."

"You did well," she reassured him, "except for the betrothal. We would not have made the same choice and I fear for my daughter."

"There is time," the tansul replied. "Now that we are together again, we can find a way to turn Surrein to our purposes or rid the clan of him."

"That is what I thought," the vellide said calmly, "but what will Torrian suffer until then?"

Aurial listened to this exchange in amazement, as she struggled to comprehend what the two were really saying. "Then you are *both* the Inayyam?" she asked.

The vellide's warm sad eyes turned in her direction. "Of course. Is the Chenni-ad one?" she responded. "Now, let us stop this arguing and come to a decision. There must be a way out of this tangle that will allow us all to benefit."

"How much did you hear?" the tansul asked.

"All of it," his wife responded. "I thought it best to hold my presence in reserve until it was needed."

The tansul nodded. "She cannot kill us both with that profane weapon," he said. "We can send her to the Raveler and cope with the consequences when they occur."

The vellide smiled and shook her head. "No, I cannot. You see, I have been speaking to my daughters and I owe this starwoman a great deal. It is she who brought our foolish Raunn back from her brush with the Tulkan's Patrol. It is she who returned me to myself. I cannot repay those gifts with a death. To do so would give the Raveler a hold on my spirit that I could never release. We have to find another way."

Aurial weighed what she heard and lowered the gun.

She said nothing, waiting to hear what ideas the vellide would contribute.

The tansul spoke again. "If you say it is so, then it is so, though I know nothing of either event. What, then, do you suggest? Do we then concede and withdraw our support from the Tarraquis?"

"Perhaps—but not completely," the vellide responded. "Too great a change carried out too abruptly could cause adverse effects we have not considered. A party which supports the sacred isolation of our world may exist without taking violent action. Is that not so?" She looked to Aurial for corroboration. Aurial nodded. "Trade may also continue with restrictions agreed upon by both sides. Is that not so?"

"That is so," Aurial confirmed.

"If the spirits of our people support the True Word as we believe they do, then we may achieve through diplomacy what we could not accomplish with force," the vellide continued.

"It will take far longer," the tansul protested.

"The Kohrable was not written in a matter of days," his wife commented. "The alternative this woman has described is something I do not wish to contemplate."

"How can we be sure that outworlders will negotiate in good faith?" he asked.

"This one who calls herself Aurial has demonstrated her goodwill already," she replied, "or we would not be talking now. She may better ask that same question of us."

Aurial agreed. There had been enough intrigue here on this one night to call into question many of the things she had thought she understood. To the Inayyam, deception was just another tactic. They had already shown duplicity toward others of their faith, and she was an outworlder, exempt from the rules and restrictions of the Kohrable. Her mother's voice spoke quietly in her ear, saying *The best strategy is partnership*. Aurial knew that was true only in certain circumstances, one had to be careful, but here it could work.

"The spirit of the Kohrable is truth," she quoted. "You said that the True Word is your life, Tansul. If you both swear on it that you will negotiate honorably, I will accept that. The word of the Inayyam must be of some value."

"It is," the tansul said. He and the vellide swore an oath on the ancient, ragged book and Aurial nodded. "Now we may talk," she said. "There is much to debate before we reach an agreement. Before we begin, however, I would like to propose that we collaborate on a different issue, one that is of great importance to you both." She had been going to do this anyway, she might as well turn it to her advantage. Aurial briefed the Inayyam on what she had in mind.

"What must we do?" the tansul inquired and she could almost detect a twinge of excitement in his voice.

"You need only speak to your chef," she replied. "I'll take care of the rest."

"Then let us begin," the vellide commented. "We have much to discuss between now and the wedding and I wish to go over the details of this plan of yours immediately. First, however, I suggest that we remove ourselves to a more comfortable room." She turned to her husband. "This one was always too barren for my liking and now that you've removed my chair, I can't even sit down."

Aurial could afford to smile at the vellide's complaint but her face, tight with tension, felt as if it might crack instead. She slipped the gun back out of sight in her pocket and followed the two out of the door. The worst was over. There was still a lot of work ahead of her but, for the first time since she had arrived on Chennidur, she was confident of success. Aurial had no intention of letting down her guard, however, regardless of their oath. From now until the morning after Torrian's wedding, she would keep the gun on her person at all times.

# TORRIAN

Torrian was numb. She had followed the advice given to her by the Voice and done everything it instructed her to do, even though staying in control of her fear was the hardest task she had ever undertaken. In the time before the wedding, she had tried to think positively and to keep her spirits up by laughing at the standard wedding jokes. She had tried to visualize herself as she wanted to be, not as she feared Surrein would make her. Yet her best efforts had not succeeded and all the while, even as she tried to rise above the desperation that flooded her, she had waited for rescue.

Torrian was not sure who or what she had expected to deliver her from the marriage, perhaps her father or the Voice, or the Chenni-ad itself. It may even have been Raunn's odd friend who had appeared from nowhere, belonged to no clan listed in the book, behaved in peculiar fashion and now lived on Cheffra Street as if she were part of the family. She had sought for a protector, waited for a savior, but none had appeared and now it was too late.

Here she stood, nearly paralyzed with fear, in the temple at Surrein's side in the midst of all the other couples being united on the fifth day of the Wedding Season. The ceremony was progressing inexorably all around her and she had no choice but to participate. Already they had drunk the Heartspring water together and sung the lines of the marriage chant. The rennish bowl was being passed down the line of white-robed celebrants so that each couple could hold it and breathe in the smoke once for each of the five members of the Chenni-ad and once for the omnipotent unity. The large censer, redolent with burning rennish, came to them and Surrein seized it in his strong hands. Torrian placed her own hands beneath the bowl, careful not to touch his, and inhaled deeply, hoping that the smoke would do its magic quickly.

Then she could stand quietly again without thinking and let the ceremony flow around her. At her back, she could feel the eyes of all the families, intent on the participants, as they followed each portion of the ceremony avidly. The heat of a temple filled with people, the droning of the six nayyat as they called the blessings of the Chenni-ad upon the nuptial participants, and the pervasive smell of rennish all washed over her. She began to feel light, as if she could rise out of her body up to the arches beneath the roof and escape through the small windows that ventilated the temple. Torrian almost smiled at the thought.

On cue, she turned to face Surrein and laced her hands through his in a gesture symbolic of their physical union. His eyes sought hers with a heaviness that compelled her to match his gaze. Instead she looked at a point just over his head. It was often obvious during this particular rite which of the couples had already become lovers and she had no wish to reveal that to anyone in either family. She took small satisfaction from thwarting Surrein's desire to announce his complete success to all watching.

Soon the wedding ceremony would be over and the nightmare of her marriage would begin. One of the nayyat approached them and lifted the ancestral, ceremonial wedding belt of Clan Cliffmaster from the cushion where it rested. He wrapped it around them twice and tied it loosely. Then, along with all the others, she and Surrein repeated their dedication to the True Word, promised to raise their children safely within its guidance, and pledged to adhere to the rules of the Kohrable and *shufri-nagai*.

The nayyat gave a final blessing and it was done. It could not be undone. Torrian felt as if the end of the ceremony marked the end of her life. She and Surrein filed out of the temple in the procession of newly-married couples and were surrounded by their joyful families. Even in her dull state, Torrian could see that the jubilance of the Fellskeeper Clan exceeded that of Clan Cliffmaster. Small wonder, considering what the upstarts had to gain. Surrein took her hand firmly in his and set out to lead the combined families through the streets to the Cliffmaster house where food and music awaited them. As was traditional, servants of both clans threw flower petals and cheered as the couple passed. Torrian could barely hear them and the flowers might as well have been ice.

## SURREIN

Surrein was euphoric. All had gone according to his plans, the wedding was over and they were married. It was irrevocable. They had stood in their plain white robes along with all the other couples being married at that day's ceremony. By his side, Torrian had been quiet, unsmiling and unresponsive except for the portions of the ceremony which required her participation. Her reticence notwithstanding, they had drunk the water together, sung the chant together, breathed rennish smoke together and dedicated themselves while the ancestral wedding belt bound them in spirit. The Clan Cliffmaster belt. He was now part of one of the most powerful clans on Chennidur and the next in line—the only one in line—to be tansul.

His elation was boundless and Surrein's exuberance overcompensated for Torrian's passivity. He hoped that her behavior now did not indicate future demeanor. He was not ready for her to be quiet and passive, not yet. He wanted anger and fear, resistance and submission, so that he would have the pleasure of forcing her to his will. The vision of her bare back, pale and vulnerable, floated before him as he mingled with the guests.

At the wedding feast, Surrein greeted people he did not know and smiled at people he disdained. With serious mien, he described Fellskeeper Citadel as equal in size and importance to the Rock. Smiling at the guests and caressing his new wife, he presented the appearance of loving son and doting husband. Wrapping himself in humility, he deferred to shallow people whose wit and intellect he knew to be inferior to his own. In a virtuoso performance, Surrein slipped masks on and off, changing his image to be what each person expected. The only thing true and honest about him was his outright enjoyment of the night and the celebration. Surrein was relishing his triumph and the successful culmination of all his efforts. Tonight was his night, the beginning of many days and nights of power, authority and prestige to come.

The food was brought out and he escorted a pale Torrian to their place at the center of a long table. Before the first course, and between every course thereafter, the new couple was served a small dish which symbolized some aspect of the wedded state. They could nibble at the rest of the feast, but these special foods they must eat completely. A servant placed a small *pittari* pastry, representing the sweetness of love, before each of them and Surrein consumed his in one moment. Torrian, chewing slowly, took longer but when both were eaten, the guests cheered. Now the feast would begin.

Food and drink were brought out in enormous quantities. Each course was of the finest provender, prepared elaborately and served in ostentatious constructions that were demolished quickly by ravenous guests. The wedding ceremony had lasted for several hours, causing everyone to inhale far more rennish smoke than normal. Surrein played the role of the delighted husband and outgoing host to perfection, seeking to create a favorable impression that would stay in the mind of each guest for years. He paced himself throughout the meal so as not to overdo anything and paid assiduous compliments to his unreceptive bride.

The fourth of the special dishes was placed before them, a cracker spread thinly with jirrifish pate. This delicacy, although popular with many of the most sophisticated troinom including the tansul, was one for which he had never acquired a taste. The fish's natural toxin permeated its flesh and could not be removed completely. Skilled chefs could prepare it in ways that altered the dose to suit the diner's taste but, despite their best efforts, it was occasionally and unpredictably lethal. Jirrifish was usually tart and caused a slight tingling of the lips and extremities that its devotees found pleasurable. Although it was a delicacy, jirrifish made Surrein feel slightly outside of himself, not completely in control, and for that reason he had always declined to eat it. Here, however, it symbolized the occasional bitterness of marriage and he could not avoid consuming a small ritual portion. He devoured the cracker, made a comical face which caused the guests to laugh, and called for a cup of Heartspring water to wash it down. The next course appeared, breast of turch with a cream sauce that he particularly enjoyed, and the feast continued.

Surrein was trying to charm Torrian into a smile when a discreet cough captured his attention. He turned to see his manservant hovering uncertainly behind the chair. "What is it?" he asked abruptly, annoyed at the interruption.

"Sri-nothi," the man began apologetically, "the porter has informed me that a man waits by the gate who must speak with you."

"Now?" Surrein expostulated. "I'm in the middle of my wedding feast. Who is it?"

The servant flinched. "I do not know, sri-nothi, but he said that it was most urgent. He insists on speaking with you right away."

Surrein thought quickly. He was not aware of any issue so critical that it required his attention at this precise moment, but one could never tell. It would be wiser to invest a few moments now to deal with this man, whoever he was, than risk a problem erupting later for lack of attention. Excusing himself, he rose and followed his manservant from the room. Outside, the air was refreshingly cool and he breathed it in gratefully. It would help to clear away the symptoms of the jirrifish pate, which were unusually persistent. In addition to the tingling in his tongue and lips, he had developed a headache from the heat and noise in the crowded room. He would have to get this errand over with quickly. He made his way to the gate and the porter hurried to open it at his approach.

Stepping out into the street, Surrein spied a man standing some distance away, close to an alley untouched by Smallmoon's pale blue light. He appeared to be a Patrol lieutenant but in the uncertain light Surrein could not be positive. It was after curfew, however, so who else could it be?

Surrein gestured peevishly for the man to approach but received no response. Stifling a curse, he strode toward the motionless figure, flexing his fingers as he walked in an attempt to rid himself of the vexatious tingling. He could not understand how anyone could enjoy such a feeling and eat an otherwise unpleasant fish in order to achieve it. The prickle seemed to spread rather than diminish and his fingertips were numb. Annoyed at the coincidence that distracted him when dealing with a problem, he called out, "You! What do you want?"

The man did not speak but turned his head slowly toward Surrein. His cap was pulled down low, shading his face, making it impossible for the troinom to see his features. Surrein raised his arm and it floated upward as if lighter than his body. The Patrolman seemed to notice him for the first time and spoke as Surrein approached. "Sri-noth Surrein. Lieutenant Zed. I regret interrupting you upon such an occasion but there is a problem with the labor shipment that must be resolved immediately."

"That is not my concern," Surrein replied and his voice was slurred by lips which refused to form the sounds properly. "I have nothing to do with labor shipments."

"That is so," Zed conceded. He nodded toward the house, "But he said you should handle it. It was a direct order. My apologies, sri-noth."

*That would be just like Verrer,* Surrein thought. *Push it off on me during my wedding feast. Probably another one of his mungering tests.* "Alright, what is it?"

"I have to show you," the man said. "Follow me." He turned and stepped into the shadows. "It's not far," his voice floated back. Surrein moved to follow him but stumbled on feet that would not quite obey his commands. Before he could fall, Zed returned and grasped his upper arm, holding him up. "Are you all right?" the Patrolman inquired with solicitude.

Surrein attempted to respond but could not. He was weak all over and then, abruptly, he began to sweat like a bluedirt farmer laboring in the hot sun. "Let me help you, sri-noth," Zed said, steadying an arm around Surrein's shoulders. The feel of the strong male arm around him, the unyielding grip of the man's hand, opened a door in

Surrein's memory that he had thought locked and bolted. Once again he felt his uncle holding him, pulling him closer. Strong hands, irresistible. An inflexible grasp. An insistent embrace. *No!* Surrein thought in panic. *Why did it have to be me? He could have taken a boy from the underranks for his pleasure. That's what drevs are there for, to please a troinom, to follow orders. I didn't want it. Never liked it. Why me?*

The memory ripped its way out and through him, bringing with it all the disgust, the pain, the helplessness and the rage. Images followed one another in rapid succession, building toward the inevitable climax of his uncle's body falling. Falling. The memory took possession of him, overwhelming what was occurring in the real world. The rage built toward a convulsive attack but he fought it, battling his way back to awareness only to find that he, too, was falling. He did not know how long the memories had dominated him but he could no longer feel anything, not even the Patrolman's support, and the man's grip was all that kept him from collapsing to the street.

As his body succumbed to paralysis, however, Surrein's mind clarified. He knew that the chef had tampered with his ritual jirrifish to increase the potency and only one person could have instructed him to do so. This was Torrian's last desperate attempt to escape him. Who else would have poisoned a food that only he would eat, a food that was always dangerous? She had risked the enormous punishment meted to a poisoner, gambling that the civil authorities would believe his death accidental. And she might have succeeded but for his extraordinary double life. He wanted to laugh, to cry out in triumph. He would still win. How could she know that he would be called at precisely the right time to meet an ally, a Patrolman who could take him to the Port for treatment by their excellent offworld doctor? How could she have guessed that her plan would be foiled by sheer coincidence and that he would live despite her murderous attempts? He would live and return to make her pay!

Surrein tried to tell Zed what had happened so the

lieutenant could arrange immediately for the right treatment but was incapable of moving any part of his body. Instead he heard Zed speak to another man who remained unseen in the shadows. "He's under. He won't be any problem now."

The other man replied, "Let's get him into the floater fast before the real Patrol comes by."

Then, with that same clarity, Surrein knew. These were not his allies. He had been doubly duped. There would be no help for him. The full extent of his betrayal was apparent.

Another man spoke but Surrein could not move and saw only darkness as he listened. "I want to be sure Dr. La has enough time to get the poison out of his system and stabilize him. If he dies before we can get him into a cylinder, we lose our bounty."

"Keep that bounty to yourself," Zed said grimly. "We're supposed to be neutral."

"But we are neutral," the second man replied. "We're just following orders," he said and laughed.

Then Surrein was lifted and carried a short distance before being slung into a vehicle. Just before the door closed, a shrill whistle sliced into his brain.

# AURIAL

Aurial heard the whistle and strolled away from the wall, through the courtyard and back to the festivities. It was difficult to keep a smile from her lips as yet another part of her plan was completed without hindrance. At this moment, Surrein ceased to be a problem for Torrian and her family. With poetic justice, he was joining the labor force created by his masters to profit from their opposition. His dramatic disappearance on the night of his own wedding would cause a great deal of confusion and consternation to those not of Clan Cliffmaster. There would be investigations, Verrer would ensure that, but no answers. Without a body, no one could prove murder and the authorities could not charge anyone with a crime.

Her elegant design had involved only three people and two of them were ignorant of the real plot, having played only small roles. Surrein's manservant could answer truthfully any question put to him about the message he had conveyed. The chef, informed of Surrein's preference for strong jirrifish, had prepared the dish to suit, but at a level far from lethal. In the unlikely event that he was questioned, the chef's loyalties were to Clan Cliffmaster and he would have no desire to face charges of even accidental poisoning. Torrian, who was ignorant of the plot, had been in sight of the guests all evening. That left the Inayyam and they would carry the secret to their deathbeds.

Aurial's step was light. Within days, she had neutralized the tansul's opposition and gained the loyal support of his wife and eldest daughter. Her objective was at hand. The tansul would withdraw his open opposition to the Tulkan's government and his covert support of the Tarraquis. The nayyat themselves could keep the fundamentalist group going for a while but, without the Inayyam's leadership, the Tarraquis would gradually lose momentum and become ineffective. Fundamentalist opposition would continue at a lower level but open conflict, at least for the moment, would be averted.

Aurial was not proud of having compromised the tansul but consoled herself by thinking that, in reality, she had only turned his own prejudices against him and to her favor.

She made her way back to the table, having absented herself from the room no longer than it would have taken for her to relieve herself. It was important that she, too, be visible to all the guests tonight so that no suspicion would be attached to her. After dawn, when the curfew was lifted, she could slip out of the house on Cheffra Street and return to the Port. That would remove her from the maelstrom that was sure to follow on Surrein's disappearance. From the Port, she could monitor the tansul's activities and write an official report while she waited for Merradrix to return. Then, her work done, she would embark on the first ship out and begin the long voyage back to the Beldame.

She took her seat at the table just in time for the next course. Already full, she had no desire for more food but protocol demanded that she at least taste each dish. She resigned herself to long boring hours sweating in the gym if she was ever going to return her body to the slenderness she preferred.

## RAUNN

From where she sat, surrounded by family, Raunn watched the comings and goings with interest. Something was up and she was offended at not being part of it. Surrein's seat was empty and had been for some time. Yet Torrian was oblivious to his absence, speaking and eating with no greater animation than she had displayed all evening. Yes, something was going on. Raunn tapped her fork on her plate as she thought.

The celebration continued, the hour drew on, and the time came for her to lead Torrian's female relatives in a procession escorting the bride to the apartments she would share with her new husband. Surrein's male relatives gathered to perform the same role for him and stopped in consternation when no one could locate the groom. Confusion broke out as they all talked, each one thinking that someone else knew where he could be found.

Standing next to Torrian, Raunn heard her tell one of the men that her husband's manservant had been sent to summon him outside. Her voice was placid and unworried but her words sent them off to pull the man from his sleep in the servant's quarters. When they had gone, Raunn

searched her sister's face and saw there no clue as to what
was happening. She wanted to follow the men and be part
of the search just for the excitement. She could not help
hoping that something terrible had happened to Surrein
and wanted to know if it had. Instead, she continued in
her role as the model sister and performed the next step of
the ritual in proper fashion. She led the procession and
sang the traditional songs but her mind was not on her
task.

As soon as she could do so, she left Torrian in the
company of the other women and went out to discover
"how long the men would be." From what she found, it
would be a long time. The men had surged out into the
street despite the curfew only to be met by empty cobbles
and blank walls. With dawn fast approaching, they searched
up and down the streets, around corners and through
alleys with no success. There were no signs of a fight, no
bloodstains, no wagon marks to give them a clue. Lacking
a trail to follow, they regrouped in the courtyard where
Raunn, standing unobtrusively in the corner, listened to
them speculate on what may have happened. Completely
stymied, they talked in circles but decided that, when
curfew was lifted, two of them would go and summon the
authorities. The others set off for the room where both
sets of parents waited for word. "I don't understand," one
of them said as he passed. "It's as though he vanished into
the sky."

The sky. Of course. Raunn gathered the folds of her
elaborate *dorchari* and turned swiftly back into the house.
Her intrigues had taught her that, in time of crisis, the
one who is not present can be more important than those
who are and two people were not part of these events.
Verrer, who could not associate himself publicly with his
minion, had simply retired for the night. Aurial, not part
of either family, had done likewise. But of the two, Aurial
was the one she had to speak with.

The door to the starwoman's room was closed but she
was not asleep. At Raunn's knock, Aurial opened it quickly.
She was still dressed and the bed was untouched. "Shouldn't
you be with your sister?" Aurial asked.

"Yes. But I had to ask you something first," Raunn said.

"Me?" Aurial queried innocently. "What would I know?"

"More than you're letting on," Raunn replied quickly. "What do you think is the likelihood that Surrein would just vanish on the night of the wedding that grants him all the power he has ever sought?"

"Very little," Aurial said succinctly.

"Correct. So if he didn't disappear and he wasn't killed—there's no body—what happened to him?"

"I really have no idea," Aurial replied. "Perhaps your father, the tansul, would know. Or Verrer."

"Whatever they know, I'm sure it's less than you do," Raunn countered bluntly. "Did you have him taken out?"

"Really, Raunn," was all Aurial would say.

Raunn was angry. Up until now, she had been included in everything and enjoyed it despite her arguments and protestations. Now, instead of trust, she encountered a blank wall. It never occurred to her that she might be kept in the dark for her own good, or that she was extraneous to this particular activity. She felt excluded and she didn't like it at all. "But," Raunn expostulated, "he can't just disappear! If there's no body, we can't know if he's dead. If he's not dead, Torrian's not a widow. If she's neither a widow nor a wife, what is she? Torrian can't just wait forever!"

Aurial's voice was calm, if slightly pedantic. "Surely the Kohrable provides guidance for this sort of thing as it has rules for everything. You know far more than I about the laws. Does it not provide for such an occurrence, no matter how unlikely?"

Raunn, surprised, thought quickly. "The law says that, when a husband disappears, the wife must wait for five years. If, by that time, the husband has not reappeared, alive or dead, the wife is free to resume her life."

"Well, then," Aurial said. "That seems quite clear."

"But Torrian cannot remarry," Raunn protested, unaware that she had been skillfully diverted from her original inquiry.

"No," said Aurial softly. "Neither can she be forced to remarry."

Understanding dawned. Raunn saw the mystery anew and, as she thought it through, her appreciation grew. She still wanted to know what had happened to Surrein but Aurial was obviously not prepared to discuss any of it with her. "I see," was all she said.

"It seems you and Torrian have five years to straighten out the Clan's affairs," Aurial added. "I'm sure your mother, the vellide, will have much to say on the subject of Torrian's future husband—and yours as well."

"Yes. I agree." Her reason told her to drop the subject but one last question forced itself out. "Do you think it likely that Surrein will ever return?" she asked.

"Not really," Aurial answered. "I think it less likely than, say, that Merradrix will return."

"Ah." Raunn thought quickly, then nodded. "Yes. I see." She wanted to laugh and shout at the thought of suave, arrogant Surrein sweating on a labor gang, far from the protection of Verrer and the Tulkan. A hundred more questions pushed at her lips. How did you arrange it? she wanted to ask. Where will he go? Tell me everything. But she did not speak, aware that Aurial had said nothing that would have seemed odd to an observer. It would be wise of her to do the same. "I think I must return to my sister," she commented. "She will need support and reassurance from her family."

"Indeed, she will," Aurial responded. "Although I think she will hold up very well. Your sister Torrian is stronger than she may appear."

"Yes, I'm sure you're right." Raunn turned, but hesitated. Something was happening here as well and she was reluctant to leave.

"I will be gone in the morning, Raunn," Aurial said. "It is time. My task has been accomplished and I must leave."

That was it. She had known, but not wanted to know. For all their arguments, Aurial was her link to the forbidden world of the stars and Raunn did not wish to be left behind. Yet there was no choice. Where would she go? Aurial could not lead her through the star trails the way

Raunn had guided her through the Perimeter. *Maybe someday*, she consoled herself. *But not now*. She did not know what to say, so she said nothing. Instead, she took two steps over to the starwoman and embraced her, surprised by the strength of those arms.

They separated and she walked from the room without looking back. Tonight everything had changed and there was much to do.

# EPILOGUE

## THE PORT

"Well," Aurial said, "both our reports are complete and they will be analyzed thoroughly before we arrive back on the Beldame. There could be some tough questions to face when we return."

Rolfe took a drink of his beverage and made a face. "Relax. What are you afraid of? You did just fine."

"I did what Mother wanted," Aurial agreed, "but it's really a temporary fix and it could come apart at any time in any number of ways. I also compromised the Inayyam, which makes the solution less than perfect."

"In retrospect, could you have done any better?" Rolfe asked.

"Me? No," she replied doubtfully. "Mother could, or Itombe, or Gwynn. I'm sure you could have come up with a better idea, too. But I did the best I could."

"Then you have nothing to worry about," Rolfe reassured her. "All they can ask you to do is the best you can do. Besides, um, Mother probably didn't expect you to be this successful when she gave you the assignment."

Aurial studied him, perplexed. "What?" she asked. "She didn't? I don't understand."

He smiled and refilled his cup. "It was your first real field assignment, right?"

"Right."

"And it was a difficult mission with an objective that was almost impossible to accomplish, right?"

"Right."

"And Chennidur is not a major source of revenue for the Family, right? I mean, if it drops out of the trade net, there won't be any huge repercussions."

"Right."

"Then it was almost certainly a training exercise, the purpose of which was to give you an opportunity to learn and grow and stretch a bit. It was like giving you a plate full of tangled noodles to get through and anything you managed to accomplish would be sauce on the noodles."

Aurial was silent. She thought about how hard she had worked physically and mentally to succeed and prove herself a worthy daughter of Nashaum il Tarz. She remembered the endless hiking up and down the Perimeter's hills, the time spent poring through the Kohrable. Then she considered her dependence on rennish and a newly-developed taste for red meat. A learning experience! She wanted to scream and laugh at the same time. Then she looked at her brother cautiously. "Are you sure?" she asked.

"No, of course not. But I understand some of the way that Mother thinks and it seems more than likely to me. If I'm correct, you're way ahead already so stop worrying."

"Hmmm. If you're so smart, then tell me something else," Aurial said.

He tipped his cup at her, "Just name it, little sister. The omniscient one will be glad to answer."

Aurial ignored his teasing and said seriously, "When all this started here in the Port, Raunn lectured me about slave trading and accused the Family of profiting from the transport of slaves. She was furious with me and self-righteous about it. But then, when I was out there," she gestured in a wide arc that encompassed all of Chennidur,

"I saw how the troinom treat the underranks. The drevs are little more than slaves here and the troinom act the part of masters."

"Do the troinom buy and sell drevs?" Rolfe asked.

"No, but the drevs 'belong' to a particular clan and live on its holding all their lives," Aurial answered. "The troinom hold virtual power of life and death over them. Granted, the Kohrable contains severe prohibitions against the mistreatment of the underranks and strict laws about caring for the drevs that are one's responsibility. The only problem is, there are virtually no penalties for troinom who don't obey the laws. So, in reality, only an individual's code of honor controls his behavior."

"Does Raunn object to this situation?" he probed.

Aurial shook her head. "No, she takes it for granted, as do all the other troinom. But she's not abusive to the drevs, nor is anyone else in Clan Cliffmaster that I observed."

Rolfe stared into his cup and thought. Then he raised his head and said, "Then perhaps she acted out Rolfe's Rule of Inverse Distress—we become angriest at behavior in others that reflects behavior we prefer not to see in ourselves. Sometimes it's too painful to acknowledge our own flaws, much less be critical of them, but it's easier and much more gratifying to reproach others for doing the same thing."

"That's not logical," Aurial protested.

"Logic has nothing to do with it," Rolfe responded. "In the long run, though, I think the master/servant classes on Chennidur will change irrespective of your agreement with the Innayyam. It's the return of Merradrix and Astin that will I predict, be a turning point in the history of this planet."

Aurial's forehead creased. "For what reason?" she queried.

"Simply because they will begin the very process you threatened to start when you confronted the Inayyam."

Aurial thought about it and then shook her head. "They don't know anything about the Nordreffian ship crashing on Chennidur. Or ecoforming. Or how the True Word became the dominant religion."

"That's true," Rolfe conceded. "But they learned other things that are also important and they are men now, not the drevs they were when they went up the well. We talked a great deal on the trip home and they asked a lot of questions. Sometimes I had the answers and other times not but I could see how they were thinking and their ideas are the kind that lead inevitably to change."

"Such as?" Aurial probed. "The drevs accepted this culture and the True Word as being divinely ordained just as the troinom do. They may be at the bottom of the social order, but they don't challenge it."

"Also true. But on Big Green, Merradrix and Astin learned to challenge everything the hard way. They did not have the perspective and the opportunity to approach a new situation cerebrally the way you did. They were thrown into crisis where survival was paramount and they had to think in different ways to keep on living. From what I can tell, the experience changed them radically. For example, they learned that the True Word is not true for every world and that *shirz* means nothing off Chennidur. They discovered new strengths, including the ability to confront a strange world on its own terms. An undeniable lesson was that those in power are not necessarily good or right. They learned about worlds where distinctions like drev and troinom don't exist. But most importantly, they broke out of the old patterns and learned to think."

"So you're saying they won't just come back here and settle into life the way it always was," Aurial sounded intrigued.

"Exactly."

"How about one other lesson—that good can come out of bad but, to make something happen, one must be willing to pay the price."

Rolfe smiled. "Very good. And that's one you shared, I think. So now you see why these two men could represent the vanguard of change on Chennidur." He drained his cup and then put it down with a sour expression on his face.

"What are you drinking?" Aurial asked. "You don't seem to enjoy it much."

"It's just water," he replied with a laugh, "but I hate water."

"Then why are you drinking it?" she persisted.

"Because it's the only thing on Chennidur that's safe," he said. "Everything else is poisonous one way or another."

"Don't be absurd," Aurial protested. "I've been eating the local food for some time now and I'm still alive. I've even gained weight. Plus, I have learned to appreciate things I never thought I'd put in my mouth."

"So this was a broadening experience?" he asked.

"Yes," she said with a rueful smile and a pat on her hips. "It certainly was."

He laughed again. "Actually," he continued, "I don't want to take any chances on upsetting my metabolism because I have been looking forward to a little R & R before returning to the Beldame's tight society. Are there any nice-looking women you could introduce me to?" He gave a cocky grin. "I can be very charming."

"Yes, I know," she replied. "Unfortunately, you are *shirz* here, not to mention an outworlder, and that means you haven't got a chance. A troinom would consider the very idea offensive and insulting. Even a bluedirt drev woman would be immune to your appeal, for purely religious reasons, of course. Sorry."

Rolfe shrugged. "I guess I'll just have to plan a layover on the trip back."

"Don't lay over too long," Aurial cautioned, "or I'll go on to the Beldame without you and collect all the glory."

"Oh, it's glory that awaits us now," he teased her. "Well, don't worry. I'll find a way to enjoy myself and you won't be inconvenienced. Tell me, are you going to miss this place?"

Aurial looked at the wall as if she could see through the Port to the streets of Nandarri and the hills beyond. "Yes," she replied, "I think I will." She admitted to herself with some surprise that there was a great deal to miss, more than she would ever have imagined at the beginning. She was about to exchange Raunn and their ongoing contest of wills between equals for the familiar company of her sisters, among whom she would probably never be equal.

The immense, awesome beauty of Chennidur would soon dwindle into the Perimeter's darkness, its bright veiled days and clear nights relegated to memory. The vitality of living on the edge, thinking fast and staying one step ahead would eventually fade.

Then there was Antikoby.

Aurial felt the usual conflicting emotions well up, but they were overlaid now with a warmth she wanted very much to keep. Although he had been her first lover and there had been only the one night, the experience could not have been better. It was distressing to think of that strong and intelligent man being treated on a daily basis as something less than completely human. If change was as inevitable as Rolfe believed, then Aurial hoped Antikoby would be at the forefront. She could picture him taking charge amid turmoil, setting new ideas into motion, and leading those who trusted him while striving to keep them safe. That was, Aurial decided, the picture of Antikoby that she would hold in her memory.

"Come on," she said to her brother. "It's time to get moving. There's a long way to go before we're home."

# APPENDIX A

## GLOSSARY OF TERMS

### CHENNIDUR

*Bikkle*—A small rounded reptile with excellent camouflage abilities. When deception fails against an enemy, it runs extremely fast and can turn in a split-second. Bikkles are dwads and form lifetime partnerships and telepathic bonds with their podmate.

*Blaik*—A musical instrument similar to the flute.

*Bluedirt*—Pejorative term, derived from the predominant color of mountain soil, for a farmer. All farmers are of the underranks and at the bottom of the social scale.

*Bonding Period*—A period of time following a wedding when the newly-married couple retreats to an isolated site where they become accustomed to living with one another without distraction. Not even body servants accompany the couple.

*Burrky(ies)*—Large ruminant mammals domesticated for riding and for use as draft animals. Burrkies are dwads, gathering only in pairs or in groups of two. They have prehensile tails and two additional prehensile appendages curled behind their jowls. They are slow-moving and extremely placid creatures.

*Clan Mark*—A tattoo of a design specific to each clan. The mark is tattooed on the left shoulder for girls and the right shoulder for boys at the time of their coming of age.

*Clickbug*—A large predatory insect that eats shell-bearing reptiles and inhabits the shells of its victims.

*Deathcatcher*—A carnivorous animal that attracts insects and small rodents to it with the appearance and smell of carrion.

*Diktall*—A carniverous avian of reptilian origin. Various species live in trees and rocky cliffs. It soars on wings of stretched membrane. Diktalls are not edible in any form.

*Dorchari*—The traditional dress of a troinom woman. It consists of a long-sleeved, hip-length tunic over a long skirt. It is often brightly colored and may be, for formal occasions, highly embroidered.

*Draks*—The laws of hospitality within shufri-nagai.

*DraksHouse*—An inn or public house, usually found on well-traveled roads.

*Drev*—Any member of the underranks.

*Dumpling Bulb*—The edible root of a wild flower. It may be harvested from the wild and roasted as a delicacy. The dumpling bulb is edible during Chennidur's spring, when all the nourishment of the plant is still enclosed and before the toxins that accompany full growth have developed.

*Durric*—A small arboreal mammal. Mults, they travel in packs of ten or more. The meat is edible: all viscera are toxic, either raw or cooked.

*Dusklizard*—A finger-length nocturnal lizard that eats insects and is tolerated in households as a means of controlling pests. It "sings" in the evenings by rubbing its legs, thus its name.

*Dwads*—Animals of any species that live in pairs or in groups of two.

*Eyestar*—The brightest object in the Chennidurian sky. It is also the polestar and its place in the heavens remains fixed. This combination of facts gives it great importance in folklore. It is supposed to be the eye of the Chenni-ad, and reports to the multiple deity on the activities of the people of Chennidur.

*Firevine*—A woody vine that grows abundantly in the wild. Its leaves and stems contain a volatile oil that is poisonous to the touch. It produces painful welts that develop into large blisters. When the blisters break, they are followed by an extremely itchy rash.

*Firstmeal*—Breakfast.

*The Great Wheel*—The Milky Way Galaxy as seen from Chennidur, located far in the Outback. The Great Wheel is the single largest source of light in the Chennidurian night sky. In legend, the end of the world will come when the Great Wheel falls and slices Chennidur in two.

*Heartspring*—A spring of uncontaminated water that forms the core of every clan.

*Januga's Pipe*—A wild herb, commonly found in shady areas. The pale shoots are edible and add flavor to food.

*Jirrifish*—A large, predatory freshwater fish with firm white flesh that is prized as a delicacy by sophisticated diners despite its tart taste. Because of its position at the top of the aquatic food chain, toxins build up in its flesh, particularly the tetrodotoxins. Eating jirrifish that has been properly prepared causes a mild "high" that is the reason for its popularity. Because the quantity of the tetrodotoxin is variable, however, the fish can sometimes be lethal.

*Jura Bush*—A perennial, evergreen shrub that is both domesticated and occurs in the wild. The buds and leaves of the bush are edible and add a peppery dash to food. The berries and all other parts of the jura bush are toxic.

*Klypt*—A tall deciduous tree with pendulous branches and fan-shaped leaves. Its bark exfoliates in patches and is eaten by a number of herbivorous creatures.

*Kohrable*—The holy book of the True Word. It encompasses all the tenets of the faith.

*Kristopresh*—A rare grey-white stone that has a luminous quality. The finest samples seem to contain their own source of light. Kristopresh can be worked and is often fashioned into ritual objects of great value.

*Lastmeal*—Dinner.

*Merrain*—A pudgy and somewhat stupid mammal hunted

for its long silky fur. Merrains adapt well to different terrains, thus there are stone merrains, grass merrains, etc. Merrains are kwads and if one is killed, the other four members of the group can also be killed easily.

*Midmeal*—Lunch.

*Mon*—An animal that is solitary except for mating season.

*Mults*—Animals that live in packs of ten or more.

*Nayya(t)*—A holy man and interpreter of the tenets of the True Word. The nayyat are male and of the troinom class.

*Parostri*—Anyone who is not a follower of the True Word or who has been separated from worship of the Chenni-ad for any reason.

*Pittarr/Pittarri*—A melon with green rind and white flesh. The flesh is edible but tasteless. The rind, when crushed and boiled, delivers a bright green syrup that is extremely sweet. It is used as a sweetener and for making candies and jam.

*Puffers*—Avians, possibly of reptilian origin, that inflate thin membranes with a gas that allows them to drift with the wind. They soar during the day and roost in trees at night. Their source of nourishment is unknown but is thought to be some form of photosynthesis.

*Rennish*—An herbaceous perennial plant that grows from rootstalk cuttings and grows approximately two meters high. The plant's rhizome, for which it is cultivated, is dried and used in religious rituals. The rhizome contains a concentrated substance which is released when the root is burned. The smoke acts to reduce anxiety, and can cause enhanced suggestibility.

*Ridgepole*—Deciduous trees with smooth greyish bark and pale yellow-green leaves. Their shallow, spreading root system creates groves where other trees cannot get a foothold. The lower branches drop off as the tree grows, leaving straight trunks that rise high up to a tulip-shaped cluster of branches at the crown. This makes the lumber useful for building, thus the name.

*Rigor Bean*—A thorny shrub that propagates through large flat seeds grown in pods. The seeds, or "beans," are highly poisonous but the fleshy pods which contain them are edible when cooked.

*Rockcrawler*—A small shy lizard that lives in rocky environments, particularly cliffs and escarpments. Rockcrawlers are mons, living completely alone within their territories, except during mating. They eat insects.

*Rugas*—A flowering plant cultivated for its large, showy blossoms. The rugas is scentless, like all flowers on Chennidur. Its flowers range in color from white to deep purple, with all shades of lavender and blue in between.

*Rugollah*—A secondary human species native to Chennidur. They are nomadic and avoid contact with the followers of the True Word.

*Shirz*—Anyone who is not and has never been a Follower of the True Word. An adherent of another religion.

*Shufri-nagai*—The code of religious laws followed by all believers of the True Word.

*Skri*—A mammal the size of a large cat or raccoon. It scavenges on the edge of fields and farms and is considered vermin. Skris are mons that can run very fast, climb trees and often outwit their pursuers. Skri hunting is a popular sport among the troinom. They are trapped and shot with blowguns by farmers.

*Springborers*—A freshwater mollusc that lives in rocky streams and pools. It scours the rock of algae and other underwater plants with sharp teeth set in a circular mouth. Over time, this erodes the stone, enlarging the pools in which the creature lives.

*Stickybush*—A carnivorous shrub that can grow to a diameter of twenty feet or more. The bush lures its prey, mostly small animals, with a strong fruity scent. When the animal is underneath the shrub, its branches release a sticky resin that traps the prey. The bush feeds through its roots, which enwrap the prey, crush it and suck out its life juices.

*Stonefather Tales*—An oral tradition of stories that teach useful rules and information valuable to children.

*Stone Merrain*—(See Merrain) The stone merrain prefers a rocky environment and eats plants and mosses.

*Stoniver*—An herbivorous ruminant domesticated for its hair, which is woven into cloth and knitted into warm clothing.

*Su-vellide*—The oldest daughter of a clan, who is trained to marry into another clan and run its holding.

*Syddian*—A deep green stone carved into jewelry and ritual objects. It is often matched with silver.

*Taki*—Small, thin sausages that are highly spiced and salted. Often eaten as a condiment or an appetizer.

*Tansul*—The oldest male and ruler of a clan.

*Tapit*—Servants who are responsible for one part of a holding's activities. They are under the direct authority of the tuupit.

*Tarmit*—A domesticated mammal that eats insects by luring them with a long tongue that is coated with a sweet-smelling, sticky substance.

*Thinning*—A natural phenomenon when the Veil is thinner than normal, thus allowing dangerous radiation to filter through to the surface. This usually occurs during Icelock, or midwinter. All humans must stay indoors and avoid unnecessary exposure to sunlight during a thinning.

*Tulkan*—The current ruler of Chennidur. His father seized power from the last conciliator.

*Tunser*—An herbivorous rodent the size of a large dog.

*Troinom*—The aristocratic class of Chennidur. When a troinom comes of age, s/he is marked with a tattoo that indicates the birth clan.

*Turch*—A domestic avian with edible meat. The viscera and eggs are toxic.

*Tuupit*—The highest-ranking servant in a clan holding. The tuupit is responsible for running the day-to-day activities of a holding within a set of very specific rules. The tuupit assumes no initiative for giving orders or making decisions outside those rules.

*Vellide*—The wife (or sister) of a Tansul. She is the primary authority on domestic matters.

*Watergreen*—A freshwater aquatic plant with tiny round leaves. Both leaves and stems are edible and have a sharp minty taste.

*Wedding Season*—A period of six months, beginning in Chennidur's spring, when all marriages take place. It coincides with a time when sexual interest is reawakened after the long winter.

*Windikins*—Figures used as scarecrows in the fields. Windikins have moving parts that rotate or revolve in the wind.

*Wordless*—A pejorative term for the Rugollah and by extension for anyone who does not follow the True Word.

*Zegwan Sauce*—A highly-spiced sauce into which vegetable cakes are dipped. Sometimes used as a marinade or a seasoning.

## BIG GREEN

*Dumaass*—The jungle which covers the equatorial belt on BG-x3.

*Reds*—The red work suits worn by laborers so as to make them easy to see in the jungle.

*Whites*—The suits worn by the guards, or screws, to distinguish them from the laborers.

# APPENDIX B

## THE KOHRABLE
## I—GENESIS

### WORLDBIRTH

Out of the timeless dark,
Out of the vastness of time,
Came the Chen-i-ad who bore first light.
The light brought forth the world.
The world was one with the darkness and the light.
All time was around it but time was not upon it.
It was completed.

Yet was the world barren:
Divided into light and shadow, heat and cold, night and
day.
Without life it was unfinished, as a rough gem or an
unbaked loaf.
Without life it waited, having no purpose and no motion.

Then did Chen-i-ad look upon it.
They walked its barren rocks and saw that nothing lived

upon the world which they had created.
Forsaking unity and the interwoven web, they sought beauty.

## MOVEMENT

Aahks the Planner moved apart, surveying what was done.
With a great twist, the Planner spun the world.
Thus exchanging light with dark,
heat with cold, and night with day.
Thus did the shadows move and time came upon the world.
Aahks entwined. It was completed.

## THE AIR

Ysn came close, seeing that all moved, yet was separate.
The Modifier spread out its form encircling the worldrock,
drawing substance from the void,
Ysn the Modifier stirred the sky.
Whirling winds of air that tempered light and dark, heat and cold.
When the blending was completed, Ysn entwined.

## WATER

Yet was the world dry, for rocks do not thirst.
Neither do rocks grow and bear fruit
and their time moves slowly.
Mchul the Maker dipped into the air,
pulling tears from the winds and the clouds,
so the rains fell onto stone.
Sinking deep within the worldrock, Mchul searched.
Finding cracks and fissures,
seeking the world's heart, tapping its beat, he drew lifewater
into the fissures so that it surged up
forming the Heartsprings.
With water above and water below,
Mchul entwined. It was completed.

# THE PLANTS

Now was the world worthy of life,
yet no life was upon it.
Chey the Quickener sought among the starminds
to know that which would be best.
This knowledge he turned to the new world,
shaping it, changing it, suiting it
to its new home.
Spreading over the worldrock Chey flew,
and in his wake life grew up.
Grass and bushes, trees and vines,
all reached out toward the web
growing high and waving in the sun.
Flowers bloomed and fruit ripened, swelling in bounty
that the Quickener should notice their abundance.
When the worldrock was green, it was completed.
Chey entwined.

# THE ANIMALS

Ewm the Animator saw further purpose.
Existing for their own sake, yet were the plants also fodder,
nesting places, protection, warmth.
Thinking thus, Ewm slept and in his sleep, dreamed.
Of creatures walking through a cleft.
In pairs and triplets, fours and sixes, the animals marched.
In sizes, shapes, colors and skins beyond count.
Past the cleft, they spread out over the rocks,
under the grasses, beneath the water, into the air.
When they were of the world, Ewm woke.
Seeing what his dream had wrought, he was satisfied.
And entwined.

# COMPLETION

Then the Chen-i-ad reunited, re-wove the web,
content with that which they had done.
All was beauty, all was peace.
The world was completed.

## II—CONFRONTATION

### THE COMING OF THE RAVELER

Then did the Raveler come upon the world.
Sensing the world, measuring, absorbing, tasting, feeling.
What is this world? it questioned.
But all was silent.
Who made this world? it questioned.
But all was peace.
What is the purpose of this world? it questioned.
But all was beauty.
The Chen-i-ad, satisfied and entwined, had no need of
questions or of answers.

The Raveler asked for the last time,
Who lives on this world?

### THE RESPONSE

Then the Chen-i-ad listened and considered.
For the animals and plants were of the world
but did not live upon it.
Thus they formed an answer:
The world is as it is,
nothing else is required.

Then did the Raveler laugh.
And that laughter rolled down from the mountaintops,
it crashed in the winds,
it swelled from the sea bottom.
The Raveler replied in the role of Adversary.
"You have done what you can.

Now shall I find a life worthy of this world.
And when that is done, I shall have taken the world from
you."

Silence.
The Raveler began to search.

# Anne McCaffrey
# vs.
# The Planet Pirates

**SASSINAK:** Sassinak was twelve when the raiders came. That made her just the right age: old enough to be used, young enough to be broken. But Sassinak turned out to be a little different from your typical slave girl. And finally, she escaped. But that was only the beginning for Sassinak. Now she's a fleet captain with a pirate-chasing ship of her own, and only one regret in life: not enough pirates.
BY ANNE MCCAFFREY AND ELIZABETH MOON
69863 * $4.95 _____

**THE DEATH OF SLEEP:** Lunzie Mespil was a Healer. All she wanted in life was a chance to make things better for others. But she was getting the feeling she was particularly marked by fate: every ship she served on ran into trouble—and every time she went out, she ended up in coldsleep. When she went to the Dinosaur Planet she thought the curse was lifted—but there she met a long-lost relative named *Sassinak* who'd make her life much more complicated. . . .
BY ANNE MCCAFFREY AND JODY LYNN NYE
69884-2 * $4.95 _____

**GENERATION WARRIORS:** Sassinak and Lunzie combine forces to beat the planet pirates once and for all. With Lunzie's contacts, Sassinak's crew, and Sassinak herself, it would take a galaxy-wide conspiracy to foil them. Unfortunately, that's just what the planet pirates are. . . .
BY ANNE MCCAFFREY AND ELIZABETH MOON
72041-4 * $4.95 _____

*Available at your local bookstore. Or you can order any or all of these books with this order form. Just mark your choices above and send the combined cover price/s to: Baen Books, Dept. BA, P.O. Box 1403, Riverdale, NY 10471.*

# Trouble in a Tutti-Frutti Hat

It was half past my hangover and a quarter to the hair of the dog when *she* ankled into my life. I could smell trouble clinging to her like cheap perfume, but a man in my racket learns when to follow his nose and when to plug it. She was brunette, bouncy, beautiful. Also fruity. Also dead.

I watched her size up my cabin with brown eyes big as dinner plates, motioned her into the only other chair in the room. Her hips redefined the structure of DNA en route to a soft landing on the tatty cushion. Then they went right through the cushion. Like I said, dead. A crossover sister, which means my crack about smelling trouble was just figurative. You never get the scent-input off of what you civvies'd call a ghost. Never thought I'd meet one in the figurative flesh. Not on Space Station Three. Even the dead have taste.

*What was Carmen Miranda doing on board Space Station Three?*

CARMEN MIRANDA'S GHOST IS HAUNTING SPACE STATION THREE, edited by Don Sakers Featuring stories by Anne McCaffrey, C.J. Cherryh, Esther Friesner, Melissa Scott & Lisa Barnett and many more. Inspired by the song by Leslie Fish. 69864-8 * $3.95

Other Baen Books by these authors:

*The Paladin,* C.J. Cherryh
65417-9 * $3.95                              _____

*Twilight's Kingdoms,* Nancy Asire
65362-8 * $3.50                              _____

*Carmen Miranda's Ghost is Haunting Space Station Three* edited by Don Sakers, inspired by a song by Leslie Fish
69864-8 * $3.95                              _____

*Knight of Ghosts and Shadows,* Mercedes Lackey & Ellen Guon
69885-0 * $3.95                              _____

# FRED SABERHAGEN

Fred Saberhagen needs very little introduction these days. His most famous creations—the awesome Berserkers—are known to SF readers around the world. He's reached the bestseller lists several times, most recently with his "Book of Swords" series, and his novels span the territory from hard science fiction to high fantasy. Quite understandably, Saberhagen's been labeled one of the best writers in the business.

These fine volumes by Saberhagen are available from Baen Books:

## PYRAMIDS
A fascinating new twist on the time-travel novel, introducing a great new series hero: Pilgrim, the Flying Dutchman of Time, whose only hope for returning home lies in subtly altering the history of our own timeline to more closely reflect his own. Learn why the curse of the Pharaoh Khufu (builder of the Great Pyramid) had a special reality, in *Pyramids*. "Saberhagen's light, imaginative and enjoyable adventures speed along twisting paths to a climax that is even more surprising than the rest of the book."

—*Publishers Weekly*

## AFTER THE FACT
This is the second novel featuring the great new series hero, Pilgrim—the Lost Traveller adrift in time and dimensionality. His current project: to rescue Abraham Lincoln from assassination, AFTER THE FACT!

## THE FRANKENSTEIN PAPERS
At last—the truth about a sinister Dr. Frankenstein and his monster with a heart of gold, based on a history written by the monster himself! Find out what happened when the mad Doctor brought his creation to life, and why the monster has no scars.

## THE EMPIRE OF THE EAST
A masterful blend of high technology and high sorcery; a world where magic rules—and science struggles to live again! "Ranks favorably with Tolkien. Exceptional in sheer unbridled zest and imaginative sweep!—*School Library Journal* "*Empire of the East* is one of the best science fiction fantasy epics—Saberhagen can be justly proud. Highly recommended."
—*Science Fiction Chronicle*

## THE BLACK THRONE with Roger Zelazny
Two masters of SF collaborate on a masterpiece of fantasy: As children they met and built sand castles on a beach out of space and time: Edgar Perry, little Annie, and Edgar Allan Poe. . . . Fifteen years later Edgar Perry has grown to manhood—and as the result of a trip through a maelstrom, he's leading a much more active life. Perry will learn to thrive in the dark, romantic world he's landed in, where lead can be transmuted to gold, ravens can speak, orangutans can commit murder, and beautiful women are easy to come by. But his alter ego, Edgar Allan, is stranded in a strange and unfriendly world where he can only write about the wonderful and mysterious reality he has lost forever. . . .

## THE GOLDEN PEOPLE
Genetically perfect, super-human children are created by a dedicated scientist for the betterment of Mankind. As the children mature, however, they begin to wonder if Man *should* survive. . . .

## LOVE CONQUERS ALL

In a future where childbirth is outlawed and promiscuity required, one woman dares fight the system for the right to bear children.

## OCTAGON

Players scattered across the continent are engaged in a game called "Starweb." Each player has certain attributes, and can ally with or attack any of the others. But one player seems to have confused the reality of the world: a player with the attributes of machinelike precision and mechanical ruthlessness. His name is Octagon, and he's out for blood.